NEVER-ENDING-SNAKE

Also by Aimée & David Thurlo

Ella Clah Novels

Blackening Song
Death Walker
Bad Medicine
Enemy Way
Shooting Chant
Red Mesa
Changing Woman
Tracking Bear
Wind Spirit
White Thunder
Mourning Dove
Turquoise Girl
Coyote's Wife
Earthway
Black Thunder (forthcoming)

Plant Them Deep

Lee Nez Novels

Second Sunrise
Blood Retribution
Pale Death
Surrogate Evil

Sister Agatha Novels

Bad Faith
Thief in Retreat
Prey for a Miracle
False Witness
Prodigal Nun
The Bad Samaritan

NEVER-ENDING-SNAKE

— ✕ ✕ ✕ ✕ ✕ —

AN ELLA CLAH NOVEL

AIMÉE & DAVID THURLO

A Tom Doherty Associates Book
New York

This is a work of fiction. All of the characters, organizations, and events portrayed in this novel are either products of the authors' imaginations or are used fictitiously.

A Forge Book
Published by Tom Doherty Associates, LLC
175 Fifth Avenue
New York, NY 10010

www.tor-forge.com

Forge® is a registered trademark of Tom Doherty Associates, LLC.

The Library of Congress has cataloged the hardcover edition as follows:

Thurlo, Aimée.
    Never-ending-snake / Aimée and David Thurlo.—1st hardcover ed.
        p. cm.
    "A Tom Doherty Associates book."
    ISBN 978-0-7653-2450-4
    1. Clah, Ella (Fictitious character)—Fiction.   2. Police—New Mexico—
Fiction.   3. Navajo Indians—Fiction.   4. Navajo women—Fiction.
5. Intimidation—Fiction.   6. New Mexico—Fiction.   I. Thurlo, David.
II. Title.
    PS3570.H82N48 2010
    813'.54—dc22

                                                                    2010033982

ISBN 978-0-7653-2453-5 (trade paperback)

Printed in the United States of America

D 10   9   8   7   6   5   4   3

To Madeline,
Your future is filled with endless possibilities.
May you always walk in beauty.

ACKNOWLEDGMENTS

Special thanks to Sergeant Ryan Tafoya for always being there when we had a question.

Thanks also to Deputies Larry Harlan and Terry Matthews for helping us keep it real.

As always, any mistakes are our own.

NEVER-ENDING-SNAKE

ONE

——— ✕ ✕ ✕ ———

SUNDAY

As the small single-engine aircraft lifted off the Albuquerque runway—next stop Shiprock—Special Investigator Ella Clah of the Navajo Tribal Police couldn't resist a smile. Even sharing a flight with a genuine Navajo war hero and the tribe's most respected attorney couldn't compare with the rush that came from knowing she was finally on the last leg of her journey home.

She'd sorely missed her daughter during her short stay in D.C. Back in her twenties, the job she'd just been offered in the nation's capital would have been a slam dunk. But Ella was twice that age now. With maturity and parenthood had come other responsibilities that surpassed even her dedication to restoring balance among the *Diné*—the Navajo People—so all could walk in beauty.

Pulling out her BlackBerry, she checked for a signal. She'd sent her daughter a tweet and wondered if Dawn had replied. Her daughter was allowed to use the strictly text message utility as long as she followed the rules that Ella had set down for her. Like her mom, Dawn had her own followers and screen name. Dawn signed in as Firstlight1, and Ella was Ladylaw.

As she thought of her eleven-year-old, Ella sighed, wondering where the time had gone. That chilly April morning when she'd first held her baby girl in her arms seemed like only yesterday. Yet today it was warm, less than a week since Labor Day, and Dawn had already started the sixth grade.

"So what do you think of D.C.?" Kevin asked, looking back to talk. He was seated up front beside the pilot. "It's an exciting place, isn't it? Could you see yourself and our daughter living there—at the center of power and intrigue for all the United States?"

Kevin Tolino was Dawn's father. Even though he and Ella had never lived together or married, they'd remained close by sharing the responsibilities of parenthood. Like most parents, however, they'd had many conflicts over the years, particularly when it came to raising their child.

"What you're really asking is whether I've decided to accept the job with John Blakely's security firm," she said with a ghost of a smile. "The answer's still no. I haven't made up my mind yet."

Ella had first met Blakely years ago when they'd both served in the FBI. He was a senior agent and she'd just come off her rookie year in the Bureau when they'd been assigned a particularly tough case in the Denver area. The results of her undercover work had made a lasting impression on Blakely.

Now, retired from the Bureau, John had opened Personnel Profile Security, PPS, an up-and-coming firm in D.C. Recently, and seemingly out of nowhere, he'd called to offer her a job. Ella strongly suspected that Kevin had encouraged the contact—a not-so-subtle attempt to bring both her and her daughter to D.C. where he spent most of his time. Kevin worked in the tribe's Washington office almost exclusively these days.

Although she had many things to take into account before making her decision, there was no denying that the PPS offer would mean a substantial salary increase for her, in addition to far less dangerous and stressful work. It was an opportunity she couldn't easily dismiss.

"The shot at a career jump like this only comes once in a blue moon, particularly in today's economy," Kevin said.

She shook her head imperceptibly, warning him to drop the subject for now. Although she didn't mind having this kind of conversation with Kevin, Adam Lonewolf, sitting just to her left, was practically a stranger. Media coverage had made Adam's face familiar to everyone, and his deeds in the military gathered attention and respect wherever he went. Yet the fact remained that Kevin had only just introduced them this morning at Reagan National Airport in Washington.

The tall, lean, ex-GI was a war hero and a big celebrity in the Four Corners, especially in the Navajo Nation. Sergeant Lonewolf had been awarded the Distinguished Service Cross after almost singlehandedly fighting off an attack on his unit's Afghan mountain outpost. During six hours of nighttime combat, Sergeant Lonewolf had been wounded several times. Yet despite his own injuries, he'd rescued three trapped soldiers and led them to safety.

After leaving the military and returning home, Adam had sought a new direction for his life. The search had eventually led him to Kevin, who'd helped him get a job as a lobbyist. Kevin had even gone the extra mile, introducing Adam to the Washington businessmen and government officials he'd need to network with on behalf of the tribe.

Recently, when Kevin had unexpectedly become the target of threats, Adam had volunteered to provide him with travel protection. Knowing Adam's reputation would be the best possible deterrent, Kevin had readily agreed.

Lonewolf wasn't much of a talker, though. Ella doubted that he'd said more than three words since they'd left Albuquerque, and even less on the flight from the capital.

"Now that you've had a taste of D.C., how do you feel about representing the tribe and its business interests there?" Ella asked Adam, hoping to draw him out a bit.

"It's a different kind of warfare," he said after a beat. "But I'll get the hang of it."

His smile never reached his eyes. The hard, yet vacant gleam there was one she recognized. She'd seen it in the faces of many veterans and experienced law enforcement officers who'd seen too much death—up close and personal. Adam's military service had been intense and extremely violent and that left major scars, not all of them visible. Ella knew it was likely he would carry some of those for as long as he lived.

"If you ever decide you want to leave a lobbyist's pressure cooker life of not-so-gentle persuasion, come work full-time for me," Kevin said.

Adam shook his head. "I'll help you with security whenever I can, you know that, but I came back to serve the *Diné*. The best way for me to do that is by advancing the tribe's interests in D.C." He paused for a moment, then continued. "As a soldier, I know firsthand what happens when word comes down from Washington. I want to give the *Diné* more input at the source, particularly when it comes to matters that'll affect The People, whether it be in business, regulation, or legislation."

"Does that mean you're going to relocate to D.C. full-time?" Ella asked.

"No, I don't think that'll be necessary. The tribe covers my transportation expenses. Staying connected to the *Dinétah* will help me keep my perspective, too."

"All the traveling . . . With family, it isn't easy," Ella warned in a low, thoughtful voice.

"After two tours in Afghanistan, my wife, Marie, is used to not having me around for long periods of time. She wouldn't know what to do with me if I decided to stay home," he added, suddenly laughing.

The gesture transformed his face, and for that brief moment Adam Lonewolf was just another young Navajo man looking forward to being home again with his family.

"As a police detective, I imagine your family's had its share of adapting to the demands of your work, too. It can't be easy for them whenever they hear about an officer involved in a shooting," he said, his expression shifting back to its somber mood.

"That's true," she admitted. "Even accepting the small things, like my not showing up for dinner or a school event, can be hard on them sometimes. But my daughter knows that if she needs me I'm just a phone call away. The same goes for her dad," she added, glancing at Kevin.

"I haven't always been that accessible to my family," Adam said, "particularly when I was on patrol or at some remote mountain outpost halfway around the world. What helped me most back then was knowing I could count on my clan to look after things for me here."

Ella nodded. The dependable support system clans provided were multilayered, more than family, and more complex than most people on the outside ever realized. "The Rez is a good place to live. It's too bad that work's always so hard to find."

"That's one of the things I hope to change, or at least influence for the better, as a lobbyist. I could make a real difference for other families, and my own, if I could bring more jobs to the Navajo Nation."

"You can be very persuasive, and people genuinely like you, Adam. That'll get you the contacts you need to advance the tribe's agenda," Kevin said. "I've seen you working those business conferences and agency gatherings in D.C. You can hold your own with practically anyone."

Adam smiled and this time it did reach his eyes. "Learning to communicate effectively, even with total strangers, is something the military teaches you. It's a survival skill as well as a tactical necessity sometimes."

Ship Rock, the ancient volcanic cone rising from the desert floor, came into view again through the front cockpit glass as the aircraft banked to the west. The pilot then circled to the right, lining up the aircraft as they lost more altitude, approaching from the south toward the small landing strip southwest of "downtown" Shiprock.

Adam grew quiet again, his hands on the briefcase on his lap as he stared out the window.

From what she could read of his body language, he was impatient, eager to land. She had a feeling that Adam had missed his wife a lot more than he'd readily admit. She smiled, sympathizing.

Ahead, to their left and far below, Ella saw a white van coming down the access road from the west. It wasn't her mother, Rose, and her husband, Herman. Her stepfather still drove his old hot rod pickup. Maybe it was cargo for the single engine aircraft's return flight to Albuquerque—or a service vehicle.

Their small craft dropped quickly, then flared out and slowed, touching down with a gentle bump of the rear landing gear. The nose dropped slightly, and the front gear touched down. The pilot cut the engine speed again, applied the brakes, and they slowed quickly. Without the roar of big jet engines and the whir from the activation of flaps and such, their landing was relatively quiet. They slowed to a few miles per hour, then turned to the right and taxied toward a small hangar.

Home. Ella's heart began to beat faster, and she looked in vain at the small parking lot, hoping to see Herman's pickup. She couldn't wait to see Dawn. Although she'd only been away for three days, it felt like an eternity had passed. Phone calls were never enough, and bulletin-style e-mails and tweets lacked a personal touch.

They came to a stop about fifty feet from the edge of the asphalt. The pilot took off his headset, unbuckled his seat belt, then half turned in his seat. "No ground crew here, folks. Sorry. You can unbuckle and gather your gear while I climb out and deploy the steps." He opened his door and dropped down to the pavement.

"Will your family be coming to pick you up?" Ella asked Adam as she reached under her seat for her purse.

"No, my wife has been helping my parents at our sheep camp up in the mountains. I expect Marie's still on the road, driving back. I was planning to ride in with Kevin, then pick up a car at the tribal motor pool on the mesa."

Ella again noted the brown leather briefcase he'd held protectively on his lap the entire flight.

Following her gaze, he gave her a quick half smile. "When I left the Army, I told myself I'd find a job where I'd never have to carry anything heavy around again. But my wife bought this for me, so I'm stuck with taking paperwork home to show her how much I appreciate the gift," he added, then laughed. "Win some, lose some."

She smiled and looked past Adam at the open cockpit door. The pilot was outside adjusting the small aluminum steps. "Every time I take a trip, I go with a half empty suitcase so I can bring back gifts for my family," Ella said.

"I may have to up-size next trip. This time, beside a special edition board game for my nephew, I've actually got some important papers crowded in here. I could have used a tote bag for the game, I guess, but I like to keep one hand free whenever I can—and I'm never going to carry anything over my shoulder again."

Kevin laughed. "When my daughter was younger, I always brought back something for her and lodged it between tribal documents." He took a deep breath, rising from his seat and crouching low, waiting for them to exit. "My job has sure changed a lot these past few years."

"For the better or worse?" Adam asked.

"Worse, particularly lately," Kevin said, following Adam out of the aircraft. "Ever since I started building my case against Alan Grady, the manager who handles our new tribal casino in Fruitland, things have been a little edgy." Kevin looked up to see if Ella needed a hand down the simple ladder.

"Something about his firm overbilling the tribe, right?" Ella asked, taking Kevin's hand for balance as she climbed down.

"Yeah, that's it in a nutshell. Right now I'm preparing a lawsuit to recover some overpayments. It's a contractual issue, but several hundred thousand are at stake. Enough, apparently, to make me a target, at least for harassment. I wouldn't be surprised if my enemies try to get me fired once they discover I can't be intimidated."

"Nice to be at an airport where there's no need for security," Adam noted, his gaze taking in the airstrip facilities.

"Just a couple of mechanics and a delivery truck," Kevin said, laughing. "Consider yourself off the clock, Adam."

Ella gazed at the Chuska Mountains to the west and took a deep breath, looking up at clear blue skies. New Mexico air smelled sweeter than the exhaust-laden oxygen substitute she'd been forced to breathe in D.C.

Life, even in the twenty-first century, was less complicated here on the *Dinétah*. Their airport, for example, was nothing more than a few narrow asphalt strips with a wide spot at one end and a hangar just large enough to provide a little shade for the mechanic. To her right, about fifty yards from the hangar, were the fuel pumps, and beyond, a small cinder block structure with a rooftop observation area. She smiled, glad to be back on her turf.

"Any sign of Rose and Herman?" Kevin asked as the three of them stepped away from the aircraft, waiting for their luggage. The pilot, Pete Sanchez, ducked under the wing and moved to the belly, where there was a storage compartment.

"No, I didn't see the pickup or Mom's old car when we were coming down." Sticking to a precise schedule was more of an Anglo preoccupation. Things on the Rez usually ran on Indian time.

"Dawn's coming with them, right?" Kevin asked.

"Yeah. Nothing could keep her away," Ella said, grinning widely. "She's probably got a million things to tell us now that she's finally in middle school. Her life seems to run at a faster pace than ours."

Hearing the faint squeal of tires, Ella noted the arrival of the white van she'd observed during the approach. It looked like a FedEx ground service van, though she couldn't see the sign from this angle. Glancing back toward the aircraft, she saw Pete retrieving their luggage, three soft side bags and two carry-ons.

"Someone was supposed to meet me here with a car," Kevin grumbled, bringing out his cell phone. "I should have called ahead to remind them when we reached Albuquerque."

"You got spoiled in the big city where there's a taxicab going by every thirty seconds," Ella said, laughing. "Maybe the tribal car's in the shop and that van's your ride."

Ella glanced at Adam. His gaze was focused on the van, which had whipped around, then come to a stop, rear doors facing them. An uneasy feeling crept up her spine and almost simultaneously, the badger fetish at her neck, a gift from her brother, became scalding hot—a sure sign of danger. Ella placed her hand on the butt of her pistol.

Adam took a step closer to Kevin, his gaze still fixed on the van.

Suddenly both rear doors flew open and two bulky men in black overalls armed with assault rifles jumped down to the pavement.

"Guns!" Ella dove for the asphalt as the men began firing from the hip.

Glancing back, Ella saw Adam yank Kevin to the ground beside the starboard side landing gear, then drop to one knee, grabbing at his thigh, instinctively reaching for the service Beretta he'd worn for years. A second later he flinched, then toppled to the pavement, blood spewing from his head.

Groaning from an apparent hit, Kevin curled up behind the meager protection of the landing gear wheel.

Ella, her nine-millimeter service pistol in hand, snapped off three quick shots, then rolled to her left, trying to use the shadow cast from the aircraft's tail for concealment. The two shooters stopped moving forward but kept their weapons up by their shoulders, squeezing off round after round. The pilot, in line when the men first opened fire, had already taken a stray bullet to the shoulder, but the assailants were no longer paying any attention to him. Their targets appeared to be the men wearing suits. As she fired at the pair, the pilot dove back into the aircraft through the open door.

Ella aimed directly at the closest gunman's chest, and fired twice. The man flinched, and staggered back. A hit.

Ella shifted, trying to get a sight picture on the second man, who was at least ten feet from his partner. Before she could squeeze off a shot, he located her in the shadows and fired a half dozen rounds of suppressing fire.

Ella rolled, the bullets digging up asphalt where she'd been an instant before, and returned fire. The man's partner, the one she'd thought she'd hit twice already, hadn't even slowed down. He took another step forward, firing four or five more rounds at Adam and Kevin, who were bunched together now.

She squeezed off more rounds. She was scoring hits, the bullets rocked the attackers, but neither would go down. They were probably wearing body armor. Out of ammo, Ella dove for the only concealment around—the luggage beneath the storage compartment. One of the shooters was reloading, replacing the spent magazine with another, but his partner kept snapping off one round at a time, and she had to roll again to stay out of sight.

On her back, she released the spent magazine and groped in her jacket pocket for the spare clip. Bullets ricocheted off the pavement, striking metal, and she wondered what a hit on the aircraft would do to her chances. Hoping the airplane's fuel tanks were in the wings, higher up, she inserted the new magazine and closed the action with a touch of her thumb.

Ella looked around the edge of a carry-on to get a fix on the gunmen. They were retreating now, walking backwards toward the van. One of them snapped off a round, which whined overhead and forced her to duck behind cover.

Ella knew she had to get a sight picture and go for a head shot. Her third magazine, the one with the armor-piercing rounds, was in her purse, somewhere over by the right wing. Rising to a crouch, she dove toward the left side landing-gear wheel. The metal post and wheel would give her more protection than a suitcase full of clothes. With a little luck, there was still an outside chance that she could take them down.

One of the men reached the van and jumped into the back, giving her an opening. She brought her weapon up in a two-handed grip, but the shooter still on the ground fired three quick shots, pinning her down again before she could squeeze off a round. One of the bullets struck the tire just beside her head and it exploded, stinging her with rubber, steel cord, or both. There was a thump on the asphalt next, and she saw a roundish object rolling in her direction. Her heart nearly stopped.

Grenade! She hugged the ground, covering her head with her arms. "Love you, Dawn." she muttered, expecting the worst.

A heartbeat later there was a loud pop instead of the earthshaking blast and scream of flying metal she'd expected. Recognizing the sound, she looked up to see a billowing cloud of white smoke. It wasn't her time—not yet—and the realization brought her hope—and anger.

Hearing the sound of closing doors, Ella fired blind at the vanishing outline of the van, screened by the smoke for obvious reasons. Her chances of scoring a head shot now were slim to none.

Realizing the smoke concealed her as well, she ran around the nose of the aircraft, angling for a clear shot. The accelerating van was already a hundred yards down the road. Ella aimed carefully, squeezed off two more shots at a rear tire, but missed. Only a lucky hit could have stopped them now, but if it had, then what? She was outgunned and low on ammo.

Hearing shouts, Ella turned around and saw three men— the landing strip's personnel—running toward the single-engine aircraft. She jammed her pistol back into the holster and grabbed her cell phone.

"We called the police," one yelled. "I told them about the white van—and the men. They're putting out an ATL, whatever that is."

"Attempt to locate," Ella mumbled, not caring if he heard.

As she jogged toward the aircraft, the first man that came into full view was the pilot, staggering away from the open cockpit door. Wounds to his upper body had now soaked much of his shirt in blood, but he was mobile. Ella shifted her attention to where she'd last seen Adam and Kevin. The asphalt around the landing gear was thick with blood.

"Call an ambulance," she shouted to one of the airstrip's men—the manager, judging from the white shirt and bolo tie.

"Already done," he answered, waving his cell phone.

As she reached the fallen men, the sickeningly sweet scent of blood filled her nostrils. She swallowed hard, trying to brace herself, but nothing could have prepared her for what she saw next.

Adam lay across Kevin's left arm, the side of his head a mass of blood and hair. Bubbles in the blood around his nose showed he was still breathing, barely. He'd also been struck on the leg, but she didn't see any wounds along his neck or center line of his back. Ella carefully lifted him enough to free Kevin's arm.

Kevin had been shot in the side, around the ribs, and had taken another hit in the thigh and one on his arm, just below the elbow. Mercifully, both men were unconscious.

Experience told her that Kevin would live if help arrived promptly, but she wasn't so sure about Adam. With head wounds there wasn't much she could do without the risk of killing him right there.

Ella looked at one of the airport workers, a man in overalls who was absentmindedly holding a fire extinguisher. "I need bandages," she called out, pressing her hand against Kevin's thigh and applying direct pressure to the wound that appeared to be losing the most blood. She could hear the sound of an approaching siren now and the tone suggested it was the EMTs, not a squad car.

"Hang on, guys," she told the wounded, hoping that some part of them would hear.

The wounded pilot came toward her, his bloody left hand pressed against his right shoulder. A large red first-aid kit dangled from the fingers of his injured arm. He held it out and said something, but she couldn't hear a word as a white and blue emergency vehicle skidded to a stop on the runway, lights flashing and siren wailing.

"Finally," she said, as two white uniformed men, one Anglo and the other Navajo, rushed up carrying large medical cases.

She stepped back to let them work. So much blood . . . It was different when it was someone you knew.

Seeing movement on the runway out of the corner of her eye, Ella turned her head for a clearer look, and saw her family driving up in Rose's white Chevy Cavalier. Ella pulled herself together quickly. There was no way she was going to let Dawn see her father in the condition he was in now.

Jogging over to her mother's old sedan, Ella motioned palm up for them to remain where they were, then realized her hand was covered with blood and put it down quickly. She stopped in front of Dawn's backseat door and stood against it so her daughter couldn't open it and get out. As she looked at Rose, Ella saw a mixture of relief and fear on her face—the latter from seeing she was all right, and the former from not knowing what had happened.

"There's been a shooting, and Dawn's father is one of the three who have been injured," she said gently. "Stay well back and let the emergency people work. I'll answer your questions as soon as I can, but right now I need to get back over there. This is a crime scene now."

Ella looked at her daughter and forced a smile. "Hang in there, Pumpkin. And don't worry."

Dawn nodded, but fear still shone in her eyes.

"One last thing," she said, giving Herman a worried glance. "We'll need statements from all of you, so you can't leave just yet."

Herman nodded, silently reassuring her that he'd take care of things here.

As her family climbed out of the car, Ella used her cell phone to call her partner and second cousin, Justine Goodluck. Getting her on the first ring, Ella gave her a quick description of the events, made sure officers in the county would be looking for the van, and requested the crime scene team be dispatched to the location.

"Are you sure you're okay?" Justine asked immediately.

"I was nicked by bullet fragments and flying debris, but that's all," Ella answered. "Right now the EMTs are concentrating on Kevin and Sergeant Lonewolf, who's in the worst condition. The pilot took a hit, too."

As Ella put the phone back into her pocket, she saw her daughter standing between Herman and Rose, watching the activity around the wounded. Blood was everywhere, and

Dawn's eyes were huge. She'd seen enough TV shows to know that violence was part of police work, but in her brief life Dawn had never seen anything like this.

Ella realized then that she'd been wrong to ask them to stay. She'd get their statements later.

Ella hurried back to where her family was and hugged her daughter tightly, careful not to touch her with her bloody hand.

"Mom," Dawn managed, her voice barely above a whisper. "You're hurt. You're bleeding."

"I scratched up the side of my head and my cheek. That's all it is, honey. I'm fine," she said, easing her hold enough to look down and give Dawn a gentle smile. "But this is no place for you right now. You're going to have to go home with your grandparents, okay? And please don't call your friends—not until your grandmother says it's okay." Ella saw Dawn holding her new cell phone in one hand.

"Okay," Dawn answered, placing the phone into her hip pocket.

Rose touched Ella on the arm gently. "We were nearly run off the road by a white van when we turned up the airport road," she said, her voice two octaves higher than usual. "I didn't notice the driver, but the van ended up going north. Did he do this . . . massacre?"

"Mom," Ella snapped, forcing Rose to focus. "I need you two to take my daughter home," she said, respecting her mother's traditionalist views by not using Dawn's name. Names were said to have power and were not to be used lightly.

"I was a medic in the Army, and I conducted a first-aid class at the senior center a few months ago. Is there anything I can do here?" Herman, her mother's husband, asked.

Ella glanced back and saw the EMTs fighting to save the most badly wounded, but Pete Sanchez was sitting alone, a compress on his arm. "The pilot . . ."

Herman nodded once, then strode off.

"What . . ." Rose began, but seeing Ella shake her head, allowed her voice to trail off.

"Mom . . . is Dad? . . ." Dawn's voice broke.

"I think he's going to be okay," Ella heard herself saying with a conviction she didn't feel. But honesty would wait. Dawn had seen and heard enough. "You two need to go home now. I'll be there as soon as I can with news."

"My husband will need a way home," Rose said, glancing at Herman, who was already tending the pilot.

"I'll arrange something, or he can ride back with me," Ella replied. "It might be a while, though."

The airstrip wasn't far from the station and as they spoke, the crime scene van appeared at the far end of the road.

"I've got to get to work, Mom, but I need you to write down everything you remember about the van and the men inside as soon as possible. Both of you," she added, looking at Dawn. "Even small details might help."

As soon as Rose and Dawn were on their way, Ella breathed a sigh of relief. Though it seemed like a lifetime ago, she still remembered seeing her father's body lying in the morgue. He'd been ritually murdered and, to this day, those gruesome images remained in her mind, imprinted there, ready to be replayed in her many nightmares.

That was why she'd been so determined to protect her child from the bloody scene out on the runway. Even in a fast-paced world—or maybe because of it—children deserved their brief time of innocence.

Now, with her child safely on the way home, Ella walked back to the crime scene, ready to resume her duties as a tribal police investigator.

TWO

— ✖ ✖ ✖ —

Ella heard the ambulance driver slam the rear door shut. Moments later, she watched the emergency vehicle racing across the strip and down the airport drive, sirens on and emergency lights flashing.

The tribal crime scene team, currently Justine Goodluck, Sergeant Joe Neskahi, and newcomer Benny Pete, were already unloading their gear from the van. Airport workers were busy examining the single-engine aircraft, obviously concerned about damage and safety issues.

"Partner, you're bleeding," Justine said as Ella approached.

"They had their hands full and needed to transport right away to save the soldier," Herman answered for Ella, then stepped toward her, first-aid kit in hand. "Let me take a look at you."

"It's nothing," Ella insisted. "When I took cover I was sprayed with flying debris, probably gravel and asphalt. And a landing gear tire popped right next to me. I got scratched up a bit, that's all, but it's already clotting," she said, dabbing at her cheek with a fingertip.

"Are you aware that you also have two bullet holes in the side of your shirt?" Justine asked, pointing to the entrance and exit holes.

"The suspects were blasting away with assault rifles. With that kind of firepower, I got off extremely lucky." Finding a third hole in her jacket, Ella gave her a rueful smile. "At least it isn't the suit I bought for D.C."

Herman had reached Social Security age in the last century, and these days his hands shook some, but equipped with antiseptic-soaked swabs he cleansed the scrapes above her ear and on her cheek. Despite his light touch, Ella flinched from the sting.

"Yow!" she grumbled.

"I've seen all the shell casings lying around and the bullet holes in your clothes, daughter-in-law. You dodge bullets without even batting an eyelash. No man could ever be tougher than you in a fight. But when I touch you with a little bit of disinfectant, you melt like butter in a hot skillet. What's wrong with this picture?" Herman asked.

Justine started to laugh, but seeing Ella's scowl, thought better of it.

"You won't need stitches," Herman said, moving away at last, "but your scalp was creased with something, probably a bullet. You should be checked by a doctor as soon as possible."

"I'm going to take a look around here first. After that, I'm off to the hospital. Once I check into the condition of the wounded, I'll get my scratches tended."

"I'd like to ride there with you," Herman said. "I have a feeling your mother and your daughter will be going there instead of home."

"Mom at a hospital?" Ella knew that would be the last place her mother would want to be. The hospital was a place for the *chindi*. According to Navajo beliefs, when a person died, the good in them joined universal harmony, but the evil side stayed earthbound, ready to create problems for the living. Since patients died in hospitals every day, Traditionalists saw it as a dangerous place to visit. Though her mother understood the need for hospitals, she did her best to avoid them.

"My wife will probably try her best to convince your daughter that home is the best place for them right now, but the girl is stubborn, like you. They might go back to the house initially, but it won't take long before she'll insist on going to the hospital so she can be near her father."

Dawn, like many young Navajos raised around Traditionalists, walked an easy line between the old and modern ways. Fear of the dead wouldn't keep her from going to Kevin's side. Dawn adored him. In her eyes, Kevin could do no wrong. As far as Ella was concerned, Dawn's view of her dad bordered on hero worship.

"You're bleeding again," Justine said gently. "Come on. I'm taking you to the hospital. The rest of the team will carry on here. The suspects didn't leave much for us except for a bucket full of .223 shell casings, skid marks, and tire tread images." She pointed to where the van had been parked.

"That's a start."

"Give me a minute, then the three of us will head up," Ella said.

After Ella briefed Joe Neskahi, the crime scene's senior officer, they left. Although only two members of her team were actively working the crime scene, nothing would be overlooked, and each piece of evidence would be faithfully recorded.

Benny Pete, their newest crime scene member, was an experienced officer who had trained and served with the Phoenix Metro department before returning to the Rez. As a crime scene investigator, Benny had already proved he was good at spotting even the minutest trace evidence. Though he was only on loan from Tuba City until Ralph Tache and Anna Bekis returned, Ella was glad to have him. Tache, their bomb expert, was still convalescing after an on-the-job incident. Bekis had taken his place as their new explosives expert, but the former ATF member's talents required her to cover a lot of ground. Right now she was on assignment with the Window Rock District.

While Justine drove to the hospital, Ella considered all the events of that morning. "Have you heard anything that might explain the reason for the attack?" Ella asked her.

"I know only what you do—that Kevin's been threatened verbally via crank calls and e-mails. It all started when he took the case against Alan Grady, the manager provided by Casino Enterprises Management, the firm contracted to run the facility. From the gossip I've heard, he's been over-billing the tribe and skimming off the top. It's also possible that some members of our tribe are on the take."

"We should make up a list of names, focusing particularly on those who might have had military training. These guys were confident, not to mention extremely well armed. And they are skilled fighters. One of them pinned me down with cover fire while the other deployed a smoke grenade to screen their escape. Otherwise, I'd have had a clear shot at their vehicle up close, and maybe taken out a tire—or more. They thought this thing through."

They arrived at the hospital less than five minutes later and parked beside the EMT vehicle in the space reserved for the police.

Paramedics were busy replenishing their supplies and putting away their gear, but seeing Ella, one of the med techs came to meet her. "Both men are now in surgery, but we've set aside their personal effects for you." He pointed to a pair of labeled and signed plastic bags.

Ella thanked them as Justine took possession of the items.

"Do you want me to stick around or should I head back?" Justine asked her.

"Go help the others at the airstrip. I'll be fine."

As Ella walked into the small emergency room lobby, she saw Dawn at the water fountain and Rose seated in a straight-backed chair, staring at her hands. Herman stood beside Rose, his hand on his wife's shoulder.

Turning at the sound of the door opening and seeing Ella, Dawn ran over and hugged her tightly. "They won't let me see him, Mom. Can't you do something? Dad would want me with him. I can't even get anyone to tell me how he's doing!"

"You're going to have to be patient. The doctors are busy and can't take time for us right now," Ella said, easing her hold.

As Dawn stepped out of her arms, her eyes grew wide and huge tears began spilling down her face. "Mom, you're still bleeding!"

Ella's stomach sank. The last thing she'd wanted to do was scare her kid even more. "Any cut on the scalp bleeds like crazy, Pumpkin. You know that. Remember when you fell off Wind in the arena and bumped into the gate? Relax." She lowered her voice, and in a whisper, added, "Right now I need you to keep it together so you can take care of your grandmother. Can I count on you?"

Her words had the desired effect. Dawn straightened and wiped her eyes. "I'm fine, Mom. I'll take care of *Shimasání*," she said, using the Navajo word for Grandmother.

"You know how she feels about hospitals, so you'll have to stay close to her."

"She hates it here, *Shimá*, but I can't leave, not until I see Dad," Dawn said in a strangled voice.

Ella heard the fear and the steely determination in her daughter's voice. Nothing was going to convince Dawn to leave.

Rose came over and joined them, strain mirrored clearly on her face. Ella found herself wishing that she could have sent Rose and Dawn downstairs to what was clearly the most peaceful section of the hospital. Her best friend, Dr. Carolyn Roanhorse, would have gladly looked after both of them. But it was completely out of the question. Carolyn was the

Navajo Nation's only pathologist, and downstairs was the morgue. Since Carolyn had regular contact with the dead, most Navajos, including Rose, assiduously avoided her, not to mention the morgue.

Ella gave her mother an encouraging smile. "My daughter just needs reassurance from the doctor. Once she hears that her father's out of surgery and in the recovery room, she'll go home."

Rose sighed. "She's as stubborn as you were at that age."

Ella chuckled, knowing it was the truth. "I'll be back in a few minutes," she said. "I need to get these cuts cleaned up."

Ella went up to the desk, then followed one of the nurses into a small examination room. An Anglo doctor she'd never met before came in about five minutes later.

His name tag read Dr. James Kelner, and from his age, Ella guessed he was one of the young doctors who came to work on the Rez as a way to pay off his student loans. Often highly skilled, though not necessarily experienced, most found the customs of a culture they'd known little about prior to their arrival, overwhelming. Though there were exceptions, the majority left as soon as they could.

Dr. Kelner checked Ella out quickly, cleaning the wounds again under bright lights and sterile conditions.

"You're hair is beautiful, but I could get a better look if you let me cut some of it away," he asked, reaching into a drawer and bringing out clippers.

Ella's black hair had lightened a bit with age—or maybe because of the job—but it had been down well past her shoulders since she'd left the Bureau many years ago. As he came toward her, she answered his question with a "how would you like a kick in the groin" look.

Kelner laughed, placing the clippers back in the drawer. "I never argue with a woman wearing a gun." He adjusted the overhead light and took another close look at her scalp.

"And a very lucky woman, it seems. I understand you were involved in that shooting at the airstrip, so I'm reporting that long furrow as a bullet graze. Your department will probably want copies. But it looks like you won't need stitches," he said at last. "I'll give you a prescription for antibiotics, and I want you to come back in another day or so. I'll take another look then to make sure everything's healing the way it should."

"The wounded men who came in first," Ella said. "Have you heard anything about their condition?"

"I only attended, but the one with the shoulder wound—the pilot—is listed as stable now. The other two went straight into surgery. Sergeant Lonewolf is in critical condition, but his companion's wounds were less serious and his prognosis is good. If you need more information, you'll have to talk to the surgical team once the patients go into recovery."

"Thanks." Ella followed the doctor out of the room. The second she was in the hall, Dawn came rushing up, looking up at her head. "Mom?"

Ella smiled at her. "I'm fine, and it looks like your dad will be, too."

"I know. *Shimasání* got one of her feelings and told me," Dawn said.

Ella smiled. Rose's feelings on matters of this kind were as reliable as the rising sun. No one had ever been able to explain it, but it was hard to argue with a track record like hers. "Your father's still in surgery, and afterwards he'll need to sleep for several hours. You won't be able to talk to him, not for quite a while."

"Maybe I can see him when they take him to his room," Dawn said in a whisper. "Will you stay with us, or do you have to go back to the crime scene?"

Ella noticed she'd said "crime scene," not airport. Dawn had learned the hard way about the demands of her mother's work. "I'll stick around for a bit."

While they waited, Ella noted that Rose sat on the edge

of her chair, never quite leaning back. Herman stood by his wife's side, scarcely moving, his hand still on her shoulder, a gentle comfort and reminder of his presence.

As the minutes passed, Ella kept checking back with her team via cell phone. Just as she took another call, Dawn went back to the vending machine for the third time. So far, her daughter had eaten three bags of potato chips and drunk a can of soda. Dawn had a very healthy appetite, but never put on weight. Whatever she took in, she burned off almost as quickly. Ella smiled wistfully, remembering a time when the same had been said about her. These days she had to work out hard or she'd pack on the pounds.

Hearing the door to the emergency room open behind her, Ella turned and saw a tired, somber-looking, middle-aged doctor in surgical scrubs approaching.

"Investigator Clah?" the Anglo doctor asked, looking directly at her. When she nodded, the man stepped forward. "I'm Dr. Sanderson."

From his age, Ella guessed he was one of the few MDs who'd chosen to stay and continue his practice on the Rez.

"I thought you'd want to know that Mr. Tolino has just been taken into the recovery room. He's stable, his signs are good, and unless there are some unforeseen complications he should fully recover."

Ella saw her daughter leap into her grandmother's arms. Reassured by Dawn's response, Ella focused on the work at hand. "And the other patient, Adam Lonewolf?"

Dr. Sanderson stepped closer and lowered his voice. "The next twenty-four will be critical for Sergeant Lonewolf. After that, we'll see where we stand. Head trauma doesn't always follow a predictable course. I wish I had better news."

Ella nodded somberly. "I'll need the slugs and any foreign fragments recovered from the victims as well as their clothing. I'll also want to question both men as soon as they regain consciousness. Can you give an idea of when that'll be?"

"I understand that you're conducting a criminal investigation, but as I said, Mr. Lonewolf's condition is far from stable. There's no way of predicting when, or if, he'll regain consciousness," he said. "And head trauma is often accompanied by short- or long-term memory loss."

As the doctor excused himself and turned away, Ella felt a hand on her shoulder. The unexpected touch made her flinch.

"Easy, Clah, it's just me," Special Agent Dwayne Blalock said.

"Dwayne," Ella said, recognizing the distinctive voice instantly and turning. Throughout the years, she and the tall, athletic FBI agent—nicknamed FB-Eyes because he had one blue and one brown eye—had worked many cases together. "It's been one heckuva day."

"So I hear," he answered, giving her a crooked smile. "Officer Goodluck called me from the scene so I thought I'd come by and give you a ride when you're done."

"Thanks," Ella said. "Right now I need to check in with my people and see if the van's been found."

"Every agency in the Four Corners has picked up on that ATL broadcast, and everyone's out looking. Roadblocks have been set up, too, but so far no luck."

Before she could answer, Dawn came up to her. "*Shimasání* wants to go home, but I want to be here when Dad wakes up. Can I stay with you?"

"That's not a good idea," Ella said. "You need to go home and help *Shimasání*. It's been a scary morning and she may need to rest. Remember that your dad may not wake up for hours. As soon as he does and is allowed to see visitors, you can come back."

"But Mom—"

"No. The nurses will call *Shimasání* when your father wakes up, and you can come back then. Sitting in a chair here at the hospital won't make things go any faster," Ella said. "I'll be leaving shortly, too."

Rose came up to join them. "My granddaughter and I will be fine. We'll wait here until suppertime, then go home. Go do whatever you have to, daughter."

Ella smiled at her mom. Rose was always there whenever Ella needed her. No one knew how old Rose really was, but her mother had boundless energy. As an active member of the Plant Watchers, Rose often went on long nature walks that would have tired even a seasoned hiker.

As Ella's family left, two Navajo women rushed in and hurried to the front desk. The younger one was wearing jeans and a tee-shirt and Ella recognized her instantly from a recent newspaper photo. She was Adam's wife, Marie. The second woman was around Rose's age and wearing a traditional long skirt and loose-fitting blouse.

The women were followed by an older Navajo man wearing jeans and a western shirt with snaps instead of buttons. He had long hair, a red headband, and boots—the equivalent of cowboy garb, Indian style. He joined them at the counter.

As Ella glanced over wondering if this would be a good time to introduce herself, the man turned around, spotted her, and approached. He smelled of hay, sheep, and hours of hard work outside.

"You're the policewoman who was on the same airplane—that nurse said. We came as soon as we could, but we were at our sheep camp in the Chuskas when the officer tracked us down. It's a long drive into town," he said, pushing back a strand of white hair that had worked free from the pony tail at the base of his neck. "My son . . . is he . . ."

Ella realized then that he was Adam Lonewolf's father. From the way he avoided the use of names, she also surmised he was a Traditionalist. "Your son is fighting for his life, but there's hope. He's young and strong. Your son's doctor will be able to tell you more." Seeing Dr. Sanderson coming down the hall, Ella signaled him.

Ella introduced the men, then stepped back as they joined the two women, who'd been watching anxiously.

Dr. Sanderson gave them the same highlights he'd given Ella earlier, then added, "He's undergoing another procedure right now but, fortunately, he's holding his own and that's a positive sign."

"We want a *hataalii* to come to the hospital and do a Come-to-Life Sing," Mr. Lonewolf said.

Ella knew that her brother Clifford specialized in those. As one of the tribe's most respected *hataaliis*, medicine men, he was often called in to perform the ceremony whenever a Navajo was rendered unconscious. Navajos believed that the living part of a man, his life spirit, sometimes became separated from the body. When that happened the proper ceremony was needed to restore order and bring about harmony.

Leaving them to work out the details, Ella joined Blalock, who'd gone over to buy two cans of soda. He handed one to Ella without comment. "Thanks," she mumbled, opening the can with a tug on the ring.

"Ready to go?" he asked.

"Let me touch base with the surgeon one last time," she said, heading toward the doctor, who'd just stepped away from the Lonewolf family.

He met her halfway. "I've left instructions for you to be called when either of the men regain consciousness."

"Thank you. I appreciate that."

He looked back at the Lonewolf family and shook his head. "I've worked here for almost ten years, but I still can't get used to giving medicine men access to my patients."

"Our tribal beliefs matter," Ella said simply.

"Yes, and to be fair, I've seen your medicine men get results I can't even come close to explaining. But in this particular case, with the chance of infection and complications so high—" Before he could finish, his pager went off. Excusing himself, he hurried down the hall.

"They always come ready to dismiss what they don't understand, and end up finding more than they bargained for," Ella told Blalock, who'd come up.

He nodded. "It's that way for most Anglos, including me."

Ella finished her soda and tossed it in the proper bin. "This case is going to bring major league pressure down on the department," she said.

"I know. The Bureau's already received a call from your tribal president. Whatever you need, you've got."

Ella glanced around. "Before we go, I need to arrange for an officer to be posted by Kevin's door and another by Lonewolf's. Hospital security has additional personnel patrolling the area whenever shooting victims arrive, but that's not going to be enough in this case."

"I agree. If this was a hit, the suspects will find out soon enough that they didn't get the job done. They might decide to try again."

Ella contacted Big Ed, their police chief, and briefed him. "We'll need plainclothes officers brought in to guard the men. Uniforms will point out the rooms to any potential assailant."

"We're fully deployed, so I'll have to pull two of our people off the manhunt," he said. "And, Shorty, I want a full briefing as soon as you can manage it."

"Copy."

After making sure that armed, plainclothes security guards would be in place until tribal officers arrived, Ella rode with Blalock back to the station. Everyone else had been notified, and by the time they reached the Shiprock police station her team had already assembled in Big Ed Atcitty's office.

Blalock took his usual seat to the left hand side of the

desk, and the tribal officers either stood or sat on the other available chairs.

Big Ed, a barrel-chested man in his early sixties, looked her over closely without speaking, obviously accessing her condition and state of mind. He leaned forward in his chair, a question on the tip of his tongue.

Seeing it, Ella preempted him. "Don't worry about me. I'm one hundred percent, Chief," she said.

"Update me on your situation," Big Ed said.

"Attorney Tolino is out of surgery and stable with a good prognosis, but Adam Lonewolf is listed as critical. The two would-be assassins remain on the loose."

"I'm still not clear on what went down at the airstrip. Fill us in, Shorty," Big Ed said, using his nickname for Ella, though she was a head taller than him. He held up a recorder so everyone could see, then switched it on.

For the next five minutes, Ella gave them a blow-by-blow accounting of the events. When she got to the part about going to check on the victims, she tried to remain cool and analytical, but her voice cracked.

Big Ed switched off the recorder. "I want our best team on this investigation, so Special Investigator Clah will be running the show despite her personal stake in this," he said, sitting back in his chair and looking at Ella.

Ella nodded once, then turned slowly to make eye contact with the others. "Let's start with motive. This wasn't even close to a random attack. Anyone have any ideas, comments, or suggestions?"

"How about some background on the incident, Ella?" Justine said. "You flew in with both men, and it appears that one or both of them were the intended targets. Did either mention being concerned about anything in particular, or maybe seem unusually tense?"

Ella told them what she knew about the lawsuit Kevin

had been preparing against Alan Grady and Casino Enterprises. "Kevin's had threats he believes originated on the Rez—which explains why he wanted Adam Lonewolf to act as high-profile security for him. Unfortunately Adam's paperwork allowing him to be armed or carry concealed through airports hadn't been processed yet, so today, he was basically providing muscle and an extra pair of eyes. I got that from Kevin earlier in the day—but he didn't seem to be bothered by that lack of protection."

"Bet the shooters didn't know Lonewolf wasn't carrying, though, which is why they came armed to the teeth. Do you have any idea on the nature of the threats against Tolino?" Blalock asked.

"They've been in the form of calls, unsigned letters, and hostile e-mails as far as I know," Ella answered.

"The outcome of Tolino's lawsuit could impact a large number of casino employees," Benny said. "If Casino Management Enterprises loses their contract and the place is forced to close down for a while, a lot of people are going to lose their paychecks."

"I've got cousins who work there, and they say that Tolino's on a witch hunt, trying to micro-manage business operations for political reasons," Neskahi said. "So what if Grady and his company are both raking in the cash? The general consensus is that since the tribe's making money, too, and the casino offers the *Diné* good jobs with benefits, why risk the entire operation? I understand that several council members are asking for a slow down on this legal action, too. They want to work it out behind closed doors, not in the press or the courtroom."

"Double billing and phony invoices hurt the tribe. They're stealing from all of us," Justine said. "It's fraud, plain and simple. A casino run by thieves is a black mark on the entire tribe."

"Maybe so," Benny said, "but some people think that the

real issue has political overtones, and the pressure to take down Grady and his people is coming from tribal members who want to shut down all gambling on the Rez."

"What does any of this have to do with Lonewolf?" Blalock asked. "Besides working security for Tolino, how does he fit into this?"

"As far as I know, that's the extent of it," Ella said. "But we shouldn't assume anything at this point. For all we know, Adam could have been the real target of the attack. Come to think of it, Adam did seem a little tense the closer we got to home. I assumed that he was getting impatient and wanting to land so he could see his family, but I may have misread that."

"Walk very carefully here, Shorty. If you start digging into Lonewolf's activities, you're going to piss off a lot of people," Big Ed said. "He's the tribe's favorite son—and not without reason. If people think you're trying to smear a fallen hero, they'll turn on you, and any cooperation you may have hoped to get will dry up instantly."

"I realize that, and we'll try to be tactful, but it's got to be done," Ella said, then glanced at Justine. "What were you able to get from the crime scene?"

Justine reached for her small notebook and flipped it open. "These are preliminary findings," she warned, then continued. "The grenade components we found are from a military surplus smoker available over the Internet—and there's no way to trace it, unfortunately. We found fifty-one .223 shell casings, plus the nine millimeter brass that came from your weapon, Ella. They must have pocketed their empty magazines because we couldn't find any."

"They had two magazines taped together. All they had to do was flip them over. A quick tactical reload," Ella said, remembering.

"That explains it," Justine answered. "We've also tagged all the hits we could find from the assault weapons. There are several in the airplane hatch, the door to the luggage compartment or whatever you call it, and some ricocheted off the landing gear, blowing out one tire. The aircraft appears to be fully functional once the tire is replaced, but there are two mechanics still looking it over. We've got tire tread impressions from the suspects' vehicle where they ran off the asphalt, and what we think is fabric from one of the gray coveralls the men wore. It's not Kevlar, or any other material used in ballistic vests—just heavy cotton. The blood splatter and pools have been typed and preliminaries suggest that it's from the four victims—you included. If the shooters were hit, we have no evidence of it."

"Adam came out of the plane carrying a brown leather briefcase," Ella said. "Where is it now, the evidence room?"

"It's in the lab. A round penetrated it and there's no exit hole, so the slug must still be inside. I haven't had time to open the briefcase and recover the bullet. Hopefully we'll get something we can use for a ballistics match. I also have the items that were in Tolino's and Lonewolf's possession when they were attacked. In addition to regular chewing gum, bus tokens, ink pens and such, there are wallets, keys, and a BlackBerry each."

"We need to check all their incoming calls to see if either of them received any threats that could point us to a suspect. They might have also made some notes that could give us a lead. Let's go sort through all that before we assign areas of investigation," Ella said. Just as she stood, Big Ed's phone rang.

As he answered, they waited, but he soon waved for them to continue without him.

Justine's small lab wasn't much larger than a walk-in freezer. As they all crowded into the room, Ella smiled, thinking of the huge, glass-walled sets on the crime lab series everyone was watching on TV these days. The one here looked like a miniature science class—without the students—and most of their equipment was on one large counter.

As all five of them gathered around the centrally located black-topped lab table, Justine put on a pair of latex gloves and examined the leather briefcase. A small bump was visible on the side opposite the bullet hole, and she felt it with her fingertip. "Here's the bullet, I think. Whatever's inside must have really slowed it down—maybe a really thick book."

Using a scalpel, she cut a circle into the leather, exposing the copper-jacketed bullet, which was almost intact. "Full metal jacket—military surplus. Cheap and hard to trace." Justine pried the bullet out gently with her fingers then, taking the evidence bag from Ella, placed the slug inside.

"Now let's find out what in the briefcase slowed down a high velocity round like that," Ella said. "I remember Adam telling me that he was bringing home some papers and a game for his nephew, but he must have had something a lot thicker than that inside."

"Want me to pick the lock? I don't have a key," Justine said. "I went through Adam's things—the ones the EMTs signed over to me—but I didn't find one there."

"Are you saying that he had a locked briefcase but no key? That doesn't make sense," Blalock said.

"Did he have a key chain?" Ella asked.

"No," Justine answered, producing the evidence bags containing all of Lonewolf's personal effects.

"What else did he have on him?" Ella asked.

Justine placed two more large, thick paper evidence bags before her. "The hospital stripped off his clothing and placed everything in here for us, according to protocol."

"Maybe Adam lost the key," Blalock suggested.

Ella shook her head. "Not likely. He struck me as a man who paid particular attention to details. In that same spirit, he may not have carried the key in a key chain, making it easy for anyone who might break into his hotel room, for example. But he would have been smart enough to keep it handy in case airport security asked him to open his briefcase."

"So you're thinking he kept it . . . where?" Justine asked.

Ella considered it as she studied the evidence bag with Adam's personal effects. One contained his BlackBerry, which had been damaged, his wallet, his tickets, and a matchbook.

Putting on a pair of gloves, Ella walked to a small closet where the bloody clothes were hung to dry before being stored. As she searched his pants, she discovered a small, deep change pocket on the right. "I've got it. It's in here."

Moments later Justine opened the briefcase. The bullet had passed through a folder labeled "Tribal Industries" that held about fifty sheets of paper, then through both sides of a special edition boxed Monopoly game. From there it had continued through to the opposite wooden panel and pushed into the leather skin.

"I can't see anything in this briefcase that could have slowed it down that much," Ella said.

"Maybe the round was defective," Justine said.

"An assault rifle of that caliber will penetrate most ballistic vests well beyond a hundred yards, and this was just a little wood and paper. The airport shooting took place at a distance of what—a hundred feet or less?" Blalock asked.

Ella nodded. "That's about right."

Justine picked up the Monopoly box, still in the shrink-wrap. "I remember these as being longer. This is nearly square. And it sure feels heavy for being a kid's board game."

"Maybe the playing board is metal, not cardboard. That would make it a special edition," Neskahi said, taking it from Justine and studying it. "I don't see a store label or price tag," he noted.

"Open it up so we can take a look," Ella said.

Using a pocketknife, Justine sliced open the wrapping and opened the box. Suddenly the room grew silent.

"This isn't play money," Ella said, studying the large stacks of hundred-dollar bills that were banded together with wide rubber bands. The bullet had passed through several of the tightly packed bundles—and a thick plastic game board folded and hinged in the middle. "Now we know what slowed the slug down to zero."

Ella pulled one of the bills out from a stack that had been untouched and held it up to the light. A moment later, she set it back down on the table. "I've seen top-grade counterfeit money before, but this looks like the real thing."

"Hold it up for me, Ella," Blalock asked. "You've got the gloves on."

She held it up to the light, giving FB-Eyes a closer look.

He studied it then finally nodded. "It's got all the anti-counterfeiting features—buried strips, special dyes, hidden faces—the whole nine yards. It's the real deal."

Neskahi whistled low. "How much do you think is here?"

"I have no idea," Ella said. "I've never been so close to this much cash."

"Me neither," Blalock admitted. "What strikes me is how skillfully this was disguised. The game cards, player pieces, and board are still in their original box. Almost everyone knows this particular game has lots of stacks of play money, so a casual look by an x-ray screener wouldn't have raised any questions, particularly because the box has been rewrapped with stretch film to make it look like the factory seal."

"But why would Adam have been carrying this much money?" Ella asked, thinking out loud.

Blalock stared at the bills, lost in thought. "He's a tribal lobbyist, right? Maybe this is bribe money for his government contacts. I don't see any logic in Lonewolf being paid off. The kickback money usually goes in the other direction."

"Following your premise, then why was he carrying it back to the Rez? That cash should have stayed in D.C.," Justine said.

Ella stared at the stacks of money. "Maybe this came from Casino Enterprises' home office. It could be part of a deal to pay back the money they took from the tribe and squash the lawsuit Kevin's throwing at them."

"This could also be the war hero's savings—cashed out," Neskahi suggested. "He might have been planning to make a down payment on, say, a condo in D.C., then changed his mind."

"A sergeant in the armed services with that much cash lying around?" Blalock shook his head. "Not likely—unless he had another business on the side. Of course soldiers sometimes bring back stuff from overseas and resell it here—legal or not. He could have been dealing anything from collector's items to drugs."

"The very existence of this much untraceable money sends out warning signals," Benny said. "Most legal businesses handle transactions through electronic transfers or checks, not with cash."

"Whatever the case, someone sure went to a lot of trouble buying the game, opening it, switching out the play money, then carefully resealing the whole thing," Ella said. "Adam told me he'd bought the game for his nephew."

"Either Lonewolf didn't know about the stash and was being played by someone who was using him as a courier, or he lied to you. Maybe *this* is what the shooters were after," Blalock said.

"No, I don't agree with that. It would have been a lot simpler for the perps with the assault rifles to demand the money up front instead of opening fire," Ella said. "Their only interest was in their targets. As soon as Kevin and Adam went down hard, their job was done and they took off. That's my definition of a hit."

"Any idea when can we talk to Tolino?" Blalock asked.

"I don't know. The hospital will call me when he's conscious," Ella said. "What we could do right now is talk to Kevin's boss, Robert Buck. He might be able to help us rule out or establish the casino payoff possibility."

"Buck, he's what . . . the equivalent of the attorney general for the tribe?" Blalock asked.

Ella nodded.

"It's Sunday so he's not going to be at the office," Justine said, then going to her computer, found Robert Buck's address in the tribal government database and wrote it down. "Here you go," she said, handing the paper to Ella. "He lives just north of Twin Lakes, not far from the turnoff to Coyote Canyon. About an eighty-minute drive one way."

"Good thing my house is on the way," Ella said. "I'll stop there long enough to shower and change. I've still got blood on me, and my shirt's full of holes." She glanced at Justine and added, "I'll bag it all for you and bring it in."

Ella looked around at the other members of her team. "Justine will take care of the lab work. Benny and Joe, start interviewing everyone in the community who might have seen that van, working from the airstrip out. The shooters were probably waiting in the area, maybe at a fast food place or beside the highway, then moved in when they spotted the aircraft circling. Their timing was precise. They also had to know we were coming in on that flight so, Benny, find out who knew Tolino and Lonewolf were scheduled to land this morning. Joe, I want you to talk to those who knew Lonewolf and see what other things he had going on in his life."

"In D.C., too?" Neskahi asked.

"Yeah. You can do that part of it by phone," Ella said. "Also interview people who knew or worked with Kevin here and over there. Benny, one last thing. Check on Alan Grady's alibi. We'll need to know where he was during the time of the incident."

Benny nodded. "I'll try to get the names of Grady's closest associates, too. If he was one of the gunmen, he wasn't alone. But this'll take a while to put together."

"We need more manpower," Neskahi said, turning as Big Ed appeared at the lab's door. The chief nodded for the sergeant to continue.

"Those immediate interviews and alibi checks are going to take time, and we may have to track down locals who saw something—like business employees whose shifts have ended," Neskahi added.

"Feel free to pull in Officer Marianna Talk for legwork," Big Ed said. "If you still need more hands, Shorty, come talk to me. I just took another call from headquarters at Window Rock. You're to have all the help you need."

"I'll get Marianna then," Ella said.

"I'll arrange for Bureau agents in D.C. to look into any possible connection between the crime and the work that Tolino and Lonewolf were doing in and around the capital," Blalock said.

"There's something else I'm going to need." Ella showed Big Ed the money Adam had been carrying, and described how they'd found it. When she repeated what Adam had told her about the game being for his nephew, Big Ed's eyebrows went up.

"Do whatever you need to keep this from hitting the fan," he said.

"I need to get all the details behind Kevin's lawsuit against casino management," Ella said. "I'm planning to talk to Robert Buck about it, but I don't think he's going to give me a straight answer."

"You're right about that," Big Ed said. "In my experience, attorneys play things like this very close to their chests, and Robert Buck is an old defense lawyer. But give me a little time and I'll see what I can do."

"I appreciate the help, Chief," Ella said.

As Ella left the building with Blalock some time later, she lapsed into an uneasy silence.

"What's eating at you, Clah?" Blalock asked at last.

"Every police officer is warned repeatedly that complacency always carries a high price. When the plane landed I was really looking forward to spending some quiet time with my family, and business was the last thing on my mind. I let down my guard, Dwayne, and that was precisely when everything went crazy."

"It happens that way sometimes. Don't start blaming yourself. You couldn't have anticipated what happened."

Ella thought of Kevin and ex-army sergeant Lonewolf, an authentic war hero who'd been awarded his country's second highest medal for his heroism in Afghanistan. Now he was fighting for his life after being ambushed, unarmed, at a small Navajo airstrip over three hundred and fifty miles inside the borders of his native land. He'd survived the war abroad, with its IEDs, mortars, snipers, and machine-gun fire, only to have to face his own mortality here at home.

It was now up to her to restore the *hózhó*, the harmony. That's what she did. In the *bilagáana* world, a police officer upheld the law. Here on the reservation, her job went beyond that. She needed to restore the balance, honoring both the laws of nature and of men, so all could walk in beauty.

As they drove south out of Shiprock, passing the airstrip on her left, she saw the airplane still sitting there. Heat waves rose from the asphalt where she'd nearly died a few hours ago. Ella forced herself to look away and focus on the job ahead. Her work had only just begun.

THREE

✖ ✖ ✖

Hey, Ella, you okay in there?" Blalock called out.

"Yeah, sorry it's taken me so long, Dwayne," she yelled from the back bedroom. "Normally I can shower and change in five minutes, but I'm sore all over. All that hitting the pavement and rolling takes its toll." She crossed the narrow hall, and entered the living room, where he was waiting.

"I'd suggest that you're getting too old for this field work crap, but I have a dozen years on you and I haven't got the sense to start looking for a desk job either," Blalock said, getting up from the sofa.

"Have a seat again while I grab a glass of my mom's herbal tea, will you? I've been looking forward to that for the past four days," Ella said, heading toward the kitchen. "Want one?"

"No thanks." He eased back down onto the soft cushion. "Have you decided if you'll be taking the job at PPS? After what happened to you today, I was wondering if working for three times the pay in an air-conditioned D.C. office has suddenly become irresistible."

Ella poured herself a glass of the cool brew from a gallon

jar her mom kept in the fridge. "I don't know what I'm going to do. The money and benefits are hard to beat, that's true, but I'd be giving up a lot."

She stopped in the doorway, looking at FB-Eyes as she sipped the cold tea. "I spoke to three of the women who work at PPS. Two of them are former police officers, and the one thing that struck me is that they're lonely after hours. They were always looking for ways to connect with other people, through clubs, churches and things like that. On the Rez that's all built in. We're all connected—part of the tribe. We have our neighbors, our clans, and our families."

"You could still stay in touch with everyone here. E-mail, phone calls, text messaging, video conferencing in front of your computer, even. It's pretty much instant gratification."

"I'm not sure that would be enough for me. But like I said, I'm still thinking things over." She walked back to the sink and rinsed out her glass. "Right now you and I better get going," she said, grabbing the paper bag that held her soiled clothing.

Blalock reached for his keys. "I've done some homework while you were cleaning up. Robert Buck, Kevin's boss, graduated from Harvard and has worked for the tribe ever since. He flies back and forth from his office in Window Rock to D.C. about once a month. He also keeps his nose clean. He doesn't even have a parking ticket, and his credit rating is excellent. No big bills, and no money problems, apparently."

Moments later, Blalock drove down the gravel road leading from Ella's home to the main highway to the east. "You've checked Buck's background via our normal channels. Now let me go through the back door," Ella said. Then, using her cell phone, she dialed her mother, who was still at the hospital.

Rose was well connected, and, more often than not, managed to get the kind of information that went well beyond legal channels.

Rose answered on the first ring. These days her mom

not only carried a cell phone, she actually kept it on. For many months, though she'd take the phone with her wherever she went, she'd refuse to turn it on. She didn't want to be bothered. Ella smiled. Dawn had finally convinced her to leave it on so she could reach her grandmother anytime in case of an emergency.

Ella wasn't sure what career her daughter would end up choosing someday, but her powers of persuasion were second to none.

Ella told her mom what she needed, asking her to keep the request totally private. "Anything you can tell me about him might help, Mom."

"I know the attorney general's grandmother. She's very proud of her son, the lawyer from Harvard. She thinks that he places too much importance on what the *bilagáanas* think, but he told her that he has to play by their rules so he can get some cooperation on matters that affect the tribe."

"Thanks, Mom," Ella said, then hung up.

"What did she say?" Blalock asked.

Ella shared what she'd learned. "Kevin's like that, too—he plays to win. The difference between men like Adam and Kevin is the site of their battles."

Blalock glanced over at her, then back at the road.

She waited for his comment, but it didn't come. "What?" she finally asked.

"For a moment there it almost sounded like you still had a thing for Tolino."

Ella shook her head. "No, we'll never be more than friends. But he's a good man, and without him, my life would be minus the one person who means the world to me—Dawn."

"Most women I know would have tossed a criticism or two in there to justify why they let him go," Blalock said. "But then again, you're not like most women."

"Is there a compliment in there somewhere?"

"Yeah, but don't let it go to your head," he grumbled, speeding up to pass a slow-moving pickup loaded with firewood.

Ella started writing down notes in the small leather notebook she carried in her breast pocket. It had been a Christmas gift from Dawn. The first page still read, "To Mom, the best cop on the Rez."

A few months ago Dawn had been fascinated with police work. Now, she wanted to become an actress. Ella had taken it as a win. Anything was better than having her daughter in law enforcement.

"Whatcha got there?" Blalock asked.

Ella looked down at her notes—most of it questions that needed to be answered. "I'm still trying to figure out if the gunmen picked up those assault rifles—the ArmaLites— locally. Since they would have been far too easy to trace if they'd come from a sporting goods store, I was thinking maybe an area gun show?"

"There are lot of AR assault rifles in the hands of civilians. You sure they were 180Bs?"

"Pretty sure. The receivers looked flat, not rounded like with the earlier AR-15s and the M-16s. There was no handle on top, and the stock looked more tapered near the pistol grip, setting them off from the earlier 180s, if I recall correctly. They're supposed to be improved models, not that I've ever fired one. I just got a good look every time they shifted targets. Lucky me."

"At least that narrows down the search. The bad part is that a lot of assault weapons are being bought and sold at the moment. The drug wars in Mexico have created a hot market and getting hold of weapons and ammunition is easy, if you know where to look. On the outside chance that the two weapons were stolen from a gun dealer, I'm having the Bureau check out reports in surrounding states. A security camera image would sure help us out."

She nodded, closing her notebook.

After a long silence, Blalock spoke. "You're right about Kevin not liking to lose. That's why he's going to want to nail whoever did this."

"I'm hoping he'll be able to give us some leads. But, if not, we'll find them on our own," Ella said. "I don't like to lose either."

This corner of the Rez was closer to the mountains. The piñon and juniper trees were taller and more numerous, scattered over the low hills and alongside the many arroyos that flowed from the south. Farther west lay the Chuska Mountains, where actual patches of forest could be found on the higher slopes.

After making a left onto tribal Highway 9, which led past Coyote Canyon all the way to Crownpoint, she saw a solitary house about a quarter mile from the road. The one-story ranch-style structure, complete with two car garage, was surrounded by junipers except for a big garden patch at the rear and a large fenced-in corral with a loafing shed on the west side.

"A big garage and no hogan in the back, so these are Modernists, right? We won't have to wait by the car?" Blalock asked as he drove down the gravel lane.

"Some of the tribal officials react badly to those who look like they're disrespecting the culture, so let's play it safe. We'll get out and wait by the car. If we put the family at ease by extending them that courtesy, things might go more smoothly."

Blalock parked beside a flagstone walk that led to the front door, then they both got out of the vehicle and stood by the front bumper. A minute later a tall Navajo man in dress slacks and a long-sleeved yellow shirt stepped out, holding a cell phone to his ear. Ella recognized Robert Buck immediately. As he continued speaking to the person on the other end, the tribe's head attorney motioned for them to approach.

When they reached the concrete porch, he opened the front door and silently invited them inside. Buck led them through an ordinary-looking living room, where a wall-mounted large-screen TV was tuned to a baseball game, then down a hall into his office. He waved them toward a small sofa and continued his conversation.

"The officers are here right now," Robert Buck told the person on the other end. "I'll let you know what progress has been made as soon as possible." Buck closed up the phone and focused on them, standing with his hips pressed against the front of his desk.

"Special Investigator Clah, I'm glad to see you're not seriously injured. And Special Agent Blalock, it's good to see the Bureau's going to work with us on this." He reached out and shook Blalock's hand, an Anglo political concession. Casual physical contact was something that didn't come naturally to the *Diné*.

Buck walked around to his desk chair, then sat. "Our tribal president is going to be watching this case very closely. A national hero and one of our tribe's most respected attorneys have been attacked here on our land. A security lapse like that should have never been allowed to happen."

Ella felt the implied criticism in his words and struggled for a moment to suppress her resentment.

"Have you uncovered a motive for the attack?" Buck asked.

"It's too soon for that," Ella said.

"Have you considered the possibility that you, Investigator Clah, were the real target?" Buck asked. "As a police officer, you make enemies with nearly every arrest."

"We haven't ruled anything out, but the events suggest that the two men wearing business suits were the focus of the attack—not me. The gunmen opened fire on Kevin Tolino and Adam Lonewolf first, though I was a closer target. Most of the shots were directed at them, too. The suspects didn't shift their aim to me until I returned fire. They also withdrew even though I was obviously still alive."

Buck nodded thoughtfully, but didn't comment.

"That brings me to the reason I'm here," Ella said. "I need to fill in some gaps."

Ella told him about the cash they'd found—$75,000 according to Justine, who'd text-messaged her the amount during the long drive. "I'll be speaking to Mr. Lonewolf's family later, but at this point we have no idea why Adam was carrying so much money, where it came from, or why he chose to conceal it from airport security."

Buck leaned back in his chair, stretching his long legs out before him. His angular features sharpened even more as he weighed what she'd told him. "That money didn't come from our office. I can tell you that much for sure. I also can't imagine that amount having come from any branch of tribal government. In a world of accountants and financial responsibility, all our tribal business transactions and payouts are conducted via money transfers or checks. Nobody in government uses that amount of cash."

"Is it possible that Kevin negotiated some kind of settlement with casino management and that was some of the money being returned to the tribe?" Ella asked. "Something done in cash might help keep the paperwork low profile and save some embarrassing disclosures."

"Just the opposite, I'd say, but either way that couldn't have happened without my knowledge." Buck regarded her thoughtfully. "Kevin's had a tough time making his case. Casino Enterprises covers their paper trail well, and they want certain things to stay hidden. I've heard rumblings about a move to get him fired, or demoted. They're also willing to play as rough as it takes to divert from the real issue."

Ella sat up, sensing there was more to the story. "What do you mean?"

"About ten days ago, Kevin was assaulted outside our D.C. office late one evening. He believed that his assailants were people hired by casino management to get him to back off, because he wasn't robbed, just roughed up. Of course that made Kevin even more determined to see the case through."

Ella glanced at Blalock and saw him nod imperceptibly at her. He'd follow up on the crime report later.

She focused back on Buck. "I'm going to need to know more about the lawsuit. What kind of evidence did Kevin have that the company was stealing from the tribe?"

Buck took a deep breath and expelled it in a hiss. "I was hoping you wouldn't ask. Your chief of police called the tribal president earlier and he asked me to give you all the details. For the record, I don't agree with that decision, but I'll go along with it."

Ella waited, knowing, eventually, he'd continue.

"The tribe ordered an audit, and every dollar we'd paid Casino Enterprises was accounted for, but when Kevin took a closer look, new details came to light. Their charges for administrative services, equipment, and supplies were often way out line compared to established rates, and some transactions looked like duplicates of earlier orders with just the dates and invoice numbers changed. Then he discovered that Casino Enterprises had been hired to run the casino through a series of smaller, concurrent contracts. That allowed them to avoid the single, larger contract amount that would have required competitive bids."

"What put Kevin onto the scam?" Blalock asked.

"An informant sent him an e-mail with copies of the invoices. When management was asked to account for discrepancies, we got accusations of harassment, then a stall, asking for time to conduct an internal audit. That's when the coverup began. Kevin learned that the manager had been allowed to use his own people to conduct the initial audit, so we decided to get informants to fill in the gaps and take the company to court once we had a case."

"So Kevin's been trying to find additional informants so he can gather more evidence?" Ella asked.

"Exactly. What works in our favor is that Casino Enterprises Management can't afford the unfavorable publicity. They're trying to close a deal with another tribe in Oklahoma. Mind you, CEM is still capable of playing hardball, but we're not sure to what extent."

"So it's possible, maybe even likely, that Kevin *was* the target and Adam got caught in the crossfire because the gunmen had to make sure they got the right guy. Both victims were dressed alike and share similar physical characteristics," Ella said. "But that still doesn't explain the money Adam was carrying."

"Adam was—is—a lobbyist, and his job is to represent tribal interests. That includes promoting the passage of favorable legislation and bringing investments and industry to the Navajo Nation. I suppose the cash could have been a payoff for one of the companies he contacted, but who funded it? Had it been a legitimate money transfer, it would have gone through the banking systems," Buck said.

"My thoughts exactly," Blalock agreed.

"I'll try to get more information for you about the government officials and business concerns he was supposed to be in contact with," Buck said, "but tread carefully. We can't risk embarrassing the wrong people."

A few minutes later, Buck saw them to the door. "Keep me updated," he added just before going back inside.

Ella remained quiet as they got back on the main highway, heading north on Highway 491.

Finally Blalock glanced over at her. "Something about

Robert Buck annoyed you big time," he said. "Don't bother to deny it. What's the problem?"

"His first priority wasn't the injured men. It was protecting the case one of his trial attorneys was working on and making sure no blame could be pointed in his direction."

"He's a politician. Covering their tails and trails is what they do best," Blalock said with a shrug.

"Maybe so, but not embarrassing the wrong people isn't high on my list of priorities. Getting answers is."

FOUR
———— ✖ ✖ ✖ ————

MONDAY

The following morning Ella awoke slowly. Although it felt as if she'd just fallen asleep, the alarm clock was ringing insistently and loudly. Grumbling, she reached over and shut it off, wishing she could just go back to sleep. As she lay there wondering if she could steal five more minutes, she could hear Rose fixing breakfast.

Ella joined her family in the kitchen a short time later and headed straight for the coffeepot. Dawn was drinking orange juice while Rose fixed oatmeal from scratch. Her mom added milk from the very beginning, then cooked it slowly and thoroughly, bringing out the flavor and filling the kitchen with the wonderful scent of home-cooked breakfast. Rose wouldn't even consider buying the thirty-second kind, much less instant.

As Ella sat down she heard a knock at the door, followed by footsteps announcing that the person had entered the house. Even before he called out a hello and came into view, Ella knew it was Ford. The sound of his footsteps were as familiar to her these days as Rose's and Herman's.

Ford came up behind Ella, placed his hands on her

shoulders, and squeezed gently. "I heard about yesterday. Are you okay?"

Ella patted his hand. That was all the affection Ford—the Navajo minister at the ultra-conservative Good Shepherd Church—would condone in public. "I'm fine."

"I went by the hospital first thing. Your child's father is out of ICU and in his own room, but he's still under sedation."

Glancing at Dawn, Ella returned her bright smile. "See that? He's going to be fine. Once he's awake, he'll want to see you, but you're going to have to keep your visits short. He'll need rest most of all."

"I know, Mom, I know. How about after school today? Can I go then?"

"Maybe, but no promises. We'll have to wait and see," Ella said.

As Rose set a steaming bowl of oatmeal in front of Dawn, Ella grabbed Ford gently by the hand and led him into the living room.

The moment they were out of view, he gathered her into his arms. "When I heard . . . ," he whispered, then kissed her gently.

"It was rough going," she answered in a soft voice, resting her chin on his shoulder, her cheek next to his.

Ford held her tightly for a moment, then eased his hold and moved away, taking her hands in his. "Your job is too dangerous and unpredictable," he said, then in a heavy voice added, "But that's exactly what attracts you to it."

"You should understand that better than most. You weren't always a preacher," she said. To this day she still didn't know what his job had been, only that he'd been part of the intelligence community and had done jobs for the FBI. When she'd tried to get answers she'd been officially warned to back off. Need to know didn't include her. She'd followed orders, but the questions remained.

"Dawn seems to be handling things very well," he said.

"So far, yes," Ella said slowly. "But I think she's role-playing, trying to meet my expectations and be tough. Inside, she's pretty scared."

"She's trying too hard to be just like her mother. But little girls need an outlet for their emotions. Big girls, too," he added with a gentle smile.

"Don't worry about me. I've got things covered. But Dawn . . ."

"Why don't we both talk to her right now? That might help."

They joined her at the breakfast table and, after Dawn finished eating, Ella asked her into the living room.

"Is it Dad? Something you're not telling me?" Dawn asked immediately, her fists clinched and white-knuckled.

"That's not it at all, sweetie," Ella responded immediately, giving Dawn a big hug. "Sit down for a moment, okay?"

"Did I do something wrong? Am I in trouble?" she asked, sitting across from them on the sofa.

"Not at all," Ford said quickly. "We were just wondering if there was any way we could help you. We know you must be worried about your father, and maybe a little afraid, too, though you're being very brave about it."

"I was scared, but not anymore," Dawn said. "*Shimasání* knows things, and she said Dad's going to be okay."

Ella saw Ford's face stiffen. Although he was a Navajo scholar with an intimate knowledge of the tribe and the Navajo Way, he didn't accept any other power, or way of life, that didn't center around the god he worshiped. Reverend Bilford Tome was a conservative Christian who preached that the *Diné's* traditional beliefs were pagan and false—a part of the tribe's history, but nothing more.

"Is there anything I can do to make the next few days easier for you?" he asked, sidestepping the issue.

Ella knew that Ford was hoping she'd ask him to pray for her dad, but although Dawn didn't dismiss his beliefs, she didn't embrace them either. Uncertain of what would happen, Ella watched the situation play out between Ford and Dawn.

"Dad's going to be fine, but the other man, the soldier who got all those medals fighting for our country, he's in bad shape," she said at last. "Maybe you could pray for him to your god."

"My God wants to be yours, too. He doesn't play favorites. He loves you. Why don't we ask Him together?"

"I don't know how," Dawn answered.

"Just repeat what I say," Ford said, then led her in the Lord's Prayer.

Halfway through, Rose appeared at the doorway, glared at Ella, then disappeared. Though Rose hadn't said a word, Ella felt the sting of her mother's disapproval. Ella's dad had been a Christian preacher, and her mom, a Traditionalist her entire life, knew that the strict demands of conservative Christianity didn't allow much room for the Navajo Way. Rose wanted her granddaughter to know and embrace her own culture before being asked to participate in what she saw as Anglo religion.

After they finished the prayer, Dawn grabbed her school bag and ran off to catch the bus.

Ford came over to where Ella stood by the living room window, watching her daughter. "I hope you didn't mind," he said.

"I didn't. And I appreciate the fact that you didn't insist that she pray *only* to your god," she added, mostly to make a point.

"It's *not* just my God," Ford insisted, then shook his head. "Never mind."

"What's next on your agenda?" she asked, walking with Ford to the door.

"I need to meet with a parishioner, then I'm going back to the hospital. I'll be there within the hour, so if you'd like, I can call you and give you updates on the men."

"That would be great. In particular let me know when Kevin's awake and alert enough to be questioned. The hospital said they would, but they have other priorities," she added. "Adam, from what I've been told, is struggling to survive. I'm hoping for the best, but I doubt he'll be coming around anytime soon."

"That's what I've heard, too," he answered. "His wife attends our church and asked me to hold a bedside prayer vigil for him."

"I got the impression that his parents are Traditionalists," she mentioned, remembering how they'd been dressed at the hospital.

"Yes, they are. I'll have to work things out so nobody's upset, but the wife's wishes come first." Ford stepped to the front door. "I better get going, but we'll talk later."

Ella was about to say something when Justine walked into the room, having entered through the kitchen. "Good morning, partner—Rev. Ford," she added, giving him a friendly smile just before he stepped outside. "Your mom offered me some of her piñon coffee," she said, holding up an empty mug, "and I'm going to take her up on it. Then I'll be ready to go, okay?"

"Sure, cuz, but what brought you here so early?"

"Big Ed reminded our team that he doesn't want you to ride alone until the case is closed."

"I don't agree with him, but he's the boss, so I guess I'll adapt," Ella said, hearing Ford drive away in his old truck. "Go get your java, then we'll hit the road."

They climbed into Justine's unit a few minutes later. "Where to first?"

Ella considered it. "My brother's. I want to talk to Clifford."

"You've got it," Justine answered, driving down the private road, which led farther west toward Clifford's home. "How are you feeling? Still sore?"

"Oh, yeah. I've got more bruises than I can count."

"Speaking of counting—the $75K Adam was carrying was cleaned. It took quite a while to dust, but there were no prints at all—not one. Not even from Lonewolf himself."

"That's some wad of cash—and no prints? That's interesting all on its own," Ella said. "Were there any leads in his notes or his wallet about how or where he got the money?"

"No, but I'm still digging into it. From what I've learned a lobbyist might buy someone a thirty-dollar gift, or maybe a fifty-dollar lunch, but the former's on the high end. Junkets and expensive vacations or 'conferences' are still around, but much lower profile than they've ever been. Next on my list is talking to Lonewolf's business contacts, but I'm still trying to find an angle. It's hard to question people effectively about the cash we found in Adam's possession without getting into specifics and putting them on the defensive. If someone was expecting a bribe, they certainly wouldn't want to talk about it to a cop—not unless they're rock stupid," Justine said.

"I hate being forced to tiptoe around issues," Ella said. "We're detectives. It's our job to get to the truth. Having to handle people with kid gloves—that's for the politicians. Most of us stink at diplomacy."

"You're right. Pushing directly for answers 'til we get them is more our style."

The dirt road they were on was rough this time of year from the seasonal rains, and Justine had to keep an eye out for sharp rocks sticking up and patches of sand that could bog them down.

"Why are we going to Clifford's? You never mentioned," Justine asked.

"Lonewolf's parents are Traditionalists. I'm hoping

Clifford's dealt with them before and I can get some insight into the family," Ella said.

"Marie, his wife, isn't a Traditionalist. She goes to my church. Did you know that?" Justine asked.

Ella nodded. "Do you know her?"

"I see her around from time to time. She and I went to high school together, but even back then we weren't close. We hung out with different groups."

"But you're a familiar face to her . . . ," Ella said in a thoughtful voice.

"Do you want me to ask Marie about the money?" Justine said, following Ella's train of thought.

"Yes. If you get the chance, go for it, but don't ask directly. You can't tip your hand. The money can't become public knowledge, at least not yet."

The drive didn't take long. As they pulled up to her brother's place, Ella noted that there was no smoke coming from the roof of the medicine hogan and took that as a good sign. She'd hoped that her brother wouldn't be busy.

As they drew closer, Ella spotted Ford's truck parked on the far side of the hogan.

"Oh-oh," Justine said, voicing Ella's unspoken thoughts. "Your brother and Ford in the same place . . ."

"Someone else is there, too," Ella said, noting a second pickup on the other side of the main house. It was well used and had a wooden stock rack around the bed.

"I think that one belongs to someone in the Lonewolf family. I saw it in the hospital emergency room parking lot the other day," Justine said.

Justine parked and Ella stepped out of the car. As she stood by the passenger's side door she heard two men arguing on the far side of the hexagonally shaped hogan. Although their voices were muted, it was impossible to mistake the undercurrent of tension between them.

"I'm going to see what's going on," Ella said. "If you get a chance, talk to Marie."

Ella walked to her brother's medicine hogan. As she drew closer she could hear Ford and Clifford clearly.

"You *cannot* do the ritual while we have a prayer vigil underway," Ford, who had his back to her, said. "The Christians in the family will object, and if there's anything they don't need, it's more tension and confusion."

Clifford saw her approaching, and his eyes diverted to her for just a second before focusing on Ford once more. "A Come-to-Life Sing is absolutely necessary right now."

"It sounds to me like the family needs both of you," Ella said, joining them.

Ford turned to look at her, then exhaled softly. "This isn't about us. It's about them—the entire family." He looked back at Clifford. "You and I have to find a way to work this out."

"You're right." Clifford mulled it over. "Since mine is essentially emergency treatment beside the patient and no sandpaintings or prayer sticks are needed, I can find a way to shorten the ceremony. With that in mind, I can do the Come-to-Life Sing *before* your prayer vigil. Will that work for you?"

Ford nodded. "After you finish, we'll begin."

"Then it's settled. Let's go back inside, talk to the wounded man's wife, and explain what we've decided," Clifford said.

Ford glanced at Ella, and seeing the questions in her eyes, answered, "The hero's wife insisted on meeting me here," he said, avoiding names out of respect for Clifford. "She wanted me to help her convince the *hataalii* not to interrupt the bedside vigil she'd already asked me to conduct."

"So she's in the house?" Ella asked, glancing back. Seeing Justine was watching her, Ella cocked her head toward Clifford's home.

Justine picked up on the gesture and headed inside.

Knowing her partner would need time to work things out, Ella decided to do her part to help. "This case has brought a lot of pressure down on the department," Ella said, looking at Ford, then Clifford. "I have to find answers quickly, but I can't do it alone. If you're willing, I could use a little help from both of you."

Clifford nodded.

"All you have to do is ask," Ford added.

"Let's take a walk. I want to make sure no one can accidentally overhear what I have to say."

With Ford on one side of her and Clifford on the other, they went down the road a short distance, then walked up a shallow wash toward a flat-topped mesa a quarter of a mile beyond.

"When we processed the hero's personal effects, we discovered that he was carrying a considerable amount of cash in his briefcase. I need to find out where that money came from and why he had it with him. You're both in professions that inspire trust, and people often confide in you rather than us. If either of you hear anything that might explain it, I'd appreciate a tip."

"How large a stash was it?" Ford asked.

"More than fifty thousand dollars," Ella said, deciding at the last second to keep the exact details within the team.

Ford's eyebrows shot up. "Do you think he was on the take?"

"The fact that it's all in cash is suspicious, but we have no evidence that anything illegal was going on."

"And to go after a man who's so respected with nothing more than guesses is going to start a war right here on the Rez," Ford added with a nod.

"Exactly. I need answers, but no one can know about the money," she said.

"I'll try to find out if the hero had someone he might

have confided in—maybe an army buddy or someone like that. I'm assuming that you've spoken to his wife, or intend to do that on your own time," Ford said and saw Ella nod.

"I'll keep my ears open and let you know if I hear anything you might find useful," Clifford said.

As they walked back toward Clifford's home, Ford spoke again. "This is in the strictest of confidence, of course, but I can tell you that he and his wife are strapped for money right now. No way that cash is his. Even with his tribal paycheck, he still has out-of-pocket expenses whenever he travels, and the reimbursement checks take months to come in. That, in addition to the regular costs of maintaining a household, means they've got an ongoing cash flow problem."

"Even with Kevin's relatively high-level position for the tribe, I've heard him complain more than once about the cost of living in D.C.," Ella said with a nod. "Money can be an issue because it takes time for the tribe to pick up the tab."

"Maybe that money has nothing to do with the war hero," Clifford said. "Everyone knows about your child's father and his legal attack on the casino's management. Maybe the cash has something to do with them."

"That's a good point. The casino would easily have access to large amounts like that," Ford agreed. "I've always said that gambling, even when the tribe makes a handsome profit, may not be worth the other problems it creates."

"Nothing to excess. That's how a Navajo walks in beauty," Clifford said in a rare moment of agreement between them.

"The promise of instant riches is a powerful lure for people living on the edge," Ford answered.

When they reached the hogan Ella saw Justine walking near the back of the house with Marie, who was crying. Wondering if more bad news had arrived, Ella increased her pace. Clifford's wife, Loretta, who was now near the entrance to the hogan, stepped over and intercepted her. "Leave them alone for a bit. Your cousin is trying to calm her down after hearing some bad news."

"What happened?"

"There was a phone call while you were gone with the men. Her husband's heart stopped not long ago, and although they were able to revive and stabilize him, she's terrified. She'd made herself believe that once her husband was finally out of surgery the danger would be behind them. Now, she's seeing that it's not that simple."

Several minutes later, Justine led Marie back to where Loretta and Ford were waiting. Saying good-bye to them, she jogged over to meet Ella. "Sorry to keep you. I'm ready to go whenever you are."

Ella didn't break the silence between them until they reached the highway several minutes later. "Once we reach Shiprock, head for the hospital."

"Got it," Justine said, turning north.

"So how did it go?" Ella asked.

"Marie's barely hanging on. When Adam was discharged from the army she was relieved, thinking they would finally have a more normal life. But things didn't turn out the way she'd hoped when Adam found work as a lobbyist within three months of coming home. For one thing, their financial situation is tighter than ever. Apparently, most lobbyists work for a multitude of interests, but the tribe wants Adam to work strictly for them, and that limits the Lonewolf income. Marie asked him to threaten to quit and pressure the tribe to either increase his salary or let him take on other clients, but Adam refused. His goal is to get into tribal politics. He wants to use his popularity to network and develop contacts in Washington, and make a name for himself as someone who gets things done," Justine said. "But, Ella, to make a long story short, no way that cash belonged to Adam."

As her phone rang, Ella answered it, identifying herself.

"It's Blalock," the voice answered. "I'm at the hospital

right now and thought you'd want to know that Kevin's awake and alert enough to talk."

"I'm on my way as we speak," Ella answered. "Our ETA is ten minutes, give or take. But while I've got you on the phone, has the Bureau in D.C. turned up anything new?"

"Nothing on the mugging or the threats with an obvious connection to what went down here. I also spoke to ATF as well as local law enforcement to see if any pawn shops and gun dealers in the Four Corners have been under investigation, or even under watch. One name came up—Dan Butler—someone I know has sold more than his share of assault rifles this past year."

"Friend of yours?" Ella asked.

"Not a friend, no, but I know him. Word has it that he's the go-to arms merchant for area militia and doomsday groups. Dan's acquired a rep for being able to get whatever weapon a client wants—just so long as they're legal. He's got a clear record and wants to keep it that way. Dan also has the skills to work on virtually any firearm ever made. That's what has made him a favorite of local gun enthusiasts, and not just the nut jobs."

"If the gunmen at the airstrip were local, then he may have done business with them," Ella said, concurring. "We need to talk to Butler. Helping us bring down those who attacked a local hero will earn him a lot of goodwill. That should give us a bit of leverage."

"Agreed. I'll see you when you get here. After we talk to Tolino, we may want to head over to Dan's shop in Farmington."

As Ella closed up the cell phone, she updated Justine. "With luck, Kevin will finally be able to shed some light on what happened."

After they arrived at the hospital, Ella followed the nurse's directions and went to a private room at the end of a long hallway. A plainclothes officer Ella recognized as Tyler

Sells was sitting to one side of Kevin's door. Ella greeted him with a nod and went inside. Justine remained at the doorway, talking to the young officer. Glad for her partner's insight into her methods, Ella went up to Kevin's bed, ready for a one-to-one with him.

"So much for coming home to some peace and quiet, huh?" he said with a wry grin.

Ella pulled up a chair. "I hope you feel up to answering some tough questions."

"I can try, but I don't know how much I can tell you. That whole thing at the airstrip came out of nowhere." He paused. "I understand Adam's in real bad shape."

"He took some nasty hits, Kev."

"Yeah, defending *me*. He's the one who pushed me down, and pulled me behind cover. Saved my life. I'll tell you one thing, I'm going to make sure that his family lacks for absolutely nothing while he's laid up. And if he needs any rehab later . . ."

"Are you two friends?"

Kevin shook his head. "Adam's difficult to get to know beyond a certain point—very private. But I understood him, man to man. He had a lot of drive, Ella, and big plans for his future."

"Funny you should say that," she answered. "Do you know he was carrying seventy-five thousand dollars in cash in that briefcase of his?"

Kevin stared at her, then blinked. "I don't think my brain's working right. Repeat what you just said."

Ella did and gave him the highlights.

"Monopoly money, right? I got shot three times, and here you are messing with my mind?"

"No, this was the real deal. The play money had been replaced with Uncle Sam's finest, all Ben Franklins. The bills were in bundled stacks thick enough to stop a bullet, as a matter of fact."

"Adam's barely scraping by right now. The cash can't be his. Do you know where it came from?"

"I was hoping you'd tell me," Ella answered.

"I always carry some cash on business trips, and Adam does, too, but we're talking a few hundred. I can't explain a sum like that. The whole revelation sounds like something out of a movie."

"I'm open to any ideas you might have."

Kevin paused for a minute or two, taking a sip out of a glass using a straw, careful not to tangle the IV attached to his other arm. "Here's a thought. Maybe Adam decided to do some freelance work—buying for a client back in D.C. Wholesalers who deal with tribal artisans often carry large sums onto the Rez. You need a big chunk to buy several Two Grey Hills rugs, or jewelry by the carload from Navajo silversmiths. Craftsmen doing wholesale business deep on the Rez don't accept checks or credit cards."

"That's an interesting possibility," Ella said. "Can you think of anyone who might have hired him to work in that capacity?"

"No, but Adam wasn't exactly chatty. I don't have the foggiest notion what he does on his own time."

"Is Adam an honest man, at least as far as you know?"

"Oh, yeah. That's why I went to bat on his behalf with Tribal Industries. In his job description they stipulated that he could only lobby for the tribe. That forced Adam to turn down offers from the city of Farmington and the state tourism board. I did my best to get that changed so he could add to his client list, but no dice," Kevin said. "Thing is, Adam could have easily handled several accounts. He can pour on the charm and multitask like a seasoned politician."

"I've been considering the possibility that Adam was acting as a courier. Informants are usually paid for information and you're building a case against one of the tribe's

most important contractors—the casino management firm."
Ella paused, then in a hard voice, added, "Are you *sure* you
don't know where that money came from, Kevin?"

"I don't," he answered firmly. "He wasn't carrying the
money for me—or anyone else I know about. Besides, the
tribe would never okay a sum like that to pay off informants, Ella. We just don't have that kind of money lying
around. And why would it be coming *from* D.C.?"

"I don't know. I'm just exploring possibilities."

"And on a personal note, I don't have that kind of cash
either. I could probably raise it by tapping into retirement
accounts and savings, but not quickly."

"I understand your case relies on well-placed sources. I
need their names."

"How did you—" He shook his head. "Never mind. But,
Ella, you know better than to ask me something like that.
They've trusted me to keep their identities secret until we go
to court and, without them, I don't have a strong enough
case to nail these rip-off artists to the wall."

"I'll protect their identities, Kevin, you have my word.
But I'm going to have to push you on this. You and Adam
appear to have been the intended targets, so I can't afford to
overlook the casino's possible connection. By holding out on
me, all you're doing is helping the gunmen get away with
what they did to you and Adam."

He exhaled loudly, then nodded. "The names are saved
on my laptop in an encrypted text file, and the computer's
stashed away in my carry-on luggage."

"Then it's in the department's evidence room," she said.
"Thanks, Kevin."

"In those files you'll also find scanned copies of receipts
for phony purchases and inflated billing invoices from CEM,
Casino Enterprises Management." He paused and she could
tell he was feeling weary. "And, Ella, one more thing. Do
everything in your power not to scare or expose them.

Without their testimony, my case may not be strong enough to prove criminal intent, only greed."

"I'll be extremely careful, don't worry," Ella said. "Now tell me, how do I access your files?"

He asked for a piece of paper, then gave her his password and the names of the folders they were in.

Ella took the information and stood. "I better get going, but I'll be text messaging our daughter next. She's very worried about you."

"She and I have grown very close," he said, his voice softening.

Ella heard the love in his voice and smiled. "She adores you, Kev."

"Take the job in D.C., Ella. You and I have had to work hard for everything we've ever gotten. Make Dawn's life a little easier by giving her the kind of opportunities we never had."

"This isn't about what's easy and what isn't. It's about what's right—for her, and for me. But I don't want to think about all that now. I've got my hands full."

"I know," he said. "And just between the two of us, I've been picking up some vibes concerning my own job in Washington. Maybe it's political pressure, or the economy, but I've been hearing that tribal work in D.C. is going to be taking some budgetary hits. I may end up without a job, or at least be kept closer to home. That would be a plus, if you and Dawn stay on the Rez. But don't let that affect your decision. My issue is still very much up in the air."

"I appreciate your honesty. By political pressure, you mean the casino lobby?"

"Exactly. I get them, they get back at me. But, hey, I'm putting my money on me—us really."

"Smart bet," Ella replied, then took a step back.

"One more thing. Before you go, Ella, I'd like you to give me a straight answer. How's Adam doing?"

"He's still in critical." She was about to make a further comment when a nurse came into the room.

"Investigator Clah, it's time for patient meds, and Mr. Tolino will need to rest after that. You'll have to leave now."

"I'm going." Ella walked to the door and as she looked back, saw Kevin's eyes close. She'd tired him out. Angry with herself, she went to meet Justine.

"I'd like to check on Adam's status," Ella said.

"I figured that, so I located his doctor. He's on this floor right now." She pointed ahead. "That's him, Doctor Ward, the curly-haired one in the Hawaiian shirt with three young interns in tow."

Ella hurried toward the young-looking doctor, and, after identifying herself, took him aside. "I'm investigating the airport shooting incident, and need to speak to the gunshot victim, Adam Lonewolf, as soon as I can. Can you give me an idea of when you think that might be possible?" she asked, hoping that he'd be able to narrow things down for her.

"I couldn't say. Traumatic gunshot wounds like this are usually fatal. It helped getting him into surgery so quickly, and he's doing better than expected, but whether he'll ever regain consciousness—it's just too early to tell."

"He's a key witness. The second he wakes up and can communicate, I need to be contacted," she said, giving him her card with her cell number on the back.

He glanced at it then back at her. "Your request has already been noted on his file, and the staff has been briefed."

"Where's Mr. Lonewolf right now?" she asked.

"Intensive care—around the corner and second door to the left. Just follow the green line on the wall."

Ella continued down the hall, but when she reached the ICU she didn't see anyone guarding the door. Stepping inside the room immediately, she looked around. Three patients were in separate, glass-partitioned sections. One was Adam, judging from the extensive head bandages. Everything seemed in order here, so she went back out into the hall.

Her temper rose quickly as she looked in both directions for the missing guard. He should have been here at his post. When she finally found him, she'd ream him out, then have him pulled from the assignment.

As Ella walked over to the nurses' station, she spotted Justine, who was at the other end of the hall, and motioned for her to come over.

Before Justine reached her, Ella saw an orderly who'd been standing near the water fountain enter the ICU. As the door was closing, she spotted the man heading toward Adam's bed.

Acting on instinct, Ella followed him inside. The orderly glanced out the window, then at the staff, who were busy with their other patients. Sensing something was off, Ella moved in closer. Despite the white coat, he wasn't acting like hospital personnel. As he stepped toward Adam's bed, his coat shifted slightly and Ella saw he was wearing a shoulder holster.

FIVE

✕ ✕ ✕

Ella leaped forward and slammed him against the wall. "Who are you?" she demanded, identifying herself.

"Officer Michael Betone. I'm on special duty, Investigator Clah. I've got my badge and ID in my pocket," he said quickly.

From the corner of her eye Ella could see the three staff members staring at her in alarm.

"I know him, Ella," Justine said quickly, hurrying inside. "Sorry about that, Mike," she added as Ella released him.

"Why were you away from your post?" Ella demanded angrily.

"I was watching the entrance from down by the watercooler," he said. "Didn't you see me? I've been moving around a bit so I don't alarm anyone." Although it was something that didn't come naturally to any Navajo, he forced himself to look directly at her. "No one will get near him, Investigator Clah, not on my watch. We owe that soldier our protection after all he's done."

Ella nodded, somewhat mollified by his response. Officer Betone's words had reminded her once again of the sensitive nature of their case. If the tribe's hero turned out to have feet of clay, whoever ripped his mask off would also answer to The People.

As another familiar voice called out to her, Ella turned her head, and saw Dwayne Blalock approaching. "What's going on?" he asked quickly, looking from Justine to the officer.

"Nothing, my mistake," Ella said. "I apologize, Officer Betone. Carry on."

Ella walked back out of the room and into the hall before speaking again, not wanting to share their private discussion with those in intensive care.

"How much checking have you've done on the pilot, Pete Sanchez?" Blalock asked her immediately.

"None. We've had other priorities. How about you? Have you looked into his background?"

"I checked with my contact in INS and Homeland Security. There's been a lot of illegal gun traffic headed down into Mexico lately and those drug cartels south of the border pay big bucks. They're at war with each other right now, and with the authorities, too."

"Are you thinking that Sanchez was involved in that, and *he* was the target?" Ella asked, surprised.

"In your report you said that the gunmen concentrated on the businessmen first, then you, when you defended yourself. Yet the fact is that you guys were between the gunmen and the pilot, and he ducked into the plane to avoid getting shot a second time, right?"

"Right."

"We need to question him as soon as possible," Blalock said.

"Sanchez wasn't critical, so he won't be at this hospital. This is a tribal facility."

"I know. He was taken to the regional medical center in Farmington. What do you say we head over there next and pay him a visit?"

"Investigator Clah?" a nurse asked, looking back and forth between Ella and Justine as she walked up from the nurses' station.

"That's me," Ella answered.

"You have a call from Chief Atcitty. Use the phone on the counter over there," she pointed. "Push the hold button first."

Ella's cell phone, according to hospital rules, had been turned off. If the chief had taken the time to track her down, something important must have gone down. Ella walked over to the nurse's station and quickly picked up the phone.

"We've got at least a dozen reporters here, Shorty," Big Ed said. "I'm going to give them an official statement, but I want you to steer clear and stick to the investigation. When you return to the station, just be warned that the press is lying in wait."

"Thanks for the heads-up," she answered.

After hanging up, Ella joined the others and told them about Big Ed's call, suggesting they keep their eyes and ears open concerning reporters. "Now we need to split up and get back to business," she advised as the three walked to the closest exit.

"I'll continue digging into the pilot's background then," Blalock said. "If I hit paydirt, you'll be the second to know."

They walked down the steps and entered the parking lot. A yellow sports car came down the lane, then stopped right in front of them, blocking their way. Ella recognized the vehicle and the driver, instantly. It was Abigail Yellowhair, classy as usual, this time dressed in a conservative gray business suit.

The widow of a former high-profile politician, she had become an extremely powerful force on the Rez, but Ella didn't trust her. Abigail had played a role in too many questionable incidents around the Rez. Ella still vividly recalled the threats Abigail had made last year when her adopted daughter, Barbara, got arrested. The woman was still in prison, and Abigail wasn't the type to forgive and forget.

"Excuse me, officers—and Agent Blalock. I just heard the news about yesterday's shootings. How is Adam Lonewolf doing? Is he going to survive?"

Abigail looked exhausted, and judging from the carry-on bag on the seat beside her—ID label still attached—she'd come directly from the airport, probably the one in Farmington, or maybe even Albuquerque.

Justine looked at Ella instead of answering, and Ella also held her tongue, leaving Blalock to take the initiative. "I'm sure the families of the victims appreciate your concern, Mrs. Yellowhair," he said, glancing over at Ella, who nodded. "Mr. Lonewolf's in critical condition—touch-and-go, unfortunately. The other victims are out of danger, but no visitors except for immediately family are allowed at this time."

"Thank you, Dwayne," Abigail responded. "I'm sure you and the tribe's finest are already making progress in tracking down the animals who conducted this brazen attack."

"Thanks for your support, Mrs. Yellowhair," Justine responded.

"Stay safe, Justine," Abigail said. "And you, too, Ella," she added. "I'll leave you to your work, then," she added, then drove away.

Blalock shook his head. "Is it just me, or do I detect a small level of insincerity in her voice when the 'she wolf' refers to you, Ella?"

"You think?" Ella replied, glancing over at Justine, who just rolled her eyes.

"Well, now that we know Mrs. Yellowhair will be closely monitoring our progress, I guess we'd better get to it, huh?" Blalock said.

They separated in the parking lot, and Ella and Justine

were soon on their way. Not wanting to waste any time, Ella pulled out her cell phone and called Rose. "Mom, just a heads-up. I'm going to text message my kid and tell her that her dad's awake."

"Then I'll have to pull her out of school early. The second she reads it, she'll want me to pick her up and take her to the hospital."

"It's almost two now, so she'll probably see the message before going to her last class. If she calls you and pushes it, take her. It'll be good for both of them."

Ella hung up, then left a text message for Dawn. The middle school—which had rules that applied to cell phone use—allowed calls and text messaging between classes as long as that didn't create other problems, like tardiness. But students caught using them during class risked confiscation and a visit from a parent in order to get them back. Ella knew that her daughter would be checking her cell phone as often as possible today.

Placing the cell phone back in her pocket, she glanced at Justine. "What did we ever do in the days before cell phones?"

"I'm permanently attached to mine these days."

Though they'd both thought they'd been prepared for the media circus, the reality hit them hard as they approached the station's parking lot. There were antenna and dish-encrusted vans from every area station—network, local, and cable. Half of the media people were carrying video cameras, and the other half were looking over their notes, playing with microphones, or checking their hair and ties.

"Let's see if we can sneak in through the back," Ella said.

Justine detoured, driving into the maintenance yard, but the press had all the doorways covered. Judging from the way they swarmed over anyone trying to enter or leave the station, they were hungry for information on the still-developing story.

"Now what, partner?" Justine asked.

"We go in and keep our mouths shut—no comments. Big Ed will be taking the heat, not us."

Ella picked up the bag that had the clothing she'd worn during the attack, then took the lead, pushing her way inside. The reporters pressed in, throwing out questions that always began with "Investigator Clah." Clear passage was nearly impossible. At one point, one of the reporters grabbed her arm, hoping to make her turn and face the camera. Ella stepped on his toe with the heel of her boot, and with a yelp, he released her.

Once they got past the outer lobby, Ella finally took a deep breath. "You okay, cuz?"

"Yeah," Justine muttered, taking the bag from Ella's hand. "I'm going to my lab. Good luck evading those reporters. They're out for blood."

Ella watched her escape, then glanced back at the mostly male, barrel-chested patrol officers who'd formed a wall, blocking the reporters from going any farther than the reception area. Life had become very complicated at the station—and things were bound to get worse before they got better.

"Shorty!" she heard a familiar voice call from down the hall.

Ella hurried to Big Ed's office.

"I've got a statement ready, and I wanted you to look it over," he said as Ella came in. "I'm going to try and shift their focus from Adam to Kevin by telling them that we suspect Kevin was the real target because of his current legal activities. I hope that'll take some of the pressure off the Lonewolf family."

"Do you think the press will buy your spin?"

"I hope so. Kevin was in the middle of a high-profile case, so it's not out of left field."

"Kevin's not going to be happy to see his case appear on the headlines and as part of the lead story tonight," she said.

"It's the lesser of two evils. I'm hoping the reporters will dig in the opposite direction so they don't mess up our investigation. If they discover that Adam was carrying cash—and how much—things are going to get much worse."

"A hero-gone-bad story would explode onto every screen and newspaper in the country," Ella said, nodding slowly.

"Before I go out there and publicly name you as the lead detective, there's something I need to know. Are you one hundred percent certain that you can investigate this case despite your connection to Tolino?"

"Absolutely. If Kevin's broken the law, I'll bring him in. But I know that man, Chief. To serve a greater good, he might cross into the gray area, but he'd stay on the right side of the law all the way."

"All right then." He picked up his notes and led the way out of his office. "Time to talk to the vultures."

Ella slipped down the hall and went straight to the lab. "Anything new?" Ella asked, seeing Justine processing evidence.

"I've checked all your clothing, but didn't find anything other than what you'd expect."

"Do you have Kevin's laptop here?" Ella asked, looking around.

Justine nodded. "It's inside the box on the second shelf over there," she said, pointing with her lips.

Ella put evidence gloves on before handling the computer. She didn't expect Justine to find anything on the laptop except Kevin's prints, but she wouldn't break protocols.

Taking a seat by the desk, Ella turned on the device. As the main screen came up Justine joined her, looking over her shoulder. "Are you searching for anything in particular?" she asked.

Ella nodded. "Kevin said that he had a file in here listing his sources."

"If that's true, he was incredibly trusting," Justine said, surprised. "Anyone could have hacked into it."

Ella shook her head. "It would have taken an expert, and even then, he would have found it a challenge. First, you need a password to get in, then another one to access his files, which are encrypted. Also you'd have to know where to look. The directory is hidden within the operating system files, and the files themselves have extensions that must be changed in order to read them using word processing programs. If you don't know the names of his sources, you wouldn't know where to look, either. The directory file is within a printer driver directory folder and has the name ix128."

Ella called up the word processing program, found the file, then changed the name so it would be recognized as a text file. Only then was she able to open it. "This is more extensive than just a list of names. He has background info here, too." Ella studied the contents for a few minutes. "He only has three major sources, but talk about well-placed . . ."

Justine pointed to the first entry. "Don Yazzie. The name sounds familiar, though I can't put a face to it. According to the note that follows, he manages the warehouse at the casino, so I'm not sure how I would have met him, yet . . ."

"I think the reason his name's familiar is because of his wife, Cornelia. Although she's battling cancer herself, she runs her own version of the Make-A-Wish Foundation for Navajo kids."

Justine nodded. "Yeah, I remember hearing about a little boy with only a few months to live. His fondest memories were of a vacation he'd taken with his family to the Grand Canyon. He couldn't be moved, so Cornelia's foundation revamped the kid's room and turned it into a replica of the cabin his father had rented there. That boy passed on in peace."

Ella sighed. "I don't know how she does it. Constantly

being with kids who are fighting a death sentence. It would destroy me one inch at a time."

"She's a Christian, Ella. That gives her a totally different perspective. Ask Ford."

Ella smiled and shook her head. "No way, partner. We avoid discussing things that we'll never agree on. Ford's beliefs don't allow him to accept any other way but his, and I'm not so quick to walk a line of absolutes. I've seen too much I can't explain. I'm no Traditionalist, but I know that my brother's ceremonies and rituals often get amazing results, yet Ford's religion insists it's all just pagan magic and superstition."

Before Justine could comment, Ella brought their focus back to the text file. "Here's another one of his sources. Angelina Manuelito is the receptionist at CEM's local office. She'd be in a position to know quite a bit." Ella paused. "I don't remember ever meeting her though."

"I don't know her either," Justine said.

"Here's the last name," Ella said a second later. "Cheryl Hoskie's the casino bookkeeper. Run these names and see what you get."

Justine went over to her computer terminal, then after a minute answered. "None have any priors. They're clean, Ella."

"We need to talk to all of them, but we're going to have to make certain we're not followed."

"With the circus underway outside, that might be difficult," Justine answered.

As they stood, Ella's phone vibrated. Flipping it open with one hand, Ella noted the caller ID. "Hey, Mom," she greeted.

"I'm at the hospital with your daughter," Rose said in a shaky voice. "We were in the downstairs lobby when there was a huge explosion outside. A car's burning and the fire department's on its way. I don't know if anyone's hurt. Everything's going crazy here."

Ella's blood ran cold. She could hear the shouts and sounds of chaos just beyond Rose's voice. "Hospital security—"

"Went outside," her mother finished for her.

"Mom, take my daughter and *stay away* from her father's room. This could be a diversion. I'm on my way." Ella immediately called Officer Betone.

"Everything's secure here, but it sounds like they could use help outside," he said.

"Stay at your post," Ella said, motioning for Justine to follow as she hurried out.

"I'm not going anywhere. Don't worry about that. Lonewolf's my responsibility and no one's laying a finger on him."

Ella noted the respect mirrored in Betone's words whenever he spoke of the man he'd been assigned to protect. In hard times, larger-than-life heroes reminded everyone of the best of human nature and gave them something to strive for. More than anything, Ella hoped that Adam would live up to the faith others had placed in him.

Ella put the phone away and checked her pistol as she walked, verifying that her third clip was there, the one with the armor-piercing rounds. "We need to get to the hospital pronto. I'll fill you in on the way."

Fighting the urge to do the opposite, they left the department at a leisurely pace and without emergency lights, trying not to call attention to themselves. When they reached the highway, Justine picked up speed and turned on the siren. "We're clear, Ella. No tail."

"When we arrive, go to Kevin's room, I'll head for the ICU. Until things calm down we'll back up the officers guarding the two men."

Chaos ruled in the hospital's front parking lot as they pulled up, with cars blocking some of the rows and people milling around. Justine circled the action and headed toward the emergency room entrance. They could see the fire department at the scene and many members of the hospital staff were on the outside steps and sidewalks. Most were trying to see what was going on, while others were making themselves useful.

Once inside, Ella raced down the left corridor while Justine went straight. As Ella turned the corner of the long hall, she spotted someone wearing a dark green hooded sweatshirt, head covered, striding purposefully down the hall toward intensive care.

The fact that the person was wearing that type of clothing inside the building—this time of day and year—immediately got her attention. It seemed doubly odd when you considered that the temperature outside was in the high seventies. As the man turned the corner, Ella noticed the large bouquet of flowers in his left hand. The way he was resting it on top of his right hand seemed odd—unless he was trying to hide something.

That thought, and the fact that the person was wearing what was practically a convenience store robbery uniform, jolted her into immediate action. Ella spurted forward and called out, "You with the flowers—stop!"

The man didn't even turn to look. Instead, he ignored her and picked up speed. He was less than twenty feet from the twin doors leading to the ICU when he suddenly turned away and raced down an adjacent hallway, dropping the flowers.

Ella saw what had changed the suspect's mind. Officer Betone, apparently having heard her shout, was peering out one of the windows in the ICU doors. Betone slipped out into the hall, his hand on the butt of his handgun. "Who was that?"

"Stay with Adam!" Ella yelled, sprinting after Hooded Guy.

As she turned the corner, a security guard came out of the stairwell door.

"What's going on?" he yelled as she ran by.

"Hooded man with a gun. Secure the exits!" she answered, not slowing down.

As she raced down the corridor, she saw her suspect nearly collide with a cleaning cart one of the janitors was pushing down the hall. The suspect pointed his handgun at the janitor, who jumped back instantly, trying to hug the wall.

Hooded Guy slid on the waxed floor, managed to sidestep the cart at the last second, then turned the corner.

"Police. Stop!" Ella ordered, but once again, he ignored her and kept running.

With only a waiting area at the end of this hall, the subject was trapped. "There's no way out," Ella called out to him, slowing to a brisk walk, pistol in hand. "Give it up."

The man turned, dropped to a crouch, and took two quick shots.

As the bullets whined overhead, she dove behind the only available cover, a potted plant. Hesitant to return fire, not knowing what was behind the wall at the end of the hall or if anyone was in the waiting area, she poked her head out slowly and carefully. In the seconds it took her to do that, he'd vanished.

SIX

✖ ✖ ✖

Figuring that he must have ducked into the waiting area, she inched down the hall slowly, hugging the wall and ready for an ambush. But how would she recognize the man if he'd taken off the hood? She'd had only one quick look at his face, and he'd been wearing sunglasses. If he was seated among others, he'd have a lethal advantage.

Suddenly the shrill sound of a fire alarm shattered the silence. Ella stopped at the entrance to the small lounge, crouched, and looked around the corner, pistol out. A fire exit she didn't remember seeing there before was ajar.

Hurrying out, she saw dozens of people watching two firemen spraying water on the burning car while the rest of the crew worked to hook up a fat hose she thought would probably dispense foam. With onlookers everywhere, half of them taking photos and video with cell cameras, the suspect had slipped out unnoticed and blended in with the crowd.

Yet Ella knew that he couldn't have gone far. She called Justine on the cell phone as she searched up and down the rows of parked cars.

"Kevin's secure," Justine said. "No trouble here."

Ella reported her location, then ended the call and continued to search the area, circling the crowd slowly on foot. After several minutes, she decided to focus on the parked vehicles. Hearing footsteps behind a van one row away, she circled for a better view, and saw a woman helping a man into a wheelchair. Ella continued to the next row and stood up on the back bumper of an old pickup, trying to get a better view.

Suddenly a car raced up from behind her. Hearing it, Ella jumped off the bumper and turned, her hand on the butt of her pistol. A second later the squad car stopped, and she saw Justine behind the wheel.

"I'm assuming Kevin's still under guard?" Ella asked, slipping into the cruiser.

"Yes. Officer Poyer is there now, along with another one of our people. Marianna Talk was here at the hospital visiting her mother and is now backing him up."

"Good. Circle the lot."

"What are we looking for?" Justine asked as she drove up and down the rows of vehicles.

"The suspect's wearing sunglasses and a green hooded sweatshirt," Ella said, giving her highlights.

"You need to start wearing a vest again, cuz. And maybe a helmet."

"No kidding." Ella reached for her cell phone. "As soon as this is over, I'm going to have Kevin moved to another room."

They drove slowly, circling the area where all the outside action was taking place, searching for anyone pulling out or acting suspicious. People crowded in from all sides, hampering the emergency crew's efforts.

"I want our crime scene team to work with the fire marshal and check out the incident with the car," Ella said. "I think it was a diversion meant to draw security away from the hospital interior. Vehicles don't generally blow up by themselves."

"Let me call Benny and Joe and have them secure the scene," Justine said. "The hospital guards are in over their heads."

"I'll make the call. Let's keep searching for the suspect." Although she knew the chances of finding him were slim, she wasn't ready to give up. Ella called her team but kept her gaze focused on the surrounding area as she spoke.

As Justine drove around to the outpatient clinic east of the main building, Ella noted a truck ahead waiting to pull out of the parking area onto a side street. The passenger in the cab was wearing what was either a black, or dark green hooded sweatshirt.

"Pull them over," Ella snapped. "It's a long shot, but it's all we've got."

"The truck's got a casino parking lot sticker," Justine said, flipping the sirens off and on to flag the driver. As the truck pulled to one side, Justine glanced at Ella, who was reaching for her gun. "You're wound too tight, partner. Ease up."

"I want the dirtbag who turned the hospital into a shooting gallery. He's not getting away from me—not for long anyway."

Gun in hand, Ella approached carefully, keeping the angle tight as she moved closer to the pickup. While Justine covered the driver, Ella ordered the passenger to step out.

The person moved slowly and climbed down from the seat. When she pushed back the hood, Ella immediately recognized Cornelia Yazzie—her hair gone from the ravages of cancer therapy. Placing her gun back in its holster, Ella apologized quickly. "I'm so sorry. There's someone with a gun running around the hospital. He was wearing sunglasses and a hooded sweatshirt."

The driver glanced over the hood at Ella. "Detective Clah? What's going on?"

Ella recognized Don Yazzie from Ford's annual church

picnic. "I'm really sorry for the mixup, but this may be a good thing after all. I've been wanting a chance to talk to you—and I think you know why. Will you come back to the hospital with me? It'll look like I've held you up for questioning because of the hooded sweatshirt Cornelia's wearing. Those inside the hospital know I've been chasing a suspect fitting that description."

"And no questions will be raised," he added softly. "Not a bad idea. But let me take my wife into an empty treatment room where she can lie down. The hospital staff won't mind, and it'll give her a chance to rest. She's always beat after chemo."

Less than ten minutes later, Ella sat with Don in one of the rooms inside the Administration offices.

"Are they after Mr. Tolino?" Don asked quickly, once the door was shut. "Is that what the explosion in the parking lot was all about? If that's the case, I'm in real trouble. If you've found out that I've been helping Kevin, maybe they have, too," he said, his words tumbling over each other. "I warned Kevin that they'd fight back—hard and dirty. CEM plays rough. They know the casino business, and they know how to get around . . . obstacles."

"And you think Kevin's an obstacle?" she asked.

"Let's say he's a problem, and they've got a lot of experience making problems disappear."

"This is now a police investigation and that's why Kevin gave me your name. Your cooperation will remain confidential."

"Good. I was helping Kevin because my bosses aren't playing fair with the tribe and I didn't want to be part of that. But Cornelia can't take any more problems, Ella. She's handling all she can."

"If things close in on you, you'll have police protection, but the incident today has nothing to do with you. They're gunning for either Kevin or Adam, or maybe both. We just don't know enough to determine that yet."

"I'm sorry to hear about Adam and Kevin, but I'm glad they didn't come after me, particularly when I'm with Cornelia," he said.

"Who do you think is running the scam at the casino?" Ella asked him.

"Alan Grady. He's the casino's business manager. Everything that has a dollar sign attached to it goes through him. He's not in it alone, but he's the one calling the shots."

"Where can I find Grady?"

"His office is at the casino, and he's usually there eighteen hours a day. He has a home somewhere near the Rez, too, within a five minute drive." He shook his head slowly. "Can you believe he was allowed to practically write his own contract with the tribe? Sweet deal, huh?"

"Sounds like it," she said. "By any chance, were you working at the casino yesterday morning?"

"Sure was, all day, from ten a.m. to six p.m. We're open twenty-four/seven, and my days off are Monday and Tuesday, normally," he said. "Yesterday morning . . . wasn't that when the shooting took place?"

"Yeah. Did you happen to notice if Alan Grady was at the casino then?"

He thought about it for a minute. "I saw him around eleven. He always walks the entire casino just before the morning crowd starts to trickle in. He then cruises the buffet with a critical eye, taste-testing as he fills his plate. After that, he goes and eats in his office. Unless something requires his presence he doesn't come back out until late afternoon. It was the same yesterday. I saw him again just before I clocked out. Were you thinking that maybe he was one of the shooters?" Don asked.

"We need to rule out people before we can narrow the list of suspects," she said, not committing herself.

"You could access the security cameras and verify where he was. Of course you'd have to get his permission."

"Okay. Thanks for your help. If anyone asks why I questioned you tell them the story we settled on."

"It's going to make you look like a fool," he said quietly.

"Yeah, and word will get around fast, too. But as my brother would say, everything has two sides. If my enemy underestimates me, it'll give me the edge."

He nodded, and as he walked away Justine came down the hall. "Joe and Marianna are outside gathering evidence and working the scene. Benny Pete's still not here, but he's on his way. The explosion was set off by a ruptured gas tank, though the reason for the fire is still unknown. A few people were struck by flying debris, but no one was seriously injured."

"Have you checked the security camera feed? Everything's monitored inside and outside this hospital." Ella knew it wasn't as secure as the casino, except in the pharmacy area, but there were still plenty of cameras in the public places.

"That's what I was doing while you were talking to Don," Justine answered. "I went to see Jonah Tom, head of security here. He's got some real old equipment—tapes, mostly—except for where the drugs are stored. He's waiting for us now," she said, and cocked her head down the hall.

As they entered the security room just off the hall, a gray uniformed Navajo man in his late forties or early fifties nodded to her.

"The tapes are lousy and grainy. Just a heads-up," Jonah said. "I've been after administration to let me update the general site recorders to match the DVD hardware in the pharmacy, but it's a hard sell. The truth of the matter is that we never have problems—not like today's anyway—and since money's always tight, things that aren't high priority usually get set aside."

Ella nodded, only too aware of what he was saying. "At least we have daylight in our favor. Let's start with the parking lot video," she said.

As he played the black-and-white tape, she realized that it was so grainy the perp wearing the baseball cap and jacket could have faced the camera, smiled and waved, and they still wouldn't have been able to ID him. She decided to focus instead on the way the suspect moved and walked as he worked on the car he was obviously sabotaging. It soon became clear to her that he was aware of the cameras, purposely turning away and keeping his face down.

"Judging from the size and overall body type, that's not the same man I chased down the hall," Ella said.

"You got ambushed at the airstrip by two men. Maybe this was his partner. Does his body type fit?" Justine asked her.

"Yeah, but what we have is still too broad a description," Ella said, continuing to study the feed. "Look at the way he checks his watch as he works. Everything was timed and done with precision." She watched the man duck below camera range. "Military-like."

After about two minutes, he walked away from the car and out of range of the surveillance camera.

"It's not much in terms of visuals," Justine said. "But we do have something. They're either pros, ex-military men, or both."

"Mercs—ex-military who need a little excitement to keep their blood flowing," Jonah said. "Many of our young men find the reservation too tame when they get back."

"Let me see the feed outside Kevin Tolino's room, say, thirty minutes prior to my encounter with the gunman," Ella said.

Jonah nodded. "I've already separated it, but it all seems routine," he added, then played the tape.

As she watched, she saw Don and Cornelia walk by,

stop to talk to the guard, then continue down the hall. Since the treatment area for cancer patients was on the other side of the hospital, questions immediately flooded her mind.

Justine, who stood directly behind her, spoke softly. "I know what you're thinking. Maybe they were just curious when they heard about the shooting and wanted to check on Kevin."

"Or maybe Don's starting to think that if that's what they did to Kevin, he's in over his head," Ella said.

Next, Ella watched the video segment taken outside Adam's room. Ella studied the man in the hooded sweats and sunglasses the second he came into view. He kept his head down, and as he walked, she saw a flash of the gun he'd held beneath the flowers. Then the scene she'd experienced played out before her.

"Look at the way he's avoiding the cameras. He's too . . . practiced," Ella said at last.

"Are you thinking that he came in earlier and studied all the camera angles?" Justine asked. "Their viewing fields are set."

Ella nodded. "Precisely. Look at how he turns away at just the right moments. We need to look at the footage taken earlier in the day and look for anyone who's paying attention to the cameras. Let's see if we can ID someone who fits the general size and shape of our suspects."

"I'll get those segments for you," Jonah said.

After a moment's pause, Ella looked over at Justine. "Pete Sanchez, the pilot who was wounded yesterday, is at the Farmington hospital. Call over there and see if they've had any problems."

As Ella was speaking, Agent Blalock came into the room. "I checked on that when I heard what was happening here," he said. "Everything's fine, but I put extra security on the job anyway—including FPD. You and I can go over and talk to him once you're finished here."

Leaving Justine to continue viewing the tapes, Ella went outside with Blalock. "Let's go see what my team's managed to get us so far," she said.

As they approached, Marianna greeted Ella with a quick half smile, while Benny continued placing numbered yellow markers by each piece of evidence, methodically working the scene.

"We don't have much to report yet," Marianna said.

"All we know is that the fire originated beneath the gas tank. It was set using a makeshift time delay and lots of flammable material," Benny said. "Maybe a hole was poked into the tank itself, or the fuel line compromised. Either way, all it took once the fire started was for the flames to encounter the fuel vapor."

"Keep at it," Ella said. "When you get more, call me. Don't wait to catch me at the station."

"Copy that," Benny answered.

"One more thing, Benny. According to one source, Alan Grady was at the casino, in or around his office, at the time of the airport incident. See if you can get anyone to confirm that."

He nodded. "Will do."

Ella glanced at Blalock and took a deep breath. "My family's still inside," she said, explaining the call from Rose that had brought her here in such a hurry. "Give me a minute to talk to them. If they're both okay, then we can take off."

"No problem."

Ella dialed her mother and Rose answered instantly. "What's happened, daughter? You told me to keep my granddaughter away from her father's room and I've done that. But she's very frightened and so am I. Somebody said there were gunshots, and a man was chased by police. I have a feeling you were in the middle of all that."

"I was. But it's over now and it's safe for you to move around the hospital. Where are you, by the way?"

"In the doctor's lounge. The door wasn't locked and no one was here, so we came in."

"Good thinking, Mom," Ella said. "Tell my daughter that her father's safe, but his room's going to be changed for security reasons and getting him settled might take a while. You should both go home for now. In a few hours, once everything calms down, you and she can return and visit."

"It's hard to keep her away from her father," Rose said softly.

"I know, Mom. Do what you can, and I'll talk to her when I get home."

"Which will be late, I'll bet," Rose answered.

"Probably so."

"Stay safe, daughter."

"I will. Bye, Mom."

As she placed the phone back in her pocket, she glanced around and saw Blalock leaning against one of the cars.

"Ready," she said.

As Blalock drove out of the hospital parking lot, Ella rubbed her side absently.

"You okay?"

"Yeah," she muttered. "By now you'd think that I'd have the art of hitting the ground and rolling behind cover refined to perfection. But I always end up black and blue."

Blalock laughed as they stopped at the main entrance. "Here's a news flash for you. The older you get, the worse it'll be. And cops age faster than the rest of the population."

"That comes with the job," Ella agreed.

"I can't count the times I've thought about retiring. I've put in my twenty years. But having all that time on my hands . . ." He shook his head. "I mean, how often can you go fishing?"

"Don't look at me. I hate fishing," she answered with a grin. "But I hear you. If I had the years in right now I'd retire just so I could be with my kid a little more. A few years from now, she won't want to be seen with me. And after she's grown . . ."

"Yeah. Retirement never comes when it's convenient."

About twenty-five minutes later they reached the western edges of the off-Rez city of Farmington. As Blalock turned south and headed for the hospital, he glanced over at her. "Here's a thought. Did the pilot escape the second attempt because they haven't found him yet, or because they couldn't pull off both attacks at once?"

"Finding him shouldn't have been that hard, so it's possible he was never a target, and got hit by a stray. But we can't say that for sure yet." She paused, gathering her thoughts. "What have you managed to dig up on Sanchez?"

"He's an ex-Army pilot with eighteen years experience flying small aircraft. He has a home in the Albuquerque area and is divorced, with no children. He makes a decent living, belongs to the Civil Air Patrol, and often assists in searches for downed aircraft. He's worked at his current job for ten years and pays into a 401k."

"So he's squeaky clean and frugal."

"Yeah," Blalock answered, "but let's go talk to him anyway. Even if he has nothing to do with what went down, he might have overheard something that'll be useful to us."

"I'd like to know how the gunmen knew about our schedule. Are Sanchez's arrival and departure times listed somewhere on the Internet, or would someone have to call in to find out? If that's the case, maybe we can trace the call."

"Sounds like a plan," Blalock said.

It was a little past seven in the evening when they parked and went inside the Regional Medical Center. A plainclothes Farmington police officer was sitting beside Sanchez's door. Recognizing Blalock, he stood and introduced himself to Ella. "I was assigned to provide security for Mr. Sanchez, but it's been quiet except for a couple of local media people. He's scheduled to be released tomorrow. Do I stay with him?"

"If there's been no incident by then, FPD's protection won't be required," Blalock said. "If something changes, I'll talk to your chief and make the request."

He nodded once, then stepped aside, letting them pass.

The moment Pete saw Ella, his face brightened considerably. "Hey, Ella! It's good to see you! I heard you were okay, but how are Kevin and Sergeant Lonewolf? I can't seem to get a straight answer from the nurses here."

She gave him an update.

"With all the shots fired, we're lucky to be alive," he said.

"Yeah, I hear you," Ella answered.

"Sorry I couldn't help out. Only the big carriers permit firearms on board. Of course I know some pilots who stash a pistol in their pocket from time to time. I mean, who's going to check? I just never thought it was necessary myself. Live and learn, huh?"

Ella sat down in a visitor's chair and Blalock did the same. "Let me ask you something, Pete. Is it possible that *you* were the target?"

"I know where you're heading. With all the drug activity and gunrunning south into Mexico, small aircraft pilots like me often get lucrative offers. But I'm not into any of that. Check with my employer. They know when and where I've taken their aircraft. And check the plane itself if you want. If I'd been carrying weapons and ammunition back and forth, you'd find telltale traces of gunpowder residue, right?"

"No one's accusing you of anything, but thanks," Ella said. Since she'd carried a pistol and ammunition on the aircraft, and he also may have transported hunters, it wouldn't have been a productive activity. "Tell us how you got the job taking us to the Rez."

He leaned back against the pillow and relaxed. "That's easy. The tribe has a contract with my company to fly folks back and forth from Albuquerque."

"How well do you know Adam or Kevin?" Ella asked him.

"I don't know either of them personally, but I've been piloting Mr. Tolino back and forth from Albuquerque for years and know he's an attorney for the tribe. Sergeant Lonewolf only started flying with me a few months ago, so I guess that means he's flown in my aircraft three or four times."

"What have you managed to learn about Adam so far?" she asked, keeping her tone relaxed.

He shrugged. "Normally he's a very easygoing guy—pumped up on flights to Albuquerque and then eager to get home on his way back. But he's been a little uptight lately."

"What makes you say that?" Ella asked.

"Right before the flight, I picked up his carry-on, ready to put it in the plane for him as usual. But he blocked my hand when I reached for his attaché case. That took me by complete surprise. Then Adam apologized, saying he'd keep his brief-case with him."

"Do you have any idea why he was so protective?" Blalock asked.

"I assume he was carrying some important papers and didn't want to let the case out of his sight," he said. "My job is to ferry passengers back and forth, not intrude on their privacy."

Instinct told her Pete was exactly what he appeared to be. "Okay," Ella said, standing. "I understand you're scheduled to be released tomorrow."

He nodded. "I'll be going home. You've got my telephone numbers, right?" Seeing Ella nod, he continued. "Do you think I should stay on my guard?"

"Be wary of strangers, and if you run into any trouble or

suspect something out of the ordinary is going on, let us know right away," Ella said, handing him her card.

"Do you think they might come after me?" he asked quickly.

"It's unlikely, but since we still don't know for sure who the target of the attack was, it's better to be cautious," Blalock said, giving the pilot his card as well.

"There's no way those two crazies came after me. It had to have been one of you guys," Pete said, looking at Ella. "Lawyers and police make a lot more enemies than pilots do."

"Maybe so, but keep your guard up," Ella said.

As Blalock and Ella headed back to the Rez, he glanced over at her. "You want to stop by my office?"

She shook her head. "Just take me home. I'm calling it a day. Unless something pops up before then, I need to spend some time with my kid. I want to see for myself how she's handling everything that's happened. Dawn's always thought of Kevin as this larger-than-life person who's somehow above the danger I face daily."

"A father-daughter relationship isn't about facts. It's about emotions."

"That's precisely why I'm worried about her. She adores Kevin. Half the reason I think she wants to leave the Rez and go to school in D.C. is because she wants to spend more time with him."

"I don't think you're seeing the whole picture," Blalock said slowly. "If you leave the Rez, you and Kevin are also bound to spend more time together—or at least more so than you are now. In a city of strangers, you'd be more inclined to hang out with each other, and my guess is that Dawn's counting on that."

Ella looked at him in surprise. "That can't be it. My kid

knows there's no hope of Kevin and I getting back together. And she likes the man I'm dating—Ford."

"You're using logic. Think with the heart of a kid who has a big imagination—one who dreams big and can see what she wants right there in front of her."

"You may have a point there." What he said rang true, but Kevin and she were nothing more than a footnote in history. Even before she discovered she was pregnant, their romance had ended.

Ella's thoughts then shifted to Ford and her chest tightened. Although she cared deeply for him, there was an emotional and physical distance between them that neither could bridge. Religion—it had divided people and nations since the beginning of time. At one time, she'd thought they'd be able to work things out, but she'd learned the hard way that in situations like these, compromises satisfied no one. In time, their different beliefs were bound to pull them apart. She suspected that he'd soon be asking her to convert to his religion—a logical assumption considering he was a preacher—and she knew already that would never happen. Ultimately, Ella realized their relationship had little chance of growing beyond the current level.

As Blalock passed through the town of Shiprock, turning south in the direction of her home, Ella shook free of the thought. Worrying about what might be was as bad as living in the past. That made it easy to overlook today, and the present was all anyone really had.

SEVEN

—— ✕ ✕ ✕ ——

When Blalock pulled up to her house, Ella said good-bye and started walking toward the porch. On the way, she saw the yellow sports car parked by the side of the house, and cringed. Abigail Yellowhair was here.

Ella had warned Rose repeatedly not to trust Abigail's friendship, that the woman had an agenda, but Rose had still been willing to give Abigail the benefit of the doubt and had welcomed Abigail into the Plant Watchers. The group Rose led shared knowledge and protected native plants that often played an important role in the tribe's rituals and healing ceremonies. Rose's expertise was so valued that she was also a tribal consultant, recording and locating plant specimens for Navajo botanists, environmentalists, and officials working to protect the natural heritage.

As Ella came into the kitchen, Abigail looked up from the table and gave her a cold nod. "It's good to see you doing so well," she said, her voice not matching her forced smile. "Since this morning I've heard a lot more about the events at the airstrip and your involvement."

"Things were touch-and-go, but I'm fine. Thank you for

your concern," Ella said, matching her tone, then looked at Rose. "Is my daughter still up?"

Rose nodded. "She's listening to music through those earphones. She says it helps her do her homework. I'm not so sure about that, but as long as her grades don't slip, I don't think we should say no."

"I agree wholeheartedly," Ella said, remembering that it was Kevin who'd bought her the iPod. Taking two of her mother's oatmeal cookies from the plate on the kitchen table, she went down the hall to Dawn's room.

As Ella entered, she saw Dawn sitting at her desk in front of her laptop computer. Ella touched her daughter's shoulder, and Dawn's jumped, startled.

"Sorry, Pumpkin," Ella said, patting her gently.

Dawn closed the lid on the laptop, shut off the tiny music player, and took off her earphones. "Hey, Mom," she said, scooting over to the bed quickly.

A wave of uneasiness suddenly swept through Ella. Dawn was only supposed to go on the Internet when an adult could see the screen as well. That was a house rule. Following her instincts, she went to her daughter's computer and opened it. "What have you got here?"

"*Mooom!* I was just talking to my friend on Facebook," Dawn said, hurrying over. "I couldn't have any privacy in front of Mrs. Yellowhair."

"This is a friend that you know and have seen in real life, right, not someone you met online?"

"It's Clara, Mom," she said pointing to the small photo of the girl Ella recognized as Dawn's current best friend.

Ella took a closer look at the dialogue box, skimming the conversation that had been going on between the two girls.

"Mother, *please!*" Dawn protested, closing the laptop once again.

By then Ella had read enough to know that Dawn had been telling Clara how worried she was about both her parents.

Although this was a subject she wanted to broach with her daughter, Ella remained silent for a few seconds, trying to figure out the best way to do that.

"Will you be taking the job in Washington?" Dawn asked, suddenly diverting her.

"I don't know yet."

"Mom, you've got to take that job! Things would be more . . . I don't know . . . normal," she said at last. "Clara never has to worry about *her* parents. They come home at five-thirty every night. They always have dinner together, too, not just at Thanksgiving or somebody's birthday. . . ."

Ella took a deep breath, then let it out. "There's more to life than living by the clock. You're very loved, daughter, and you have your *Shimasání* here when you come home."

"Yeah, but if we made a few changes and worked a little harder, things could be even better. Think of all the stuff you and I and Dad could do in D.C.! And *Shimasání* could come with us, too, and maybe stay for weeks at a time. We could help all the *Diné* just by being us. Some people in the Anglo world think 'Indian' means 'stupid.' Or they think we're like those people who play Indians in the movies. To them, every tribe is the same."

"There's some truth in what you're saying," Ella admitted slowly.

"You and Dad work for the tribe, and you want to make things better for all of us. If you work together, there isn't anything you couldn't do for the *Diné*."

"Whoa! I'm a police officer, not a politician," Ella said with a ghost of a smile.

"But in our nation's capital, you could do even more important things for the tribe. And it's not like you couldn't ever see your boyfriend, Ford," she added. "Of course he's not like you and Dad but . . ."

Ella looked at her daughter and waited, hoping Dawn would finish her thought. She didn't want to guess what was on her kid's mind.

"The thing is, Mom, he doesn't work for the tribe, not really," Dawn said at last. "He works for his church—preaching and trying to get other Navajos to join. Stuff like that. He does a lot of good things for people, but mostly it's for the ones who go to his church."

"He practices his own beliefs, sure, but there's nothing wrong with that," Ella argued. "This country gives everyone a chance to express their religions, or choose not to have one."

"Okay. But you and Dad are Navajo first, and Mom, that *matters*."

Ella stared at her little girl. She'd voiced some very adult ideas. Yet as the computer made a dinging sound, and Dawn opened it to see the screen, it was almost as if someone had flicked a switch. "Oh, Mom, look! Jane got a hamster! Isn't he cute? Can we get one?"

"We'll see," Ella said with a sigh. Kissing her daughter's forehead, she stepped out into the hall. If this had been a preview, she was nearly certain she wouldn't survive Dawn's teenage years.

As Ella entered the kitchen once again, Abigail stood. "I'll be going now and let you two have some time together." Abigail gave Rose a warm smile, then slipped out of the kitchen.

Moments later they heard her car pulling away.

"So what brought your friend over tonight?" Ella asked.

"She's working with me on the Prickly Weed Project." Rose took a deep breath. "If anyone had told me that I'd actually be growing *ch'il deenîni* in my garden, I would have told them they were crazy."

Ella chuckled. "I've read the newspaper articles. It's supposed to be a potential source of ethanol, which is added to gasoline to reduce fuel consumption. If it works, and they can stop using corn to produce fuel, that, in turn, could lower food and animal feed prices."

"And become a huge crop for our tribe," Rose added. "Unlike the casinos, this can bring us nothing but good. We'd be making use of something that's readily available to lessen the nation's dependency on foreign oil. I'm proud to be able to take part in this. Some of the Plant Watchers are now busy trying to find places on the Navajo Nation where tumbleweeds already flourish. That hasn't been difficult, the weed grows almost everywhere, but we also need to see how easy it is to grow them where we want them to be. That's why there's a crop planted in our backyard."

"You may regret that decision," Ella said with a wry smile.

"If this works, Navajo families who don't have other job skills may be able to grow prickly weed and earn a living," Rose said.

"Isn't there some hitch in the pilot project right now, something to do with the project's location?"

She nodded. "The land the tribe wants to use is ideally situated, adjacent to the current Navajo Irrigation project and close to a road network near Farmington. Unfortunately, that has also been occupied by the same Navajo family for years and they don't want to turn the bulk of it back to the tribe."

"Well, if they're using it, why should they?"

"That's just it, they aren't, and since no individual owns tribal land, they have to abide by our laws. They can't keep those parcels unless they're farming the land or using it for grazing," Rose said. "Of course they claim they still have animals, but they let their grazing permits expire years ago. There have been chapter house meetings about this already, but I don't think anything's been resolved. Of course it will be eventually, and once it is, the Prickly Weed Project will undoubtedly become an incredible gift to the tribe."

"And that's why the new Plant Watcher has decided to take part in the project," Ella said, referring to Abigail. "If there's good publicity to be had . . ."

"Daughter, you're too hard on her," Rose answered. "We have our family. Our lives are full, but she has very little except for money, which, in this case, I understand she's invested every last dime in the project. It explains her enthusiasm, I suppose. Her biological daughter passed on years ago in that accident, then her husband was shot dead. She adopted that other girl, who turned out to be a criminal. Poverty isn't the only evil among us."

"Mom, you've got too good of a heart, but don't trust her, okay? People don't change," Ella added, recalling with amusement Blalock's description of Abigail as the "she wolf."

"Some do," Rose answered quietly, not noticing the hint of a smile on Ella's face. "But let's not talk about this now. I'm too tired." She stood and walked to the doorway. "I'm going to bed early. I've had a very long day."

Ella said good night, then as her mother disappeared from view, went down the hall. To her disappointment Dawn had already turned off her lights. She'd hoped to spend a little more time with her daughter tonight.

As she went to her own room, she tried not to think about Abigail Yellowhair or the PPS job that hung in the balance. These days, it was always there in the back of her mind. But there were other priorities now. She had to find whoever had attacked Adam and Kevin before she could shift her attention to anything else.

Police work—she lived it and breathed it on a daily basis. It defined her and filled her with purpose. And sometimes it was the only thing in her life that made perfect sense.

TUESDAY

Ella woke early the following morning. The household wasn't up, so she made coffee as she phoned Justine.

"I was just about to call you," Justine answered. "Need me to pick you up?"

"Sure do. Then we'll go over to the casino's business offices. Let's see if we can figure out where the money Adam was carrying came from."

"We need to find out more about Grady," Justine said. "Benny said that he followed up on what you'd told him and that Grady's alibi seems to check out. But that doesn't mean he didn't set up the hit. We need to find out more about the man—unofficially."

"Do you know someone who could help us do that?" she asked, sensing what Justine had left unsaid.

"I sure do. My second cousin, Martin, on my dad's side, works for the casino."

"What's he do there?"

"He's the assistant office manager—and as honest as the day is long, Ella. I don't want to approach him at the office because I wouldn't want to jeopardize his job. But it's barely seven now. If we hurry, we might be able to catch him before he leaves for work."

"Where's he live?"

"In Fruitland—not far from the casino, actually."

"Then get here as soon as you can," Ella said, knowing it was a half-hour drive from her house. Fruitland was east of Shiprock and adjacent to Kirtland. The casino was south of that valley community, just across the San Juan River and on tribal land.

"I'm on my way to your house now," Justine said. "I should be there in ten or less."

Ella stepped outside and Two came out with her. The old mutt—a rescue who'd just shown up one day—loved the early morning sun. He usually lay out on the hard ground beside the porch, soaking up the rays. Ella bent down to pet him. Though Two was getting up in years, he was in remarkably good shape.

"Hey, buddy," Ella said softly.

The mutt wagged his tail furiously, then lay beside her as she sat on the porch swing Herman had built for her mother.

Two was the perfect family dog. Whenever anyone was sick or troubled about something, Two would remain with them until the crisis passed. He was a good friend to each of them, but he favored Rose. Her mother, in turn, adored the dog and was always cooking or buying special treats for the guy.

A short time later, just as Ella finished her coffee, Justine pulled up. Ella scratched Two behind the ears one more time, got into the car, and fastened her seat belt. "Tell me more about this cousin of yours," she said as they got underway.

"He and I have always been good friends. I called right after I spoke to you, just to make sure we caught him. He said to come over and he'd do his best to help us."

They arrived at a small house below the mesa along the San Juan River a short distance from Kirtland. There was a well-tended apple orchard surrounding the white cottage, and the apples looked ready to drop. A young Navajo man in his late twenties, short like Justine, came out to meet them as the vehicle tires were crunching in the gravel drive.

"I've got fresh coffee inside," he said, opening the gate on the white picket fence and gesturing for them to follow him.

As they sat around the kitchen table, he placed mugs of fresh coffee before them. "I don't have to be at work until nine, and the drive takes less than ten minutes. That means I've got plenty of time, so fire away."

Ella sipped the coffee and found it incredibly good. Choosing to take it as an omen, she leaned back in her chair. "You've heard about the shooting outside Shiprock, right?"

"It even made CNN—of course I know about that," he answered. "And since Kevin Tolino's the one after Grady, people are saying that Alan's behind it somehow. But I don't believe it. It's too obvious, and my boss isn't stupid."

"Then who do you think is responsible?" Justine asked him.

"I don't think it's got anything to do with the casino. If I had to guess I'd say it's an enemy one of you guys made, you in particular, Ella. Talk to Grady yourself, you'll see. The man's too smart and too smooth to pull something this brazen." He paused. "Of course, all the talk going around took its toll, so right now he's going to be hard to find."

"Why's that?" Ella asked. "He's not going in to work, or what?"

"The tribal president called Grady yesterday at work and placed him on a paid leave of absence until the investigation is finished. Mind you, Grady doesn't take me into his confidence, I'm just a minor league player, but I know his assistant. Betsy Dodge and I get along great, and she and I talk all the time."

"Do you have any idea what the reason was for the leave of absence?" Justine asked. "It can't be just because of the talk."

"You didn't hear this from me, okay? But here's what went down," he said, leaning forward and lowering his voice, though no one else was around. "According to Betsy, Grady got a call last week from BIA honchos in Washington. Some of Grady's business contacts are suspected organized crime figures in Arizona who—as it turns out—have investments in a tribal casino. There's already an investigation underway in that state about money laundering and political corruption associated with casino activity, and Grady ended up in a BIA report as a person of interest. The tribal attorney general's office found out about that almost right away and since the tribal president had asked to be kept in the loop, they informed him shortly thereafter."

"Is there any proof connecting Grady with the corruption in Arizona?" Ella asked.

"Not enough to obtain warrants or bring charges, but the tribal president is being extra careful, politically speaking, and wants to cover his butt. That's why Grady's on paid leave."

"Does Grady have any close contacts on the tribal council, people he might want to rely on now to keep him in place?" Ella asked.

"The only person in the council I know he's tight with is Cardell Natani. They often have dinner at the casino."

Ella knew Natani. He'd been pro-casino since the very beginning, seeing it as an expedient way to raise cash and give the tribe a steady flow of income. Although she'd also heard that he had a bit of a gambling problem, no one had ever tried to use that against him.

"So the person we need to talk to is Grady's assistant, Betsy," Ella said, thinking out loud.

"Yeah, but don't tell her you spoke to me. In fact, don't tell anyone at the casino office that you even know me, okay?"

"No problem," Ella assured him.

Martin glanced at Justine. "I owe you big time, so whenever you need my help, just ask. Thanks to you, I was finally able to get Dad to accept the fact that I wasn't going to join the military." He looked at Ella and continued. "My dad spent his entire life in the Army and he always assumed that I'd follow in his footsteps. But I'm not cut out for that kind of life."

As they got back into the car, Justine glanced at her and explained. "Martin's a gentle soul. He never even went out for sports—too much competition. His dad thinks he's a wuss, but Martin's just a nice guy who happens to hate violence of any kind."

"I hate it, too, but it's part of life," Ella answered.

"You and I are cut from a different mold."

On the way, Ella used the onboard computer and printer to generate photos of the shooting victims. "Let's see if Betsy has seen Kevin or Adam at the casino or with any of the employees." Ella then accessed some of their available databases.

They arrived at the casino a short time later. "I ran a check on Betsy. She's clean," Ella said. "According to what I could find, she's in her mid-twenties and has been working at the casino since it opened. Everyone employed by the tribe, especially at one of the casinos, has had background checks."

"Let's see what Betsy can tell us," Justine said. "If there's one thing I've learned over the years, it's that if you want details about the boss, you should ask his assistant."

They found Betsy Dodge typing away at a computer keyboard, a stack of colored folders on the desk beside her. When Ella introduced herself, Betsy stiffened noticeably and quickly exited the program she was running—something that looked like a personnel file.

"How can I help you?" she asked coldly.

"We'd like to talk to you about an ongoing criminal investigation. Is there someplace we can go?" Ella asked.

"Right now's a real bad time. My boss is going to be away for a while and I need to get some last minute details sorted for him."

"Then take us to see him," Ella said, immediately taking advantage of this unexpected stroke of luck.

As they walked inside the spacious office, they saw Alan Grady, a short, balding Anglo in his sixties, placing several file folders into an expensive looking alligator-skin briefcase.

Seeing Ella and Justine, and noting the badges clipped to their belts, he smiled. "How can I help you two officers?"

"We have a few questions for you," Ella said, closing the door as soon as the young woman stepped out.

Grady sat behind his enormous ebony desk, which was accented by a small bronze sculpture of a spear-wielding warrior on a horse. "Make yourselves comfortable," he said, waving them to a couple of chairs. "At the moment I'm on paid leave, so I'm in no rush."

"We understand that you've come under investigation by federal and state agencies for your business contacts and operations. But we're more concerned about offenses you may have committed here."

Grady steepled his fingers. "If you think that a man in my position has no secrets, then you're very naïve—which contradicts what I've heard about you and your reputation as an investigator for the tribe, Ms. Clah. I'm well aware that there have been some misunderstandings about the compensation I receive for my work here at the casino, but with a lawsuit pending, my attorney has advised me not to comment on these matters. I will tell you this much: I haven't broken any laws, and no criminal case can be made against me."

Ella studied Grady. He was calm, almost cocky. This was a man used to bending the rules when it suited him, and one who enjoyed an occasional challenge to his authority.

"Mr. Grady, have you heard about the incident at the airstrip?" Ella asked.

"Who hasn't?" he countered, and shrugged. "One of the tribal attorneys was attacked—the same one, Tolino, who filed the lawsuit against me and my company. But that's got nothing to do with me or my people. You need to look to your own backyard for answers."

Ella's gaze narrowed. "Do you know something about these crimes that we don't?"

"You had two very ambitious men on board that plane,

and ambitious men *always* have secrets and enemies," he answered.

Ella tried to figure out if he knew about the money, but it was impossible to read him. She waited, wondering if he was going to get curious and ask her a question, but he just sat there, staring at his fingernails.

After a minute or two of silence, he stood up, dismissing them. "I'm not in a rush, but I do have some plans today, Detectives, so if you don't mind . . ." He went to the door and held it open.

Ella and Justine walked out and remained quiet until they were well out of earshot.

"Any vibes?" Justine asked at last as they stopped by a soft drink machine in the wide hall well beyond the office area.

"Nothing. He's one cool customer—like a professional poker player who knows how to avoid the tells."

"Well, considering the environment," Justine replied, waving her hand toward a double row of slot machines, half of them in use by mostly Navajo guests.

A short, big-chested Navajo man in a bolo tie, fancy belt buckle, and expensive-looking suit was standing beside one of the machines, looking in their direction. From this distance she didn't recognize him, but his posture and casual attentiveness suggested he was undercover security.

"Try to find out if the tribe has anything else on him besides what we already know," Ella said, avoiding mentioning Martin's name or even the possibility of a source. With so many security cameras, there was also the possibility of hidden microphones or trained lip readers, and she suspected the guy with the bolo tie was watching them, perhaps because they'd just met with Grady.

Moments later, as they stood drinking sodas, they saw Grady hurry down the other end of the hall carrying his briefcase and a cardboard box.

Justine gave Ella a quick nod, and followed Grady until he went through the last door at the end. After waiting a couple of seconds, she opened the door and took a quick look.

Satisfied, she returned to where Ella waited. "There's a low-profile employee entrance that requires a security code to open from the outside. He left the building."

"Let's go find Betsy," Ella said, glancing around but no longer seeing the Navajo with the bolo tie.

They found the young woman at her desk. Grady's office door directly behind her was wide open, but no one was inside.

Noticing Betsy tensing up as she approached, Ella smiled. "Relax. We're going to keep this informal."

"I don't know what I can tell you. Mr. Grady's a good man. He came here to make sure the *Diné's* casino runs smoothly, and he's got years of experience managing gaming operations. He was involved with helping some of the Rio Grande Valley pueblo casinos get set up, and look how successful they are."

"Does Mr. Grady feel that the tribe is targeting him unfairly?" Ella asked.

"No, not at all. He says that the casino business is tough and there are always going to be people in the community opposed to gaming for religious or other reasons. The way he sees it, his goal as casino manager is to make sure the tribe turns a healthy profit. He's done it for other tribes, and plans to do it here, too. That's why he's not worried. He knows he'll be back at his desk soon."

"Do you like the way he's running things?" Justine asked.

Betsy considered it for several long moments. "Yeah, I do. The casinos are in the business of selling dreams. Get rich quick—all it takes is a coin or token in a slot, or a lucky hand with the cards or throw of the dice. The tribe, of course, *will* make money because people refuse to see the reality of it—that casinos are a business with a built-in profit. The tribe operates this casino to make more money than it gives away. But those who come here to play get something out of it, too. They get hours of excitement dreaming about all the 'what ifs.' "

"You said that Alan believes he'll be back at his desk before long. Do you think he's right?" Ella asked her.

"Oh, yeah. He's got enemies—all successful entrepreneurs do. But it's results that matter in this business, and he's getting results."

"How long have you known Alan Grady?" Justine asked her.

"Since he came on board as casino manager. He trained everyone before opening day."

Ella reached for the photos she'd printed out. "Do you know either of these men, and have you ever seen them here?"

"I know both of them. That's Kevin Tolino," she said, pointing, "the attorney representing the tribe in the lawsuit against Mr. Grady and Casino Enterprises Management. The other man is that soldier who won all the medals fighting in Afghanistan, Sergeant Lonewolf—Adam, I think. I don't know him personally, but every news program in the state has carried a story about him. He's an honest-to-gosh hero. There's a photo of him by the entrance, next to the tribal president and the Council member from this district."

"Have you ever seen Mr. Tolino here at Mr. Grady's office?" Ella asked her.

"Sure. He's been here several times, the most recent being a few weeks ago. The door to Mr. Grady's office was closed so I didn't hear what they were saying, but by the time Mr. Tolino left, Mr. Grady was in a really bad mood. He hung up on someone, and yelled at the cleaning crew. I stayed out of his way the rest of the day. A few days later we heard about the lawsuit."

"What about Adam?"

"I've never seen him here—and I would have remembered him," she added. "Good-looking, but he's married. Such a tragedy—him getting shot, I mean. I hope he makes it."

"Me, too," Ella added.

Ella and Justine left the office and headed for the exit at the far end of the enormous facility. "We need to find out when Kevin learned about Grady's suspected ties to the mob," Ella said.

"You're thinking that was the reason Kevin came by a few weeks ago?" Justine asked.

Ella nodded. "He must have already known. Lawyers are like cops, most of the time they already know the answer to a question and are just looking for a reaction, or setting a trap."

"Kevin might have been pushing to get Grady out of the casino as soon as possible so he wouldn't be in a position to cover his trail, or intimidate anyone who might testify against him."

"I'm sure Grady gathered his own forces just as quickly," Ella said. "Kevin's got clout, but Grady's no pushover. Look at the facts. He managed to stay in control and maintain the status quo—until *after* the shooting, that is. That incident was what finally motivated the tribal president to remove Grady from the public eye."

"So where to next?" Justine asked.

"The hospital. I want to talk to Adam's wife, Marie, then follow up with Kevin."

Ella and Justine walked down the outside steps and into the parking lot, passing casino patrons along the way. Business seemed to be thriving despite the economy, Ella surmised, noting the cheerful expressions on the faces of the mostly Navajo crowd.

They were nearly to the car when she heard steps coming up from behind. In a heartbeat, an arm snaked around her throat. "This is just a warning, whore!"

Ella instantly slammed her fist back, hammering him in the groin. As he gasped, doubling up, she stomped hard with her heel on his instep, then spun and punched up, catching him in the throat. He staggered back, dazed and off balance.

Justine was fighting her own battle. Her partner had been lifted off the ground, but she immediately kicked back, whacking her attacker on the kneecap. He yelled and dropped her.

The attackers, Anglos, not Navajos, had clearly come looking for a fight—and they wouldn't be disappointed.

EIGHT
——— ✕ ✕ ✕ ———

We're cops. Back off," Ella shouted.

"Yeah, and I'm with the 'effing bee eye," her attacker replied.

Having recaptured his balance, he came at her, swinging. From his unpolished assault, he was obviously an untrained street brawler used to relying on his bulk.

Ella ducked beneath the blow, and kicked, sending him sprawling back. As Ella reached for her holster, the man bolted to his feet.

"Look out, this hooker's got a gun!" he shouted.

"Dude, run," the other man yelled. The two raced away, heading down the row of parked cars.

"Get to the cruiser and cut them off," Ella yelled to Justine as she sprinted after the men. They were faster than Ella had expected them to be, but kept making the mistake of looking back. As they raced around a curve in the lot, Justine cut them off, blocking the way.

The first man was going too fast to stop, but as he tried, his partner collided with him and they both tumbled to the pavement.

Justine was out of the vehicle in a second and grabbed

the big man's hand, forcing him to stay down with a painful twist of his wrist.

Ella caught up to the other as he rose to his knees, and kicked him in the chest. He bounced off the car, falling onto his back. Ella cuffed him while Justine did the same to the other suspect. Their prisoners secure, Ella recited the out-of-breath thugs their rights, and together with Justine, shoved them into the back of their tribal unit.

"You're both going down for assault on two police officers," Ella said.

Judging from their calloused hands, work shirts, pocket-knives in holders, and extra belt loops on their carpenter-type pants, and, more importantly, their lack of fighting skills, Ella figured the men were probably blue collar workers from a nearby site.

"The Indian dude said you were hookers, doing guys in the parking lot," the big man argued. "This is a mistake."

"Attacking prostitutes is okay, then?" Justine replied.

"No, that's not what he's saying," the other man blurted out, slamming his buddy on the shoulder. "The dude . . ."

"*What* dude? Somebody put you up to this? Tell us everything you know—now. This is your only chance," Ella added

"We're not criminals, we just . . . never mind, we'll talk," the bulky, blond-haired Anglo man said. "What do you need to know?"

"Start with your names," Ella said.

"I'm Larry Brown," the big man said.

"I'm Gene Murphy," his redheaded partner added. "Cut us some slack, okay? Some Navajo guy from casino security said you were hooking up with the patrons, and that was giving the casino and the tribe a bad rep. He paid us to scare the hell out of you, you know, so you wouldn't come back. Honest, we didn't know you were cops."

"*Who* hired you?" Ella demanded.

"A short Navajo guy built like a wrestler. He was wearing a suit and one of those turquoise bolo ties. He said he was working security, and that he'd warned you two before, but you keep coming back. He said that lately you'd just take off every time he got close. He pointed you out inside, then paid us two hundred dollars to put a scare in you. We owe the casino some money, so . . . ."

Ella thought of the guy who'd been watching them earlier inside, and Cardell Natani came to mind. "Did he show you any kind of ID?" she asked, bringing out her handcuff key to tempt them.

They both shook their heads. "No, but he was carrying a gun and stuff. He acted legit, and we thought it was a good way of clearing our debts with the tribe. Sorry," Murphy said.

"That's not enough information to keep you out of jail, boys. We need more," Ella said, putting the key back into her pocket.

"We've told you all we know," Larry said. "Can't you cut us a deal?"

"If you want a deal, you've got to give me something to work with," Ella prodded. "Tell me more about this Navajo man—a lot more."

"His belt buckle was gold, with a cowboy roping a calf. There was some kind of lettering on it, too, like it was a prize. Maybe he competes at the rodeo," Larry suggested. "His suit was pin-striped and his boots were custom-looking, snakeskin, maybe."

"Since when did you start checking out men's fashions, bro?" Gene said, rolling his eyes. "I saw his wheels, because he came out ahead of us—said he wanted to watch, from a distance. Climbed into a nice lowrider Dodge with a custom bed liner, black leather interior, under-sized wheels. It was hard to miss, too—yellow, with that pearl kinda finish, and parked in one of the security parking slots. Sweet ride for picking up the ladies."

"There are lot of trucks in this area, and yellow isn't exactly uncommon," Ella countered.

"Maybe not, but this was auto-show quality, like you'd see cruising in Albuquerque—or more likely, L.A.," Gene added.

"Come up with something else," Ella pressed. The description she'd been given matched the guy she'd seen near the slot machines. If only she'd been a little closer.

"That's all we've got," Gene insisted. "But I'd trade my old lady for that ride."

"Your old lady dumped you during the last Super Bowl, loser," Larry sneered.

Justine shook her head and Ella groaned in disgust.

"If all you've got is B.S., boys, this interview is over," she said, reaching for the front door handle.

"No, wait, I just remembered something," Larry added quickly. "That belt buckle backs up something else I noticed. He had a tribal rodeo booklet in his shirt pocket. They have a bunch of them inside the casino to advertise upcoming events, remember, Gene?"

Gene looked confused for a second, then nodded. "Oh yeah, by the ATMs."

"All right," Ella said, helping them out of the cruiser and taking off their cuffs. "We're going to cut you loose but don't make us regret it."

"Sorry for the trouble, officers. You'll never see *us* again—promise," Gene said. The men walked away briskly, never looking back.

Justine glanced at Ella. "Let me run a check and see who among the casino security staff owns a fancy yellow truck—for cruising the 'hood.'"

Ella nodded, then told Justine about the man she'd seen watching them earlier. "Start with the younger men—they're the ones with the biggest case of wheel envy. Somebody's got to remember seeing it. Who knows, it might point us in the right direction for more than one crime. Check on Cardell Natani's vehicles in particular."

Several moments later, Justine looked up from the computer terminal in the center console. "Several yellow trucks listed here. I'll send this on to Marianna for follow up. Cardell's got a pickup, all right, but it's a white Ford 150 with a crew cab."

"Okay. Then let's get back to Shiprock and focus on Marie and Kevin. I have a feeling that neither one is giving us the whole story."

They arrived at the hospital twenty minutes later. "Do you want me to talk to Marie while you interview Kevin?" Justine asked as they stepped inside the main entrance.

"That's a good idea, but I want you to really press her. We need to find out everything she knows, starting with the obvious—if she can think of any reason why Adam might have been a target. If so, we want to find out who she thinks the shooter was, or who might have ordered the attack."

"To me, it's looking more like Kevin was the intended target and the hit on Adam was just a way of making sure the right man went down. Once on the scene, the gunmen might have had trouble figuring out which professional-looking Navajo man in the suit and tie to kill. Kevin and Adam are about the same build, and both were carrying briefcases. At a hundred feet . . ."

"True, and the more I hear about what Kevin was doing, the more I tend to agree with that, especially after all the trouble we've had today," Ella said. "But the money Adam was carrying . . . that still doesn't add up. We're missing something and that's what worries me."

They split up in the hall, going down opposite corridors. Ella went directly to Kevin's room. He looked up and smiled as she knocked lightly on the door. Several boxes of chocolate-covered piñon nuts, Kevin's weakness, were on the side table. He was just reaching for one when she came inside. He held out the box, inviting her to take one.

She took three, then pulled up a chair beside his bed and sat down.

"Have you made any progress?" he asked. "My laptop's at the crime lab, there's nothing to read, television programming this time of day is women's talk show nonsense, and I'm going stir-crazy in here. You need to close this case so I can go back to work without having to wear a suit of armor."

"With that in mind, what I need from you is a more detailed idea of what's going on with Alan Grady and Casino Enterprises Management."

He shook his head. "You know better than to expect any details from me on that, Ella. It's an ongoing legal case."

"Right—a legal case, not a police investigation. I need answers, Kevin. We're not exactly in a courtroom, and we both work for the same tribe."

He remained silent for several moments, then at long last, nodded. "I've been giving this a lot of thought, and the way I see it, I don't merit this type of attack. Adam, on the other hand, was carrying what, around here, is considered a king's ransom. You know I'm right."

"Maybe, but without any information on where that money came from, I have to work the only leads I've got. Talk to me about what you're involved in," Ella said, refusing to let him sidetrack her. "Start by telling me about Cardell Natani."

Kevin made a face. "Natani's a thief and a con man. He's part coyote and just as tricky. But I don't have anything solid on him, and, believe me, I've looked."

"You—personally?"

"No. I hired Bruce Little. My offices use his services from time to time."

Ella had known the former police officer since high

school, when his nickname had been Teeny. Bruce stood nearly seven feet tall. Far too big for the basketball court, Teeny was built like the perfect defensive tackle, two oil drums with a soccer ball on top, and arms as large as most people's legs. Her childhood friend often had a spaced-out expression that made him look like he had the IQ of a stump, but that was far from the case. Teeny was highly intelligent, very inventive when it came to working cases, and his security and PI firm had prospered as a result.

"All I can tell you for sure," Kevin continued, "is that Cardell's very much pro-gaming and wants Alan Grady to remain at the helm of the new casino. That's why I began to suspect that Cardell had something more at stake. Teeny thought it might be related to the source of some of Councilman Natani's campaign contributions. Donations just seem to appear when his funds get low, and always come in small amounts from a large number of individuals—all Navajos. Those who'll talk say that the money was given to them to contribute, but nobody will say by whom. We think it's Grady, but we can't prove it. That tactic also manages to evade the disclosure rules that would lead us to the actual source," he said. "So, basically, all we have is a contributor we can't identify, one who provides money and remains anonymous."

"So Grady's possibly involved in a pay to play. That's common in New Mexico. Even our governor was accused of that," Ella said.

"Yeah, and though none of that is enough to charge either of the parties, those donations raise interesting questions. Teeny's still digging, but here's the thing. The general consensus among people who know Cardell is that he always works for the good of the tribe—that, in spite of the fact he appears to be paying off friends and taking a little off the top for himself. He's got some fiercely loyal friends, and allies, too, and that cuts him a lot of slack around here. I can't touch him."

Ella leaned back in the chair, and stared off into space. "Tell me more about Grady," she said finally. "How well placed are his allies—not including Councilman Natani?"

"They're high up on the food chain, Ella. Keep in mind that casinos mean money and jobs for the tribe. Most people don't really know, or care, how the business is run as long as the tribe benefits and there are enough jobs to go around. Unemployment has always been the big problem on the Rez, but that situation's eased up in the communities surrounding the two casinos in operation now. As long as the jobs are there, and our people are benefiting, the tribe, as a whole, is happy to overlook what they consider minor improprieties, just as long as the situation doesn't get out of hand."

"Before I go," Ella said, standing. "Do you know if either of those men drives a fancy yellow pickup? Like one of those lowriders?"

He shrugged. "I have no idea."

Ella walked out of the room and down the hall. Justine was waiting for her just outside the ICU door.

"What's going on?" Ella asked her.

"They're having a prayer service," she said softly. "Adam's still unconscious and things don't look good for him."

Ella glanced inside the room and saw Ford and the family gathered by the patient's bedside. "As soon as Marie comes out into the hall, let's take her aside. After Adam, she may be our best hope of finding out where that money came from."

"She may not know," Justine warned, "especially if it was a business bribe or a payoff. Secrets like that can be embarrassing to admit, even to a loved one."

"Sometimes wives aren't aware of how much they really know. If we ask the right questions . . .," Ella answered.

Moments later Ford came out, Marie half a step behind him.

Ford gave Ella a warm smile. "It's good to see you," he said quietly.

Ella felt him brush her hand with his own. The barely noticeable gesture, typical of Ford, had not caught anyone else's attention.

"We need to speak to you, Marie," Justine said softly. "Will you come sit with us for a few minutes?"

"Sure," she said, her voice betraying a deep weariness. Marie was small and fragile-looking for a Navajo woman, with pretty, delicate features and deeply set, dark eyes.

As the family moved away, Ford lingered behind, staying close to Ella. "When are you going to move him?" he asked in a barely audible voice.

"Where did you get the idea that we're doing that?" she asked, surprised. Although she'd given that some thought, she hadn't mentioned it to anyone.

"It's what I would do in your shoes. He's too vulnerable here."

She nodded. Logic was a trademark of Ford—except when it came to his religion. Faith seemed to fill in a lot of gaps for him then. "I'll tell you more as soon as I can. In the meantime, don't mention that possibility to anyone."

"No worries there." He glanced over to where Justine now sat with Marie. "My impression is that Adam didn't confide in Marie—he took care of her. Do you understand the distinction I'm making?"

"Yeah, but I've got to say, I've never understood women who encourage that kind of thing—or more to the point, put up with it. Marriage is made up of two people, not one and a half."

"Everyone has to find their own path to happiness. Don't judge—not unless you've walked in their shoes."

"I'm not judging. I'm stating the truth as I see it." She took a deep breath and focused back on business. "Time for me to get back to work."

Ella sat on the chair across from Marie and Justine. Marie's eyes were swollen and a trail of tears still moistened her face.

As Ella looked at the young Navajo woman, compassion filled her heart. No matter how strong you were, the ravages of grief spared no one. Ella kept her voice soft as she spoke.

"I'm going to have to ask you some tough questions, Marie, and I want to know anything that comes to your mind. Even something that seems trivial to you could help us find whoever did this to Adam," Ella said.

"I'll do what I can, but Adam's always kept his work to himself. I think that dates back to his military training. If he hadn't been awarded that medal and everything he'd done made public, I probably would never have known about it. He doesn't talk to me about what he does outside the house."

"I know that his job for the tribe didn't pay as much as he'd hoped. Did that put a strain on your finances, or do you have enough set aside to get by?" Ella asked.

Marie shrugged. "Things are tight. He gets his paycheck at his Washington office, then transfers the funds I need to pay bills into our local credit union checking account. When there isn't enough in the checkbook to cover everything, he takes the money from our savings."

"So you have substantial savings?" Ella asked.

The woman shrugged. "The tribe matches our contribution to a retirement account, but I don't know how much is in there right now, or how to get the money out if we need it. We have a regular savings account, too."

"How much is in your savings account right now?" Ella pressed.

"Around four or maybe five thousand, but that's just a guess. I'd have to look in our file cabinet at home, or check online. There are things he takes care of and things I handle myself. Anything outside the checking account is his responsibility."

"Was there anyone he might have confided in, a coworker, maybe?"

Marie tugged at the small cross she wore around her neck, then clenched it in her fist. "Adam knows a lot of people, both in and out of the military, but he's not the kind who talks to anyone about his personal business. If he has a problem, he takes care of it on his own."

"So what does he do for fun?" Ella asked, hoping to get Marie to relax a bit.

Marie smiled. "He loves hiking and camping. Sometimes, when he has time off, he'll go off by himself for a few days carrying nothing more than a backpack, a few survival items, and water. He said that it's good for a man to test himself from time to time. For a while, when he was just back from overseas deployment, I worried he might have some of those post-traumatic stress issues to work out. He saw a lot of combat, as you must have heard."

"Yes, I have. Does he ever open up to you about it?"

"No, he still keeps everything inside. But Adam handles it, I guess. He seems happy."

"How does he like his job as a lobbyist for the tribe?" Ella asked, switching back to the issue she needed to pursue.

Marie hesitated. "He told me that it was a different minefield than the one he'd been trained to clear, but he likes challenges. He says that's what keeps his blood pumping." She paused then added, "That's probably the main reason he agreed to do some bodyguard work for Kevin."

"Are the two good friends?" Ella asked, mostly to get her opinion.

"They haven't known each other long, but they get along well. Adam really approves of how hard Kevin works for the tribe."

"How does Adam feel about the tribe's casinos?" Justine asked.

"Adam says that poverty is The People's greatest enemy.

That's why he's in favor of this new casino, so close to home, and the Prickly Weed Project, too. A lot of people think it's a crazy idea, but Adam says it's definitely something worth exploring."

"Who's your husband's closest work associate?" Ella asked.

Marie smiled. "His BlackBerry."

"Thanks, Marie," Ella said, chuckling. "I appreciate your help."

"I know you've still got questions about him, but my husband's completely loyal and dedicated to our tribe," Marie said. "When he gets better, he'll tell you everything you need to know."

"One last thing," Ella said, lowering her voice. "Your husband's safety is our first priority. That's why I'm going to arrange to have him transferred to a military facility as soon as his doctor okays it. He'll be under guard there, and considering it's nearly impossible for anyone without credentials to even get on base, let alone into the hospital, I believe Adam will be safest there."

"You're right. Where's this place, and how soon do you think we can do this?" Marie asked.

"Let me handle the arrangements. I'll be in touch, hopefully very soon," Ella said. She already had a place in mind, Kirtland Air Force Base in Albuquerque, but for security reasons, didn't want to say anything to Marie until the last minute.

As Marie returned to the ICU, Ella glanced at Justine. "We need to coordinate this. I'll want one of our own people to accompany him on the flight and remain with him in Albuquerque."

"I can take care of all the details as soon as his doctor okays the move. Big Ed will also have to make some calls—that's assuming he gives us his approval," Justine said.

"Let's go back to the station so I can talk this over with

him," Ella said. "In the meantime, I want everything that's in Adam's BlackBerry."

"I've been trying to recover the files and data, but remember it was damaged. On top of that, it's all encrypted."

"If you can't figure out a way to pull out whatever he stored in that thing, get Teeny to do it." Experience had taught her that Teeny, who specialized in electronics, could make computers do just about anything.

"All right," Justine answered.

Ten minutes later they were back at the station. As they walked into the lobby, Ella stopped by the vending machine and bought colas for Justine and her. "I need what's in Adam's BlackBerry, partner," Ella said, handing Justine the soda can. "Make that your top priority."

As Justine hurried down the hall, Big Ed came out of his office. "I thought I heard your voice out here, Shorty," he said, motioning for her to join him.

"Let's hear what you've got so far on the victims and the investigation," he said once they were both inside and the door was closed.

Taking a seat across from his desk, Ella first gave Big Ed an update on Kevin and Adam's condition, then filled him in on what they'd learned about Alan Grady.

Big Ed rocked back and forth in his chair as he stared at the wall behind her, lost in thought. "Are you sure Tolino's playing it straight with you?" he asked at last.

"Kevin's answered my direct questions, but if he thought he could better serve the *Diné* by holding back some of the details, he'd do that without hesitation."

"Any leads on the cash Adam had on him?"

She shook her head. "That whole money issue still remains a question mark. All I know for sure is that both Kevin and Adam are still targets. Kevin will be released soon—the hospitals aren't keeping them long anymore—and I can make sure he's got protection at home or at a safe house. But Adam's a different story. He needs constant medical care, and may need more surgery—at least that's my guess."

"So what's your plan?"

"I want to have him transferred to Kirtland Air Force Base as soon as he's stable enough to be moved. I think that's the safest place for him here within our state, and it's a direct flight. Blalock can help me with the red tape. Albuquerque can provide more medical expertise, when and if needed."

"But there's more to your plan, isn't there?" Big Ed said, observing her closely.

Ella nodded, then after pausing to gather her thoughts, continued. "Once he's on base and secure, I want to release the story that he passed on, and that his family has gone into seclusion to grieve."

"What about the funeral? He's a public figure now, and people will want to acknowledge his passing with some kind of ceremony. There'll also be a horde of politicians wanting to be seen in the patriotic glow cast by a fallen hero," he said with an expression of disgust.

"Getting cynical, Chief?"

"Getting real, Shorty, and you know I'm right. Elections are coming up soon."

"Then we'll have to sidestep that issue. The easiest way will be to say that Adam will be buried in a private ceremony, and let it go at that."

"I've got news for you. The press isn't going to let it go," Big Ed said.

"If they can't get to the family, they won't have a choice," Ella answered.

"Do you intend on placing the family in protective custody?"

"No, I just want them out of the way. I was hoping you could talk to the base commander and arrange for them to be given temporary on-base housing. That way they can stay close to Adam—and be out of our way. That'll free up officers from protection duty, too."

"I may have to go through the tribal president, but I'll see what I can do. Give me a couple of hours, then come back to my office," Big Ed said, picking up the phone.

Ella walked down the hall to Justine's lab. As she stepped inside she saw her partner standing at the counter, conferring with Benny Pete. The BlackBerry had been taken apart and the memory card data downloaded to a lab computer.

"How's it going?" Ella asked them.

"I don't think any data was lost, but this level of encryption isn't something we can break here," Benny said.

"Teeny's our best bet now, Ella. I've already transferred the data onto a flash drive," Justine said.

Benny nodded. "I hear Mr. Little's got some software that rivals CIA and NSA sources."

"He writes his own, and his hacker friends design special programs for him that are nothing short of amazing," Justine said with a nod.

"I'll take it over to him," Ella said, and held out her hand.

Justine entered a few commands, then removed the small flash drive from one of her computer's USB ports. Placing a cap on it, she handed the data storage device to Ella. "Benny can take care of things here at the lab. I'll go with you."

"That's not necessary," Ella said.

"It is, actually. Remember Big Ed's orders? For all we know, you're still one of the targets," Justine answered. "You need backup."

As much as she hated to admit it, Justine was right. "We have to find a way to identify the actual target of the attack. Otherwise, it'll tie up an officer every time I go out."

"Teeny's our best hope right now, and he's already working the case."

"You mean because of his involvement with Kevin?" Ella asked, wondering how Justine had found out.

"What involvement?" she asked, then seeing Ella's expression, shrugged and continued. "You know that Teeny and my sister Jayne are still seeing each other, right?" Seeing Ella nod, she added, "Jayne told me that Teeny's mad as hell that someone used you for target practice. He's stirring up the bushes, hoping something will poke its head up. And if it does, blood's gonna flow." She shrugged. "Jayne's a little on the overdramatic side, but from what I know about Teeny, I don't think she's far off the mark."

Ella's knew her friendship with Teeny was special. They had a bond that was hard to describe, but was as dependable as the morning sunrise. "Teeny and I need to talk. Let's go."

NINE

✖ ✖ ✖

Justine pulled up next to the cameras at the gate of the fenced compound Teeny called home and waved into the lens. The home-slash-office, a metal warehouse, was located east of Shiprock but still on the Rez. A moment later Teeny pressed the buzzer and the gate swung open.

"I'm sure glad to see you, Ella, and you, too, Justine," he said, meeting them at the door and inviting them inside. "Have you ladies had lunch yet?"

"No, we haven't eaten," Ella answered. "If you're inviting us to lunch, we accept." Teeny was a world-class chef and the temptation was too much to resist.

Teeny laughed, his gaze taking in the wound on her scalp. "It's good to hear that you're back to normal."

As Ella brought out the flash drive containing the Black-Berry's stored memory data, Teeny waved them to a chair.

"I need your help," Ella said, giving him the highlights. "Justine was able to transfer this from the memory card on Adam's BlackBerry, but the files are encrypted."

"We were hoping that your skill can do what our programs can't," Justine added.

"Count on it," he said, studying the flash drive Ella had

handed him. Moments later, the device was connected to one of Teeny's computers. Rolling his chair back away from the desk, he glanced at Ella. "I'm glad you came. I've got some information you might be interested in. As I'm sure you've heard, I've been asking around about the incident at the airstrip."

"You really should have checked with me on that first. You're not with the department anymore and this is police business," Ella said. "Okay, now that I have that out of the way, what did you find out?"

He grinned at her, but the problem with Teeny's smile was that it looked more like a sneer. It was nothing short of frightening to anyone seeing it for the first time. The expression contorted his features into something sharp and deadly, and could make even hardened criminals spill their guts.

"Kevin's made himself some serious enemies over the years, and he knows it," Teeny said. "Not just with Casino Enterprises, but with a goodly number of our own people. He put the Aspass brothers away for skimming from the tribe, remember? Then new information came to light later on, and they were released."

Ella nodded. "I remember that case. It looked like Aspass Construction had been embezzling from the north San Juan bridge project. Then the money was found in the wrong bank account and the screwup traced to an accountant Kevin had recommended. Kevin nearly lost his job after that mess."

"He got lucky when word finally got out that it hadn't been his choice, that Robert Buck, his boss, had ordered him to take the men to court. But the fact remains that Kevin won the case and the Aspass brothers spent nearly three months behind bars."

"So you're saying that the Aspass brothers were behind this incident?"

"No, not at all. I'm saying that's only one of many possible motives for the shooting—and that's in addition to the casino lawsuit. Through his work as an attorney, Kevin has cost people their money, and sometimes their freedom. You've got tons of enemies yourself, too, Ella, because you're a good cop who closes most of her cases. And Adam . . . he's a hero all right, but everyone who's human has made a mistake or two in their past. Maybe he's not as squeaky clean as people would like to believe he is."

"You've got something on him?"

Hearing his oven timer go off, Teeny walked into the kitchen. As he pulled an enchilada casserole from the oven, a wonderful aroma slowly permeated the entire warehouse.

"Adam invested his own money in the Prickly Weed Project via a tribal partnership program that allows private citizens, even non-Navajos, to buy in. Since he's being paid to push the project for the tribe, his financial involvement could lead him to make certain agreements that might favor him and his co-investors at the expense of his employer. Technically, though, what he's done is not illegal. And he's not the only one. There are a lot of others who represent the tribe in one way or another and have serious money invested in the success of the Prickly Weed Project," he said, looking up at them as he placed the hot dish on a wooden trivet to cool.

"Like whom?" Ella asked.

"Robert Buck, Kevin Tolino, Billy Garnenez—even our tribal president. And Abigail Yellowhair, the late state senator's wife, has close to a quarter million sunk into the project, if you believe the stories. I've even got six figures out of my own pocket on this venture. Think of it. The Southwest is filled with that damn plant. This project could be the best thing that's ever happened to our tribe. Forget the casinos. If we can get economical levels of fuel from a weed that's as common as sand, those Middle Eastern boys are going to be weeping into their *thobes*."

"Huh?" Justine's eyebrows shot up.

"Those white robes the Saudis wear," Teeny responded.

"You learning about Saudis' dress codes now?" Ella asked.

"One of my employees just returned from eighteen months in Iraq. I pick up trivia here and there."

Teeny placed a huge portion of the casserole onto a plate and handed it to Ella. He then served up an identical portion on a second dish and gave it to Justine.

"What are you really saying, Teeny?" Ella asked as they ate. "About the tumbleweeds, I mean. You lost me."

"Tumbleweeds, Russian thistle, prickly weed, *ch'il deenini*—same plant, different names. To get off the ground, the Prickly Weed Project needed some serious energy-industry backing. The choice was eventually narrowed to one company, called Industrial Futures Technology, IFT. They had experts in the field as well as the technology to carry it through. But getting them on board has been nearly impossible. It's not the science that's in question—it's the money that the project will take to get off to a good start. IFT didn't want to commit that much time and money into an unproven venture like this one. But something changed their minds. It's not official yet, but an agreement has been reached, papers signed, and they're now ready to get moving."

"How good are your sources? Do you trust this information?" Ella asked.

"Yeah, absolutely."

Although he'd taken a portion at least three times larger than what he'd troweled onto her plate, Teeny had finished lunch. He stood and walked over to his computer keyboard.

Meanwhile, Justine and Ella practically licked their plates clean. The combination of salsa, beef, cheese, and freshly made corn tortillas could not be beat.

"You could make a killing if you ever opened your own restaurant," Ella said.

"No way. Cooking's what I do to unwind. I'm a cop—private these days—but investigative work's in my blood. You, more than anyone else, should be able to understand that."

Ella nodded silently. As much as she loved being a mom, she needed her work, too. The challenge, the demands, the danger—they got under your skin. Law enforcement was as much a part of her as breathing.

And that was the problem with the job she'd been offered in D.C. Though it paid a generous salary, and would allow her to give her daughter things she'd never been able to before, it would put her behind a desk most of the time. More importantly, it would also take her away from the place where her skills were needed most. Tribal officers were in short supply these days, and critical to the *Diné*.

Yet, being honest with herself, she had to admit that the major hold-back had little to do with all that. On the Rez, the connections between people were real and nearly tangible. The clans linked almost everyone, giving each person a feeling of belonging that was unrivaled on the outside. She truly wanted her daughter to grow up feeling those ties, and with a real sense of who and what she was.

"Okay, I've got some partial information," Teeny said reading the computer screen. "Some of it is still garbled, possibly from physical damage to the device, or maybe just another layer of subtle encryption, but I was able to run a program that reconstructed most of the data. It looks like the list of companies Adam contacted in D.C. on behalf of the Prickly Weed Project—before IFT took over, I would imagine. The company names seem to fit with energy production or technology."

"That's all that's on the chip?" Ella asked.

"Of course not. But if you want the rest, I'm going to need a few more hours so I can run some programs that'll reconstruct the portions that are still garbled."

"I've got someplace else I've got to be right now, so that works for me," Ella said, noting that more than an hour had gone by. It was time for her to return to the station and check in with Big Ed.

Once in the cruiser and on the way back to the station, Justine gave Ella a worried look. "What are you so tense about, Ella?"

"I'm not ready to talk about what I've got in the works, partner. Once I'm clear about our next step, I'll explain."

Ella joined the chief in his office a half hour later. Blalock was already there. As soon as Ella was seated and the office door closed, Big Ed spoke.

"The medical staff here says a transfer is possible, so I've arranged for the county's medical evac helicopter to take Adam Lonewolf directly to Kirtland AFB. That'll avoid the Albuquerque commercial terminal altogether," he said. "Residents are also used to seeing Angel Hawk on the hospital landing pad, so it won't attract any undue attention. I'm having a couple of officers send in a fake call preceding the run in case the media is monitoring emergency radio traffic. We'll just have to be careful while getting Adam out of the hospital and loaded up so he's not ID'd. Of course we'll have to get the final okay from his doctors before we actually put him on the chopper. Last time I checked, he was critical but stable, and he'll have a doctor with him on the flight."

"Bureau agents and an Air Police detail will meet the chopper when it lands on base," Blalock added. "Along with a medical team."

"It's a solid plan," Ella said, nodding thoughtfully, "but another diversion can't hurt. Could you call a press conference at the station at the same time the airlift is happening, chief, and tell the reporters that Adam passed away during surgery? That way, if anyone does notice the chopper, we can stall for a few hours, then finally confirm that his body is being delivered to the Office of the Medical Investigators at UNM Hospital for an additional forensic examination. Dr. Roanhorse will back us up if necessary."

"I hate to put out a false report, but I'll make an exception under the circumstances," Big Ed said. "Once the doctors have him ready to move, I'll make sure radio traffic about the transfer of the deceased goes out as well—using a patient number, not a name, of course. Once Adam's underway, I'll call and give you the word. Then you and Blalock gather up the family. They'll be making the trip there with one of our officers, who'll be driving an older model SUV. You two will follow in something nondescript and provide an escort."

"We'll get to it as soon as the press conference starts," Ella said, reading the chief's plan clearly.

"Looks like you and I are going on a road trip, Clah," Blalock said, heading out of the office and toward the side exit. "We'll want to stay undercover and look like Mr. and Mrs. John Q. Public all the way. I'll dress like 'Bubba' on the weekend, dig up an old married-couple sedan, and throw my golf clubs in the back. Make like you're a housewife traveling to the big city to visit your in-laws. Maybe you could even wear a dress. No one will recognize you then. Including me. But wait . . . you *do* own a dress, right?"

"Let me surprise you," she said.

"Bring some luggage we can throw in the back, too. That'll cinch our cover."

"I'll meet you at your office in an hour," Ella said. "I'll bring some extra nine-millimeter magazines with AP ammo, just in case. You should pack some extra firepower, too, maybe an M-16."

"I see you've met my family," Blalock said straight-faced.

Three hours later, as they entered the hills and winding highway near the remote community of Counselor, Ella's cell phone rang. About an eighth of a mile ahead they could see the lead vehicle's brake lights come on, and the car begin to slow quickly. A large, foreign object was just off the highway to the right.

"TA to the right. Looks like the vehicle rolled over, scattering debris," the officer riding shotgun with the Lonewolfs reported. "Appears to be injured at the scene, too."

"Don't stop, keep going," Ella ordered the lead car as she glanced over at Blalock, who was driving, then at the traffic accident ahead. "It could be a diversion—a setup to take out your passengers. Call it in, but keep moving. That's an order."

"What if—" the officer replied, but she cut him off.

"*My* responsibility. Get out of the area, and be on the alert for a second vehicle. I'll check out the traffic accident. Stay on the line," Ella snapped.

She could see the vehicle clearly now, upright, but with a badly dented roof and a broken windshield. The left front tire was in shreds—a blowout, apparently, judging from the chunks of rubber along a hundred feet of highway. To the left of the vehicle, the ground was littered with what looked like body parts. Her stomach sank. Considering the alternative, she almost hoped it was an ambush, but there was no way the gunmen she'd dealt with could have known about this trip and had time to set this up.

"What now, Clah?" Blalock said. He'd slowed down to fifteen miles per hour as they approached the scene. "Looks nasty, but it could still be a setup. We gonna stop?"

Ella reached for her handgun, ejected the magazine, and replaced it with one containing armor-piercing rounds. She then checked the highway ahead, and behind them. "We've got to check this out. No options."

Blalock braked to a stop, looking out on the scene. His service handgun was out and on his lap now. "Those aren't body parts, they're pants and shirts. There's a closet full of clothing spilling out of that old Chevy, and stuff in boxes, too. Looks like everything they own is in and around that wreck."

"Somebody's still alive. There's a woman sitting in the shade over there, with a child, I think," Ella said, wishing she hadn't worn a dress now. "We've got to go over there and make sure."

"*I'll* make sure," Blalock replied, reaching down to his left and bringing up a Bureau issue HK MP-5 submachine gun. "Take this and cover me while I walk over for a look-see."

"Yeah. You've got the vest, not me," she replied, looking down at her outfit. She was wearing a dusty rose knit top with an ornamented V-neck, and a long crinkle skirt in coordinating dusty rose and sand, with a tiny pattern of Southwest plants and animals in matching hues. The silver concha belt added to what her daughter called "the hot Navajo momma" look. Last time she'd worn it was to an evening program at Dawn's school. It definitely didn't shout "cop," and that had been the idea.

Taking the weapon and extending the stock came automatically for Ella, who would never become a soccer mom with this set of skills. Her window was already rolled down, so all she had to do was swing it around and aim.

"Watch for a third party," he warned, climbing out.

Blalock walked around to the front of the vehicle, his hand resting on the butt of his pistol. "Ma'am, I'm with the FBI, and help is on the way. Are you injured?" he called out, watching the woman closely as he stepped off the shoulder of the highway.

"I don't know. I bumped my head and everything is foggy. My husband said he was going for help, but I lost track of him. And my little girl, I think her arm's broken." The woman tried to stand, then slumped back to the ground.

Blalock stopped. "Where did you last see your husband?"

"By the road, I think."

Ella, who'd been looking for someone hiding behind the car, saw movement on the ground to Blalock's left. As an arm came up from behind a bush along the drainage ditch, she swung the HK around.

"To your left, Dwayne." Her sights captured a man's head and bloody arm.

"Help," he called, his voice weak.

Blalock, his pistol out and ready by his side, walked toward the man.

Ella covered him until she saw him stop and holster his handgun.

"It's for real, Ella. Go help the others."

Ella thumbed the safety on the automatic weapon, then placed it on the floorboards and climbed out, bringing the first-aid kit from underneath the seat. Pistol jammed into her belt, she hurried toward the woman and child, grateful to hear a siren in the distance. Help was on the way. Now if she could only avoid getting her skirt caught on the brush. . . .

Fifteen minutes later, they caught up to the rest of the transport team and the Lonewolf family. Much to Ella's pronounced relief, the rest of the trip to Albuquerque went without incident.

Once the Lonewolf family was settled in base housing and the patient secure at the hospital, Blalock and Ella hit the road back to Shiprock—a three-hour drive on Highway 550 with little more than the beautiful desert scenery to keep them distracted.

"That was top-notch housing the base commander chose for the family," Blalock said.

"Sergeant Lonewolf's not just a tribal hero—he's the country's hero, and a real one, too. A quarterback who passes for the winning touchdown, or the forward who scores the most three-pointers in a come-from-behind victory isn't a hero. They're just skilled athletes—and maybe a bit lucky. A real hero is someone who chooses to put his own neck on the line in order to save others—above and beyond what's expected of him, or her," Ella said. "Sadly enough, war and real heroes all too often go hand-in-hand."

A long silence stretched out as they each remained in the privacy of their own thoughts. Ella stared at the desert outside her window wishing there was something more to see than dry grass and the ever-present mile markers.

Never comfortable with long silences, Blalock finally spoke. "How are you planning to handle the issue of trust when your team finds out that you didn't tell them about Adam's transfer to Albuquerque?"

"Hopefully they'll understand that they had to be at the station and on hand for that press conference. If the reporters decided they wanted to speak to a member of the crime scene team, and we were all gone, questions would have been raised, and we probably wouldn't have been able to pull it off."

"Having Adam secure and out of the way should simplify our job. We have only one guy to keep out of harm's way now," Blalock said.

"That's assuming Kevin was ever really the target. . . ."

"The shooters at the airstrip were hired guns, Ella. We're in agreement there. Since we still aren't sure who the intended target was, we should concentrate on finding the motive behind what went down. Who might have wanted, one, or both, of those men dead, and why? We need to start pushing people harder," Blalock said.

"I agree. I'm also hoping Teeny will be able to get something from the scrambled data on Adam's BlackBerry," she said, giving him the details.

"I've been talking to gunshop employers who are active with the shooting clubs and service most of the gun owners in the area. I'm hoping lady luck will smile and one of them will be able to give us a lead to the two gunmen. My guess is that the pair practiced the hit, and that means they consumed a lot of ammunition. The rounds recovered and the cartridge cases have established that their the ammo was military surplus, probably bought in bulk. There should be a record of that somewhere, or, if not, a record of the theft."

"That's a good angle. The problem with the Four Corners region is that among the mostly honest, legitimate sportsmen and gun owners, there are still a few hardcore nut jobs worried about Armageddon or who believe the urban legend of impending gun confiscation. Of course a lot of those guys already have more firearms and ammo than most small town police departments."

Blalock laughed. "Truer words were never spoken."

Ella mentally went over the details of the incident once again. "I still can't wrap my head around what happened at that airstrip. Nobody in his right mind would go gunning for Adam. He's the pride of the Navajo Nation—and New Mexico. They'd have to know that every department in the area would go after them."

"So you're thinking it was a mistake?"

"Or a total lack of common sense by someone who was desperate. To me, it sounds like somebody panicked," she said. "Maybe it has something to do with the money he was carrying. But we still can't dismiss the possibility that Kevin was the real target all along. There's a chance he's holding out on us—with the best of intentions, mind you, but still not telling us everything."

"What's going to make things really tough is your personal connection to him," Blalock said.

"If you think I'm going to cut him some slack, you're crazy. I'm on the job."

"So there's nothing between you two anymore?"

"He and I have a connection—our daughter. But we're not romantically involved, and haven't been for ages," Ella said. "And even if I cared for him, that still wouldn't stop me from doing whatever I'm sworn to do."

"Are you sure?"

"Let me make this easy for you. If you feel you could question him more effectively than I could, then go for it," she said without hesitation.

"That's an excellent idea, all things considered." Blalock started to say more when his cell phone rang. He kept one hand on the steering wheel and used his free hand to flip the phone open. "When and where?" he said, listening for only a few moments.

Noting the abrupt change in his tone, Ella's sat up a little straighter.

"Understood—just information and no guarantees," Blalock said, then after a moment added, "No problem. I'm on an errand right now, but give me an hour and I'll meet you. I'll have to stop by my house to change clothes."

Blalock hung up and glanced over at her. "You might want in on this, Ella. That was Dan Butler, one of my most reliable sources. He runs that little Farmington gun shop on east 550 past the country club."

Ella nodded. "That's the Double Barrel, right? He carries everything from Old West antiques to urban assault weapons."

"That's him. With the gun business booming in this uncertain economy, he doesn't want anyone to see him talking to law enforcement, local or otherwise. Dan's concerned that it'll look like he's an informant to those 'storm troopers' who'll soon be breaking down doors and taking away their guns. Something like that might cost him business—or his life."

"So he wants to meet out of town somewhere?" she asked, finishing his thought.

"Yeah, at a place where a few of the locals go for a little informal target practice. But we can't come looking like cops. I used that stopping-by-the-house excuse for your benefit. With my bubba outfit I'm pretty much set except for some boots and my shooting jacket, but you might want to change out of that dress into jeans and a tee-shirt so we can join him for a little late afternoon target practice. I should have something that'll fit you well enough. You're not nearly my weight, but you're tall enough." He glanced over at her. "It's a shame, though. I may never see you in a dress again."

"At your funeral, maybe, particularly if you mention it to anyone on my team," she joked.

"You're safe. Nobody would believe me."

"I actually put some of my clothes, including jeans and a jacket, in the suitcase I brought along for show. I also packed my boots and socks, so I'm set on clothing. But if you have one, I'd like to borrow a baseball cap. Between that and my sunglasses, my face will be all but covered. That'll give us a little added insurance, especially after that photo of me in the paper and my appearance on the TV news recently," Ella said.

"No problem," he said. "I've got a Springfield M1903A4 sniper rifle from WWII that you can show off, too, and we can fire a couple of clips if you want. I'll also take the M1 carbine I picked up years ago and throw a couple of targets into my old SUV. I've got an NRA sticker on the back bumper for street cred."

"Why didn't Butler just talk to you over the phone and save us all some time?"

"He was still in the shop, with a customer due to pick up a rifle Dan's been working on. My guess is that he didn't want to take the chance that he'd be overheard. Dan's as close to paranoid as you can be and not get locked up," Blalock added.

"And a licensed gun dealer? In a way, I guess that makes sense, doesn't it?"

They soon reached Blalock's home. Although he'd lived in a Farmington apartment for almost as long as she'd known him, Blalock had recently taken advantage of a slow real estate market and bought himself a home farther east, outside of Bloomfield. The commute to his Shiprock office was longer, but once through Farmington, traffic was easy.

As they drove up the long driveway, Ella studied the house. It seemed large—three or four bedrooms—a lot for just one person.

"Is there something you haven't told me?" she asked.

"Like what?"

"A large house like this one . . . for just one man?"

He laughed. "I got it for a song. It was too good a deal to pass up."

"No new lady love?" she pressed, more curious than ever.

He grinned. "Her name's Cat. You'll meet her when we go in. She's perfect."

She knew that Blalock didn't care for felines, so this wasn't likely to be a stray he'd adopted. It was probably some kind of nickname—short for Cathy or maybe Katrina. "What makes her perfect?"

"No demands and no expectations. I'm too old a horse to learn new tricks, Ella. I need someone who can accept me the way I am."

"Old and crotchety?" she baited.

"Honorable and wise, trying to make the most of that special time in my life—after birth and before death."

She laughed.

"But she's not much of a housekeeper, so don't expect everything to be in place," he said. "Not that I care. We don't get much company."

Ella gave him a surprised look, but didn't comment. If Cat was the love of his life, being critical at this early stage in their relationship made no sense to her. A man in the middle of a passionate love affair—or even a lukewarm relationship—didn't see his lady's flaws.

As Ella glanced at Blalock, she suddenly had a hard time visualizing the possibility of passion and romance from the man. Blalock was dependable, but as methodical as time. Passion wasn't a quality she'd ever associated with him—except for his work. He was a good agent who honored his duty. But Mr. Romance when it came to women? *No way*.

When they arrived at the house, Ella saw Blalock's old SUV, but that was the only vehicle. Too bad. The woman's choice might have revealed something about her personality. For example, country women in New Mexico drove pickups most of the time. But there were no other vehicles parked outside and the home only had a carport. Wondering if his lady love had gone shopping, or just didn't have a car of her own, Ella waited as Blalock opened the door.

As it swung open, she heard a strange sound. It was as if someone with a truly wretched voice was attempting to sing. A heartbeat later, Ella came face to face with a dog with the size and stature of a horizontal fireplug. The bulldog, with its massive wrinkles and severe underbite, had a weird looking smile on her face.

"Don't try to pet Cat," Blalock warned. "Wait 'til she comes to you."

"Cat's a dog?"

"She's my son's pet, really. Her name comes from 'Cat 9,' a Marine Corp reference to someone beyond dumb. Apparently, Category 5 is the lowest score you can get in the entrance exams. Needless to say, Cat's virtually untrainable."

"How did she end up here with you?"

"Andy conference-called his mother and me. They were deploying him overseas where he couldn't take Cat, and he didn't want to give her away. My ex, Ruthann, isn't big on pets so I ended up with the dog-sitting gig." Dwayne looked down at the dog and smiled fondly. "Cat's a bit on the crabby side and dumb as a stump, but there's something about her that gets to you. The best part of it is that Andy drove her here and we all got to visit for a while. Ruthann came, too, with our boy facing deployment in a combat zone."

"When's the last time Ruthann, Andy, and you all got together?" she asked, petting the dog, who'd finally decided to come over.

"Years. Andy's a captain in the Marines now, and after two tours in the Persian Gulf he's been stateside, training future Marines. But the Corps came up with new orders for him, and he's now going to see more action. As far as seeing Ruthann again . . . I forgot how much we had in common."

Blalock led the way into his den, opened a tall weapons safe tucked away in a closet, and brought out the rifle, carbine, and ammo for both. The targets were on a shelf. With Ella's help, they carried them out to his SUV, adding a couple of realty signs that the man obviously used to hold his targets, and two headsets for hearing protection. Once everything was loaded up, they transferred their department weapons, except for their handguns, into the trunk of the sedan.

Five minutes later, after changing clothes, they left Cat behind the sofa chewing a rawhide bone roughly the size of Ella's forearm and drove off, heading north out of Bloomfield.

"You never told me how it went with you and Ruthann," she said, still curious.

He took a deep, steadying breath. "That's one of the reasons I asked you about your connection to Kevin. You know that Ruthann and I called it quits a long, long time ago. Our grown son is really the only tie that binds us. Yet when we were all here under the same roof . . . it just felt good.

"I know. It's crazy," Blalock continued. "We were ancient history, Ella. But with Andy, Ruthann, and me all together and the dog running around—we were like family again. All the anger and nonsense that led us to the divorce didn't seem so important anymore." He paused for several moments. "I haven't been that happy in a long time. The really strange thing is that we all felt it. Ruthann and I . . . Well, we've kept in touch since then, and she's been back twice already."

"And that's why you bought the house?"

"I moved in right before my family arrived, and I think that's what helped me see things in a new light," he said. "Or maybe I was already in the right mind-set, so things fell into place."

"So, are you and Ruthann thinking of getting back together?"

He paused. "Three months ago if you'd asked me that same question I would have burst out laughing. Now, I can't answer that. I'm not sure what's going to happen."

"Do *you* want to get back together?"

He hesitated. "Well, I've kept the house, and it's not just for the dog."

Ella shook her head. "Here's a hint. When you talk to Ruthann, phrase things differently. Women like to have things spelled out a little more, shall we say, romantically?"

"I suck at that," he muttered.

"She knows that already, but she'll appreciate the effort."

Blalock adjusted his baseball cap. "There's a UNM Lobo cap in the glove compartment that'll fit you. Harmless enough unless Dan's an Aggie fan."

Ella slipped it on, then pulled her ponytail out the gap in the back. "What's your plan when we meet this Dan guy?"

"We're going to have to play it by ear."

"Good enough. Now tell me about this place we're going."

"There's a mesa a few miles ahead where people go and shoot across a ravine into the opposite side. Somebody has set up a few old, sand-filled oil drums painted white with big black Xs. It's just a safe place for locals to go plinking or check out their hunting rifles. But here's a heads-up. People have a tendency to bring just about anything, from black powder muskets to machine guns. One time someone actually brought a Civil War cannon."

"Wait—how do you know this place so well?"

"Dan Butler's helped me out on a few cases, and this is where he likes to meet. I've been here before, so even if someone were to see him and me out there we'd blend in with the other good ole boys."

"What about women? I'm assuming some hang out there, too?"

"Enough so that you'll fit in, particularly wearing jeans and that Lobo cap. Here's the turnoff."

He slowed, left the highway, and headed northeast down a dirt road. Low, wide junipers dotted the gently rolling hills, and knee-high sagebrush provided cover for cottontails and jackrabbits. It was close to sunset, and though the daylight hours were long this time of year, they only had usable light for perhaps another hour.

After a bumpy two-mile drive along fresh and well-defined tire ruts, Blalock turned up a long, gentle rise. Once at the top, he parked beside two pickups. Beyond was the rim of a steep drop-off, more of a cliff, and below a small canyon. On the far side was another steep mesa. The wide ravine made a perfect bullet trap as long as shots were directed into the base of the opposite slope. Three bullet-ridden barrels rested at that spot, though one had managed to get tipped over.

As they climbed out, three men also exited a red and white Dodge Ram and walked in their general direction. They all had what looked like military handguns at their waists. Dan, whom Ella recognized, wore a black German leather holster, probably containing a P-38 pistol or a Luger. His companions had M1911 .45 autos in GI style leather holsters with U.S. stamped on the flaps. One of them also carried a late World War II German assault rifle slung over his shoulder. It was either an MP-43 or 44, she couldn't remember which, though she was pretty current on the last hundred years of weapon history.

"Dan," Blalock greeted, shaking the offered hand. The gun shop owner was a tall, slightly balding male in his mid-forties, wearing a red pullover shirt and yellow-tinted shooting glasses. "This is a friend of mine, Ella."

"Good to meet you," Dan said, with a raised eyebrow that suggested his cop radar had just gone off. "These two pistol-packing bozos claim to be friends of mine. Gary and Dennis," he added, "meet Dwayne and Ella."

His companions, both about Dan's age and looking fit in jeans, tee-shirts, and open windbreakers, shook hands with her. Although Navajos generally avoided physical contact with strangers, Ella went along with it. Silently noting the automatic weapon Dennis was cradling over his forearm, she said, "I saw one of those in that Private Ryan movie. A German assault rifle, isn't it?"

"You know your firearms, lady. This is an MP-44, one of the *first* assault rifles. This particular baby fires a 7.92 short from a 35 round magazine. The Russians used it as inspiration for their AK-47. Ever fire a full automatic?"

"No, but maybe I'll get the opportunity someday. I like weapons with a bit of history behind them." Playing innocent and letting herself be impressed seemed the best strategy at the moment. "My dad fought in World War II, and he owned a surplus M-1 that he let me fire several times. Dwayne's brought me out for the chance to shoot his Springfield .30-06 with the original Weaver scope, too. Supposed to be a fine sniper rifle."

"Sure was, but you've got to see my MG 42. Best rifle-caliber machine gun ever made—in my not-so-humble opinion," Gary added with a grin. "Sweet and reliable, though it goes through ammo like there's no tomorrow. It's over there in my pickup bed. Wanna take a look?"

Ella glanced at Blalock, who was trying to get a few quiet words with Dan. Deciding that he'd do better getting information from his source if he got some time alone with Dan, she walked over with the others to admire the big World War II–era German machine gun. It was mounted on a bipod and resting inside an open wooden crate. A canvas tarp tossed to the side obviously served as a dust cover during transport.

"I'm afraid one of these days I'll get pulled over by a deputy and he'll freak out when he looks under the tarp," Gary said with a chuckle. "I can't exactly carry it on a rack behind the seat rest, and my old lady won't let me drive her minivan off-road since I trashed the oil pan a few months back."

Back in the days when she'd served with the Bureau, Ella had received extensive firearms training, and she'd taken it upon herself to learn how to operate virtually any firearm she might encounter. Although she didn't have any actual experience with a belt-fed machine gun on a tripod or bipod, she'd fired several submachine guns and assault rifles, all at semi and full auto.

Ella kept Dennis and Gary busy, flattering their egos, and revealing just enough background knowledge to keep the conversation going.

"So, Ella, ready to work your way up to fully automatic? You might want to start out with Dennis's machinenpistole. It's easy to aim and control. Then you can explode some targets with the big girl, if you're still eager," Gary said. "We've got fresh targets taped onto two sand-filled fifty-five-gallon drums down there in the wash."

Ella was interested, and nodded, having never fired a World War II German weapon other than nine-millimeter pistols and a Mauser rifle. But she'd found the Russian designed AKs she'd handled accurate and reliable, and was genuinely looking forward to firing its German predecessor. "Let me get some ear protection first."

Five minutes later, after emptying a full magazine into the target on the left, she lowered the MP-44 from her shoulder and turned her head to gauge their reaction, pleased with her accuracy. The assault rifle was noisier and had a little more kick than the MP-5, a much more recent design submachine gun in pistol caliber, but it was still easy to aim and control. For a weapon produced in the mid-1940s, it could still hold its own with any iron-sighted automatic weapon she'd ever carried, and it didn't look as crude and simple as the AK-47. She could have blown away targets for hours with that bad boy.

"Real skill or beginner's luck, you dun good, Ella." Dennis, who'd been watching the target with a pair of fancy binoculars, laughed as he tried to read her expression. "Every time I see someone fire full auto for the first time, there's that same smile on their face."

Ella carefully handed the empty weapon back to Dennis. "There was a lot less recoil than I expected, and it has a really natural feel to it. Sweet and easy to aim. But I'd go broke buying the ammo, not to mention the expensive federal permit needed to own one of these babies."

"Just wait 'til you work a few seconds of full-size 7.92 rounds through 'Bertha over there," Gary waved toward the bed of his Dodge. "Better than sex—well, close."

The sound of a vehicle driving up got their attention. Ella noted two men in the cab of the gold Chevy Silverado as it swung to the left and came to a stop fifty yards farther along the edge of the cliff. "This must be a popular hangout," she said.

"Sure is. No problems with the law, no neighbors to complain, no gun club dues, and no rules except mutual respect and common sense," Gary said, watching the truck. "I think those boys have been here before."

One of the men waved as he climbed out of the passenger side, an assault gun in his hand, barrel pointed skyward. Ella stared, recognizing the silhouette of the weapon. It was something in the ArmaLite, M-16 family. Then the driver stepped out of the cab, and looked right at her.

"Cop!" he yelled, then jumped back into the truck. His partner followed.

"What the hell?" Dennis said, taking a step back and raising his binoculars.

Ella reached down for her handgun, then realized it was in the SUV instead of at her hip. By then, the driver was already whipping the Silverado around in a panic.

"Dwayne, that's them!" Ella yelled, racing toward his vehicle.

Twenty seconds later they were bouncing along the dirt track, branches from juniper trees whipping the sides of the SUV as Blalock struggled to maintain speed and control over lousy ground. Visibility was poor among the junipers and he was cutting corners whenever he could, in hot pursuit.

After retrieving her handgun and holster from beneath the seat, Ella struggled to get Blalock's out of the glove compartment where, thanks to the rough road, it had become buried under several maps. The sniper rifle and carbine were in gun cases in the back, out of reach, but her nine-millimeter was loaded with AP rounds now.

"Did we really get that lucky and cross paths with the pair from the airstrip?" Blalock asked, not taking his eyes off the truck ahead. "I thought you hadn't been able to make an ID."

"I still can't. They blew it when they recognized *me*. Add to that the fact that they were carrying the right weapons, and I'm willing to bet we hit pay dirt."

"Let's catch up to them first, then we'll sort this out," Blalock said, then began to cough from the cloud of dust that the truck ahead of them was kicking up. Their windows were wide open.

Ella sneezed as they raced up a steep hill, then swerved hard to the right, going back down into an arroyo. To remain steady she had to grab on to the door handle despite her seat belt. The pickup was now out of view, somewhere ahead.

"Bad place for an ambush," Blalock said.

"Or good—for them." Ella reached up to grasp the turquoise badger fetish around her neck—a gift from her *hataalii* brother—and immediately felt the heat, a warning sign.

"Ambush!" she yelled. "Take evasive—now!"

Blalock hit the brakes, throwing them into a controlled slide. Shifting the vehicle into reverse, he jammed on the gas.

Suddenly bullets tore into the front end, ripping up the hood.

"Hit the floor," Blalock yelled, letting go of the wheel and diving in her direction as the windshield exploded, raining glass down on them.

They bumped heads, but the sound of bullets tearing through the vehicle numbed every other sensation. Ella attempted to cover up with her arms, but Dwayne was already on top of her and she couldn't move.

The five-second barrage seemed to go on for an eternity, but just as suddenly as it had started, it grew still. The engine had long since died, and the only sound she could hear was Blalock's breathing and her own pounding heartbeat.

"Clah, you okay?" he said at last.

"Yeah—once you get off me, that is."

"Which way?" he whispered.

"Out your side. Then cover me when I follow."

Ella felt the pressure ease as Blalock lifted off her, then heard him grope for the door handle.

Seconds later, she crawled out and fell to the ground on her hands and knees. Hearing a vehicle racing up from behind, she instantly dove into the brush beside the front door, flattened, and brought her pistol up, taking aim. Blalock, who was still crouched by the front bumper, aimed his weapon in the direction of the sound and braced for a fight.

TEN
—————— ✖ ✖ ✖ ——————

Seconds later the red and white Dodge Ram from the firing range raced up, sliding to a stop only ten feet away. Dennis jumped out first, holding the German MP-44 at his hip, Rambo-style, as he emerged from the cloud of dust thrown up by their approach. He was joined by Dan and Gary, pistols in hand.

"Glad to see you two are still standing. It sounded like you might need some extra firepower," Dan said, looking past them. "I see dust down the road, so it looks like the dudes in the Silverado are taking off."

"Now that they're outnumbered and outgunned," Ella said, standing up and tucking her handgun into the holster at her belt. "They're the same dirtbags who shot two men at the airstrip the other day."

"Who *are* you?" Gary asked.

"The tribal detective they've missed twice now," Ella answered. "And, yes, this is out of my jurisdiction."

Ella walked up the road, cautiously, and found one of the gunmen's ambush positions—obvious from the glint of metal on the ground beside the twisted juniper stump. Everything was in shadow now and it would be dark soon, but she could see plenty of spent brass—in .223, again. Maybe they'd be able to match it to the rounds at the airport—or, if they got really lucky—lift a print or two. She picked up two casings with a small stick, one at a time, and dropped them into her pocket.

"Tribal detective," Gary mused, watching as she returned. "Interesting. And you?" he asked Blalock. "You aren't with the tribe. So that makes you . . ."

"FBI," he said, cell phone out and already on the line with the jurisdictional law enforcement branch—the county sheriff. "Armed and extremely dangerous," he added after describing the pair.

As he put the phone away, Blalock looked at Ella and added, "A deputy is on the way with a crime scene team following. You and I are grounded for now. My SUV is a Swiss cheese piece of crap."

Gary and Dennis, who'd slung his assault rifle over his shoulder, both had their eyes on Dan.

"Yeah, so he's Fibbye. So what? He's a friend and he wasn't here to harass any legal gun owners. Agent Blalock and the lady are after the men who killed that Navajo Army Sergeant, Adam Lonewolf, the GI who was awarded the Distinguished Service Cross," Dan said.

The men still looked uncomfortable, so Ella smiled at them. "Those two didn't know we were out here for target practice when they pulled up, but you boys got lucky, too. Once they saw what you brought to the range, those crazies might have turned their guns on you. Then they could have driven away with some real heavy firepower, leaving you either dead or in pieces."

"Point noted," Dennis said with a nod. "You're that hotshot Navajo cop, the one that keeps showing up on the news, right, Ella Claw?"

"Yeah," she confirmed.

"No wonder you can shoot like a man," Dennis said.

Not really knowing how to accept the backhanded

compliment, she didn't comment. "I got the idea earlier that you guys have seen those men before. Is that true?"

Dan nodded. "Two or three times, at least, but only from a distance. They never do more than wave or nod, and they don't drink beer while shooting like I've seen a few idiots do. They keep to themselves, minding their own business and cutting loose at silhouettes with assault rifles. They're pretty good at it, too, so they either get a lot of practice or have military experience. You agree with that, boys?" He turned to Gary and Dennis, who both nodded.

"We appreciate you three coming to the rescue," Ella said, still doing her best to set the men at ease. Witnesses who didn't trust her invariably locked up or gave out bad information. Right now she needed them relaxed and talkative. Even the most minute detail could turn out to be extremely useful.

"So, you gonna tell her?" Gary prodded.

"Yeah, yeah," Dennis muttered, then looked back at Ella. "I have new digital binoculars I was trying out today. Great in shadow and low light conditions, like now. I got shots of your target shooting. I also managed to get photos of the pair and their pickup as they raced off." He handed her the binoculars, letting her see the LCD display.

The angle had been bad and she couldn't see their faces directly because they were looking away as they fled, but their profiles gave her a general description. Yet it was the Silverado itself that held her attention. "If you can go back and forth between those last shots of them driving off, I think I'll be able to read that license plate."

Blalock came up, looking over her shoulder. As Dennis manipulated the display, they were able to get all the letters and numbers.

Blalock called it in immediately.

"You can take the memory card—until you're done with it," Dennis said, then removed it from the binoculars.

"Anything I can do to help nail the bastards who killed Sergeant Lonewolf—just say the word."

"Thanks. This'll help us a lot," Ella said.

"I saw the weapon the passenger had," Gary said. "It was in the M-16 family, probably a civilian ArmaLite—semi-auto."

"I agree. That's the same type of weapon that was used at the airstrip," Ella said.

"I have something else that may help you," Dan said. "A week ago, maybe a little longer, I did some work on an AR-180B for a customer. I can't remember his name off the cuff, but I have twenty-four/seven surveillance in the shop interior. His face is going to be in there somewhere. He might be one of your attackers."

"We'll need to go through that," Blalock said, but before he could say anything else, his cell phone rang.

As Blalock turned away and focused on the report he was getting, Ella questioned Dan further. "Think hard, and try to recall the name of the ArmaLite's owner."

Dan stared at the ground for several long moments. Finally looking up, he shook his head. "I'm sorry. I get a lot of business. The economy and the talk show hacks are all generating a lot of fear—and that means sales of guns and ammo are way up. All my business is legal, but a lot of people come through my doors."

Ella was about to press him when Blalock took her aside. "We got a hit on the Silverado. The tags are in the name of a Shawn O'Riley. A deputy's on his way over to the residence. He'll maintain surveillance until we arrive. SWAT's on the way, too—and the Bloomfield PD has been notified."

Blalock gestured toward the approaching emergency lights flashing in the distance. "That's probably the deputy they dispatched. He'll take over here until the county's crime scene team arrives."

"We still need transport," Ella pointed out, gesturing to their bullet-ridden SUV.

"We'll ride in with Dan and Gary, and Dennis can walk back and pick up Dan's pickup at the bluff," Blalock said. "Another deputy will meet us at the gun shop with an unmarked vehicle we can use." As his phone rang, Blalock placed it to his ear. "Stand by. We'll be there shortly."

"The deputy's in place at O'Riley's. There's a dark blue sedan parked in the driveway, but no Silverado."

"Either that's a second car, or they may have ditched the wheels, figuring we'd have an ATL on the truck. They don't know we got the plates and can ID the person, not just the truck, so we might get lucky and catch him at home," Ella said. "And it's not likely the truck was stolen. Those guys were just out here for some target practice."

As they rode back into town, Ella was squeezed between two large, heavily armed men with barely enough room to breathe. Gary, who was driving, looked uncomfortable, and Dan, on her other side, was almost sideways in the seat. Blalock was lodged against the far side, his elbow resting against the door frame of the open window.

"You realize that it's going to take me some time to go through my surveillance video, right?" Dan asked. "I keep everything in case I discover someone was shoplifting, but I don't always take the time to store the disks in any particular order. At least everything is dated and time-stamped and I don't record over any of the disks until after I file my quarterlies."

"Pull out all the stops and find what we need," Blalock said. "Those guys are bad news and you've seen them now."

"No warning's necessary. They know me, so that's going to put my shop in their line of fire. I have a vested interest in helping you find them," Dan said.

The ride took about a half hour. It was completely dark

by the time they arrived at the Double Barrel, but the outside of the building was well illuminated by a pair of powerful lights on a metal pole in the parking lot. A sheriff's officer was already there, standing beside an unmarked vehicle.

"Our transportation," Blalock said, then glanced at Dan. "The deputy will remain here at the shop to keep an eye out while you search through your surveillance images, Dan."

Dan gave Blalock a half smile. "I appreciate that, but I've got to tell you, if those bozos make a move on my gun shop, they're going to regret ever having been born. I could hold off a platoon in there."

"Once we unload Bertha, hell, that gun shop'll be like a bunker. Let 'em come," Gary said, then looking at Dan grinned and added, "On a lighter note, our waitress, Denise, AKA Dennis, should be showing up in a half hour to make coffee and fetch doughnuts. Not to worry, people."

With glass cubes from the windshield in her hair, her arms all scratched up from diving into the brush, and a pound of dust in her clothes, Ella still couldn't avoid a hearty laugh.

Once inside the shop, Blalock exchanged a few words with the deputy while Ella walked around, checking all the camera angles. "Looks to me like you've got a good view of your entire shop."

"I do. That's why I'll probably have multiple angles to show you once I get a hit on the day and time. The time-consuming part will be looking through hours and hours of surveillance to get there. At least I have a name to look for in my records."

"Clah, we gotta roll," Blalock called out to her.

The route to O'Riley's place took them out Farmington's east side, down highway 64 to the eastern outskirts of Bloomfield, then onto the road to Navajo Lake. The residence, not far from the main highway junction of State Highways 44 and 64, was actually a mobile home in a small court with several units—which increased the risk of civilian injuries if shooting broke out. A row of outdoor lights around the perimeter helped with resident security, and many of the units had porch lights on. On the plus side, they'd have plenty of concealment with the single-wides in rows barely twenty feet apart.

The deputy who was watching the blue trailer in space twelve had parked his unit between numbers seven and nine, and waved them off the center access road when they came into the main drive, headlights off.

Ella and Blalock jumped out immediately after coming to a stop and the deputy hurried to brief them. Ella silently noted that the residence the deputy had parked next to was currently unoccupied, with the porch light off. A big nickle padlock was on the front door, glistening in the light from the street lamps.

"I'm Deputy Salazar," the skinny, barely twenty-one-year-old kid in the black-and-tan uniform said.

"FBI—Blalock," Dwayne identified himself, offering a quick, firm handshake. "This is Special Investigator Clah from the Navajo tribe. What's the situation?"

"No sign of activity at number twelve, but there's light and a TV's on. The rear entrance to the suspect's trailer backs up to that tall cinder block wall, so anyone leaving the unit will have to come around the front or back end. The sheriff dispatched SWAT and their ETA is . . . ," Salazar checked his watch. "Eight minutes."

"Can you connect me with your SWAT commander?" Blalock asked.

Salazar handed Blalock a handheld radio. "Already done."

Deputy Salazar started to put his hand on Ella's arm,

then pulled it back. "Um, ma'am, I'm sorry about the loss of Sergeant Lonewolf. I heard about his death this afternoon. Is this O'Riley character a suspect in the shooting?"

"That's what we're trying to find out. Stay focused. O'Riley and his companion are well armed, and they've already ambushed two law enforcement officers today," she warned.

Salazar nodded, then walked over to his vehicle, brought out his department-issue shotgun, and fed a round into the chamber.

While Blalock was coordinating the arrival of SWAT on the tactical radio, Ella walked to the back end of the mobile home and checked the alley noting that, while dark, there was still enough illumination to see anything that came through. A quick walk up to number eleven, and she could see the opposite view of unit twelve.

Ella returned to where Blalock was standing, studying the area. "I'm going to cover the back door, Dwayne, just in case," she said. "They could have parked the Silverado on a side street and walked in."

Blalock nodded. "I'll be in touch as soon as SWAT arrives on scene. Then we'll have to evacuate the neighbors as quickly and quietly as possible."

Ella hurried to the back row of odd-numbered spaces. From where she stood near number eleven, she had a clear view of number twelve's back entrance. It was closed and she could see that the entire length of the single-wide was clear of everything except for a humongous dried-up tumbleweed that had blown in and become jammed between opposing walls.

A little over five minutes later Blalock gave her a heads-up, and she joined him to help evacuate the trailer court residents. Once that was done, SWAT advanced in teams of four, armed with shotguns and protected by thick body armor. From farther back, the team leader, using a hand mike, ordered the occupants to surrender and come out, unarmed, with their hands up.

Someone parted a curtain in the window and looked out. Ten seconds later, a terrified young woman, carrying an infant, opened the door of number twelve and stepped out onto the wooden porch. She had one hand raised, and the other around the child. She was either the world's best actress, or truly in fear for her life.

An officer came up and led her and the infant away to safety, then SWAT officers rushed into the mobile home, covering each other as they entered.

"Clear!" came the call three times. Then an officer appeared at the door. "That's everyone," he reported.

Blalock and Ella went up to the woman, who was standing with two officers. Her child, an infant probably a year old, was screaming at the top of his lungs.

"This is Patricia Arens," the SWAT leader reported. "She's given one of our team members permission to retrieve her purse and ID from inside the residence."

"Ma'am, we're looking for Shawn O'Riley," Blalock said in a voice loud enough to be heard over the baby's wails.

"You're not the first to come by looking for that man. He has some strange friends. They drop by at all hours. Last time it was two huge bikers. I called the Bloomfield Police Department but, by the time they got here, the bikers had already left. Check it out if you don't believe me."

"You sure you don't know O'Riley? This is the address listed on his vehicle registration," Ella said, wondering if the woman was his girlfriend.

The woman rocked the crying child. "All this commotion woke Donnie up, and he's like this whenever he gets frightened. Let me put him back in his crib with his teddy bear, then we can talk."

While deputies on the scene interviewed the returning neighbors about O'Riley, Ella and Blalock joined the woman in her living room. The little boy, back in his crib now, had quickly fallen asleep.

"All I really know about O'Riley is that he rented this unit before I did," she said.

"How long have you occupied this residence?" Blalock asked.

"Three weeks now, I think. I haven't even finished unpacking," she said, waving a hand at the boxes against the wall. "My boyfriend took off the day after we moved in, and working a split shift at the truck stop I've had a terrible time finding a reliable sitter. I've barely had time to take a breath."

Ella sympathized with her. If it hadn't been for Rose, she wasn't at all sure how she would have coped with the demands of being a single mom.

"Do you know anything about the former renter?" Blalock asked. "Any idea where he lives now?"

"No to both questions. All I know is his name, something I learned fast enough from his friends, if that's what they really are. The manager lives in the unit closest to the park's entrance, you might ask him."

"Please don't take offense, but how thoroughly have you cleaned since you moved in?" Ella asked.

"Not very," she answered honestly. "I wiped the bathroom and kitchen down with disinfectant to protect Donnie, but except for sweeping and cleaning up spills, that's about it. I haven't washed the walls or cabinets."

"We'd like your permission to come in and check for fingerprints the former renter or his guests might have left behind," Blalock said.

"No problem, but do you think you could come back in the morning to do all that? I'll leave the key in the mailbox. My son and I will be gone by seven-fifteen."

"That'll be fine," Blalock said.

As they turned to leave, Ella was surprised to see Justine

standing on the porch steps, waiting. Ella walked down to join her. "What's going on?"

"County called Big Ed and he briefed me about your operation here. Once I got the name of the suspect, I ran him through NCIC, NIBRS—and basically every database available. We already had something from the New Mexico DMV, but I got a lot more. DOD has records because O'Riley served with the Army—in the infantry." She took out the man's photo and handed it to her, along with a printout of the man's military record.

"Thanks," Ella said. He wasn't the guy who'd carried the ArmaLite, but from the quick glance she'd had of the man behind the wheel, she could make the ID. "This matches the driver of the Silverado."

Justine nodded. "Good. I'm off to talk to the county crime scene team. We're going to pool our forensic information and see if the slugs retrieved from the incident today— assuming they can find one sufficiently intact—match the ones from the airstrip. There are plenty of casings to check for ejection and firing pin correlations as well. We also have the round they took out of Adam. That one was pretty much intact, with clear rifling marks."

"Justine, there's something you need to know about Adam Lonewolf," Ella said, her voice barely above a whisper as they walked down the drive.

"No need. I know where you're headed with that. Big Ed brought us in on it after the press conference and told us what was really going on. Good strategy, getting him out of the way."

"How did the other officers on the team handle the little deception? We had to make it look real."

"We knew right away that something was going on when you and Blalock didn't show up at the press conference, so everyone took the news in stride. But you might want to reassure the new officers on the team that it wasn't a trust issue, just an operational maneuver," Justine said. Seeing Ella nod, she continued. "Big Ed also told us that we'd be kept up to speed on Adam's condition, but warned us not to try and contact the family. Makes sense."

"Have you heard if Adam's made any progress?"

"No change—and I've been told that's not a good thing," Justine answered in a somber voice.

After Justine left, Ella joined Blalock and headed to the manager's unit. SWAT was already packing up and would be gone in a few minutes.

With jurisdiction needed, Blalock took the lead, and after informing the man about tomorrow morning's return visit by deputies, they returned to the unmarked vehicle they'd borrowed from county.

Ella checked her watch. It was close to 10.00 P.M. now. "It's late, but I say we keep going. What say you?"

"Let's go back to the Double Barrel and see what, if anything, Dan's managed to find for us."

"Do you think he's still going to be there working?"

"Oh yeah. That shop's his entire life. He even lives above it. That man was raised dirt poor and worked hard so he could have his own business. The Double Barrel is his American Dream. He loves that gun shop and it's as much a part of him as law enforcement is to us."

"And an incident like this threatens it," Ella said, nodding slowly.

"Exactly. You can bet he's going to do everything in his power to protect it, and that means making sure people like O'Riley and his partner don't end up giving his shop the kind of reputation that'll send him into bankruptcy."

Ella looked away from the headlights and stared blankly out the window at the businesses and homes that lined the highway between Bloomfield and the much larger city, Farmington. As her thoughts drifted, she considered her pending job offer in D.C. Among its many advantages, conducting background checks and evaluating security procedures promised regular hours. She'd be able to spend more time with her daughter, something she'd welcome wholeheartedly. This was the time to enjoy their special mother-daughter closeness and it was slipping right through her fingers.

"You're thinking of John Blakely's offer again, aren't you?" Blalock said.

"Yeah," she admitted. "From a logical standpoint alone, it makes a lot of sense for me to accept it and move on."

"But your heart's not really into it. That's the real problem, right?"

She nodded. "I have a life here, one that I happen to like. D.C., on the other hand, is a great big question mark."

"But with solid career opportunities at every bend."

"Sounds like, but there's more than the financial bottom line at stake. I really need to figure out what's best for Dawn, and me, in that order."

The drive didn't take long. Once they arrived at the Double Barrel, Dan unlocked the door and let them inside. Dan's friends had obviously gone home but the county sheriff's deputy was still on duty. He stood to one side of the solitary barred window, looking outside, while Dan walked back to his console and scanned through the images, fast forwarding when possible.

"Any luck?" Ella asked.

Dan looked up from the display—an LCD monitor connected to a small computer. "I'm getting close to the right time. I was able to screen my work orders and finally narrow down the day."

Ella brought out O'Riley's photo. "Do you recognize this man?"

"No, can't say I know him—which doesn't mean he hasn't been here before." Dan continued to run the images fast forward, focusing on the time display, then suddenly hit the pause button. He looked it over a moment, then put the feed on manual, running one frame at a time. "This is the guy. His name's Carl something," he said. "Now that I see him, I remember he paid me in cash for six twenty-round magazines for an ArmaLite AR-180B. This weapon uses standard AR-15 magazines, but I was out of the twenty-rounders and had to place a special order. He wanted them FedEx next day, so I asked for a credit card because I needed advance payment. Instead, he reached for his pocket, took out a roll of bills, and peeled off the two hundred and ten bucks just like that."

"Am I right in assuming he's not a regular?" Blalock asked him.

"He's not from around here. I don't remember doing business with him before. I know almost all the assault weapon guys—they buy a lot of ammunition and extra magazines. This guy Carl spoke with a different kind of accent, too. More like up north, like maybe Wisconsin. I lived there once, so I'm familiar with it."

"If it was a special order, shouldn't there be an invoice?" Ella asked.

"There is. I place my orders via the Internet, so I can call up the file." He moved the computer mouse, and in a few clicks located the supplier. Checking the date, a form appeared on the screen. "His name is Carl Johnson, and I have a phone number, no address. Let me print you out a copy."

Five minutes later, after making a call to Justine with the suspect's information, they got a reply. Carl Johnson matched up with dozens of men statewide, but none local. The phone number was a phony, belonging to a law firm that advertised heavily on local television. Blalock then called it in to the Bureau and requested that agents run down the name Carl Johnson and see if anyone in the system fit the description.

A half hour later, Ella and Blalock were riding back to the reservation. "There's no doubt in my mind that the shooters are ex-military misfits turned small-time hoods. Guys like these never stay anywhere for long. They're undoubtedly feeling the heat now that the news of Adam's death has become public. That's going to make them nearly impossible to locate unless we get very lucky," Blalock said.

"And so far . . ."

"Yeah, I know. Our luck stinks," Blalock finished for her. "Home?"

She was about to suggest that he drop her off at the station so she could get some paperwork done when her phone rang. It was Justine. "What's up, partner?"

"We have a new problem by the name of Norm Hattery. He's that reporter who was fired a couple of years ago after blowing a lead story for one of the TV stations in Albuquerque. He's now working for the Farmington cable station news and is looking into the shooting. He cornered me when I left the lab and told me that he knew Kevin would be going into protective custody after his release from the hospital tomorrow. He wanted to interview me on camera."

"He couldn't have known when Kevin was going to be released. Kevin doesn't know that yet, I don't think. Norm was fishing."

"Yeah, I figured that, too, so I didn't respond. That's when he told me he was going to stake out the hospital until he found Kevin's room. Then, he'd wait us out as long as necessary to get the jump on the transfer."

"Reading between the lines, what that really means is that he has no idea where Kevin lives. That's the benefit of having a post office box for your mail and not being listed in the phone book," Ella answered.

"No, he *does* know Kevin's address. He read it off to me to prove he wasn't bluffing, and more importantly, so that I'd see that his sources are solid. He wanted to cut a deal with us. He passes information along to us as he gets it, and we give him an exclusive when it's all said and done."

"No deal," Ella snapped.

"Wait—you haven't heard his parting shot. He told me that he knew Adam had been carrying something with him that's going to create a storm of controversy the second the news is made public. When I asked him what he meant, he just smiled. He told me that he's going to get all the facts one way or another, and we could all come out ahead if we work together."

"What happened then?"

"Nothing. I didn't answer him. I went back into the lab. But he's still hanging around the lobby. If you come in, be on the lookout for him. He's hard to miss and easy on the eyes, like most on-camera reporters."

"I think I'll avoid the station for now. You and I will handle this new problem tomorrow when we can think more clearly," Ella said. "Does Kevin still have security around him?"

"Absolutely. In fact, after I told Big Ed about Hattery, he decided that it's not a good idea for Kevin to go to his own home to convalesce. He'd be too easy a target. Big Ed's trying to find a safe house for him."

"Okay, partner. One last thing. Have you heard anything from Teeny?"

"Not yet. That means he hasn't finished restoring the data from Adam's BlackBerry files."

"He won't sleep until he does," Ella said. She was well aware of how her friend worked. "Pick me up at the house at seven tomorrow. We'll get an early start."

"Done."

Ella hung up, then glanced at Blalock. "Looks like I'm heading home. From the way things are shaping up, tomorrow's going to be another fun-filled day."

ELEVEN

—— ✕ ✕ ✕ ——

It was close to midnight when Ella stepped through her front door. With the lights out in the kitchen, she'd expected her family to be fast asleep, but to her surprise, Rose was sitting in the living room alone, knitting. Her mother was far from an avid knitter and, in fact, had been working on the same sweater for the past four years. Rose only knitted when she was worried, and from the furious clicking of her needles, Ella could tell something was wrong.

Herman was nowhere to be seen. That meant he'd gone to bed, not wanting to be around for reasons Ella knew she was about to discover.

Ella put her pistol and ammunition up on the high shelf, then sat down silently and waited.

Rose said nothing for about five minutes. Finally, she set down the needles and looked at her daughter. "Your child's father spoke to her this afternoon and told her that he was going to be released from the hospital tomorrow. You daughter became all excited about that, and as soon as she hung up, came to find me. She said that her dad needed her so she'd be staying with him for a while. I told her that was out of the question, and suggested she talk to you about after-school visits."

Ella sat back in the chair. She should have expected something like this. "Visits won't be possible because, for security reasons, Kevin won't be going home when he's discharged. He'll need to stay at a safe house until we're certain that he's no longer a target."

"Even if he goes to the moon, your daughter will want to be with him. As far as she's concerned, the sun rises and sets on her father. Unless we lock her up, or keep her with us all the time, we won't be able to stop her from going to look for him. That's especially true now that these rumors have surfaced. . . ."

"What rumors?" Ella asked immediately.

"Her father's the one under a cloud of suspicion now. People don't want to believe that a war hero could have done anything to merit such an attack from other Americans in his own country. They're looking for someone to blame for his death and many have decided that the attack must have been the fault of your child's father—the lawyer. A lot of people dislike and distrust lawyers, you know."

"If you follow that logic, it makes even more sense to assume *I* was the target," Ella said, surprised. "As a police detective, I've put a busload of people behind bars."

Rose shook her head. "Word has it that you're not important enough to be assassinated, but your child's father is."

Annoyed at the way she'd been dismissed by the tribe, Ella tried to push back her irritation. Her reaction was human, but it was also petty.

"Mom, I'm not even sure *where* my daughter's father will end up going to convalesce," she said, and explained, "If my kid tries to go out and find her father, she could lead the killers right to him, placing them both in danger."

"I know, but your daughter will want to be with him, and if you say no, she might sneak out anyway and try and find him on her own," Rose said in a heavy voice. "That's why I think he should stay here with us. I can cook for him, and my husband can help him out of bed."

Ella stared at Rose, accepting the logic of her mother's suggestion, yet searching fast for a different answer that would effectively solve the problem.

"One of us is generally home, and my husband knows how to use that rifle of his. He'd have protection here, and your daughter would be at peace," Rose added. "No one would ever think that you'd allow him to come here, so it may be the best place for him, all things considered."

"Mom, what you're suggesting . . ." Ella ran a hand through her hair.

"I'm aware of the problems it poses, but I also know your daughter. Would you like her to go out searching for him, maybe ditching school and riding around in cars with her friends' older brothers, or hitchhiking? No matter what, she's going to find a way to see him," Rose said.

The possibility jolted her awake. She could see Dawn doing just that. It wasn't just Rose's crazy idea, it was completely in character with her daughter's already strong sense of independence. When Dawn thought she was in the right, nothing stopped her, and stepping up as a parent would only serve to damage their relationship.

"We could put up with him for a short time, daughter. We'd just have to make sure he stayed away from the windows and remained indoors."

"I'll have to think about this," Ella said at last. "But before I crawl off to bed there's something I've been meaning to ask you. Can you give me a better idea of how the Prickly Weed Project got started and how The People are reacting to it?" When it came to getting a fix on public opinion, there was no better source than Rose.

"The man who thought up that entire project is well respected and his word carries clout. He came from nothing, pulled himself up by the bootstraps, and now owns a chain of gas stations and convenience stores. He also serves on the tribal council," Rose said.

Ella knew from the description that Rose was referring to Alfred Begaye. The man was practically a legend on the Rez. His efforts with hydrologists and the local community had enabled the tribe to double crop yields on the Navajo Irrigation Project acreage.

"When he first suggested the Prickly Weed Project, people rallied around the proposal," Rose said, "so he began to get some investors, like the late senator's wife—our new Plant Watcher. The family who occupies the land now—a widower, his daughter, and her husband—don't want to give up a single acre of land. They're fighting every inch of the way, though they aren't really farming or grazing. They could stay where their houses are now, if they'd be willing to compromise. Normally, the tribe can do whatever it wants, but the residents have allies in their fight—a group that opposes the entire concept. They're said to be against all unconventional agricultural or industrial operations—basically, anything that's not in line with the traditional way of doing things."

"So it's the Traditionalists who are against the Prickly Weed Project?"

"No, not all Traditionalists—not necessarily, anyway. The group supporting the family calls themselves the *Ha'asídís*, the Watchmen, and they look after all things Navajo. They've made their presence felt, but the ones who are for the project are better organized, so things continued to move forward, working under the assumption the tribe would get use of the necessary acreage, one way or the other. Then the project ran into money problems."

"Do you know the details about that?" Ella asked. At the mention of money, her ears perked up instantly, having already heard of the big investments made by Abigail

Yellowhair, Robert Buck, Billy Garnenez, the tribal president, and even Kevin. There were still no leads on the cash Adam had been carrying, but it had to have come from somewhere. . . .

Rose pointed down to the *Diné Times*, the tribal newspaper. "You can find what's been made public there."

Ella glanced down at the article, an interview with Billy Garnenez, one of the Tribal Industries bureaucrats and the director of the Prickly Weed Project. Garnenez was claiming that the land would soon be available and that financial backing was securely in place, despite rumors to the contrary.

"But that's not the truth, daughter," Rose said. "A private company called Industrial Futures Technology was approached to partner up with us and supply the tribe with experts and the equipment to make things happen. But then cost estimates soared—or IFT got greedy. Whatever the case, the tribe has limited resources, so we couldn't meet their new price. Our new lobbyist was working hard to get IFT to meet our terms—at least that's what I heard. But with his death, who knows what will happen? If the tribe can't find a way to get energy industry backing and support, the Prickly Weed Project will have to be put on hold indefinitely, or dropped."

Ella recalled that Teeny, who was seldom wrong about things like these, had told her that the deal had already been cut with IFT, but it wasn't official. That suggested that Adam Lonewolf had succeeded in bringing the energy company on board. "Some of the investors must be sweating this. A lot of money could be lost if the deal fell through."

"The ones in tribal government are pushing as hard as they can to keep things moving forward. But they may be fighting the impossible. The money's either there—or not," Rose stood. "I'm going to bed now, daughter, and I suggest you do the same. You're going to be putting in some very long hours—particularly if your daughter's father moves in."

"Mom, I haven't—"

Rose smiled, then crossed through the kitchen into her and Herman's wing of the house without looking back.

Ella stood. She needed a chance to think things through, but she was too tired right now. Maybe things would make more sense in the morning. As she went to her room, she thought about Ford and wondered how *he'd* react if Kevin moved in. Even if his religious beliefs demanded charity, she had a feeling he wasn't going to like this at all. Ford was a jealous man.

WEDNESDAY

By six-thirty the following morning, the kitchen was buzzing. Dawn had just sat down in front of her oatmeal and Rose was busy preparing scrambled eggs for herself and Herman.

"Mom, Dad's in real trouble, isn't he?" Dawn asked as Ella took a seat, cup of coffee in hand. "I heard that the soldier who got shot trying to protect him died yesterday. That means Dad's their next target, right?"

"Your father is being kept safe. Don't worry," Ella said.

"Mom, he's stuck in a hospital bed, all shot up. Even you'd be scared if you couldn't move."

It was her use of the word "even" that made Ella smile. "Everyone feels afraid at one time or another. It's perfectly natural. Without fear, we wouldn't have courage. One gives way to the other."

Dawn stared at her cereal, then picked up a piece of toast, holding it in her hand but not taking a bite. "Mom, you have us—but Dad only has . . . me. His parents died, and his relatives don't live around here anymore," she said at last. "I should go help him out until he heals up and can go back to work."

Rose glanced at Ella with a look that clearly said "I told you so."

Ella took a deep breath. At least the conversation she'd had with her mother had prepared her somewhat for this. "Daughter, that's not a good idea. Your father's still in danger, and I don't want you to be at risk, too."

Dawn glanced at her grandmother, then back down at her bowl. For several long moments she said nothing.

For those few wonderful minutes, Ella thought she'd managed to get Dawn to understand and drop the subject, but her hopes were soon dashed.

"When bad things happen, *Shimá*, families have to stick together. That's what you've always said, that I can count on you no matter what, right?" she asked Ella.

"Yes," Ella said, sighing. She knew where this was going, but there was no way to head it off at the pass.

"You and Dad aren't together anymore, but he's still my dad. He should be able to count on me, just like I count on you. If I can't go to him, will you let him stay here with us? He can have my room."

"He might be safer someplace farther away, maybe even another state."

"Mom, if you take care of things like you always do, there's no better place for Dad than with us. We're his family."

"Let me think about this," Ella said at last.

As the rattle of an old diesel pickup announced her ride to school had arrived, Dawn kissed her mom, and ran outside, grabbing her book bag along the way.

"If you don't bring her father here, you're asking for trouble," Rose said.

Ella knew her mother was right. "Mom, I'm just not sure what to do." Hearing the approaching deep rumble of the police unit, Ella glanced out the window. "My partner's here.

I'm going to meet her outside and save some time. We have to go to Window Rock sometime this morning."

Ella grabbed her handgun and hurried out.

Justine was just getting out of the SUV when Ella joined her. Without a word, Ella climbed in on the passenger side.

"What's up, partner? You have an argument with your mom or something?" Justine asked.

"Or something," Ella said, then shook her head, signaling Justine to drop it.

"Where to first?" Justine asked, switching on the ignition.

"Teeny's."

When they arrived, Teeny quickly ushered them inside. Seeing the pot of coffee next to the computers, Ella smiled. "You haven't slept, have you?"

"I caught a few winks," he answered. "While the computer's running, there's not much I can do."

From his reddened eyes Ella guessed that he'd slept an hour, maybe two. But puzzles, and computer problems, were addictive to Teeny. He couldn't back off until he'd mastered the challenge.

"The deceased—hell, we're not Traditionalists here—*Adam's* BlackBerry files are encrypted with a program I've never seen before. Most of what we retrieved earlier was a deliberate giveaway meant to misdirect hackers. I wasn't as far along as I thought. My own programs, ones I wrote myself, will decode nearly everything, but it's going to take time because I keep having to tweak the parameters."

"Do you have anything you can give me right now?" Ella asked.

"I've managed to isolate his schedule for the last several days. That part wasn't encrypted at the same level." He handed her a list. "Adam met with Billy Garnenez and with Alfred Begaye during his last visit to the Rez, then flew back out to D.C. hours later. The next day he had two meetings.

The first was at IFT, the second with a group of lobbyists attending an energy seminar. After that, he caught the flight back here with you and Tolino. What surprised me was that even though the Prickly Weed Project is at such a critical juncture, he had no local appointments scheduled—or maybe he hadn't gotten around to entering them."

Ella studied it, wondering if Adam *had* sealed the deal with IFT. Yet he hadn't been in a cheerful mood on the flight back, something she would have expected from a man who'd just closed the biggest deal of his new career. This case was getting stranger and stranger. Maybe Teeny's sources were wrong and her mom was right. "Thanks. This is a start."

"I'll have the rest of the files from that BlackBerry within hours."

"If you can cut corners . . ."

He nodded, then after a pause, added, "I heard that Kevin's due to be released from the hospital—today if his doctor gives a thumbs-up. Word's also out that he's still a target. If my sources are right and Kevin's planning to go home, consider borrowing a couple of my men to keep him safe."

"Kevin can't go home, the risk is still too high," Ella said. "I'm not sure where he'll end up."

"The tribe's going to need Kevin accessible and so are the police, so your best option is a safe house. But that also means that some skillful surveillance is all it'll take for the wrong people to track him down. You're going to have to watch your backs," Teeny said.

"I hear you, and that's just one of many things I need to take into account." The idea of having Kevin at her house was making more sense now, but she still wasn't comfortable with that. "Call me directly as soon as you've broken the encryption," she said, heading toward the door.

As Justine stepped out, Teeny put his hand on Ella's arm. "Something's really bugging you. Can I help?"

"It's this case," Ella said. "Every time I think I've got a handle on it, it weaves like a snake and goes in a different direction."

"Never-ending-snake . . . the inevitable struggle against evil," he said quietly.

"What keeps a cop in business," she answered with a grim smile.

Saying good-bye to Teeny, she joined Justine in the SUV. "Head for Window Rock. We're going to pay Billy a visit."

As they traveled south down the long, lonely stretch of highway, Ella leaned back. Traveling great distances was as much a part of the reservation as summer thunderstorms that evaporated before they ever reached the ground. Today's trip was taking them deeper into the Navajo Nation, across the state line and to the tribe's capital and government center, Window Rock, Arizona.

"Remember the reporter who's been hanging around the station?" Justine asked.

"Norm Hattery, right?"

"Yeah. While you were speaking to Teeny, I heard from my sister, Jayne. That reporter's sure resourceful. He found out that Jayne and Marie Lonewolf are friends and since he hasn't been able to find either Marie or Adam's parents, he's following up with family friends and trying to locate them that way. Jayne told him that they're probably holed up somewhere to get some privacy, and that talking to people about Adam now isn't going to get him far because the *Diné* don't speak of the recently deceased."

"How did Norm track down the Lonewolf family's friends? Do you have any idea where he's getting his information?"

"From what Jayne said, Norm has been going out with Mavis Neskahi."

"*Joe's sister?*" she asked surprised. "Ah, now I get it. She works at the hospital, doesn't she? In the business office."

Justine nodded. "Admissions. Jayne made it a point to go talk to Mavis and warned her that she's being used, but Mavis told Jayne to back off. Jayne wasn't about to do that, and kept pumping her for information. Eventually she found out that Mavis had met Norm in the elevator the day the wounded were brought in. Mavis also admitted that she's gone out with Norm for meals a couple of times since then, but insisted that she's done nothing wrong. She said they weren't dates or anything like that, just for lunch and dinner."

"I have a bad feeling about this. . . ."

"So did my sister. Jayne kept pressuring her, and managed to find out that Norm had heard the helicopter take off from the hospital while everyone was at the press conference. Since he picked up a call on his scanner for that time interval, he'd asked Mavis later who'd been transported. Mavis told him somebody had died and let it go at that. She used that as an example of how careful she was about giving out information."

"So Norm must have instantly assumed it was Adam because of the timing," Ella said with a nod. "We have to talk to Mavis and make sure she understands how easy it is for an experienced reporter to get answers even when she doesn't reply directly. But let's not mention this to Joe. It'll just create more problems."

"He already knows. Joe saw them together and nearly exploded. He knows precisely what Norm's trying to do, so he cornered Hattery and warned him to steer clear of his sister."

"That may have made things worse," Ella said, reaching for her phone, intending to call Joe. Then, changing her mind, put it away. Some things were better said in person.

"How much do you think Norm's managed to put together?" Justine asked her.

"I'm sure he now suspects that Adam's not really dead, and may have other sources that can tell him where the helicopter *didn't* go—like to any off-base hospital within flight range. If he's smart enough, and has enough contacts, he'll eventually find out that Angel Hawk landed at the Air Force base, not the public terminal, in Albuquerque."

"Sounds like he gets the same kind of gut feelings we do when we're close to something important," Justine said. "If Hattery's sensing a big story now, there's no way he's going to back off."

Ella leaned back in her seat. "The main problem with this case is that all the players, including Kevin, are holding back on us at some level. We need to identify what's pertinent to the case and set everything else aside."

"So where do we start?" Justine asked.

"With the cash. We need to follow the money. We have to pinpoint where it came from and where it was going. Adam can't help us with that, so we have to concentrate on the people Adam works for, or had contact with, and push them hard. We also have to figure out who has the most to gain by taking Adam—or Kevin—out of the picture. This wasn't a robbery—it was a hit. So we'll start by talking to Billy Garnenez, who's one of Adam's most important local contacts."

The drive was uneventful, and they arrived at the tribal government offices among the beautiful, piñon-covered sandstone mesas south of the Chuska Range. The complex, overlooked by the massive Window Rock formation, was quite modest considering it served the largest tribe in the country. The Navajo Nation itself was larger than some states. Finding Garnenez's office was easy, and they were soon seated there.

Billy leaned back in his chair, his expression sober. "All the tribal employees have been looking for a way to honor our fallen hero's service to his country and the Navajo Nation. Do you have any suggestions?"

"The best way to honor him is to help us find the people responsible for what happened," Ella answered. "I know it's not in keeping with traditional beliefs to discuss him so openly this soon after . . . but we have a duty."

He opened his hands in a gesture of assent.

"I know that he'd been serving as a lobbyist for the tribe these past few months," Ella continued. "In your opinion, how successful was he at that job?"

"He was the perfect tribal representative. He could open any door on reputation alone. He also had a very sharp intellect and knew instinctively how to make the most out of every opportunity. Once the family currently on the project site is either removed by the tribe or compensated, there is nothing to keep the Prickly Weed Project from moving full speed ahead, thanks largely to his efforts. The deal was closed the day after the attack. What's sad is that he'll never know that now."

"It was my understanding that IFT wanted far more than what the tribe was able to offer them," Ella said.

"There *were* bumps in the road," he admitted. "But all that's history now. With IFT on board, we can go on to the next phase of the planning."

"What finally broke the impasse?" Ella asked. "I understand funding was the major stumbling block, and there was no more money to sweeten the deal."

"Business negotiations can be difficult sometimes," Billy said, hedging her question, then standing. "I'm sorry, but I've got to leave if I'm going to make it to my next meeting. The Prickly Weed Project is only one of several new investments the Navajo Nation is currently exploring."

He ushered them out of his office quickly, then closed the door. Ella glanced at Justine. "We've been given the brush-off, partner."

"Yep, that's the way it felt to me, too."

"Well, since we're already in Window Rock, let's go by Councilman Begaye's office," Ella said.

The office building was close enough that they could

walk, and it was still pretty cool outside here among the mesas. "There's something I still can't reconcile," Ella said, lost in thought as they walked down the sidewalk side by side. "Why was Adam bringing that money back from Washington? It makes far more sense to assume the cash had been meant for someone at IFT. Bribes are a worldwide tradition when it comes to greasing wheels in business and government."

"Maybe IFT paid Adam, though I can't think of any reason for them to do that," Justine said.

"A crooked hero. . . . I sure hope we're wrong about that." Ella paused, then added, "Have you looked into this company, Industrial Futures Technology?"

"Yes, I have. Basically, they're clean, with no lawsuits, government inquiries, or hint of scandals. They do business all over the country. With the big push for alternate energy solutions, they've recently moved their corporate headquarters to the Washington, D.C., area."

"It makes sense. That's where many of the big energy projects begin, so why not? Do they have anything to do with casinos or gambling?"

"No. They're a solid part of the science and engineering business community. Their current focus is on testing and implementing alternative energy solutions—wind, geothermal, ethanol, you name it," Justine said.

They were coming up the steps of the council office building when Abigail Yellowhair came out the door. Ella wasn't surprised to see her least-favorite Plant Watcher. The day hadn't been going well anyway.

"Abigail, good morning," Justine said with enthusiasm. "We're all a little far from home today, aren't we?"

"Justine, and Ella, good morning. Working on your investigation, I hope? I'm so sorry to hear that Sergeant Lonewolf's killers are still on the loose. Those men you went up against yesterday—they got away again, right, Ella?"

Ella held her tongue—reluctantly. Although Abigail's tone was neutral, the implications were snarky, to say the least.

"At least we have a name to go with one of those suspects," Justine said.

"The rest of the details are being withheld as we pursue the new lead," Ella said, cutting her partner off. "Are you here to meet with anyone in particular, Mrs. Yellowhair? Our own councilman does have an office in Shiprock. . . ."

"Just touching bases with an old friend. But don't let me keep you." She nodded to Justine, then strode away.

"Okay, what's up?" Justine asked as Abigail hurried off. "I know you two don't get along, but why the sudden surge of hostility?"

"I got the feeling that she's disappointed I dodged bullets again. You know that she still blames me for what happened to her family, don't you?" Ella said, opening the door to the small lobby.

"You're way too hard on her, Ella. That woman has been through a lot, and she's had to toughen up just to survive," Justine said. "Despite Blalock's description of her as a 'she wolf,' she wasn't always that way. When I met Abby years ago, she still had a kind heart."

"You're the one with the kind heart now, partner," Ella said quietly. "Try to find out who she came to see."

"I'll ask around."

Ella stopped and studied the sign on the wall which indicated the office numbers of the various council members. "Now let's get back to business."

They spent the next hour trying to locate Councilman Begaye. First, they stopped by his office. There, they were told by his staff that he'd left after his meeting with Mrs. Yellowhair, but they'd be able to find him at the telecommunication commission office. Once they arrived there, they were told that Begaye had just left, but they'd be able to find him at the Division of General Services. The story repeated itself two more times.

"Billy must have warned him that we're in town. He's obviously ducking us. We could spend all morning going around in circles. Let's head back to Shiprock," Ella said. "We need to gather up everyone on the team and pool our information."

"Well, at least one of your questions was answered. Mrs. Yellowhair was the last person to meet with Councilman Begaye before he stepped out," Justine added, starting the engine and pulling out into the street.

"She's one of the Prickly Weed investors, and with the business losses she's rumored to have taken the last few years, she's probably keeping in close touch with the project leaders to protect her investment. You notice that she's dressing down? A year ago, she wouldn't be out in public wearing anything less than a thousand-dollar suit."

"You really dislike her, don't you?"

"It's more of a trust issue, cuz. But yeah, okay, she wouldn't be my first choice as a companion on a deserted island. In fact, she wouldn't even make the list."

"Who would you pick to be stranded with on a deserted island?" Justine teased. "Ford, Kevin, or Teeny?"

"Actually, I'd rather have Two. Dogs offer unconditional love and a lifetime of loyalty in exchange for a scratch behind the ears, a drink from the water hose, and a bowlful of kibbles."

As Justine drove east toward home, Ella used the wonderful scent of piñon pine trees drifting in through the window to help her relax. Leaning back, she sorted through her thoughts. The deal with IFT *had* gone through according to Garnenez, so the cash couldn't have been tied to that.

"That seventy-five thousand . . . we need to find out once

and for all who that was meant for—and who bankrolled it," Ella said, thinking out loud.

"Joe and Benny have been looking through Marie's and Adam's bank accounts. Marie gave us permission. Maybe they've come up with something."

"When we get back, I'm going to need some time to talk to Joe in private," Ella said.

"About Mavis?" Justine asked.

Ella nodded.

"Joe's mom and sister are living with him at the moment. Did you know that?" Seeing Ella shake her head, she continued. "His mother's house got damaged when an irrigation ditch overflowed. I found out about it when Mavis came to the station looking for Joe, and she and I talked for a bit."

"How old is Mavis?" Ella asked.

"Nineteen or twenty. She's only worked at the hospital for about six months. It's her first job out of high school."

"At that age, someone like Norm might seem like high adventure and romance all rolled into one package," Ella said.

"Mavis came across as pretty levelheaded. Don't sell her short."

"We've all been played at one point or another in our lives," Ella said. "Eventually, we come to our senses, but not before someone's taken full advantage of the situation."

"Like that blood-sucking parasite who's preying on women half his age?"

Ella laughed. "Come to think of it," she said, growing serious once more, "now that Joe's got his family at home, he's going to have to watch what he says. That's not always easy for a bachelor who's used to speaking freely on the phone."

"I don't think you have anything to worry about on that score, Ella. Joe—Benny, too—are both quiet by nature. Loose lips won't be a problem." She paused, then in a softer tone, added, "Benny's more laid back than Joe, but with both those guys, what you see is what you get. We've got a great team."

There was something about the way Justine's tone had changed when she'd spoken of Benny that instantly caught Ella's attention. She glanced at her partner. "Do you and Benny have a thing?"

"No, there's nothing at all going on between us. He's the most unromantic man on the planet," Justine said with a hint of a smile.

"And that's precisely what interests you."

"I find someone like Benny—who's up front about everything—a breath of fresh air." Glancing at Ella, she continued, "Let me give you an idea of what I mean. Last week the computer in the lab crashed, taking hours of work with it. It was backed up, but restoring it all again took a lot of time. Then I spilled coffee all over some papers on my desk. It was a piece-of-crap morning, so I left Benny in the lab, and stormed outside, needing a break. Benny followed me out about twenty minutes later, holding a mug of freshly brewed coffee. He picked a sunflower that had been growing near the door, then shoved the coffee and the flower in my face, and said, 'Here. Cheer up.' Then he went back inside."

Ella laughed. "Mr. Romance!"

"Yeah, but it was sweet."

They were forty minutes south of Shiprock, just passing the Newcomb Chapter house, when her cell phone rang. Ella recognized Blalock's voice instantly.

"I've got a positive ID on O'Riley's partner. I'm working on getting a current address, but the man's moved around a lot."

"What have you got so far?"

"His name's Carl Perry. He's ex-Army, from the same platoon as O'Riley. He was booted out with a dishonorable discharge for sexual assault of a woman soldier. Once we have a twenty on him, bringing him in is going to be tough.

He qualified expert on the range, and barely missed the cut for sniper school. My gut tells me that he'll be armed to the teeth."

"We're going to need SWAT," she said, "and vests."

"Yeah and to stack the odds in our favor, we should make our move at four in the morning when he's likely to be asleep."

"On or off the Rez, I want to be there for the takedown," Ella said.

"You've got it."

Placing her phone away, Ella filled Justine in. "Let's get our team updated. Looks like we're in for another long day."

TWELVE
————— ✖ ✖ ✖ —————

It was after one when they walked through the doors of the station. Ella glanced at her partner. "Find Joe and have him meet me at my office in ten minutes. I'm going to talk to Big Ed."

"All right," Justine replied.

"Also, I want the whole team in my office in a half hour."

Ella turned down the hall and headed to Big Ed's office. The chief was just finishing a phone conversation when she knocked on his door and stepped inside.

Ella updated him. "Once we get an address for Carl Perry, I'm going to take part in the takedown and sit in on the questioning."

Big Ed leaned back in his seat. "Do whatever it takes to clear Adam—or get me the information that conclusively proves he's guilty. The pressure's really coming down on this one, Shorty," he said. "And I don't want to hear that the Farmington reporter broke the story before we closed our case."

"You've already heard that he's been talking to Sergeant Neskahi's sister, haven't you?" she asked, studying his expression.

"Yeah. Then he spoke to my wife," he said. "He found out where I lived and showed up on our doorstep," he added, biting off each syllable.

Ella could feel his anger. She didn't blame him. "How did Hattery get your address?"

"I don't know, but if I find out that one of our people—or a relative of theirs—gave it to him, I promise you, heads will roll."

"None of us here would ever disclose that kind of information. You know that, Chief. But depending on how he phrased things when he spoke to Joe's sister . . ."

"Pretending to know more than he did, then letting the subject fill in the gaps," Big Ed said with a nod. "Yeah, I'm way ahead of you."

"I was going to meet Joe in my office. Shall I have him come here so we can both talk to him?"

"Do it," Big Ed said.

Ella went to her office, found Joe waiting, and walked back with him to the chief's office.

Visibly uncomfortable, Joe sat down, looked at Big Ed, then at Ella. "This is about my sister, right?"

Big Ed nodded, but said nothing.

"That Hattery creep kept joining her for coffee breaks and lunch at the hospital cafeteria. She was flattered that a television personality found her interesting, and figured it was okay to trust him after he made it sound as if the department was keeping him in the loop about the case. I set her straight on that, and pressed her to remember everything she'd told him, but she assured me that all she did was make a few comments here and there," Joe said, then shook his head. "Either way, she won't be talking to him anymore."

"He showed up at my door," Big Ed said.

Joe's mouth fell open. "You think Mavis told him where you live? But how, she doesn't know herself—I don't think."

"Hattery's a skilled game player," Ella said. "Now we

need to figure out how much he knows. Maybe Mavis can help us there. Why don't you ask her to come down to the station?"

"My sister would protect confidential information. She's not an idiot."

"It's not a matter of intelligence. It's experience that counts in something like this. You know how questioning works," Ella said. "You don't ask the suspect if he killed the victim. You ask what he was thinking about when he shot her. Hattery probably used the same technique. If Mavis passed on information, she probably never realized what she was doing."

Joe sat there, his expression becoming increasingly hard. "I'll find out what we need to know," he said flatly, then in barely audible voice, added, "Then I'm going to duct tape her mouth shut."

"Go easy. She was manipulated by a professional," Ella said. "Once she figures out that she was played, she'll be more careful. It happens to all of us at least once."

After Joe left, Ella shut the door and turned to her boss. "There's one more thing I'd like to run past you, Chief," she said, then told him about Kevin and Dawn and her plan to keep them together to avoid jeopardizing their safety.

"Do you really think your daughter would try to find him?"

"Yes, I do, and that may end up creating an even bigger problem. I need to focus on catching the gunmen and whoever paid them, not worry about my family."

"Rose may be right, then," Big Ed said after a beat. "Your home may be the safest place for Kevin simply because it's not expected. But you'll have to find a way to transport Tolino without being spotted."

Ella nodded. "I'd like to turn that assignment over to my partner. It'll be better if I'm nowhere around at the time."

"Agreed," Big Ed said. "But first make sure Mavis Neskahi didn't also give that reporter *your* address."

Ella exhaled loudly. "How could she know? Never mind, you're right. That'll be the first order of business."

As Ella went down the hall, Justine stepped out of her lab to intercept her. "What's with Joe? He was like an angry bull when he left the station."

Ella gave her the highlights.

"Wow. That explains his mood—and the message he asked me to give you. He said he's going to pick up his sister and bring her to your office. He wants you present when he questions her. He said it'll make the point far better than he could alone."

"Good. I'd like to know firsthand how much harm's been done," she said. "Put off our team meeting until after three."

Ella returned to her office and, eating a sandwich that tasted like the machine it had come from, began to work on the pile of case reports she'd set aside. She hated the tons of paperwork associated with police work. For every hour of actual work done on a case, there were at least two of related paperwork.

Before she knew it, Joe knocked on her open door. Two steps behind him was a thin, petite young woman wearing a colorful blouse and skirt. "This is my sister, Mavis," he said to Ella, then gestured to Mavis to take a seat.

Mavis was her brother's physical opposite—model-like in shape compared to Joe's burly, wrestler's build. Her face was attractive, but long for a Navajo, which made her somewhat distinctive.

"We've met before, haven't we, Mavis? Do you recall where it was?" Ella asked.

"Um, Joe didn't have a date, so he brought me along to the barbeque on the Fourth of July at Chief Atcitty's home.

Most of the officers were there, including your second cousin, Justine," Mavis said, looking up at Joe, who'd rolled his eyes. "What, Joe?"

"Never mind. Just answer our questions, okay?" Joe said. "Sorry. Go ahead, Ella."

"Tell us what you know about Norm Hattery," Ella asked.

"We met in the elevator the day the shooting victims were brought to the hospital. I was on a coffee break and we just hit it off right away."

"What did you tell him about the wounded men?" Joe asked her.

"Just that two Navajo men had been shot at the airstrip and were in bad shape. That was all I knew at the time. Someone else had handled the admission forms. We also talked a bit about the hospital and my job, and just general stuff about Shiprock and the tribe."

"But you saw him again?" Ella pressed.

"I guess, but it wasn't like we were on a date. We had lunch yesterday while I was on break, and last night when I got off work he took me to the Totah for dinner. After that, he drove me back to the hospital so I could pick up my car and go home."

"What did you two talk about?" Ella asked.

Mavis shrugged. "Nothing important. He told me about his job—working at a TV station, meeting celebrities. Norm's really interesting and he knows a lot about our tribe. It turns out he's a friend of Chief Atcitty's."

Ella saw the flash of anger in Joe's eyes, and shot him a quick, hard look, shaking her head in a silent warning.

"He's not a friend of the chief," Ella answered, her voice calm.

"Sure he is. He knew that Big Ed lives out on Highway sixty-four past the high school, not far from Rattlesnake.

He commented on the chief's sheep, too. He told me that he'd been invited to the chief's house this past spring when he'd been working on a story for the Farmington cable news."

"A lot of Navajos have animals—horses, cattle, sheep, goats. Let me guess. *You* mentioned the Churro sheep, not him?" Joe countered in a loud voice.

Mavis gave her brother a look of utter confusion. "Maybe I did. All I know is that we started talking about how different Churro sheep are from the other varieties. I was just making conversation. Was he pumping me for information? Is that what you're implying?"

Joe threw his hands up in the air, then, shaking his head, walked over and closed the door.

"Mavis, you were tricked. You gave Hattery just enough information for him to figure out where Big Ed lives," Ella told her gently. "He actually showed up at the chief's house asking questions, and that's made your brother look very bad to this department."

"But—"

"But nothing," Joe roared. "You all but put a sign in front of the chief's home. What other addresses did you give out?"

"*Nobody's!*" she said, but her voice broke at the last syllable and tears began streaming down her face.

"It's okay, Mavis. Relax and try to focus," Ella said firmly. "In your conversations with Hattery, did you, or he, ever mention other members of this department?"

She nodded. "He asked me about you once," Mavis said looking at Ella. "But I told him the truth. I barely know you."

"I need you to think back—hard. What *exactly* did he ask you? Did you get the impression that he knew me?"

"He *did* know you. He mentioned how pretty you are and how surprised he was that you aren't married. He also really admires your brother. He said that it takes a special man to become a *hataalii*," she said, then added, "Norm loves the Rez, but I don't think he really understands life here. He kept telling me how terrific it was that families lived so close together."

"And you said—what?" Joe snapped.

"I told him he was wrong about that. Some of our clan members live all the way out in Arizona. It's a big reservation, but everyone has a pickup nowadays so families can still get together."

"Did he mention knowing where my brother lived?" Ella asked quickly.

"All he said was that he was surprised a *hataalii* had time to keep sheep."

"Sheep?" Joe asked, glancing at Ella.

Ella shook her head. "He was fishing."

"Did he, or you, talk about anyone else in this department?" Joe pressed her, his voice hard.

"No. Mostly we talked about the Rez."

"Be specific," Ella said.

"I can't remember everything," she said, her voice rising. "We talked for hours."

"Try," Joe said, anger giving that one word a power all its own.

Mavis took a deep, unsteady breath. "He was interested in Navajo businesses and wanted to know how they raised cash when the need was there. Since no one owns land here, he knew equity wasn't something people could use as collateral."

"What did you tell him?" Ella asked.

"That I had no idea. I worked for a salary and didn't have much in the bank."

Ella leaned back in her chair. That line of questioning supported her theory that Hattery had known about the money Adam had been carrying. But there were other possibilities, too.

"What else?" Ella asked, pushing Mavis more gently than Joe had done.

"That's it, I swear. Most of the time I'd try to get him to tell me about his work. Being in front of a camera, and doing all that traveling for stories is a lot more exciting than my job."

"Hattery's not the guy you thought he was," Ella said. "For one thing, he used the information he got from you to find Big Ed's home. Things could have gone very wrong after that. We all got lucky."

While Joe escorted Mavis out, Ella remained seated. The comment about a *hataalii*'s sheep told her that Norm had no idea where her brother lived, at least at the time he'd spoken to Mavis. Presently, Clifford only had horses, so it had been a calculated effort to elicit information. It also meant he had no idea where her home was—a few miles from Clifford's and down the same road.

Ella thought about Kevin, and, after considering all the arguments for and against it, made up her mind. Picking up her phone, she called Justine and asked her to come to her office. A few minutes later Justine arrived.

Ella closed the door to give them complete privacy. "Partner, I need a favor," she said, and explained that she'd need Kevin transported in secret to her home. "The safest thing will be for me to stay away from Kevin. You'll have to handle all the transportation details. I'm also going to take Teeny up on his offer. A plainclothes guard not connected to the department, stationed somewhere outside the house in addition to the one inside, should be all that's needed."

"I'll make the arrangements," Justine said.

"Depending on the timing, I may be involved in a SWAT operation with Blalock when you move Kevin, and that'll keep me out of touch. That's just a heads-up in case you can't get hold of me."

"And you're *sure* you can trust Dawn not to tell any of her friends that her dad's at the house?"

"You wouldn't be able to trust most kids with vital information like that, but Dawn's been raised differently. Having a police officer mom gives her a whole new take on things," Ella said. "But the bottom line is the way she feels about her father. She'd do whatever she could to protect him. To her, he's number one."

Justine's eyebrows rose. "Doesn't that bother you just a little?"

"Sometimes it does," Ella admitted softly. "But the fact that Kevin loves her as much as I do makes it . . . almost bearable," she added with a tiny smile.

As Justine left her office, Ella stared at the phone for several long moments, wondering if she was making the right decision. Finally she sighed. It was time to focus on the business at hand. Ella called Kevin at the hospital and he picked up on the first ring.

"Hey, good news! I'm getting released today," he said, hearing her voice. "My body still has some mending to do, but the doctors say my vital signs are strong enough for the move. It'll be good to get out of here."

"I'd heard rumors. Are you sure it isn't a little too soon?"

"Hey, I can already make it to the potty and back on my own—well, with a cane at least. I figure I'll do a lot of sleeping at first, but that's what I'm doing now. I can do that at home, as long as someone can come by and keep me fed. I'm not up to puttering around the kitchen quite yet."

"Which brings me to the reason I was calling." Ella explained the situation and her concerns over Dawn.

"I can forbid her to come see me," Kevin said. "She wouldn't like that and neither would I, but she won't disobey me." After a pause, he added. "She wouldn't, would she?"

"She's your daughter and mine. What do you think?" Ella said, then not expecting an answer, continued. "My job's to keep everyone safe, so I'm going to propose something that's a little unusual." She told him what she had in mind, then waited.

A long silence followed. "I'd be bringing danger right to your doorstep. That's not acceptable to me."

"If you sleep in Dawn's room and stay away from the windows, everyone will remain perfectly safe. And we'll have guards on duty, too—inside and out," she said, explaining about Teeny's men. "The catch is that once you're in place, you won't be able to leave the house—at all. But someone will always be there. And Herman can help you get around if you need it, I'm sure."

"That'll be tough but, okay, we'll go with your plan," Kevin said. "Rose will be doing the cooking, right?"

"Is that a backhanded shot at me? Not that I'd offer."

"Just kidding. I'm hoping you'll be out hunting down the bad guys." After a beat, he changed the subject, "What about Reverend Tome? Are you going to tell him?"

"Yeah, but believe me, he's very good keeping secrets. In fact, it's one of the things he does best," Ella said.

"Do you really think the Reverend will trust me—us—living under the same roof?" Kevin said somberly, then burst out laughing. "Just kidding."

Ella didn't comment. Joke or not, he'd made his point. "Justine will be handling your transportation and working out the time schedule. Obviously she'll pick an hour when very few potential witnesses are on the road," she added.

"I'll be ready whenever you guys are," he said.

Ella hung up and considered calling Ford next, but she had more pressing work to do at the moment. It would have to wait.

After another meeting with Big Ed she returned to her office. By then, the crime scene team had gathered and was waiting for her.

Ella took a seat and began the meeting by warning

everyone about Norm Hattery. "He's as slippery as a snake, and highly intelligent. I want everyone to stay on the alert for him," Ella glanced around the room, and noted the absence of one of their members. "Where's Marianna?"

"She drove to Window Rock to question a man who was supposed to be a close friend of Adam's, but it turned out to be a dead end. Adam and the guy were close in high school, and went into the military after graduation, but they ended up in different units and rarely saw each other after being deployed overseas," Benny Pete said.

Ella nodded. "Okay, then. Let's move on."

"We've checked all of Kevin Tolino's bank accounts, with his permission, of course," Benny said. "There's no way the seventy-five grand Adam was carrying belonged to Kevin. He's got some modest savings, and decent credit, but most of that is unused. He has no debts to speak of since he always pays off the balance on his charge bills. I also decided to check and see if his office had authorized that kind of money outlay recently for whatever the reason. That's when I ran into a wall."

"So I took over," Joe said. "Since that kind of money has to go through the comptroller's office, I checked with my cousin, who works over there. Everything comes across her desk, except for a few petty cash accounts. I told her I was working a case, so she checked for me. She found no withdrawals in the range we were talking about, except as tribal-issue checks that are part of existing purchase orders," he said. "But the trip wasn't a complete waste. I found out Norm Hattery's been asking about recent, substantial cash outlays, too. He has no authority to make those inquiries, but he's been sweet-talking one of the office workers in accounting."

"*How* did that man find out about the cash?" Ella glanced around the room, but no one had an answer.

"Here's what we do know. That money didn't originate

with the tribe or come from Kevin Tolino," Benny said. "So that leaves Adam."

Justine spoke then. "I checked into that possibility. Nothing about Marie's recent purchases indicate a windfall—or the expectation of one."

"When I went through their trash, I found several past due notices, and an Insufficient Funds notice from their bank," Benny said. "The total amount was less than a thousand dollars, so he's not in any deep trouble—apparently."

"Then we're back where we started from," Ella said. "Either Adam was paid 75K for services yet to be determined, or he was bringing the money to someone here on the Rez. Either way, that cash is the key to our investigation."

"It doesn't make sense that Industrial Futures Technology would pay the tribe—or Adam. They already had the tribe's best offer on the table. In exchange for their financial and technical support, they'd become an equal partner with the tribe and share in the profits," Justine said.

"Do we know for sure that Adam was only lobbying on behalf of the tribe? Is it possible he was freelancing and getting paid to bring tribal contracts to other outside parties? Or maybe buying from our craftsmen for someone back East?" Ella asked, looking around the room.

No one answered immediately, then Joe spoke. "I can see what other contracts the tribe has recently signed with outside firms. Business is kind of slow with the economy like it is, and there shouldn't be too many coming in right now. Maybe I can get a list to follow up on from my cousin."

"I can check on the artisans angle," Benny said.

"There's also the possibility that Adam was shaking someone down," Ella added reluctantly. "He might have needed the bucks, and as a lobbyist, found himself in the position of knowing something he shouldn't. Dig into that, too, but tread carefully. We're not out to destroy a reputation.

We're out to get the suspects responsible for what went down."

As her team left her office Ella held Justine back. "Transport Kevin to my place before dawn tomorrow. Double- and triple-check to make sure you're not followed." Ella was about to say more, when Blalock called on her cell phone.

"Meet me at my office. We've got a lead on Carl Perry's residence, and we'll need to coordinate the takedown."

"I'm on my way." Ella flipped the cell phone shut, and gave Justine the highlights. "Once I know where I'll be, I'll phone in the location to dispatch. Call me on my direct line if you need me, but be prepared to leave a message."

"Wear a vest this time—okay cuz?"

Ella nodded. "Count on it."

THIRTEEN

─────── ✖ ✖ ✖ ───────

Ella sat behind the unoccupied desk inside Blalock's office. Over the years, he'd had several partners, but none had stayed more than a year or two. To move up the promotional ladder in the FBI you needed to handle high-profile cases, and those were found in big cities like Dallas, Los Angeles, and New York. To a young agent, the reservation was the equivalent of a career death sentence.

Coordinating county's SWAT and getting the permissions necessary for Ella to take part in the Bureau-directed operation took time—and, more importantly, a hefty dose of patience.

"Do we know for sure that he's there?" Ella asked Blalock. Nothing could move forward without first confirming Perry was present at the location.

"The first address we attributed to him was a phony, so was the second, and now we're working on the third. But it looks promising. MVD just sent his vehicle registration tags to that address, though his current driver's license lists one of the other two locations. County's using Google to check the layout right now for a tactical plan, but I think we need to take a real-time look for ourselves." He stood, and she joined him at the door. "Are you making any progress on the case from your side?"

As they walked to his vehicle, she briefed him on the dead end they'd reached following the money trail, but didn't bring up Hattery. That was a departmental issue, and Blalock already knew how to deal with the press. Basically, Dwayne never commented until an arrest had been made.

"I've got a feeling that once we narrow down the motive, everything else will fall into place," Ella said. "Right now, I'd settle for just knowing if the crime's connected to the casino or the Prickly Weed Project."

The drive took them east, off the Rez, and through the old farming communities of Waterflow and Fruitland.

"Carl's made darned sure to place himself well away from curious neighbors," Ella said, riding with the Bureau agent down a narrow two-lane paved road, heading north from Kirtland. They'd just passed Flare Hill, an enormous mound of dirt crowned with a derrick that gave off a flame of waste gas. "We're getting close. The building's northwest of this road, about a mile beyond the asphalt," she said, looking at the color printout of an area photo sent to Blalock's computer by County.

Blalock looked over at her. "The pavement peters out just ahead."

"There's something off to the west—the house, I think. It's hard to make out from this angle because of the setting sun."

"We'll have to move slow. It's too sandy out here. We haven't had any rain for a few weeks. Good thing I've got extra wide tires on this car," Blalock muttered.

"Desert smart, and it only took, what, fifteen years? You could have saved yourself a lot of digging if you'd have wrangled a four-wheel drive from the Bureau instead of this town car," Ella said. "Have you ever considered a body armor upgrade? On operations like this one, it would be nice added insurance. Our suspect's bound to see us coming up that track, and an assault rifle can cut this car to pieces. Think of your SUV."

"I thought of that. Once I get to that small rise, I'm taking a short cut and making my own road. As for the body armor, I've got myself covered—literally." He thumped his chest with his knuckles. "I'm wearing the upgrade."

"The Bureau shelled out for that?" Ella thought about the twenty-year-old department ballistic vest she had on.

"They probably would have covered it, but by the time the paperwork went through, I would have been collecting my pension—or my son, his inheritance," Blalock said, making a face. "I had some extra bucks, so I bought my own. I know a guy."

Ella looked at him thoughtfully. That wasn't at all like the Agent Blalock she'd grown to know. "Does this new attention to self-preservation have something to do with Ruthann and Andy?"

He shrugged.

Ella heard volumes through his silence. Though she still hated wearing a vest during summer, she, too, had grown more cautious over the years, mostly because of Dawn. "After my daughter was born I stopped taking unnecessary chances. Family changes your perspective on everything."

He exhaled softly and nodded. "They're my new beginning, Clah, just when I thought I was too old to care about stuff like that." He shook his head. "Forget I said anything. I'm going senile. That's all there is to it."

"No, you're realizing what's important—and what isn't. About time, too."

He laughed. "Yeah, yeah. Maturity—it's a real pain, at any age."

Blalock slowed as they neared the rise, then inched around the base of the hill, making sure he didn't present a silhouette of the vehicle against the skyline. Although the route was bumpy they didn't bog down. Finally easing over the top for a quick look, they spotted a small white house to the north in what could only be described as the middle of nowhere. The only other sign of civilization in the shallow depression was the forest green Jeep parked just out in front of the building.

"This guy sure knows how to take care of himself," Ella said. "Sneaking up on him here would only be possible after dark."

Though they now had the setting sun to their left, and the chances of being spotted at the moment were close to nil, Blalock eased back down the slope. The house was only a quarter mile away, but there wasn't much they could use to hide their approach. The tallest vegetation consisted of knee-high shrubs and even shorter tufts of dry grass.

"We left a trail of dust in our wake. We had no choice. You think he knows we're coming?" Blalock asked.

"There's only one vehicle, but that doesn't mean that O'Riley's not here with him. If he is, then one of them would have been keeping watch for sure," Ella said. "Either way, we shouldn't go in any closer—not without backup. We could get picked off with one of those assault rifles before we make it halfway down the hill. Once it gets dark, we'll have a much better chance."

"You don't think this is going to go down easy, do you?" he said, after radioing their position.

"It's not," she said, feeling the warmth coming from the badger fetish around her neck. She'd never figured out if it was simply her own body temperature that heated it up, but it never failed to predict trouble.

"I can see a light, so it's likely somebody's at home," he said.

"Let's try and confirm that we're not just staking out some hermit oil field worker. Do you have a good set of binoculars?"

"Sure," he said.

"Let's circle left and get the sunset to our backs. We should be able to get a look through one of those windows," Ella said. "At the same time we can study the rear and west end of the building before we move in. If I were him, I'd have a back door and an escape route that would keep me out of view of anyone approaching down the driveway. If there's an arroyo behind that house, for example, he could take off and we'd never know."

"Good idea," he said, getting the binoculars out of the glove compartment and handing them to her. "I'll notify SWAT. They can stay out of sight below the ridge until we give them the signal to move in."

Ella left the sedan and circled left, staying low. Once she had the sun to her back, she crawled forward on her stomach, minimizing her profile.

Blalock followed ten feet behind her and to the left, wearing a cap and holding an M-16 assault rifle with a small, newer-model night scope. "Just in case," he said. "By the way, we need to pace ourselves. SWAT has been delayed by a TA."

"Can't they just go around the wreck?"

"*They* were involved in the accident. A truck driver ignored their emergency lights and spun the van completely around in an intersection."

"Any injuries?"

"That's not clear, but a backup unit has been dispatched from Aztec."

"That'll take an hour, maybe."

Blalock nodded. "So we take it slow."

The sun was at about the right angle now, making them hard to see from the house, and even harder to shoot. But their opponent, or opponents, were well trained and even better armed. She'd faced these men before and had been lucky to walk away both times.

Hoping her luck would hold, Ella switched magazines

in her pistol, choosing the rarely used clip with the armor-piercing rounds. Though a head shot would be her best option, she'd have to be too close for comfort to rely on that tactic, and in low light, the upper torso was the target of choice.

They took turns advancing, staying low and covering each other as they moved to new positions. "He chose this place carefully, and yet I can't locate a back door. What is it that we don't know . . ."

". . . that could get us killed," Blalock added in a whisper, finishing her thought.

Ella worked her way toward the west side of the house. About two hundred yards from the building she found a shallow wash that ran parallel to the structure and circled around to the south-facing entrance. She slipped down into it, then circled to the right, trying to get a close-up look at the front. Once in line with a window, she rose to her knees and brought the binoculars up to her eyes. "He's inside—Carl Perry. Right now he's pouring coffee into a thermos bottle. There's no back or side door. The house looks like one big living area and a bathroom. That door's open, and it's unoccupied."

"It sounds to me like Carl's getting ready to leave," Blalock commented from about ten feet to her left. "Do you see O'Riley anywhere?"

"No. Carl may be going to meet him. We need to move fast and take him into custody before he gets to the highway and can endanger someone else. Where's SWAT?" She turned and looked up the slope. The sun had set minutes ago and everything was in shadow down in this low spot.

"They were going to give me a buzz when they were within a quarter mile. They've got us on their GPS—at least my cell phone. They sure picked one helluva time to be running late."

"Stay low," Ella whispered as the house went dark.

"Carl's going to be taking a close look around before he comes outside."

"If he reaches that Jeep, it's over. He'll take off and we're not going to be able to catch him. By the time we get back to the car, he'll be long gone," Blalock said.

"So we have to make our move before he gets to the Jeep."

"Okay, let's do this. Since it's my jurisdiction, stay where you are, and cover me," Blalock said.

"No, let me do this. I'm closer, faster—and less bulky."

"All right. Go for it. I've got your back," Blalock whispered.

Ella sprinted to the now-darkened house, crouched low, and as she glanced around the corner, Carl stepped out the door holding something in each hand. He turned in her direction, and she was suddenly blinded by the beam of a powerful flashlight.

Ella ducked back just before he fired several shots at her. The bullets from his pistol struck the corner inches from her face. Then she heard the front door slam.

"You okay, Clah?" Blalock called out.

"Yeah. His flashlight blinded me for a second, that's all," she said, edging around the corner of the house. "He's back inside, right?"

"Yeah. He screwed up my optics and I didn't have a shot. Damn nightscope." Blalock was at the passenger side of the Jeep now, down on his knees and using the vehicle for cover. "Guess we wait for SWAT."

"At least we know we have the right guy," Ella said.

"And he's not going anywhere," Blalock answered. "No back door."

Suddenly the glass on the front window shattered and a burst of bullets erupted from within, striking the front of the Jeep. A few bullets went high flew across the flats, whining into the distance.

Ella recognized the distinctive whistle of a .223 round. He was using the assault rifle now. She looked over to see if Dwayne had been hit, and saw him turn toward her and shake his head.

Ella considered her options. She couldn't return fire, the angle was wrong with him still inside and at the far end of the building. The window at the east end, behind her, was too small to enter or exit, and too high off the ground to give her a shot to the interior.

Stepping to the back corner of the house, she checked the rear. The small window back there was closed, covered by a curtain she couldn't see through. Returning to the front corner, she looked over at Blalock. He was on one knee beside the passenger-side front tire, protected by the engine block, his M-16 held at eye level. He gave her a thumbs-up.

Ella crouched low and kept her aim on the front door, grateful she'd settled years ago on a tritium night sight system for her pistol that gave her the edge in low light conditions. But she might not need to fire a shot tonight—SWAT would arrive soon. All they had to do was keep Perry pinned inside.

Suddenly something flew out the broken window, bounced off the Jeep, then burst into flames. Three seconds later Perry rushed out the door, firing from the hip. Ella returned fire instinctively, aiming at the body mass. Blalock was shooting back as well.

Their enemy fell to the ground, then rolled to a sitting position and swung his assault rifle around in Ella's direction.

She fired twice in rapid succession aiming at Perry's head. Blalock, on his feet now, continued to shoot across the hood of the Jeep. Perry pitched forward, dropping the rifle as he fell on his face.

For a moment Ella remained frozen to the spot, her hand shaking. Then, at long last, she moved her finger away from the trigger. Taking a breath, she stepped forward, pistol still aimed at the body.

Blalock came around the front of the bullet-riddled Jeep and studied the burning object Perry had thrown out. "It's a kerosene lamp," he said, though no explanation was necessary. The scattered flames leapt off the ground and gave an eerie surrealism to the whole scene.

The awkward angle of the body lying on the ground assured Ella the man was dead. Up close now, she could see a pistol sticking out of his jacket pocket. It was a Beretta Model 92 similar to U.S. Army issue. The assault rifle in the sand was an AR-180B, just as she'd expected.

Blalock crouched, felt the pulse point at Perry's neck, and cursed. "We needed him alive to find O'Riley and whoever hired both of them."

"He didn't give us a choice," Ella said.

Blalock nodded. "Carl must have known he had to make his move before our backup arrived. I might as well call off SWAT and get a crime scene team here."

As Blalock called it in, Ella holstered her gun and brought out two pairs of latex gloves from her jacket pocket. Fumbling to pull them on over still-shaking hands, she stepped past the shot-up front door and switched on the lights.

The kerosene fire on the ground outside was smoldering now but another, acrid scent caught her attention. A ribbon of black smoke was curling upwards in a corner of the kitchen. Ella soon spotted an odd-shaped object burning on top of one of the burners of the stove.

Rushing over, she grabbed a dish towel and pushed the smoldering mass into the sink, then turned on the water. There was a rush of steam and the fire went out, revealing the melted remains of a smashed cell phone.

Hearing footsteps, she glanced back and saw Blalock. "He obviously didn't want his cell phone to fall into our hands," she said.

"So he knew we were out there, and that he might not get away," Blalock said in a low, thoughtful voice. "Loyal to the end."

The entire cottage consisted of the combination living, sleeping, and cooking area, and a small bathroom with a tiny shower. There wasn't much space to search. While she went through the cabinets, Blalock looked beneath the bed and found Carl's food supply—boxes of military surplus MREs. In the wardrobe against the wall were several shirts and pairs of jeans along with underwear and socks, all folded neatly, but no more weapons. The contents suggested that Perry had lived alone.

"The only thing in here is an empty twenty-round .223 magazine. The metal's bent, which probably makes the feed unreliable," Blalock said.

As Ella's gaze traveled around the small living room, what struck her most was the total absence of personal items. She was about to comment to Blalock when she realized he'd gone back outside and was crouched by the body.

He looked up as she came out. "Assuming he was planning to make a run for it, he would have probably grabbed whatever was most important to him." He reached for Perry's wallet, opened it, and whistled low. "This is some wad of cash."

"Getting clear prints from bills is nearly impossible," Ella said. "Maybe the crime scene team will be able to lift other prints inside the house that'll lead us to whoever paid Perry and O'Riley."

Blalock removed a worn photo showing two soldiers from the victim's wallet. "Perry and O'Riley, in their younger days," he said.

Less than ten minutes later, the county's crime scene van arrived.

Time slipped away as the house, Jeep, and the surrounding grounds were swept for evidence. The findings would take even longer to process. Knowing that, Ella glanced at her watch, then at Blalock.

"What's on your mind?" he asked.

"If ballistics confirms that Perry's weapon is a match for either of the guns used in the previous incidents, we should keep that information under wraps. We might be able to use it to our advantage somewhere along the way."

Blalock considered it, then nodded. "Let me go talk to the crime scene supervisor, then I'll call Sheriff Taylor."

"It might also be good to hold off releasing Perry's identity for the same reason. The public information officer could say that the name of the deceased is being withheld pending notification of next-of-kin."

"Good strategy, Clah."

As Blalock went to talk to the others, Ella touched bases with Justine and asked how the plan to move Kevin was going.

"It'll happen at around two-thirty a.m. I'll leave my house driving my pickup, and head over to the hospital. Joe's going to cover my back and make sure I don't pick up a tail."

"Excellent plan. Have you let Kevin know?"

"Yes, it's only a matter of telling Rose now."

"I'll handle that." Ella telephoned her mother next, and quickly told her what to expect.

"I think this is the right step, daughter," Rose said.

"So do I, but I'd like Dawn to spend the night with her friend. That'll keep her out of the way. Can you arrange that?"

"Getting her over there to spend the night won't be possible. She's not talking to her best friend right now. They had an argument. But I have another idea. I can ask her if she'd be willing to sleep with me and let my husband have her room just for tonight. I can tell her that I haven't been able to sleep because he snores so loudly. She wouldn't question it."

"Of course not. She knows he snores like a buzz saw," Ella said, laughing. "And since she's such a sound sleeper she'll never hear her dad arrive."

Blalock joined her just as Ella hung up. "What are you up to?" he asked.

She told him about Kevin's move.

"You're planning to keep Kevin at your place, and you don't think Ford's going to find out?" he asked incredulously.

"This has to be a need-to-know only."

"Your call," he said, checking his watch. "It's close to nine now. Why don't I drive you home? Maybe you can get at least a few hours of sleep tonight."

"No, I have a better idea. Let's go pay Councilman Begaye an impromptu visit. He should be home and tired after a long day of trying to ditch me."

"I'm game. How do you want to play this?"

"I want him to think that the Prickly Weed Project is now getting Federal attention—from the Justice Department, not the Department of Agriculture. If there's something dirty going on, maybe that'll rattle him, particularly if he's involved."

"The county has matters in hand here now, so let's go," Blalock said. "I've also placed an ATL out on O'Riley, so everyone will be on the lookout for him."

As they headed back to the reservation, Blalock glanced over at her, then back at the road. "It's going to hit you hard later—just as soon as you sit down and get more than three seconds to yourself. And we may never know which of us fired the fatal shot," he said in a barely audible voice.

"I know. Even if it was a clean shoot, the dead follow us in nightmares we never outrun," Ella said.

"You're right, it never gets easier no matter how many years you've been carrying the badge," Blalock said.

"Our own humanity won't let us forget." Ella thought of Dawn, her mother, and Herman. "But knowing that what we do keeps others safe—that's what ultimately keeps me going."

"There are lots of people out there who never have to deal with this, Ella. They get up, go to work, come home tired, and sleep easy. Do you ever wish you were one of them?"

"You and I would have died by inches in a job like that," Ella said with a rueful smile. "When I get up in the morning I know why I'm bothering to kick the covers aside. What we do carries a price, but it also makes a difference. You and I need more than the length of days to be happy."

"True," he admitted.

"What makes us good at what we do is our ability to brush the crap off ourselves and keep going."

"Or maybe it's just fear," Blalock said. "Without the rules we've chosen to follow, we'd push the limits and become the enemy we're fighting."

Ella said nothing for a while, just staring at the road in the headlights. "The same rules that bind us also define us. All in all, it's not a bad trade-off."

FOURTEEN
——— ✕ ✕ ✕ ———

After picking up some coffee at the Totah, they set out to find Councilman Begaye's home. Soon they were in a rural area of narrow roads and farms.

"Maybe this wasn't such a good idea. How are we going to find the right place at this time of night?" Blalock muttered. "The GPS is not much help on these unnamed lanes."

It took them another half hour, but they finally found the residence, a ranch-style house with a metal roof, surrounded by fruit trees. "It's the one with the coyote fencing around it," Ella said, pointing. "Justine told me that the Begayes have been having problems with coyotes and the councilman's wife is terrified of them."

"Why? They're less aggressive than most dogs. They usually run when they see a human."

"I dunno," Ella said with a shrug. "You see them so often around here they're just part of the landscape, as far as I'm concerned. And like you said, they run."

Moments later, Blalock pulled up to the front of the house and parked. "Do you want to extend them the same courtesy we would Traditionalists, even though they're probably not?

Or should we just go up and knock on the door? Their porch light came on when I turned up the drive."

"Looks like we won't have to decide," she said, pointing with her lips to Alfred, who'd stepped out to his front porch and was waving an invitation.

Ella and Blalock left the car and went up to join him.

"Good evening, Investigator Clah and Special Agent Blalock. You two get lost?" he asked.

Since he'd recognized both of them, Ella dispensed with the formalities. "Councilman, please forgive the late hour, but we need to speak to you tonight."

"Then come in, but please be quiet. My wife has already gone to bed," he said, leading them down the hall to his home office, then shutting the door behind them.

"How can I help you?" he asked, taking them to a sitting area across the spacious room where there was a fireplace, a large leather sofa, and four overstuffed chairs.

Ella took a seat on one of the easy chairs, as did Blalock. Before she could ask the councilman anything, Alfred spoke.

"You must be here about Sergeant Lonewolf. That man was a real American hero—a Navajo patriot who honored us all. He deserved to be put to rest at the National Cemetery—buried with respect and dignity. But, according to the hospital administrator, the family left word that they wanted to grieve in private and that the body would be buried at a family site according to the Navajo Way. They wouldn't even respond to a request to allow our leaders to place a flag on his coffin. That's what makes it so frustrating. The People need to honor their heroes at times like these."

Ella nodded, but didn't comment. The strategy they'd chosen had allowed them to explain away the absence of a body. Adam's parents were Traditionalists, and the Old Ways still carried weight, even with Modernists and those who followed new religions. Only people like Begaye, hoping to make political points, would dare to even question it.

"Do you think his death was linked to the Prickly Weed Project?" Ella asked him directly.

"Why would you even ask that?" Alfred's eyes grew wide and he shook his head adamantly. "That deal closed while Adam was still in D.C. It was his last victory."

Ella instantly noted the discrepancy in timetables. Billy had told her that the deal had gone through the day *after* Adam's death, and Teeny's source had also suggested that things hadn't been settled the day of the shooting. "I was led to believe that the agreement with IFT had remained on hold until recently. Do you know what finally changed that allowed the tribe to close the deal?"

"I'm sure there'll be others who'll try to take the credit, but it was Adam's efforts that made all the difference," he responded.

Ella regarded him thoughtfully as he continued singing Adam's praises.

"We needed IFT's cooperation, but we first had to convince them that there was going to be a reasonable return on investment," Alfred continued. "Right now the only cost-effective ethanol extraction comes from corn, but that's a necessary food crop—not just for humans, but animals as well. Although we'd all save on the cost of gasoline, we'll be paying through the nose for food. On the other hand, extracting ethanol from tumbleweeds doesn't have much of a downside. Though the yield will be lower and require a higher biomass, tumbleweeds are a nuisance and almost grow themselves, even on land where nothing else seems to thrive. And if it turns out ethanol fermentation has too low a return on investment, we can always switch to biofuel or biodiesel. The plant is suitable for those alternatives. This pilot project investigates all the options."

As she listened, she was sure this had been his sales pitch. It appeared to be well rehearsed.

"So who would *you* suggest was responsible for the shootings at the airstrip?" Blalock asked when Alfred finally finished.

"I think the killers were hired by those casino hoodlums. As a council member I'm very much aware of the lawsuit Kevin Tolino has pending, and it's clear to me that they went after him. With Kevin out of the picture for good, management would have had even more time to cover their tracks."

Ella noted that he'd made the assumption that the armed men had been hired. The possibility that they were the result of a personal problem facing one of the victims hadn't even entered his mind.

"The FBI might want to take a closer look at Grady. I've heard he keeps in contact with some underworld figures," Alfred added.

Alfred couldn't be moved from that position, so a short time later Ella knew it was time to leave. She walked with Blalock to the door, then stopped, and glanced back at Alfred. "One more thing, Councilman. I've heard that the Prickly Weed Project was almost shelved because the tribe couldn't come up with the necessary funds. Does money continue to be a problem?" It had been nothing more than a shot in the dark, but seeing Begaye's expression run the gamut from alarm to anger, Ella knew she'd scored a hit.

"Everyone knows that tribal resources are stretched to their limit right now. Between the new casino and the vast outlay of resources required to open the nuclear generating station near Hogback, our cash balances are at a historical low and the budget's naturally very tight. But if our partnership with IFT is successful, we should be showing a substantial ROI, return on investment, within three years—five years tops. Alternative energy markets have no way to go but up."

Ella blinked. He'd said nothing of import. Lots of words, but no substance.

Alfred politely reached for the door handle. "I'm sorry, but it's late and I have a very early schedule."

Blalock said nothing else until they were back in his sedan. "I'm going to check the casino's surveillance videos—including those for the parking lots. If Perry and O'Riley were working for Grady, it's possible we'll see them there."

"I'll follow some of this up, too, by talking to some of Kevin's sources."

"Home?"

"Yeah, finally. I'll need at least a couple of hours of sleep before everything there starts going to hell."

THURSDAY

Ella's alarm clock went off at 3:30 A.M. She'd just pulled on a pair of slacks when Justine called on the cell phone.

"I'm on my way," Justine said. "I've got Kevin, and we haven't picked up a tail. With the roads as clear as they are, it would be easy to spot one."

"Neskahi's watching your back?" she asked.

"Yes, and Herman's nephews, Philip and Michael, despite being off duty, are watching the road coming in from the west that goes by Clifford's house. Marianna Talk's staying on Hattery. He's a guest at the Turquoise Nugget, and his SUV's parked in front of his motel room as we speak. He hasn't come out since nine p.m., and his lights are out."

"Good. Excellent idea getting Marianna to cover him, partner."

Justine pulled up with Kevin less than fifteen minutes later. Herman was in the kitchen, in the dark, sitting there with his rifle on his lap. Rose went to the door to greet their guest, her expression unreadable in the dim lighting Ella had requested.

"Mom, you're sure my daughter's asleep?" Ella asked her.

"Yes, and don't worry. She sleeps very soundly, particularly when she has her earphones on."

Ella smiled. Dawn loved going to bed playing her music. Although normally they didn't allow her to do that, she could see why Rose had relented today.

"I'm going back to check on her one last time," Rose said. "That'll give you and your daughter's father a few minutes to talk privately."

Ella gave Kevin a hand as he struggled to walk the short distance to the back door, his path illuminated by the beam of Ella's flashlight. From the look on his face, Ella could clearly see that the trip had exhausted him and he was still in pain.

"Do you want to rest for a second before we go down the hall?" she asked softly.

He nodded, his breathing heavy. "I didn't want to risk taking painkillers because they dull me out. I need to be on my guard."

"No one will think of looking for you here," Ella said, nodding to Justine, who went by them carrying Kevin's suitcase.

"I agree with you there," he said with a weary grin. "Me, staying in the same house as your mother and you . . . No one who knows us would ever think that was possible."

"You'll still have to be very careful to stay away from the windows," Ella whispered as they continued to the back bedrooms.

"I'll be on my guard, don't worry. But what about Dawn? Does she know I'm taking over her room?"

"No, I haven't even told her that you'll be staying here. I figured it could be a surprise, and you and I could talk to her when she wakes up tomorrow." Ella sat on the edge of Dawn's bed, noting the men's toiletries on the night stand—purchased by Herman, no doubt. "The bed's a twin-size, but it's very comfortable and low to the ground, which should make it easier to climb in and out. I've slept in it myself from time to time."

He took a deep breath and pointed to the bag Justine had just placed in the room. "I've got some clothing one of the officers picked up at my house earlier tonight, including a set of pajamas. Care to give me a hand putting them on?"

Ella brought the bag closer to him, chuckling. "I'll get Herman to help you."

"That won't be nearly as much fun."

"Do you really need help?" she asked him seriously. "I don't want to get Herman unless it's absolutely necessary."

He nodded reluctantly. "Yeah, as much as I hate to admit it. I can't move my left arm, and my right leg is stiff where the muscles were damaged. With a hole in my rib cage that has a matching exit in my back, it also hurts like crazy if I even try to turn to the side. But what the hey, at least I have one functioning arm and I can feed myself. And hobble to the bathroom."

"Okay, hang tight. I'll go get him," she said, heading to the door.

"The worst part is having to ask for help. You should understand, you're not big on that either," he muttered as she reached the door.

"True enough," Ella answered, turning and giving him a sympathetic smile. "But look at it this way. We had to have had *something* in common, right?"

It was six-thirty by the time Dawn's alarm clock went off. Fifteen minutes later, she was in the kitchen, still in her robe and pajamas.

Ella and Rose were already there and, gathered around the breakfast table, told Dawn what was going on.

"Dad's *here*?" A smile of pure happiness instantly formed on her face. "We'll take great care of him, Mom. *Shimasání* can make her special teas for him, and I . . . won't play my music out loud, even during the day, because I know he'll have to sleep a lot," she added.

To Dawn, there was no greater sacrifice. Ella bit back a smile. "Your father's stay will have to remain a secret. You can't tell *anyone* he's here, and you can't mention anything in e-mails or text messages. Even the tiniest hint could endanger his life—and ours. That also means your friends won't be able to visit you here after school, not until your dad's well and able to return to his own house. And one last thing. You'll have to sleep with me in my bed, or on the living room couch. Your choice."

"I'll take the couch—you squirm too much."

"There's a guard inside the house right now," Ella said as Rose went to fix herself another cup of tea. "His name is Preston Harrison, and his job is to watch over us. Don't talk to him or distract him. He's on the job."

"Sure. I'm cool with that, Mom." Dawn stared at her cereal bowl, deep in thought, then looked up and in a hopeful voice, added, "If I could stay home from school, I can help *Shimasání* take care of Dad."

Ella smiled. "Nice try. But you're not missing classes."

"How about if I stay home just for today? Dad might get lonely. His guard's on the job so he won't be good company," Dawn said.

Ella knew from the intensity in Dawn's eyes and the way she waiting for her reply, scarcely breathing, that this was important to her. But their safety was even more important. "You'll have to go to school, daughter, and pretend that everything is normal here. We don't want to risk anyone who's looking for your father to guess why you stayed home. That means no calls home, or texting anything that might give a clue. If you slip up and tell anyone, even your best friends, your father will have to be moved for his own safety—and ours. And if that happens, you might not be able to see him for days."

"Mom. Can I stay home for just *one* day?"

"Afraid not. And he'll probably spend most of his time sleeping. What he needs most is peace and quiet," Ella answered. "You can see him before you go, and as soon as you get home this afternoon."

"But . . ."

"No, it's settled. Now hurry and get ready so you can spend a few minutes with him before you have to leave," Ella said. "And no texting your dad either, in case you'd thought of it."

Dawn sighed loudly. "Okay. If Dad wants to borrow my laptop, can I loan it to him?"

Ella considered it, then nodded. "All right. Just don't be surprised if he never gets around to it. Besides, I don't want him tempted to work. He needs to rest."

Dawn wolfed down breakfast, then went to see her father.

A short time later Justine drove up. Ella went to check on Kevin one last time, but found her daughter in the hall, school bag over her shoulder, watching him through the door.

Dawn placed both palms together, held them to the side of her face, and tilted her head to one side, signaling that he was asleep.

Ella smiled and blew her daughter a kiss, then hurried outside.

When they reached the highway, Justine glanced at Ella. "Where to next, boss?"

"There seems to be some confusion about when, exactly,

IFT signed on with the tribe. Those mixed signals are coming from people who should know, so that makes me curious, particularly because that's what Adam was working on when he was shot. I'd like to track down some of the lesser-known members of the Prickly Weed Project and see what they have to say. I figure we can go to the project's office in Shiprock and introduce ourselves. I think they're located across the street from the community college in that old warehouse."

"They are. A lot of the people who did the research and the grunt work on that proposal came from the community college."

When they arrived, the enclosed parking area was nearly empty. They entered through a side door and found a young Navajo woman in her early twenties busy on the phone. A middle-aged Navajo woman with an air of authority came into the room just then, saw them, and smiled.

"Hi, I'm Professor Frieda Beard. I teach botany at the college and volunteer here. Can I help you . . . officers?" she asked, noting the sidearms at their belts.

Ella introduced herself and Justine. "We need to learn more about the Prickly Weed Project, Professor. Can you help us?"

"You certainly came to the right place," she said, taking some coffee from the pot in the corner of the room and offering them some.

Ella and Justine accepted, taking foam cups of the hot brew.

Moments later, they were sitting around a circular table on the shaded concrete loading dock, which looked down on the parking area and their vehicle. It was a beautiful sunny day, the temperature cool and pleasant, and to the west they could see the Carrizo Mountains, which lay over in Arizona.

"Where would you like to start?" the professor asked.

"I understand that the project has many staunch supporters," Ella said, sipping her coffee, which, though dreadful, was marginally better than that available in the machine at the station.

"Most of the support comes from people like myself who understand what's at stake. There's a real need for new ways to fuel our cars and our machines. This project could make our tribe a player in the energy industry."

"Yet, there's some opposition to it," Ella said. The Navajo Way taught that everything had two sides, and it was so with this, too.

"Yes, but having people like Councilman Begaye and the late Adam Lonewolf in our corner has allowed us to push this forward. Adam, in particular, never hesitated to face the opposition and stand his ground." She paused, then in a soft voice, added, "The tribe really suffered a loss with his death."

"Do you think Adam made some enemies because of where he stood on this?" Justine asked.

"Oh sure," Professor Beard said without a second's hesitation. "In fact, I was with him at one chapter house meeting when things got especially ugly. But Adam stood his ground and argued the point through logic—not anger—which is more than I can say about some of the others who spoke. The land use issue is the biggest single obstacle this project's faced. Unless the current occupants agree to turn over the necessary acreage, the tribe will be forced to take the fight to court and a ton of bad publicity is sure to follow. Mind you, it's still a small price to pay considering the potential payoff, but our politicians are hoping to find another solution."

Ella heard a car pulling up down below in the parking lot next to the loading dock. Glancing over Frieda's shoulder, she saw Alfred Begaye climb out of his late-model luxury sedan and head toward the steps leading up to their level.

Frieda followed Ella's gaze. "If you push Alfred to give you the details, he'll fill you in. Or you can just ask people who attend the East Fruitland Chapter House meetings."

A second later Alfred stepped up onto the concrete loading dock. "I didn't expect to run into you again so soon, Detective Clah," he said coldly, not even acknowledging Justine.

Frieda got up, and with a hurried good-bye, made a fast exit through the open doorway leading back inside.

"We've been looking into the land issue, Councilman Begaye," Ella said. "You never mentioned that the Prickly Weed Project had stirred up a serious controversy."

"It's not our project that's the cause of the violence you're investigating. It's that damned casino. Gambling—it never brings anything good."

The young Navajo receptionist they'd seen earlier stepped outside and looked at Alfred. "I thought I heard your voice, Councilman. You have a call from the tribal president, sir," she said. "Something about a meeting?" Then, as the phone began ringing again, she ducked back inside.

Alfred looked at Ella, then Justine. "I've got business. Are we about through here?"

"Sure," Ella said, standing.

As Begaye hurried inside, Ella took a deep breath, wishing the coffee had been stronger. "Partner, before we do much of anything else, I need to stop by the Totah for a double shot of their brew. This java is not only dreadful, it's weak."

"You didn't get much sleep last night, I take it?"

"No, not really, which is why I need strong coffee right now." Ella walked back to the SUV with Justine.

They were only a few feet away from their vehicle when Ella noticed an elderly man making his way slowly across the asphalt. In his late seventies or thereabouts, he moved carefully, as if his body were a mass of aching joints. Ella watched him step closer to Begaye's sedan, and bend over. His back was to her so she couldn't see what he was up to.

As she narrowed the distance between them she suddenly realized that he was scratching something onto the side of the car. "Hey, you, stop that!" Ella yelled.

Ella was less than ten feet from him when he spun around and began waving an ice pick back and forth in a clear, threatening gesture.

Ella froze in mid-step. "You don't want to do that, sir. I'm Special Investigator Ella Clah of the Navajo Tribal Police, and waving an ice pick at someone carrying a gun is *not* a good idea."

The man's eyes widened, and an instant later, he took off in what was probably his version of a run.

"Stop where you are," Ella ordered as Justine circled around, blocking the way out the open gate. "Don't make things worse for yourself," Ella added. Even from several yards away she could hear him breathing—wheezing was more like it.

The man suddenly stopped, and leaned over, hands on his knees. For a moment, Ella thought he was having a heart attack, but as she approached, his breathing evened and he stood up straight again.

"Begaye had it coming. He's a traitor to all the *Diné*," he managed, his breathing still labored, but less raspy. Then he lifted his arm, still clutching the ice pick in his hand.

FIFTEEN

—— ✕ ✕ ✕ ——

Justine reached for her pepper spray, but Ella signaled her to wait. "You're already having problems breathing and a shot of pepper spray will make things a lot worse for you," Ella said. "Drop the ice pick, sir."

"Yeah, do it or she'll drop *you*," Alfred said, from somewhere behind Ella.

Forcing herself not to react to Begaye, Ella met the old man's gaze. "*Now.*"

With a long sigh, he did as she asked.

Ella stepped up and quickly kicked the ice pick away. "What's your name, sir?"

"I'm known as *Dinéchilí*," he said, opting for the traditional way of introducing himself.

The nickname meant "stockily built man." "My clan is the Salt People, and I was born for the Black Streak Wood People," he added, referring to his father's clan. He gestured to what he'd scratched into Begaye's car. It was the word *anaashii*, the Navajo term for squatters. "That's exactly what his people will be if they move into my clan's land with those prickly weeds of theirs."

Ella was familiar with the term etched into the vehicle. With no place to go, and the population of the tribe soaring,

Navajos sometimes moved onto unused land that wasn't theirs, setting up trailers or building hogans. "Ownership" of land on the Navajo Nation had always been a complex— and volatile—issue.

Alfred stood by his car studying the damage, then muttered a loud oath. "Emerson Lee, you crazy old man! Ruining someone's car isn't going to get you sympathy from anyone," he said, then spat out another curse.

A security guard came up to them and took Emerson's arm, but Alfred shook his head. "No, just let him go."

The guard looked at Ella, waiting for her reaction, and she looked back at Begaye. "Are you sure you don't want to press charges?" Ella asked. "Two police officers were witnesses to the vandalism."

"No way I'm pressing charges," Alfred said, biting off each syllable, then looking at Emerson, he added, "Just get out of here."

The old man smiled at Ella. "Can I have my ice pick back now?"

"Forget it, old man," Alfred answered before Ella could speak. "Leave it right where it is, or I'll have them put you in jail right now."

Emerson looked at Ella, and seeing her shake her head, walked away, muttering in Navajo.

"Why did you let him go?" Ella asked Alfred, more curious now than ever. "Those scratches are going to take serious bucks to fix—for you or your insurance company."

"The old man doesn't have the money, and if I'd sent him off to jail he would have become a martyr to those standing in the way of the project." Alfred shook his head. "No way I'm giving him any more ammunition."

Alfred took several photos of the damage with his cell phone, then glanced at his watch. "I've got to get going. I just found out I'm needed in Window Rock. Are we through here?"

"Sure. I can find you if I need you," she added with a smile.

Alfred glared at her, then taking one last look at the word scratched on his car, cursed and slipped behind the wheel. "I'm sure we'll see each other again," he said, then drove off.

Justine came up. Until now, she'd purposely stayed back, not wanting to interfere with the way Ella was handling the situation. "I think we need to find out more about the ones who oppose the project. If Emerson's willing to break the law in broad daylight in front of witnesses, what are the others capable of doing? And who are they?"

Frieda Beard came up behind them. "That's an easy enough question. At the heart of the problem is a local contingent of the Salt People Clan and a parcel of land that has been theirs to use for decades. When Eleanor Lee was alive she had grazing permits and lived off her sheep and a bit of farming. When she passed away, her son Emerson turned the place over to his daughter, Trina Morgan. Since she has a full time job, Trina sold off her grandmother's sheep and let the grazing permits expire. That's why the tribe can now legally take back the land. It isn't being used and the tribe has plans for the bulk of it."

"Yet Trina and Emerson are still planning to fight?" Ella asked, confused.

"Oh yeah. The second Trina heard what we were planning to do, she and her husband Chester immediately brought in sheep. Then they took their dispute to the chapter house, so they could get public opinion on their side. After hearing their story, a lot of others who live in the area suddenly panicked, thinking that the same thing would happen to them. Face it, lots of people forget to renew their grazing permits—lack of money or just not paying attention—so they don't want her to lose. But the laws regarding land on the Navajo Nation are clear—basically, use it or lose it. Bringing in sheep after the fact isn't going to change anything."

"What's to fight? Unused parcels of land serve no one, and the Tribal Council can do whatever it wants," Ella said, still trying to understand.

"You're right. The tribe could just take the land like it did before when the coal companies moved in. But people still remember all the bad things that happened after that particular land grab. In exchange for some jobs, we ended up with poisoned water wells, dead livestock, and land no one could use even after the mines shut down. People were victims of so-called progress once before and those memories linger," she said. "Of course this is a totally different situation. Our politicians are spearheading the project and placing their reputations on the line. That's one reason everyone wants to go the peaceful route—to convince people instead of forcing something down their throats. And that was what Adam Lonewolf did best."

"I'm surprised that any politicians are taking a stand on a volatile issue like this one," Ella said.

"If the opposition gains enough strength, the support the project currently has will disappear. That's the nature of the beast, so to speak." She glanced at her watch. "I have to get going. I teach at the college and I've got a class in another half hour."

"Thanks for your help," Ella said, standing up.

Five minutes later, they were on the way back to the station. Blalock had requested a meeting to update them on the Bureau's efforts to track down leads in D.C. "I wonder if he got anything from the surveillance video at the casino," Ella said.

"I guess we'll know soon enough," Justine answered. After a brief pause, Justine added casually, "How do you think it's going to work out with Kevin in the house?"

Ella heard the unspoken thought within the question. That was the advantage of knowing your partner well. "It's an interesting setup, I'll say that much. Of course Dawn loves having her dad at home. But Kevin knows he and I won't ever rekindle our old relationship, I've made that clear."

"Others may not be so convinced. Have you thought about how Ford's going to react once he hears about this?"

"As much as I trust Ford's ability to keep a secret, I'm not going to share police business with him unless he's directly involved—and this time, he's not."

"Do you remember when we tried to look into Ford's past and get more details on the kind of work he'd done? The Feds' warning to back off really took me by surprise," she said, laughing. "Has he ever told you more about his past, off the record?"

"Some. I know he worked in Intelligence, but for the most part those years are still a mystery to me. That's a book he either doesn't want to open, or can't. I honestly don't know which it is."

"So there's always going to be a side of Ford you'll never know," Justine said. "There are a lot of women who'd be intrigued by that."

"Ford's secrets aren't the problem in our relationship. It's what I already know about him," Ella said softly. "His beliefs require him to at least try and convert those around him, and when it comes to dogma he's not big on compromise. The few times I've heard his sermons that's come across clearly. Up to now I've pushed all that aside, figuring it would work itself out, but I'm not sure that's something we can do in the long run."

As they pulled up to the station, Ella noticed that Blalock's vehicle was already there. "I hope he's got some answers for us. This case keeps winding around itself and we need a solid lead that'll help us break that cycle."

Less than three minutes later Justine and Ella walked into Big Ed's office, closing the door behind them and taking a seat. Their chief was behind his big desk, talking to Agent Blalock, who was seated in one of the small armchairs.

Glancing to Big Ed, who nodded, Blalock began. "Bureau agents in D.C. have been checking places where Adam hung out—starting with the extended-stay hotel he used. They were given access to his room and, there, found receipts and vouchers that marked a trail they could follow. They've been trying to determine where he purchased the board game he had with him at the airstrip. Since there's no label on the box, that made things tougher. Agents have visited every retailer within walking distance that might offer that game, but they've had no hits. They're now checking area office supply and shipping outlets that offer shrink-wrapping service. So far we've got zip."

"That board game is the key to the suspect and the money," Big Ed said.

"I agree, and so does the Bureau," Blalock answered. "Our agents will keep pounding the pavement."

"I still can't think of any legitimate reason why the man was carrying that much cash," Big Ed said. "As a lobbyist, Adam doesn't finalize deals or contracts. His sole job is to promote the interests of the tribe. He can't even accept an offer on behalf of the tribe, and he's not a tribal lawyer who could walk a client through the actual process. If someone in D.C. is paying nearly a hundred thou to someone who basically only makes suggestions and talks up the tribe, I'd sure like to meet him."

"Stand in line, Chief," Ella said. "But there *is* another way of looking at this," she added slowly. "What if a coconspirator of Grady's—operating in the nation's capital—bribed Adam? It's possible Adam was recruited to keep an eye on Kevin and his investigation—maybe even sabotage it by getting the names of Kevin's sources, for instance. The threats Kevin received previously could have been designed to allow Adam to get closer to him."

"You're going back to our first theory then—that the

hired guns were after Kevin, but Adam got in the way?" Justine said. "Maybe Adam passed along Kevin's travel plans not realizing that there was going to be hit. It's possible Grady gave up on Adam, wrote off the seventy-five K, and went with Plan B—killing Kevin."

"That's a theory we can't afford to drop, and it would explain the cash," Blalock said with an approving nod. "I'm just hoping it's a dead end, that Lonewolf wasn't—isn't—dirty."

"Speaking of that, did you ever check the surveillance system at the casino for any signs of O'Riley or Perry?" Ella asked Blalock.

"I'm still working on that. There's a lot of footage to cover."

"You've got to narrow this down, Shorty," Big Ed said, looking at Ella as he stood, signaling they were done. "This case is shining a spotlight on our entire department."

"We'll do our best, Chief," Ella said, then followed Justine out of the office.

Once in the hall, Blalock touched Ella on the arm, motioning her aside. "I'm going back to join two Bureau agents I got on loan from the Albuquerque office. They're screening the casino video as we speak. I'll let you know if we find anything."

After Blalock left, Ella met with the SI team in her office. Marianna was at home catching up on sleep after last night, but Benny, Joe, and Justine were there, waiting. "Anyone know Norm Hattery's whereabouts this morning?" Ella asked the gathering.

"I do," a familiar voice said from the doorway.

Ella looked up and saw Ford. "Come in," she invited.

"I thought you might like to know that he came by the rectory this morning. He wanted to ask me about you and Kevin."

"That's strange. What kind of questions?" Ella asked, suddenly worried that Norm might have figured out Kevin's whereabouts.

"Hattery's looking into the possibility that the hit was a result of domestic violence—something between you and Kevin. He pointed out that there are several recent examples in New Mexico of spouses who hired, or tried to hire, thugs to kill their spouses or exes."

"You're kidding," Ella said after a beat.

"I told him he was nuts," Ford said laughing. "Then he asked me about the others in your unit." He glanced around the room. "You're all the focus of the reporter's interest now, so I thought I'd better come by and warn you. If he hasn't already, he'll soon be nosing into your private lives."

"We can't stop Hattery, nor should we allow him to distract us. The only thing we can do is warn our families," Ella said, looking at her team. Joe gave her a silent thumbs-up, a positive sign concerning his sister.

"Could I speak to you privately for a moment?" Ford asked Ella.

She stepped out into the hallway with Ford, then reaching for his hand, gave it gentle squeeze. "So why did you really come in?"

"Part of it was to warn you and your team to watch yourselves. But, you're right, that wasn't the only reason." He stared at the floor for a long moment.

Ella waited, not interrupting him.

"I've learned that Adam's immediate family isn't on the Rez anymore," he said in a whisper-soft voice. "That makes me suspect that Adam's still alive, under protection elsewhere. And if I put that together, so can whoever's threatening . . . them."

"Them?" Ella pressed, trying hard not to give anything away.

"Tolino's also gone. I was at the hospital visiting a parishioner and decided to check on him. The nurse said that Kevin had been released, so I drove to his house. Though he's not of my flock, I thought he might need an errand run, or maybe enjoy some company. I *am* my brother's keeper," he added with a gentle smile. "But Kevin wasn't there either."

"Security measures on this case are extremely tight. That's all I can say."

Ford nodded, but his expression grew distant and Ella had a feeling he'd already put things together.

"You're the best at what you do, but when the personal and professional cross in the field, it never leads anywhere good. Be very careful," he said at last.

Ella stared at him as he walked away. She still wasn't sure how much Ford really knew. As it usually was, he had the ability to show only as much as he wanted you to see.

"We've got a twenty on Hattery," Justine said, coming out to meet her. "You're not going to like it."

"Give."

"He was at your daughter's bus stop this morning asking the children their names. One of the parents told him to get lost. He made excuses, saying that he was doing a story on how Navajo children pass the time riding long distances to and from school, but didn't stick around after that."

"If he gets within a mile of my kid, I'm arresting him on the spot and he'll be cooling his heels in jail," Ella said. "Notify the school that he's hanging around elementary school bus stops."

"Already done," Justine said.

Ella stepped back into the room and looked at her fellow officers. "Hattery's going to be a pain. But if he's looking for my kid, he doesn't have a solid lead. He's just fishing."

"So are we," Benny said.

"Yeah, and we've got to keep casting out our lines," Ella

said. "Get me whatever you can on Grady's finances. Also search the background of anyone with a financial link to the Prickly Weed Project."

As her team left, Ella sat back in her chair and tried to figure out her next move. Hattery was a complication she didn't need right now, and when he started messing with her family . . . Brushing aside her anger, she tried to stay focused, going over her notes.

A half hour passed, then, feeling her cell phone vibrating, Ella flipped it open.

"I've got a problem," Marianna told her. "A while ago I got a call from Angelina Manuelito, the receptionist at the casino office. Earlier today the casino's security chief, Rudy Nez, overheard her saying that she and I are good friends so he took her aside a few minutes after that. He warned her that she'd leave herself open to lawsuits if she spoke to me about the casino's private business, and that her job, too, would be history."

"Interesting."

"Then he told her that he'd be keeping his eye on her. Too rattled to work after that, she decided to go home early. But once she left the casino grounds, she discovered Nez was following her. Since she doesn't have any close neighbors, she was afraid to go home. She stopped at the Totah Café and called me. She's still there. I don't have the clout to make Nez back off unless he does something else, but if you go . . ."

"No problem. I'm in town and at the station, so I can be there in five. Give me her cell number," Ella said, standing.

Marianna gave it to her, then added, "I've got a photo of her on my cell phone and I'm going to forward that to you next."

Ella hurried down the hall, stopped by the door to the lab, and called Justine. "We've got to roll," she said, filling her in on the way to the parking lot.

As Justine got underway Ella looked at the image of Angelina on her cell phone, then called the number she'd been given. Angelina answered immediately, and from the tone of her voice Ella knew she was badly frightened. "Calm down and tell me why you're so scared of him," Ella said.

"Rudy's a jerk. At the office he told me that people with loose tongues should use their talents in other ways, then he made some really disgusting remarks. I told him he was gross, but he kept hanging around my office, so I took sick leave and headed home. I was driving down the highway when I spotted him behind me. I never thought he'd follow me home," she said, and her voice broke.

"Just sit tight, and put me on speaker. Order lunch—and stay inside. He won't do anything to you inside a crowded café."

"Then what? Are you going to arrest him?"

"Let's see how things play out, but either way, I'll make sure you're safe. Will you trust me?"

"Yes," came the whisper-thin reply.

Less than two minutes later, Justine drove into the Totah's parking lot via the back way. As they pulled into an empty parking space, Ella watched for Rudy. "I see him, he's in the bright yellow pickup. It's mustard, actually, a lowrider. Looks like the same guy I saw at the casino, the one who set us up to get jumped."

Justine nodded, following her gaze. "Now it fits. How do you want to handle this?"

"I want a reason to confront Rudy openly. He obviously likes to bully the ladies, so I'm going to set him up." Ella brought out her phone. "Angelina, I'm right outside, on the west side of the restaurant. I want you to come out into the parking lot."

"I can't," she said, her voice rising an octave. "He's still out there. I can see him from where I'm sitting. He's waiting for me." Her voice broke. "He parked next to my car."

"The silver sedan?"

"Yes."

"Okay. Listen to me carefully," Ella said firmly. "I won't let him hurt you, but I need you to come out and walk to your car. I'll be there if he tries something."

She took a deep unsteady breath. "Okay. If you can throw him in jail, this'll be worth it."

A few moments later Angelina pushed the glass foyer door open and walked out of the café. Seeing Rudy coming straight for her, Angelina froze.

Ella was only a half-dozen feet behind Rudy when a familiar face suddenly came out of the restaurant. Ford spun around Angelina just as Rudy reached for her arm.

"Hands off." With lightning fast reflexes, Ford grabbed Rudy's hand and twisted it to the outside, applying a pinch grip.

Rudy tried swinging a roundhouse punch, but sagged to his knees in agony instead.

"Stay down and calm down," Ford ordered. "Don't injure yourself."

"Good to see you, Reverend," Ella said, coming up.

"I hope I haven't interfered with a police matter, Investigator Clah. I noticed the young lady was upset, so I decided to follow her out and offer my support," Ford said softly.

Ella smiled, noting the not-quite-convincing apologetic look on his face. "I've got him now, Reverend Tome. Thank you."

"You're very welcome," he said, stepping back.

Ella identified herself—though Nez apparently knew who she was already. After she cuffed him, she removed the pistol he carried in his shoulder holster. The description she'd been given by the pair who'd come after Justine and her at the casino fit Rudy to a tee, belt buckle and all.

"You're making a real big mistake," Nez growled.

"I hope that's not a threat," Ella said smoothly.

"No, it's a fact."

"You can tell me more about that once we get to the station," Ella said, then turned him over to Justine, who read him his rights.

While Justine took Nez back to their unit, Ella joined Angelina. "He's going nowhere for a while."

"I can file charges against him, but with his credentials . . ."

"You don't have to be afraid of him. We'll make it very clear that if anything happens to you—even if all you do is trip and fall—we'll go find him," Ella said. "Leave it to me."

Ella glanced at the police unit where Justine had placed Nez. It was easy to see what had drawn him to the casino job—power.

"Do you want me to go to the station to give you a statement?" Angelina asked.

"Yeah, just follow us in," Ella said. "Making this official will put even more pressure on Nez to leave you alone."

As Angelina walked to her car, Ella joined Ford, who'd been standing back. "You're really something, Reverend."

"Glad you think so."

Ella touched the side of his face in a quick caress, then turned and walked away. That was the limit to any touching he'd permit, and that was a problem. He followed rules she wasn't prepared to obey.

SIXTEEN

—— ☓ ☓ ☓ ——

Later at the station, Ella and Justine went into the small interview room where Rudy Nez had been placed. He'd been cooling his heels for about two hours.

As they stepped inside, he sat rock still, glaring at them.

"Would you like something cool to drink?" Ella asked. "Feels kind of warm in here—stuffy."

"Spare me the games."

Ella shrugged. "Explain to me why you went after Angelina Manuelito."

"I didn't go after anyone. The woman looked like she was about to faint, so I reached out to keep her from falling. The preacher must have misunderstood and assaulted me. Then you came over."

"That doesn't mesh with the story she told us. And she wasn't even close to fainting. I was there, remember?"

"I don't care what she told you. It's all an act, you know. She has a thing for cops, and ever since she realized I wasn't interested she's been looking for a way to get back at me."

"You're no cop," Ella said calmly.

"I'm the head of security at the casino. That qualifies."

"Rent-a-cop's more like it," Justine added. "A wannabe."

Anger flashed in Rudy's eyes, and his hands curled into fists. "You two make peanuts compared to what the casino pays me, and you know the saying—'pay peanuts and you get monkeys.' At the end of the day, I drive off in a custom truck with a state-of-the-art sound system, and my three-story brick home just south of the Piñon Hills golf course belongs to me, lock, stock, and barrel. You *wish* you had my life."

"A fat wallet still doesn't make you a police officer, and you act like a pimp. If I had to take a guess, I'd say you don't have what it takes for law enforcement," Ella said.

He bolted to his feet so fast, the chair crashed to the floor.

"Sit down," Ella said firmly. "You don't want to get Tasered."

He picked up the chair and sat back down slowly, giving them a mirthless smile. "I get it. You push my buttons, then nail me for assault on a police officer. But over what—that brainless girl? Please."

"She says you threatened her and her job because she spoke to one of our officers. So that brings me to my next question. What are you trying so hard to keep secret over at the casino?" Ella leaned back, and not waiting for him to answer, continued. "Then again, I'm probably wasting my time looking to you for answers. You're just muscle—if that."

"Do you know *anything*, or do you just do what Grady tells you?" Justine asked.

"I take care of security," he growled.

"How do you define that—hiring two deadbeats to assault a couple of tribal officers who came to interview your *superior*?" Ella said, goading him. "You couldn't handle us by yourself, could you?"

"My job's to keep deadbeats *out* of the casino. I don't *hire* them."

"See? He just follows orders," Justine said. "Come on. We're wasting our time."

Nez gave her a look of utter contempt. "The casino's a good thing for the tribe. You're messing with things you don't understand."

"The same could be said for you—but, then again, understanding isn't your gig. Following orders seems closer to it," Ella said. "You're Grady's lapdog."

"You've got your bosses, I've got mine. Except for our income, we're the same," he snapped.

Ella laughed. "You're clueless. Face it, Rudy, telling that kid, Angelina, to keep her mouth shut, then trying to intimidate her? Big mistake. It's the same as pointing a finger at the one you've been hired to protect."

"Leave Grady out of this. He's a good man and has made millions for the tribe," he said. "You're trying to find out who's behind the shootings; I get it. But that has nothing to do with the casino, Grady's company, or Alan Grady himself. Quit wasting your time and mine and get on with your job."

"So then why are you leaning on people like Angelina? What are you trying to keep quiet?" Ella pressed.

"Mr. Grady's people shouldn't be talking to outsiders. At the casino we have our own way of taking care of trouble—and troublemakers," he said. "If you think about it, you'll know it's true."

"Let me guess. We're troublemakers, and that's why you set those two bozos after us?" Justine said.

"What's the complaint? If you two couldn't handle two crazy Anglos, you're in the wrong job. Where's *your* training?"

"So you're confessing?" Ella countered. "I never said they were Anglos."

"You sure? It seems to me you're losing your edge. You're having so many problems holding your own out in the field, you're even using a preacher as backup," he shot back with a sneer. "But I'm getting tired of all this harassment." He sat back and crossed his arms in front of his chest. "I'm done here. I'll wait for my attorney before saying anything else."

Ella stood. "This incident's probably going to be swept under the rug. But hear me. If anything happens to that young woman—if she even scrapes her knee—I'm going to be all over you. Life as you know it will cease to be. You get me?"

He looked at Justine. "This is harassment, pure and simple. You gonna let her get away with this?"

Justine yawned. "Excuse me, I wasn't listening. Did she say something?"

Rudy looked back at Ella and grinned slowly. "Looks like you and I have a lot more in common than you want to admit."

"What we have is a connection—people like you belong in cages, and I'm good at putting them there," Ella said.

As they left the room and stepped into the hall, Big Ed came out of his office and motioned to them. "Abigail Yellowhair just called," he said, closing the door behind them. "Someone spray-painted the word *anaashii* on her garage door."

"Sounds like Emerson Lee's work," Ella said thoughtfully.

"Abigail asked for you specifically. She said that since your mother's also part of the Prickly Weed Project, you need to see what Rose is going to be up against. I don't take requests when it comes to assigning officers to a case, so it's up to you, Shorty. I can send another officer."

Ella's expression hardened. "I'll go. There's a reason behind her friendship with my mother, and I need to figure out what that is."

"One more thing. That reporter, Hattery, showed up at Abigail's."

"Did she speak to him?"

"Yes. She said it was time someone told the general public that the project leaders are being victimized."

Ella rolled her eyes. "All right. I'll handle this, Chief."

As they turned toward the door, Big Ed spoke again. "There's one more thing."

Ella and Justine stopped and glanced back.

"Hattery's agreed to help the *Diné Times* by passing on information as he gets it. Jaime Beyale, the editor, has been forced to cut staff and agreed to use him as a stringer."

"Things must be really tough if she's using Hattery."

"Don't kid yourself, Shorty, he gets results. Lots of press awards next to his name if you Google him."

"Yeah, but he got fired from one of the Albuquerque TV stations a few years ago for screwing up big time," Ella replied.

"That's why he's working so hard to rebuild his reputation. He wants to break a story certain to make the national news," Big Ed said.

"Just the kind of reporter I need underfoot," Ella muttered.

"Tread carefully. Even with that black mark against him, he's still got connections in the industry," Big Ed added.

"Thanks for the heads-up," Ella said.

"I know you don't like Hattery nosing around our case, but you heard the chief," Justine said as they headed to the car. "We've got to treat him with kid gloves."

"So what do you propose?"

"Let *me* handle him while you question Mrs. Yellowhair."

"Partner, that's a great idea. I'll get more from Abigail if we go one-to-one," she said, then with a mischievous smile, added, "And who knows, Hattery and you might hit it off. He could even give Mr. Romance some competition."

Justine choked. "Forget it. I like to keep things simple.

One guy at a time is more my speed." She paused and in a soft voice added, "I wouldn't want to be in your shoes."

"Huh?"

"Cuz, I've known you all my life. No matter what you say about Kevin being out of the running, he's never given up on you. With him, what you see is what you get. The problem is that you don't like to play it safe, and Ford fascinates you. Behind that conservative, pious image is a brilliant man with a hidden past. Unfortunately, it seems you need more from a relationship than Ford can give you."

"And less. Before we'd go the next step, he'd insist I marry him and join his church, and that would end it, I'm afraid," Ella said.

"Maybe he'd change his mind—about the church thing. It's clear he's in love with you."

"No, that wouldn't work for him—or for me. I keep thinking of my own father and mother. They loved each other, too, but I'd never want to live that way again and have my daughter caught in the middle, like Clifford and I were. Clifford chose the Navajo Way and fought with Dad constantly. I ran off and got married."

"Yeah, and when your husband was killed, you joined the FBI," Justine admitted. "Took years before you came back. So, are you really going to leave again?"

"I still haven't decided about the D.C. job. Let's stick with nostalgia, okay?"

A short time later they arrived at Abigail's home, a modest frame structure west of the river in an area of small farms. A new-looking SUV was parked on the street in front of the house, and Abigail's fading yellow sports sedan was on the left side of the concrete driveway in front of the double garage's door.

As Ella parked across the road from Abigail's house, she took in the scene. Abigail was scrubbing off the painted, foot-high letters with rags and a strong solvent, judging from the scent that wafted over. Norm Hattery, dressed in tan slacks and a tropical-pattern shirt, was beside her, ostensibly helping.

Seeing Ella as they climbed out of the vehicle, Abigail waved. "Do you know each other?" she asked gesturing to Norm as Ella and Justine crossed the street.

"We've met Mr. Hattery." Ella gave Norm a nod, then focused on Abigail. "Do you have any idea who might have done this?"

Abigail took a few steps away from Hattery, turned her back to him, and lowered her voice. "My money's on someone from Emerson Lee's clan. Ever since that last chapter house meeting, they've been busy stirring people up. They present themselves as martyrs—you know, poor Navajos out to protect their way of life from tribal politicians—but the truth's a lot simpler than that. They don't want to relinquish that land to the tribe."

Still pretending to be scrubbing the paint, Norm edged closer to them.

Noting it, Ella glanced at her partner, then back at Abigail. "Why don't you and I go inside and talk in private for a bit?"

"I'll help Norm with the scrubbing," Justine said, picking up a pair of rubber gloves resting on the rim of a plastic bucket.

Abigail led Ella into the kitchen and offered her a seat at the table. "Things are going to get worse before they get better. That's why I'm so worried about your mother. Rose is a beautiful, gentle woman who doesn't deserve to become a target for these idiots."

Ella knew that Abigail had gone to Rose a few months ago and convinced her to participate in the Prickly Weed Project. "I recall that *you* were the one who got her involved in this."

"At the time, the only clear risks were calluses accompanied by sneezing," Abigail said. "But if your mother wants out, all she has to do is tell me. . . ."

"We're getting sidetracked," Ella replied. "Did you see anyone hanging around when you came home? Also, was Norm already with you or did he arrive afterwards?"

Abigail smiled slowly. "To answer your real question, Norm and I aren't hanging around together. He showed up about twenty minutes after I got here. I was already outside scrubbing the graffiti."

"What did he want?"

"He was very interested in Adam's role in the Prickly Weed Project, but we haven't had much of a chance to talk. I wanted to scrub that paint off my garage door before it set up. I find that particular word highly insulting. I belong to the Navajo tribe, and I grew up on tribal land. I am *not* an outsider or a squatter."

Ella nodded slowly. "Does it strike you as odd that whoever did that came all the way out here? Scratching Begaye's car was one thing. He was in a parking lot in the center of Shiprock. You've got, what, three neighbors on this street?"

"I see your point. The message was obviously intended solely for me." Abigail stood. "Let's go back outside so I can work on that paint."

Moments later as Abigail bent down to put on her rubber gloves, something thumped against the garage, and a shot rang out.

"Gun!" Ella yelled, forcing Abigail to the concrete and reaching for her pistol. A bullet had struck the garage less than two feet away from the woman. "Abigail, get behind the hedge and stay out of sight." Ella reached over to push her in the right direction, but Abigail was already on the move.

Justine rolled away from Norm, who was flat on his belly. "Get over there with Mrs. Yellowhair," she told him. "But stay low and move fast."

The farmland in this neighborhood lay atop a low mesa that rose to the north and west, but the shot had come from the river valley. Ella ran in that direction, zigzagging randomly to throw off the gunman. Too angry to be scared, she used the extra energy to give her strength and speed.

Justine followed, angling to the side so the sniper would have to choose between targets.

They were about thirty yards away from the rim of the bluff that defined the outward reach of the river when Ella heard a vehicle starting up below. She raced forward, hoping for a glimpse at the suspect's vehicle, but by the time she reached the edge of the embankment, there was nothing on the gravel road below them but dust. The vehicle had gone west and had disappeared in a farming area covered with a network of roads.

Walking along the embankment, Ella and Justine soon found the location the sniper had used to target them.

"He didn't even leave a shell casing behind," Ella said, looking to what would have been the shooter's right, the direction most firearms ejected spent cartridges.

"The sand's soft where he scrambled up and down the bank, so it buried his boot prints," Justine said.

"Let's check at the bottom, by the road," Ella said, making her way down the ten-foot-high slope.

Not finding anything but smeared-over prints and impressions in the gravel, they climbed out of the old river bottom onto high ground and walked back to the Yellowhair house. Hattery's SUV was gone from the driveway.

Ella knocked on Abigail's door, and hearing the invitation to enter, went inside, followed by Justine.

Abigail was sitting on the couch, a large shotgun on her lap.

"You won't need that," Ella said, deliberately keeping her voice calm. "Why don't you put it away?"

"It belonged to my husband. He used it to chase away

coyotes," she said, then propped it up against the wall in one corner of the room. "These people are animals, too. They're never one bit sorry for the trouble they cause."

Ella took a seat. "Where'd Hattery go?"

"Norm said he had to go file his story," Abigail said. "He didn't think you'd catch the gunman, and it looks like he was right. This is the third time you've let these criminals get away, isn't it?"

Ella refused to take the bait. "To your knowledge, has anyone else in the Prickly Weed Project been the target of violence?"

"Adam and Billy Garnenez had some problems at the last chapter house meeting." She paused, gathering her thoughts, then continued. "Someone took a swing at Billy after Emerson got the crowd worked up, reminding them about the mess the coal and uranium mines left behind. But Adam stepped in, and since nobody wanted to raise a hand to him, things calmed down."

"Do you think Emerson was responsible for the shot fired at you today?" Ella asked.

"Not Emerson himself, no," Abigail said. "The man's sight is all but gone. I doubt he could hit my house from across the street. But his son-in-law . . ."

"What do you know about him?" Ella asked.

"Until recently, Chester Morgan worked at the government offices in Farmington, but he lost his job when they cut back at the beginning of the fiscal year. He's the one who decided to plant a vegetable garden and turn out a few head of sheep to graze on the property. He told everyone that was the only way a Navajo could guarantee that neither he nor his family would go hungry," she said. "Mind you, he's got a point."

"So a part of you thinks they're right and should fight to keep their land?" Ella asked, sure she wasn't seeing the whole picture.

"We never wanted *all* their land, just, say, seventy-five percent of it on the side closest to the existing Navajo Irrigation project. Compromise is the only way to go on something like this. But the family refused to even consider the options. With only Trina working full time now, they're afraid of what the future will hold for them. It's not that they're in dire straits—they're not—but it's pretty clear that the 'what-ifs' terrify them."

When Ella's phone began to vibrate, she left Justine to finish taking Abigail's statement and answered the call outside.

"I've got good news, but you'll need to come over." Teeny's unmistakable sotto voice came through clearly. "This isn't the kind of conversation we can have over an unsecured line."

"I'll be there in twenty, maybe sooner." Ella shut the phone and signaled to Justine, who had just stood. "Time to go."

SEVENTEEN

—————— ✗ ✗ ✗ ——————

Ella followed Teeny inside the main office, and waited as he settled his enormous bulk onto the chair closest to his favorite desktop computer. He'd had special programs uploaded into multiple hard drives, added a host of peripherals, and had tweaked every component until it had practically become an extension of Teeny himself. As she looked at him staring adoringly into the screen, she had no doubt she was witnessing a case of compumance—that special romance between a man and his computer.

"I have the information you need from Adam's Black-Berry. I've made a printout of the content—names and address, his schedule, meetings, and his daily notes—kind of a log, or diary. It all came out to around forty pages when I copied everything into one text file. I've also downloaded everything onto a flash drive and placed it inside the same envelope."

"As you retrieved the information, did you take a look at it, and if so, is there anything you can tell me?"

"I skimmed some of it to make sure I'd broken the encryption, but that's about it. My job was to make it readable, so I focused on that."

"Anything particularly interesting that stuck in your mind?" she asked, hoping for the short version.

He considered it for several moments. "It's clear to me that Adam had divided loyalties, Ella," he said at last. "He was frustrated with the way the Prickly Weed Project was being handled and wanted to do things his own way. He felt that the project leaders were holding him back, yet still expecting him to get results. He couldn't do both and the guy liked to win." He met her gaze. "I can understand that. I'm the same way."

"Me, too," she admitted.

He handed her the padded envelope with the information. "I heard what happened at Abigail's."

Ella wasn't surprised. Teeny's sources—electronic and human—were second to none. "We told Abigail to lay low for a while, but I have no idea if she'll do it or not."

"Here's something you *can* count on. No one's getting near your mom's place without our knowledge. I've increased security just to stay on the safe side. Mack Kelewood will be inside your home, and take turns with Jimmie Harvey and Preston Harrison. Outside, you'll have a man who's had extensive sniper training in the Rangers, Eugene Nakai. He's the only person I know who can pick off a target the size of a baseball at a hundred yards—while it's rolling."

"That's some marksman."

"Which is why he's there," Teeny answered. "He'll have the others as backup anytime, but he told me that he rarely sleeps more than four hours a night when he's on the job. With anyone else, I would have said that's a bad idea, but not with this man. He goes by different rules."

Ella stood. "By the way, we've lost track of that pain-in-the-butt reporter, Norm Hattery, after he left the Yellowhair residence. If you hear anything about his whereabouts, let me know. I don't like not knowing where he's at, or where he could pop up next."

"You've got it."

As Ella walked to the door, Justine, who'd been in the next room talking on her cell phone, joined her. "You ready to roll?" she asked Ella.

"Yeah. Let's get back to the office. I want to go through what Teeny handed us and update Big Ed."

They were on the highway a short time later. Not wanting to waste time, Ella pulled out the printout as Justine drove. "There's nothing here that links Grady to Lonewolf. From what I can see here, Adam was completely focused on getting IFT to work with the tribe. The IFT rep, a man named Williams, was his contact, and Williams was being a hardass."

Hearing her phone ring, Ella picked it up, hoping it was Teeny and he'd found a lead to Hattery. But it was Blalock's voice she heard at the other end.

"We've got a minor problem," he said. "Marie Lonewolf went over my head and got permission to leave Kirtland Air Force Base. She's on a special flight back as we speak."

"What happened?" Ella asked.

"Since Adam hasn't regained consciousness, the family hired your brother to make a special medicine pouch for him. Marie's landing in a half hour, so I'm on my way to the airstrip to pick her up."

"So that means she's spoken to Clifford and he now knows for sure that Adam's alive," she said in a thoughtful voice.

"No, not quite. All she told your brother is that she needed a medicine bundle that would restore the *hózhǫ́*."

Medicine to restore beauty and harmony. That made sense. "My brother wasn't fooled, believe it," Ella said.

"Yeah, he's too smart for that."

"Whoever's watching her back also needs to make sure she doesn't come across Norm Hattery. I don't know where he is right now."

"Noted. I'll be taking her by her home first, so that'll buy me time to spot a tail and deal with it, if necessary," Blalock answered.

"The family's cover story has been that they went up to one of their sheep camps in the Chuskas to grieve in private. If you need to, say Marie came back to gather up her husband's belongings so she could give everything away to a church group off the Rez. Adam's parents are Traditionalists, so people would understand that they wouldn't be comfortable visiting Marie at her home if Adam's stuff was still there. Traditionalists avoid all contact with the possessions of the deceased."

"Okay, got it."

"I'll meet you at the Lonewolfs' home." Ella hung up and glanced at Justine. "Change of plans," she said, updating her partner.

Once they were headed in the right direction, Ella called her brother. Though their conversation was brief, she learned all she needed.

They met with Blalock and Marie Lonewolf thirty minutes later at the Lonewolfs' home, one of many small houses in an old tribal housing development on Shiprock's east side. The fact that every house was painted the same color, and had the identical basic design, gave it a certain amount of anonymity. Also a plus was the fact that there were no mailboxes at the curb that would make the Lonewolfs' home easier to spot.

While Ella went into the house, Justine stayed outside in the vehicle, watching the solitary road that led from the highway into the neighborhood. The landscaping was limited to one drought-resistant willow tree per yard, and the streets were wide. No one would be able to sneak up on them. If anyone tried, Justine would be there to stop them.

As she entered the living room the first thing that struck

Ella was how exhausted Marie looked. The woman took a seat on the couch and invited Ella to do the same.

"How's your husband?" Ella asked, avoiding the use of a name. Although none of them here were Traditionalists, when someone's life was so precariously balanced it seemed far better not to take any chances.

"No change. Those doctors . . . ," she said, shaking her head slowly. "You can ask them a direct question, but they never give you a straight answer."

"Maybe they have none to give you. They have to wait, too," Ella said gently.

"That's why I came to see your brother," she said. "As soon as I get what I came for, I'll go back to my husband's side."

"I've arranged for him to bring the medicine bundle to you here."

"Good. My husband needs help. Anglo medicine isn't working," Marie said. "Sometimes the old ways can do things no one can explain, but there's never any arguing with the results."

"I know," Ella answered. On the Rez she'd often seen things that defied logic.

"We need to restore his *hózhó*. He can't get well until that's done," Marie said. "I'm a Modernist and a Christian, but sometimes the old ways call to us." She touched the wedding ring on her finger, stroking it lightly with her right hand. "Now I understand what my husband has been saying all along."

"And what's that?" Ella asked her.

"What saw him through the toughest battles was respecting the connection between all things, and knowing that man's greatest responsibility is to walk in beauty. That eventually led him to become a New Traditionalist."

"How did the Prickly Weed Project fit in with his new views?" Ella asked.

"He thought it was the perfect blend of harmony and balance. But then things changed. He wouldn't go into it, but I got the idea that there was some problem involving money. Maybe it had to do with funding for the project. I don't know."

"Did he ever mention receiving, or expecting to receive, a large sum of money for his work?"

Marie shook her head. "No, in fact, it was the opposite. He called me from his hotel room to tell me he would probably be losing his job, but I shouldn't worry. He said that if he did, he'd find something else and asked me to trust him." Then she added, "He didn't have to ask. I do—and always have—trusted him."

Hearing a vehicle pulling up outside, Ella glanced over at Blalock, who was looking out the window.

"It's your brother," Blalock said looking back at her.

Clifford came in a minute later, walking with measured, purposeful strides. He was a shade taller than Ella, lean, and carried the faint scent of piñon smoke on his jeans and cotton shirt. Right now he was also wearing the white headband that marked him as a *hataalii*.

"I wasn't followed," he told Ella and Blalock. "I made very sure of that."

Trying to tail her brother was nearly impossible. She'd tried it herself several times, not only in vehicles, but on foot, and all her training and expertise had amounted to nothing more than a waste of time. If he hadn't chosen the path of a medicine man, Clifford could have been a fearsome warrior.

Clifford then focused solely on Marie. "I've brought you a very special medicine bundle. The collected substances inside it are ones that repel evil and attract good," he said, handing her a small leather pouch. "It also contains something extra—a small, carved flint shield. Flint is very powerful because it emits a light that frightens evil away. Keep this bundle with the one still unable to protect himself."

Marie thanked him, and as she reached for her purse, Clifford shook his head. "No. Later. *After* the work is done."

"I didn't tell you who it was for, but you already know, don't you?" Marie asked, gazing at the bundle.

Clifford nodded. "The bundle will help him."

Ella walked back outside with Clifford, her gaze taking in the street and houses around them. The badger fetish around her neck felt cool. "It's vitally important that you keep this meeting a secret, brother."

"Done," he said. "You need to watch out for yourself, too, sister."

Ella searched Clifford's face for any indication, however minute, that he knew Kevin was at her house—and only a few miles from his own. If he did, he gave her no sign of it.

"I've been meaning to ask you," she said, diverting him. "How do you feel about the Prickly Weed Project?"

"The tribe needs money, and putting our agricultural land to better use is a good idea. The key is balance. Until the project is well underway, we need to make sure our people don't rely on it."

As usual, her brother made perfect sense. "Watch your back and keep a close eye on your home and family. This case is . . . complicated," she warned, knowing he'd fill in the blanks.

Ella watched her brother drive away in his old pickup, then went to check with Justine. Her partner quickly assured her that no other vehicles had entered the development, and no curious neighbors had stepped outside for a look.

Reassured, Ella walked back into the house. Marie was ready to go, so they loaded two large laundry bags filled with clothing into Blalock's car in case they needed to back up their cover story. Shortly afterwards, Marie and Blalock set out, heading west.

Ella and Justine followed them until they reached the airfield road, making sure they didn't pick up a tail. Once

Blalock turned east of the main highway. Ella looked over at Justine. "Keep heading south, I need to stop by my mother's house."

The drive took less than ten minutes. When they arrived, Ella left Justine in the kitchen, greeted Teeny's man, and went to look in on Kevin. She found him convalescing in bed and playing a video game with Dawn. Ella stood just outside the doorway and watched them for a while, unnoticed.

"They've been like that since she got home from school," Rose whispered, coming up behind her.

"Let's leave them to it," Ella said softly, then slipped back down the hall with Rose. "Mom, I need to ask you something," she said as soon as they reached the living room. "I understand that there's some trouble brewing with the Traditionalists and the Modernists concerning the Prickly Weed Project. What do you know about that?"

"Daughter, I've been so busy I didn't realize how bad it really was—not until I learned that *chiishch'ilí* was attacked earlier today," she said using the nickname she'd given Abigail Yellowhair. It meant the one with curly hair, and referred to Abigail's frequent perms.

"Have you—"

Before Ella could say more, Dawn came out of her room and ran down the hall toward them. "Mom, I thought I heard you!"

Ella gave her a hug. "I can't stay. I just stopped by to talk to your grandmother and I'll also need to talk to your father privately for a few minutes. Why don't you get yourself a snack in the kitchen while I'm doing that?"

"I made some of your favorite piñon nut chocolate cookies," Rose added.

Dawn, whose appetite was never really satisfied, dashed off into the kitchen.

"I'll keep her busy, daughter. Do what you have to do."

Nodding to Mack Kelewood, who was standing next to the window and looking at the rear of the property, Ella went back into her daughter's room.

Kevin was propped up against the pillows, using their daughter's laptop. As Ella stepped closer, she saw that he was working on a text file. She knew he backed up nonsensitive files on a secure Web site, easily downloaded. Kevin was as addicted to his work as she was to hers.

Kevin smiled at her. "I thought we'd heard you out there."

Ella sat down on the edge of the bed. "I needed to talk to Mom, and figured I'd see how things were going here, too."

"Dawn's been keeping me company since she got home from school." He sagged back against the pillows.

Ella suddenly realized how tired he really was. "Don't let our daughter wear you out."

"She's not. If anything, she's the high point of my day. It feels really good to be able to spend some uninterrupted time with her."

"Dawn's really something, isn't she?" Ella asked with a gentle smile. "She can drive you crazy, but there's just something about her that wraps itself around you."

Kevin reached for Ella's hand. "You took a chance bringing me here, Ella. I'll never be able to repay you for that, or for the extra time I'll be able to spend with our daughter.

"So tell me, what brought you back home this time of day?" he added.

"I want to ask you a question about Adam," she said, relieved to get back to business. "In your opinion, how likely is it that he might have accepted a bribe?"

"No chance," he said flatly. "Let me tell you something about Adam. If there's such a thing as a completely honest man, Adam's it. As I've told him from time to time, he has almost too much integrity to work in the nation's capital," Kevin added with a wink.

Ella noted that he'd referred to Adam in the present tense, but decided not to let it slow her down. "Is it possible that he could have been convinced, or tricked into carrying an illegal bribe to someone here on the Rez, maybe in connection to the Prickly Weed Project?"

"The thing is, Ella, there's no one here who needs to be bribed. The majority want the deal to go through with IFT. What you found can't be linked to something like that."

"All right. Thanks." Ella stood. "Time for me to get back into the field."

"How did the Reverend take the news that I'm here?"

Ella stopped at the door and glanced back. "I don't know. I haven't told him."

As she walked down the hall, she heard him chuckle. Annoyed—with herself and him—she met Justine and cocked her head toward the door. "Let's go."

They were in the car heading toward the highway moments later. "Where to next, partner?" Justine asked.

"I want to talk to Emerson Lee. I need to find out if he considered Adam Lonewolf his enemy."

Even before they reached Shiprock, which was along the route, Ella grew aware of the odd, surreptitious glances Justine kept giving her. "What's on your mind?" Ella asked her.

"I still want to know about you and that job in D.C. We've had so many people leave our department in the past few years. We need you here more than ever."

"Seriously, I haven't had much of a chance to think much about it. I've had too much other stuff coming at me."

Justine nodded.

"You'll get the bug eventually, partner. Whether you'll actually go through with it like I did, that's another matter. Ever consider leaving for a job, say, at the sheriff's department, like your roommate Marianne? Or maybe the FBI?"

"I suppose it could happen. I've spent my whole life in Shiprock, Ella," Justine added softly. "Maybe I *should* see more of the country, like you did out of high school. The older I get, the less likely I am to invite change."

"I didn't mean to put ideas in your head, Justine, but here's a piece of advice, for what it's worth. If you ever decide on a career change, know what you're looking for before you set out after it," Ella said in a thoughtful voice. "Sometimes when our goals are vague—when we're searching for something we can't define—we end up someplace we never intended to be. I was running from something when I left the Rez, not toward anything, and that was a mistake. Don't do what I did."

They arrived at Emerson Lee's place forty minutes later. To the south and east lay the irrigated fields of the Navajo Irrigation project. No vehicles were visible around the main building, but Justine gestured to a *casita* by the rear of the property at the end of a narrow lane bordered by stunted Russian olives. "Emerson is supposed to live back there."

"Park in the driveway and we'll walk up," Ella said.

As they climbed out about twenty feet from the main house, Ella suddenly felt a ripple of unease. "On second thought, let's wait here until he invites us up. That little courtesy might make things easier in the long run."

Ella moved into the shade the trees offered, ready to wait, when she heard a window being opened. Glancing back, she suddenly saw the barrel of a rifle being shoved out the opening.

"Gun!" she yelled.

As she and Justine dove to the gravel, a bullet whistled by, striking something solid several feet behind them.

"Get your butts off my land," Emerson's voice called out. "Screw your promises about tribal industries. You want this land? You'll have to kill me first!"

EIGHTEEN

— ✕ ✕ ✕ —

Ella glanced around for Justine and saw her crawling into a low ditch that ran along the row of trees on the right side of the road. "You okay?" she called out.

"Yeah," came the answer.

Ella studied the house, looking over the sights of her service pistol. The barrel of the rifle was no longer visible at the window. "Mr. Lee, this is Ella Clah of the Tribal Police. Put your weapon down and come out with your hands up."

"Huh?"

Ella repeated herself, this time even louder.

"Okay, hold on." Emerson came out seconds later, squinting and holding his hand over his eyes to shield them from the setting sun.

Ella and Justine came out from behind cover, holding their weapons by their sides, but ready for anything.

"Hey, I remember you two ladies. You can put away your guns. I left the rifle on the table inside. It's empty now. I'm out of bullets," he said.

Once in the shade of the tree-lined path, he stopped and waited as they drew near. "I can't hit anything, you know—I'm old and have the shakes," he said in an apologetic tone.

"*Why* did you shoot at us?" Ella demanded, motioning for Justine to check out the *casita*.

"I thought you were that squatter, Billy Garnenez, and his coyote pal, Alfred Begaye. If I'd known it was you, the medicine man's sister, I wouldn't have fired. I wouldn't want to make the *hataalii* angry. He's helped me and my family a lot."

"I'm arresting you for assaulting a police officer," Ella said, reaching for her cuffs as she informed him of his rights. "You're not allowed to shoot at people whenever you please." Ella led him, cuffed, to their vehicle, and placed him in the backseat.

Justine, who'd returned from the guest house, took her aside and showed her Emerson's rifle, which she was carrying in her gloved hand. "It's empty now, like he said. He only had one round in it." She held out the empty thirty-thirty shell casing.

"We're still taking him in for assault on an officer," Ella said.

"Are you sure that's a good idea?" Justine asked, dropping her voice to a barely audible whisper. "That's bound to stir things up even more. His supporters will say that the police are siding with the Modernists on the land issue."

"Too bad. We can't allow Emerson to take potshots at whomever he pleases," Ella said. "While we're at it, let's also check on his whereabouts when Abigail was attacked."

They returned to the station, and while Justine booked Emerson, Ella returned to her office. Before she'd even taken a seat, Joe Neskahi walked in.

"I've got some news you'll want to hear. Several tribal businessmen here on the Rez have banded together on behalf of the Prickly Weed Project. They're organizing a big push, urging the tribe to take whatever unused land is needed from Emerson Lee and his daughter. They want the project in gear by next year's growing season," Joe said. "Lee and his clan are getting ready to meet them head-on at the next East Fruit-land Chapter House meeting."

She knew the location of that particular chapter house—less than ten miles from the Lee-Morgan residences. "When's that taking place?"

"Tonight," he said, giving her the time.

"Are you sure they're meeting that soon?"

"Both sides wanted the matter brought up as quickly as possible. From what I've heard here and there, there's going to be an all-out war."

"Thanks for the heads-up, Joe. I'm going to let Emerson cool his heels for a bit then see what I can learn from him."

"You got him here?" he asked, surprised.

Ella told him about the incident and Joe whistled low. "He comes across as a crazy old coot, Ella, but just so you know, I've heard he can make a lot of sense when he wants to."

"Then it's all an act?"

"So I've heard," Joe answered. "Just think about that shot he took at you. With the right spin he can get a lot of mileage out of that. Norm Hattery's already outside, ready to pounce on you and Justine, and pushing to interview Lee."

"How did Hattery find out about it so quickly?" Ella asked. "Nobody except Lee, Justine, and I were there."

"Emerson called him—that was his one call. Sounds like you and Justine were set up."

She'd been played, but the game wasn't over. "Thanks, Joe."

Ella walked down to the interview rooms and met Justine by the closed door. They could see Emerson inside, sitting alone in front of the bolted-down table. He was killing time cleaning his fingernails.

Stepping away from the interview room door, Ella updated Justine, adding, "Did you check Emerson's whereabouts when the incident at Abigail's went down?"

"Yeah, and his alibi is rock solid. Emerson went with his son-in-law and daughter to a prayer meeting at The Good Shepherd."

"Ford's church?" She stared at her partner for a second. "You're kidding."

"Nope. Chester's a member, and he takes his wife and father-in-law with him to church from time to time."

Before Ella could process it, someone entering the hall called out her name.

"Special Investigator Clah!"

She didn't have to turn around to know who it was. "Shoot me now," Ella muttered, closing her eyes for a moment, then opening them again.

Norm Hattery caught up to them a second later. "I hear that you've arrested Emerson Lee. What are the charges?"

"Assaulting an officer," Ella said. "And you're not allowed in this part of the station without an escort, Mr. Hattery."

"I'm with you right now. Getting back to my question, I've heard that he was trying to run off a coyote and you just happened to be in the area," he countered.

"You've been lied to, and you should be careful about reporting a false statement as factual," Ella snapped, walking away from the interview rooms, knowing he'd follow.

"Where do you stand on the Prickly Weed Project issue?" he asked, undeterred. "And do you think what happened today is connected to the shooting that cost Adam Lonewolf his life?"

"At this point, I can't say one way or the other," Ella answered through her teeth. "And you need to leave this area *now*. Otherwise, I'm going to have you escorted out of the station."

"About Adam Lonewolf—"

Ella held up one hand. "I have work to do. Excuse me." Without giving him the chance to say another word, she held a side door open for Hattery, then urged him out. Once he was gone, Justine and she went back down the restricted corridor to the interview rooms.

As they stepped into the mirrored room, Emerson grinned widely. "Good seeing you again, ladies."

Ella sat across the table from him, and seeing the look on his face, realized she'd been played all the way back to the episode at the parking lot involving Begaye's sedan. "You made a big mistake taking that shot at us," she said, her unwavering gaze on him.

"It *was* a mistake. I'd never shoot at people. I was trying to chase away a coyote."

Ella glared at him. "That's not what you said before."

"You obviously misunderstood me," he said with a ghost of a smile. "When do I get my attorney?" he added. "That's in all the police shows on TV, and when you told me about my rights, you said I could have one if I wanted. So I'm asking. I'd like a lawyer."

"I can take you to a telephone, or have a clerk make the call for you. Who's your attorney?" Ella asked him in an ice cold voice.

"I don't have one yet. I haven't got any money, just my Social Security check, so the tribe will have to pay for the lawyer. But he better be a good one. I have a lot of relatives and they'll be watching over me."

"The tribe will provide you with an attorney," Ella said, and as she stood to leave, Emerson continued.

"I'm not your enemy, you know. I'm trying to protect all of us. Every time Anglo industries come here, the land—and us—pay the price in contaminated soil, water, or air. Think about it. How many years did the *bilagáanas* spend among us before we discovered that their uranium tailings were killing The People?"

"The Prickly Weed Project isn't like that," Justine said.

"You're not thinking far enough ahead. Just wait until

they decide that the weed doesn't grow fast enough, or doesn't have enough of whatever they want it to have. Then they'll start adding things to the water, or the soil, or maybe use sprays on it. That'll continue until they get tired of what they're doing here. Once that happens, they'll take off, and we'll be the ones who have to cope with the mess they leave behind. If we don't learn from the past, we'll keep repeating the same mistakes over and over again."

There was no trace of the crazy old man they'd met before. Ella regarded him thoughtfully for a long moment. "You took a shot at me and my partner," she repeated. "Why?"

"No, it's like I told you, I was trying to run off some coyotes," he replied with a grin. "And you weren't hurt."

Ella swallowed her anger and in a calm voice continued. "How do you feel about the war hero, particularly since he was fighting for the Prickly Weed Project?"

Emerson took a deep breath. "He risked his life for our tribe and our country, and that's worthy of respect. But somewhere along the way he forgot he's not a *bilagáana*."

"So you considered him your enemy?" Justine pressed.

Emerson didn't answer right away. "An enemy is someone who purposely tries to hurt you knowing the consequences of his actions. That wasn't the case with the hero. He just didn't realize the real cost of what he was trying to sell."

"The cost to himself, you mean?" Ella asked leaning forward and resting her elbows on the table.

"I didn't know that someone was going to shoot him, if that's what you're really asking me. But he was involved in something that affects, or will affect, a lot of people. Actions like his always have consequences."

"Who do you think may have wanted him dead?" Ella asked.

"No one in my clan," he answered firmly. "Ours isn't that kind of fight. What happened to him . . . it had to do with something else. That's what I think."

Ella stood up and signaled Justine to follow. They were passing through the lobby moments later when Norm Hattery rose from one of the chairs and joined them.

Ella felt her muscles tense. "What can we do for you now?"

He shook his head. "It's what I can do for you," he countered smoothly. "Just so you know I'm not working against the police, I'm going to pass along a tip. The Salt People Clan pulled a lot of strings and managed to get Judge Goodluck for the arraignment this afternoon. Court will convene in an hour. And you better hang on to your hat, because Lee's clan, the Salt People, are coming out in full force. There's a rumor that they've even managed to get Reverend Tome to speak on behalf of the defendant."

"When did all this happen?" Ella asked him.

"Almost as soon as you arrested him. And here's another heads-up. You questioned Lee before an attorney was present, and that's going to cost you."

"I read him his rights, and he waived representation at that time. Where are you getting your information?" Ella demanded.

"My sources are confidential, but I'll be happy to pass on information you might find useful if you agree to reciprocate. You could start by telling me what you think happened to Adam Lonewolf. Who wanted him dead?"

"I won't comment on an ongoing investigation," Ella growled, nodding to the duty officer and motioning toward the door.

While Hattery was being escorted from the building, Ella and Justine walked down to Ella's office. "I underestimated Emerson badly. He's one crafty old man," Ella said, shutting the door behind them. "I need to start carrying a recorder again for times like this."

"I still do, so we can prove you read him his rights, and

he waived counsel, if it comes to that," Justine said, pointing to the small device in her shirt pocket.

"Good. Now, what do you think we'll be facing at this arraignment?"

"Grandpa G's a New Traditionalist who believes our land is a living entity with rights, and that The People are its caretakers. When he hears that the Salt People Clan are trying to protect our Earth Mother, there's no telling how he'll rule."

"This arraignment isn't about the land, or a cause. It's about someone taking a shot at two law enforcement officers."

"Yeah, you're right, but there are other factors—"

Hearing a knock at her door, Ella went to open it. Her boss, Big Ed, was standing there.

"We have a crowd of about sixty outside," he said. "They're holding up signs that read things like 'Save the Land' and 'Begaye=Betray.' There are even a few with the ever-popular 'Police Brutality,' " he added sarcastically. "Hattery's out there, too, getting quotes from anyone with a pulse. Camera crews are rumored to be on the way."

"Wonderful," Ella muttered.

"Reverend Tome arrived about five minutes ago. He's trying to keep people calm," Big Ed added.

"Is it working?" Justine asked.

"Not from what I can see. The demonstrators are trying to provoke a confrontation with the police so they can use it to publicize their cause."

Hearing another knock at her door, Ella looked up and was surprised to see Ford standing there.

"Things are getting really tense out in the parking lot, and the situation is going to get out of hand real soon unless someone in authority goes to speak to the crowd," he said as he entered the room. "Trina Morgan made an impassioned speech saying that this is a classic example of big government taking away the rights—and property—of the working class. She's got her people fired up."

"What could we possibly say to them that would diffuse this now?" Ella asked, running an exasperated hand through her hair.

"Insist that Emerson's arrest has nothing to do with the land issue. Emerson fired on two police officers, that's against the law, and he needs to answer for that in court," Ford said.

"Do you think that'll calm them?" Big Ed asked, his doubts reflected clearly in his voice.

"It'll help settle people down some," Ford said. "But I've got a feeling that crowd's going to stay right where it is until Emerson's released on bail."

"He's facing a serious charge," Justine said. "He may not get bail."

"He will," Ford said. "They have a string of people—including me—who'll vouch for his character. Emerson's many things, but he's not a murderer."

"*You* think it's okay for an old man with questionable eyesight to fire a high-powered rifle at two police officers?" Ella demanded, her eyes shooting daggers at Ford. "Just what makes that okay? The fact that he was hoping to miss? That bullet came real close to us."

"What he did was dangerous and stupid, but he wasn't out to hurt anyone," Ford said, his voice purposely soft and low. "A little forgiveness could restore some calm, and that's badly needed now."

"You're being manipulated. He's not the crazy old man he pretends to be. Are you aware of that?" Ella countered.

"I know. He mostly plays the part because it buys him some leeway. People don't expect much from an elderly man they believe has the beginnings of dementia," Ford answered.

"But here's the thing—it's not completely an act. He has his crazy moments. You've seen that yourself."

"Then what makes you so sure he's not capable of murder?" Big Ed countered.

"I trust my instincts. In my current line of work—and my previous one—I developed the ability to read people accurately, and I'm good at it." As he spoke, he looked directly at Ella.

He held her gaze and something in his eyes made Ella wonder if he knew about Kevin, but this wasn't the time to probe.

"Emerson's a sad, simple man," Ford continued. "Before the tribe made it clear they wanted to take away most of his daughter's land, he'd led a quiet life. He was content with his tiny garden and the couple of fruit trees there. He had all he wanted and was coasting through the final years of his life. Then the tribe stepped in and everything changed. His wife's land was the only important thing either of them ever had to leave to Trina. That's why he decided to fight back. He figured that if his clan could make enough noise, the politicians would feel the weight of public pressure and rethink their positions."

"So that's why he took a shot at us?" Justine asked. "For the publicity?"

"Yes, I'm convinced of it," Ford answered. "Look at the gathering outside. Do you know it's going to hit the national news?"

Ella sighed. "Just what we need, right in the middle of our most public case in years."

"At the last chapter house meeting the Morgans and Garnenez were told to work out an agreement between themselves," Ford said. "But the Morgans refused to meet with Billy. They wanted to push this issue out into the open and create as much controversy as possible."

"I'll go talk to the crowd, but nobody takes a shot at my officers and gets a free pass," Big Ed said.

Once Big Ed left, Ella glanced at Ford. "Do the Morgans want you at the chapter house meeting?"

"No, just the opposite. They're hoping it gets out of hand, which could bring in even more support from across the Navajo Nation. Either way, it's going to provide a lot of fodder for the regional press and media."

Ford went back outside but, knowing that dealing with the media wasn't what she did best, Ella remained in her office.

For the next thirty minutes, she worked on gathering background information on all the people associated with the Prickly Weed Project. Frustrated by her slow progress, she finally leaned back in her chair and rubbed her aching neck.

The problem with this case was that it crossed lines between personal and business. Ella thought of Kevin back at her home, then about Ford, here in the center of the conflict. Both men were a part of her life and each wanted her—but only on their own terms.

As Justine walked in, Ella brought her focus back onto the case. "The arraignment's been moved up again and it will start in another twenty," Justine said. "The crowd out front is heading to the courthouse. You ready to go over there, too?"

Ella let her breath out in a hiss. "No, but we better get going anyway."

"Do you want to enter the courthouse through the back?"

Ella shook her head. "The prisoner, in this case Emerson, will be brought in that way because it's the most direct route. I'll bet you dollars to doughnuts that the crowd and the reporters will all be there. You and I should go in through the front."

Less than five minutes later they arrived at the courthouse, and as Ella had predicted, the crowd had gathered out back. Ella and Justine left the SUV and strode quickly to the front entrance.

Suddenly Norm Hattery came out the door, mike in hand and cameraman beside him. "Special Investigator Clah, do you think Mr. Lee should be shown leniency by the court because of extenuating circumstances?"

"Mr. Lee fired at two tribal police officers with a hunting rifle. The court will decide what to do about the charges."

"But how do *you* feel about it?"

"My job is to arrest anyone who breaks the law, and that's what I've done. The legal system will decide what to do next."

"Meaning that if the court lets the accused back out onto the streets, it's not your fault?"

She stopped in mid-stride and faced him squarely. "Mr. Hattery, do *not* put words in my mouth. I told you exactly what I meant."

Not giving him a chance to come back at her, Ella pushed her way past him and into the building.

"Phew," Justine muttered. "For a minute or two I thought you were going to shove the microphone up his—you know what."

"I considered it," Ella grumbled.

"We better hurry," Justine said, gesturing ahead. "Court's about to go into session."

Ella and Justine sat in the last row and stood as Judge Goodluck entered the courtroom. Seconds later as they sat back down, Ella glanced over to the defendant's table and saw Emerson Lee's attorney for the first time.

Martin Tallman, called "the hammerhead" for his wide, flat forehead and his shark-like demeanor, sat beside the defendant. Tallman, a young, ambitious attorney, always made it a point to get involved with cases that brought him publicity.

This case was practically made to order for him, so she had no doubt that he'd volunteered his services.

As the proceedings got underway, the charges were read and Judge Goodluck looked at the defendant. "How do you plead?"

Tallman stood. "Not guilty, Your Honor."

Judge Goodluck's gaze took in the crowded courtroom, then focused back on the defendant. "Mr. Lee, do you understand the charges against you?"

Emerson stood up then and, oblivious to his attorney, spoke. "Your Honor, I'm sorry. I had no idea it was illegal now to shoot at coyotes."

"Do you have a hearing problem, Mr. Lee? You're charged with shooting at two tribal police officers, not coyotes."

"That's not what happened, Judge. The officers stepped in the way after I'd taken aim at that danged coyote. He's been hunting my daughter's sheep."

Tallman stood. "Your Honor, this is clearly a misunderstanding. We're asking that you dismiss the charges."

"I have no patience for games, Counselor," Judge Goodluck said. "You'll have the opportunity to present your defense during trial. The clerk will set the date for the hearing." He paused for a moment, then continued. "Since Mr. Lee has long ties to the community and no criminal record, I'm going to set bail in the amount of two thousand dollars—cash only."

Outside the Rez this would have seemed ridiculously low, but on the Rez it was a princely sum. Ella glanced at Justine, who shrugged and shook her head.

"But I'm going to set down some additional conditions, Mr. Lee. If you wish to avoid having your bail revoked, you must attend tonight's East Fruitland Chapter House meeting. You'll discuss the issues peacefully and in good faith, and reach an agreement with the tribe concerning the land issues currently under consideration. This has gone on for too long." Judge Goodluck glanced around the courtroom and his gaze fastened on Ford. "Reverend Tome, I'd like you to serve as chairman throughout the land issue segment of that meeting. Your job would be to maintain an orderly discussion. Will you agree to this?"

"I'll be there, Your Honor," Ford answered.

Tallman shot to his feet. "I will personally provide bail for my client, Your Honor, but I want to officially protest. These conditions have nothing to do with the shooting incident."

"Noted, but it's at the root of what happened. My decision stands," Judge Goodluck said, then tapped the desk with his gavel, signaling an end to the proceedings. "Next case."

Ella ducked out with Justine as quickly as possible. There'd be a lot of grandstanding outside the courthouse next, and she wanted to be long gone when it started. Ella had one hand on the exit door when Ford caught up to her.

"Can I assume you'll be at the chapter house tonight?" he asked, placing his hand on her arm.

"Count on it," she said.

As others hurried over, Ella slipped out quickly. Ford would excel at the job Judge Goodluck had given him. Though he'd be sitting on a powder keg, the role of peacemaker would appeal immensely to his Christian side.

Ella was just getting into the SUV when her cell phone rang. She answered it and heard her daughter's excited voice.

"Mom, *Shimasání* said I should call you. Someone's putting signs up on the road leading up to our house. The person's still about a mile away, but moving in our direction."

"Where is your *shimasání* now? Can you take the phone to her?"

"Okay, but she's talking to Mr. Kelewood. He's watching the door."

Moments later, Ella heard her mother's voice. "Daughter, I wanted to go down the road and see what the signs say, but the man guarding the house won't let me go outside."

"He's right. Listen to him and keep everyone, particularly my child's father, away from the windows. I'm on my way," Ella said, then added, "How did you find out about the signs?"

"Your brother and his son were out horseback riding and saw a woman putting them up, so he called right away and spoke to the guard."

"Step on it, partner," Ella said, hanging up and filling Justine in.

"Did you tell Clifford that Kevin was staying at your house?" Justine asked.

"No, but my guess is that he's been keeping an eye on Mom since the Prickly Weed Project began to make enemies. Considering how observant my brother is, he undoubtedly noticed the differences in behavior at the house, like the closed curtains during the day, and put things together on his own."

"Closed curtains won't give anything away to those who don't know you or your mom, but maybe you should make sure that Rose and Herman act as normal as possible and keep to their routines."

"You're right. I'll talk to them. But right now let's go see what's going on."

NINETEEN

——✕ ✕ ✕——

As they turned off Highway 491 and raced toward her house, Ella saw the first of many signs stuck beside the roadside. The message, product of a computer printer, read TRAITOR TO THE *DINÉ*.

"Guess we know where that comes from. Emerson's friends move fast," Justine said. "Want to stop and pull it up?"

"Not yet. First I'm going to nail whoever's doing this. And there she is," Ella added, pointing.

About a quarter mile ahead someone standing next to a late-model silver pickup was hammering yet another sign into the ground. They passed two more signs, identical to the first, as they approached the middle-aged Navajo woman doing the work.

Justine pulled up behind her and parked. Having heard them coming—no other vehicles were on the private road— the woman straightened her long, traditional-style skirt and glared at Justine and Ella as they got out.

"You know who I am." Ella held up her badge.

"Yes, I know you. You arrested my father's second cousin. My name's Kate Lee. I suppose you want to arrest me, too?" She set down the hammer and held out her hands to be handcuffed.

From her gesture Ella realized that it was exactly what she was hoping would happen. Ella shook her head. "No, we're not taking you in, but you're going to remove the signs, then go home."

"Nothing doing. The signs stay, and I'm going to keep hammering them into the ground all the way to your house. So you gonna arrest me now?"

"No," Ella said flatly. "But the signs *are* going to be taken down. If *you* do it, you can keep them. If I have to do it, then they're mine to use as kindling this fall. Either way, you're trespassing on my mother's land and you're leaving."

"I'm not going anywhere. I have more signs to put up," Kate countered stubbornly.

"Not anymore." Ella yanked out the sign Kate had been hammering into the ground, broke the stake in half with her knee, then tossed the two pieces into the backseat of the SUV.

"You can't do that. You were supposed—" Kate suddenly grew silent.

Ella shook her head. "I'm *not* going to arrest you, so if you're looking to grandstand for your relatives, you're out of luck."

Kate walked over to the bed of her pickup, grabbed a sign, then walked toward Justine, cocking the sign back like a batter at home plate.

Justine slipped around to the other side of the truck, then snapped a photo of the woman with her cell phone camera.

"You're not going to hit one of us with those signs either. If you tried, we'd just take it away from you," Ella said. "Photos will also prove who was attacking whom, so don't plan on telling any lies about this."

"This isn't over. You haven't seen the last of us," Kate answered, and stormed back to her pickup, tossing the sign back in through the open window.

As Kate drove off in a huff toward the highway, Ella looked at Justine. "She doesn't know it, but she's just given me a brand new opportunity. So far I've been careful to keep Kevin's guards out of sight, not wanting to give away the fact that he's staying with us. But I don't have to worry about that anymore, given that we've had trespassers."

They removed the sign closest to the highway. Kate Lee had taken the others, but had deliberately left the one most visible from the main road. After that, they drove to the house. While Justine updated Mack Kelewood on Kate Lee and the possibility of continued problems with Emerson's relatives and supporters, Ella went to talk to Kevin.

As she stepped into the room she was surprised to see him struggling to put on a pair of pants, probably borrowed from Herman. None of his clothes were here. "What do you think you're doing?" she demanded.

"If people know where I am, I'm putting all of you in danger. No way that's happening. I'm going home."

"No you're not. Relax," she added, and explained about the signs and the apparent strategy of those backing Emerson Lee and his family.

Before Kevin could reply, Dawn came in. "I heard you talking, and Dad, if you're leaving, I'm going with you."

Ella stared at her daughter. "What on earth are you talking about?"

"Dad needs someone to take care of him, doesn't he?"

Kevin bit back a smile. "I appreciate the offer, Dawn. It shows a lot of courage, and I'm proud of you. But it's not necessary."

"I'm just a kid, Dad, but I can help you keep watch, and nobody will even notice I'm there. I'm small, and I can slip in and out of places more quietly than any adult. Mom and my uncle have taught me a lot about survival skills."

Ella was torn between overwhelming pride and a nearly paralyzing fear. "Your father is staying here and so are you," she said firmly. "There's no reason for him to leave, no one knows he's here. Let's just make sure it remains that way."

Dawn looked at Ella. "Don't try to keep things from me, Mom."

"I'm not. The person putting up those signs was hoping to make me angry so I'd do something stupid, but it had nothing to do with your father. Now go do your homework. You can bring your father dinner later."

"Okay," she answered with a smile.

As Dawn left, Ella glared at Kevin. "Did you think you could just leave, like checking out of a hotel? And what were you planning to do when Dawn found out?"

"I was hoping to get away before she noticed," he answered, spreading open his hands, palms up, in a gesture of total helplessness.

"Don't *ever* underestimate Dawn. But there's something I need to know right now. *How* were you planning to get away? I can't see you stealing a horse or Mom's car, and with that bad leg you can't get much further than the bathroom."

"I was going to call Mona Todea. She could sneak me out in her car."

"Your secretary?" Her voice rose and she took a breath before continuing. "And you didn't think anyone would see her arrive, or you leaving with her? There are armed guards in and around this house who are watching *everyone*."

"Give me some credit. I had all that covered. I was thinking that Mona could bring a wig and a loose dress. I'd intended on wearing a disguise."

"Mona is six inches shorter than you, and doesn't walk with a limp, and you'd never be able to pass yourself off as my mom—or get past the guards. Did you honestly think that Mack would have fallen for that?"

"Legally, he can't keep me here," he said, then grinned. "I'm an attorney. I know these things."

Ella stared at the floor, trying to control her temper as she paced.

"What?" he insisted. "Dawn wouldn't have come with me. I would have stopped her."

"You hope. She's a sharp kid, and like she told you, kids can sneak by an adult who's not looking for them. And let me tell you something else. From the moment she noticed you were gone, I wouldn't have been able to even let her go to school, because she would have taken off looking for you the second her teacher's back was turned." She stopped pacing and faced him. "If you ever pull a stunt like this again, Kevin, I swear I'll shoot you myself."

Just as Ella finished speaking, Dawn stepped into the room. Instead of being upset, she looked at Ella, then at Kevin, and smiled broadly.

"What's so funny?" Ella demanded, annoyed.

"You two sound like those married couples on TV who love each other but still argue all the time."

"It's not like that," Ella answered.

"And it wasn't really an argument. Your mom's got a foul temper, that's all," Kevin said with a grin. "More like reality TV."

"Is that what you want? Reality?" Ella visualized Kevin on some remote island, thirsty and hungry, picking leeches off his neck. "Not that you could handle it."

"Mom, are you hungry? I made Dad some coconut cookies but there are some extras, if you want."

"Sure. That would be great," Ella said, mostly to get her daughter out of the room.

As Dawn went down the hallway, Ella focused back on Kevin. "You need to be a lot more careful around her. For some reason that escapes me, Dawn's convinced you're perfect."

"Little girls and their dads . . . it's a complex relationship."

Just then, Dawn came back into the room holding a plate stacked with cookies. "Here. We can all have some," she said, then proceeded to give her dad first pick.

Kevin looked at Ella, and although he struggled not to smile, lost the battle. "Thank you, daughter," he said, looking up at Dawn.

Ella took a cookie from the plate. "I've got to get back to work. Is there anything *else* I should know before I leave?"

Ella looked at Kevin, then at Dawn.

Avoiding her mother's gaze, Dawn glanced down at the floor.

"*Yesssss?*" Ella asked, stretching out the word.

"I want to learn how to shoot," Dawn said at last. "Guns, like the one you carry."

Ella stared at her daughter in stunned silence. "Why would you want to do that?" she asked, finding her voice at last. "There are plenty of people in this house who can fire a weapon if—heaven forbid—the need ever arose. There's absolutely *no* reason for you to get involved in anything like that."

"But I need to know how to defend myself and my family," Dawn insisted, a stubborn set to her chin.

"I can teach you how to protect yourself in a fight, and how to throw a punch, but using a firearm is an entirely different matter," Ella answered. "Guns are a last resort—always—and should never be used unless a life is at stake."

"But what if you or Dad were in trouble and depending on me?"

"If your dad and I were in danger, the best thing you could do is sneak away and get help," Ella said.

Dawn shook her head. "You wouldn't run and leave me behind, and neither would Dad. I won't do that either."

"Your mom wouldn't run, kiddo, but I sure would. I'm a lousy shot, but a *great* runner. Once I get better, I'll teach you to run like a deer. Or maybe a jackrabbit," Kevin said. "A quail?"

Kevin's answers were so outrageous, Ella burst out laughing.

Dawn laughed, too, then hugged Kevin. "Okay, Dad. We'll start running together—once your leg is okay."

Ella watched them, smiling. The men in her life seemed to hold nothing but surprises for her these days.

Later that night after dinner, Justine picked Ella up at the house. Considering that she had no idea what to expect at tonight's chapter house meeting, Ella was glad to have her partner's company on this particular trip.

As they pulled up to the plain stucco building, the Stars and Stripes were atop the center flagpole, and the red Zia of New Mexico to the right. The Navajo Nation flag was of equal stature to the left of center, symbolizing their culture through its rainbow and four sacred mountains.

As always, kids were playing outside, chasing each other and laughing with a joy most adults had long forgotten.

Ella noticed a table set up to the left of the main entrance. Draped over the top was a plain white cloth with the words *Ha'asídí*. So the "Watchmen" were here. The group of mostly Traditionalists stood against any unconventional agriculture or industry on the Rez. The Salt People Clan had found their perfect ally. The group was currently busy handing out pamphlets calling for the promotion of weaving, smithing, herding, organic farming, and other similar activities on the Rez.

The space next to the building normally reserved for the tribal police was occupied by an old pickup, so Justine was forced to park some distance away. As they exited their vehicle Ella spotted Frieda Beard standing on the front steps, waiting near the crowded door for her opportunity to enter. The professor was all dressed up, wearing a long skirt, satin blouse, and a gorgeous squash blossom necklace that looked like it had been in her family for generations. Considering why she was here, dressing traditionally had been a nice, wise touch.

As they approached the porch—really just a concrete slab under a sloping metal roof—Justine pointed ahead with her lips. "There's Billy. That suit he's wearing must have set him back some."

Ella glanced at the man. Despite its sheen, she doubted the western-cut suit was silk. Yet it was clearly well made and looked expensive. The silver bolo tie he'd chosen looked brand new.

As people continued to enter, Ella and Justine joined the crowd and went inside, choosing folding chairs in the last row close to the left corner so they'd have a clear look at the entire room with a turn of their heads. The chapter house was full tonight, and that meant late arrivals would be forced to stand at the rear or on the porch. Fire regulations required the center and outside aisles to be clear, and two uniformed tribal officers stood up front, their backs to the opposite walls. They provided an extra measure of security, being in a position to watch the faces of the crowd without seeming to support either position in the upcoming debate.

Lee, his family, and supporters had arrived early and sat on the right hand side, to the left of the speakers. The opposition was there, too, as evidenced by the many businessmen she recognized, most seated on the opposite side. The Prickly Weed Project would mean an increase in employment, and with more money to spend the economy would be fed from top to bottom. With the question of land use and permits certain to come up, too, select members of the grazing committees were also present, seated at a table to the left of center, facing the crowd. At least three different television stations had sent camera crews, but chapter house officials had, as in the past, forced them to take positions at

the rear of the room. There were, however, four microphones at the center podium.

As Ella's attention shifted to the right, she saw Ford,
seated at a second table with other officials she didn't recognize. He was studying his notes.

The head of the action committee, who'd been on Ford's
right, began the meeting by leading the pledge of allegiance.
While everyone was still standing, he recited a Navajo prayer
asking *Nilch'i Diyinii*, the Holy Spirit, to make everything
beautiful so the *Diné* could walk in peace and harmony.

Once finished, he glanced around the room and waited
for everyone to take their seats again. "As you all know, this
is a very special meeting. Tonight we have to bring together
two opposing sides of an issue that affects all of us, if not
now, then certainly in the future. In keeping with a request
made by tribal district Judge Goodluck, I'm turning things
over to Reverend Tome, co-minister of the Good Shepherd
Church in Shiprock."

There were a few boos when Judge Goodluck's name
was mentioned, but the dissenters were quickly hushed by
others in the crowd by the time Ford reached the podium.

"Good evening, friends. My clan is Bitter Water People
and I was born for the Black Sheep People," Ford said, introducing himself in the traditional way. Though his voice was
soft, it had a compelling quality that caused all eyes to shift
to him.

Ella smiled. She knew The Voice. Like her father's, it
would start low and gentle, then grow to earthquake propor-
tions, shaking even the mountains that surrounded the *Dinétah*. She'd only heard a couple of Ford's sermons, but they
were awesome.

"Representing the tribe's position on the issue before us
are two Navajos you all know," he said, waving his hand toward Billy Garnenez and Frieda Beard. "The family who occupies the land in question is also here," he said, gesturing

to Emerson Lee and his daughter. Ford grew silent for a moment, and in that silence, no one even stirred.

Ella smiled. Even without words, he had control of the room.

"I'll now ask the ones who occupy the land to speak," Ford said, then nodded to Emerson.

Ella watched Emerson Lee carefully, curious to see if he'd use his crazy old man act tonight. It took her only a few seconds to realize it would be just the opposite. As he stood and went to the podium she saw that there was a quiet dignity in the way he walked, allowing his daughter to steady him.

Emerson took his place behind the mike, looked at those gathered there, and in a strong voice began. "Before the Anglos came up with the idea of grazing permits, the land belonged to all of us. We honored the Earth Mother and she, in turn, took care of us. She fed our animals and they provided us with their meat and wool. The circle renewed itself and we walked in beauty. Now we depend on outsiders and their jobs to buy what we need. If we keep going down that road, we'll eventually forget who we are and lose everything that matters."

Trina, who'd stood beside him, spoke now. "Our elected officials represent us, not the other way around. Family traditions, our way of life, need to prevail. If we lose that, we'll lose ourselves. Then it won't only be the old ones who'll die of the ch'ééná, that sadness for what can't return. All of us will wake up one day, after it's too late, and see that the invisible line that separated us from the Anglo world has disappeared. We've become them, and they are us."

Ford stepped up as the small building went from utter silence to a thunderous round of applause.

"Those representing the tribe will now be given the opportunity to speak. Remember that, as Navajos, we're taught that *everything* has two sides. Honor our ways by listening to both."

The statement coming from Ford surprised her, but as she heard the ripple of assent that ran through the room, she knew that once again The Voice had struck a victory.

A new silence descended over the room as Frieda Beard stepped up to the podium.

"What has been said here today is all true," Frieda said, and a murmur of surprise went around the room. "The old ways define and sustain us. They *are* us." As she paused, all eyes were on her. "Using the land to grow plants that can bring jobs, and put food on our tables honors the Earth Mother. Everyone wins when we take a nuisance weed with little or no value and make it serve us on otherwise unproductive land. Unlike the mines, where we robbed from the earth, this allows us to work in harmony with it. Compromise on the issues—where all parties sacrifice just a little so that everyone wins—is within our reach tonight. Certainly land can be set aside for development without displacing a family, and the tribe is willing to guarantee such a solution. But in order to feed our children, provide for our elderly, and ensure the independence of our Navajo Nation, the *Diné* have to stay in step with the times. We need the dollars the Prickly Weed Project will provide."

Ella closed her eyes, then opened them again. Frieda had been doing great—especially with the hint of a compromise—till those last two sentences. Almost as her thought formed, a man on the front right of the crowd jumped to his feet.

"Compromise—just to feed the tribe's endless quest for money? I say no. Those dollars will take away more than they give us. If we don't hang on to the grazing land that feeds our livestock, we'll all go hungry."

Others began to shout in assent, drowning out Professor Beard as she tried to respond. Ford took the podium again, but the chaos that had already erupted was hard to control.

"Where are those cowards—Yellowhair and Begaye? Do

they think they're too good to listen to the voices of The People?" a woman in the front row shouted.

Ella looked between the heads in the way, but it was impossible for her to ID the person who'd just spoken, and she didn't recognize the voice.

Ford tried to calm the crowd, but his words were drowned out despite the speaker system. Suddenly he stuck both pinkies in his mouth and let out the shrillest cowboy whistle she'd ever heard. People covered their ears, cringing.

A moment later Ford smiled as he faced the gathering. "Now that I've got your attention . . ." As he took a breath, the man in the back began shouting again. Ford immediately demanded that he identify himself. When the man refused, Ford nodded to one of the uniformed officers up front, who responded by escorting the man out.

"We stand for balance and peace. If we forget that, we all lose," Ford said.

Billy came to the podium next and took the mike. "Friends, we need to face some hard facts. Most of our young people don't raise livestock anymore. It's hard to make a living farming these days. That's why our children leave the reservation in search of new lives and a way to support their families. The Prickly Weed Project can raise cash for scholarships and other services that'll nurture a better future for everyone on the *Dinétah*. We have to stop looking to the past for answers and move forward. That's the only way our tribe can continue to walk in beauty."

"We're becoming so much like the Anglos, our young people don't know who they are anymore. That's the real problem we're facing. Can't you see that?" a man shouted. When he refused to sit down, another officer escorted him out.

Billy continued. "The land in question doesn't support alfalfa, corn, or melons—only wild grasses and weeds. It wasn't until a week or two ago that sheep were brought in to graze there. The residents gave up their grazing permits years ago. Up until last month, two of the three current residents *left* the reservation every morning to go to their jobs—working *for* Anglos in the city. Tonight, they tried to tell you that they support the old ways, but they don't walk their talk. That proves they aren't part of the solution—they're part of the problem. A compromise is possible, yet they walk away, hands over their ears so not to listen to reason."

More shouts followed, and throwing his hands up in the air, Billy moved away from the podium.

Trina Morgan quickly stepped up to the microphone. "This is *not* the time for anger. Clear heads are needed, now more than ever."

For a moment or two Ella thought that Trina had reached them, but the man seated next to Emerson suddenly jumped up and yelled at Garnenez, calling him a liar and a traitor. Then a second man in the row behind him stood, trying to force Emerson's supporter to take a seat.

Ella wasn't sure who threw the first punch. All she knew was that in the blink of an eye, everything fell apart. People were pushing their way to the exit as cameras rolled and officers waded into the fray.

"We need to get Frieda and Billy out of here in one piece," Ella shouted to Justine. "There's an emergency exit on the south side of the room."

"We'll never make it to the podium," Justine said, trying to push forward through the crowd.

Before Ella could reply, someone hurled a folding chair at Ford. He ducked, deflecting it with his forearm. As it bounced away, it nearly struck Frieda, who'd come up behind him.

Taller than most, Ella fought her way through the throng. By the time she reached Frieda, who was trapped in a corner, Ella had nearly been knocked down twice. Refusing to let anything deter her, she grabbed Frieda's arm, took the lead, and worked a path toward the south exit, their backs to the wall.

Justine joined them, having located Billy, who'd been knocked to the floor and had a bloodied nose. As they reached the side door, one of the men who'd previously been escorted out suddenly appeared, blocking their way. Ella warned him to step aside, but instead of giving way, he pulled back his fist, ready to throw a punch.

Ford stepped past her in a heartbeat and grabbed the man's wrist, bending his elbow inward. As the man yelled in pain, Ford shoved him clear.

Ella smiled. The training Ford had received in his previous career sure came in handy sometimes. Within seconds, Justine, Ford, Ella, Frieda, and Billy were outside, moving into the parking lot.

"What now?" Frieda asked.

"We wait," Ford answered. "After the police regain control and remove everyone who's still resisting, we go back inside and finish what we came here for."

It took close to twenty minutes, but when they reentered the room, the mood had grown far more subdued. Judging solely by the size of the crowd that remained, one out of every three had either left or been arrested.

Ford, undaunted, took the podium again. "Now that both sides have been given the opportunity to speak, it's time to settle the issues." He turned to Emerson and Trina. "Keeping in mind the potential consequences, do you offer any suggestions or solutions to the question at hand? Will you talk to tribal representatives and work out a compromise?"

Looking at Garnenez, Emerson answered for both of them. "Our position hasn't changed. We won't give up a square foot of our land. We'll fight for what's rightfully ours."

"Then this matter will go to the tribal council, and if

necessary, the tribal courts," Billy said. "But be aware that the interests of the whole tribe carry more weight than the needs, or the wishes, of one or two families."

People stood, most of them shaking their heads sadly as they prepared to leave. Trina wiped at the tears that fell down her face. "You're taking our heritage."

Ella stood and walked toward the podium, her eyes on Trina and Emerson, then Billy. "If you won't discuss a compromise with the tribe, how about discussing one now with me, in front of the public, so that everyone knows what was said, and what's at stake?" she announced loudly, getting their attention. "I'll start with a suggestion I think is worth considering. What if the tribe cuts back on their own acreage request and leaves the family with a zone surrounding their current structures, including space for the garden and a few fruit trees? Maybe the tribe could also agree to put up a wall, or tree belt to give the families some privacy and buffer the noise."

Several in the departing crowd stopped, turning toward Ella and nodding or mumbling their agreement with the concept.

Trina glanced at Garnenez, the first sign of hope on her face. "That's already more than I would expect from the tribe. What about it, Mister Director?"

"Such a thing might work, but I can't approve any of that on my own. There are budget considerations to take into account, too. Let me talk to the others and study the site plans," he said. "There are legal hoops the tribe must jump through, but what Officer Clah suggests just might be within reach. I'll give you a call once we come up with a formal offer."

As Billy left, Ford walked over to Ella. "I'm glad you spoke up. People are stubborn sometimes, and it was clear that no compromise suggested by the 'enemy' was going to be considered. You and your family are very respected on this side of the Rez—even though you're a police officer, no offense. Our tribal attorneys could learn a thing or two from you."

Before Ella could figure out if he'd been alluding to Kevin in his own oblique way, Ford turned to speak to Dr. Beard.

Hearing the shout of a reporter, Ella turned back to the business at hand. Hattery was trying to interview the people who were leaving, his cameraman tailing along right behind him. Other reporters were clustered around Billy and the Morgans, like bees around honey. From the looks of it, this was going to be a very long night.

TWENTY

—— ✖ ✖ ✖ ——

The following morning Ella and Blalock sat in Big Ed's office. The chief looked tired and was a little short on patience.

"We still need answers, people. Last night's chapter house meeting is all over the news—including three network outlets in Albuquerque. Norm Hattery's article about Prickly Weed's possible link to the attack on Adam Lonewolf is enough to give me an ulcer. I've had calls from practically everyone in the tribal council, even the tribal president. Every last one of them is demanding to know if the connection between the shootings and the land issue is real. What's your theory, Shorty?"

"I just don't see a link between the two, Chief," Ella said. "Where's the motive? If anything, Begaye and Garnenez would have been more believable targets, not Adam."

"Have you reconsidered the possibility that they were aiming at the pilot, Pete Sanchez? Maybe we've misread this all along," Big Ed said, looking from Ella to Blalock.

Ella spoke first. "No, the men wearing business suits were the targets. I have no doubt about that. My guess is that O'Riley and Perry weren't sure who was who. Or maybe their employer ordered that the hit go down that way to confuse the issue. If so, it worked."

Blalock cleared his throat. "I've personally gone through casino security video searching for O'Riley and Perry. They're not there, so if they've got a link to Grady, it's not an obvious one. And I looked at their service records. From what I read, the two could follow orders, but neither of those men is the brightest bulb on the Christmas tree."

"*Someone* hired those hoods," Big Ed boomed out. "Any reports on what happened to O'Riley?"

"Every law enforcement agency within a thousand miles has been sent the most recent photo we have of him, but so far, nothing. He's gone to ground," Ella said. "We're working on this, Chief, but some things can't be rushed."

Big Ed ran a hand through his hair. "How's Adam doing?"

"I checked this morning, and he's regained consciousness, though he seems disoriented and is having problems communicating. He seems to recognize his wife and parents, but that's about the extent of his memory, at least so far. I've been told this is normal with brain injuries," Ella said.

"I've heard of cases like this before. His memory might take weeks, months, or even years to completely return," Blalock said. "Or it may never come back."

Big Ed steepled his fingers and stared at his hands, lost in thought. "So we're still on our own. There's another, newer complication that could also impact your investigation— particularly if the Prickly Weed connection is real. IFT has asked to survey the proposed land for the project. They need to plan utility installations and draw up more detailed designs— including the site modifications intended to protect the family living there now, if such a deal is eventually worked out. IFT has agreed to work well away from the Morgan house, but the fact that they're coming on the heels of what happened last night worries me. Opinions?"

"I agree that it's a bad idea, Chief," Ella said slowly.

"From what I understand, no discussion between the two parties has taken place, which means Emerson Lee and the Morgans haven't signed off on anything yet. This survey could create even more problems. The situation's too tense to move forward right now, at least not until a formal agreement is agreed upon."

"Do you think there'll be violence associated with it?" Big Ed asked Ella.

Ella considered it before replying. "It's a crapshoot. The family's bound to take offense if IFT makes an appearance, especially at this crucial moment. It shows a lack of respect."

"What would you recommend?" Big Ed asked.

"I would strongly advise IFT to do their planning completely off-site until tribal officials either act on a formal offer or get orders from the council to take over the property—assuming discussions fail to reach a compromise."

"All right. I'll pass that along to Begaye, Garnenez, and the others running that show."

Ella was about to say more when her cell phone vibrated. She'd intended to ignore it, but Big Ed's phone rang at the same time.

Big Ed picked up the receiver, and as he did, Ella glanced down at her own phone. Her call had come from the tribal government offices in town, only a few miles away. Before she could listen to the voice mail Big Ed looked up at her. "There's some trouble at Begaye's local office. Go see what's going on. You'll have details on your own voice mail."

Ella hurried down the hall with Blalock. "Anything from the Washington side of the investigation that might explain the money Adam was carrying?"

"No, and believe me, we've been looking under every rock."

"Let me take care of this problem at the tribal branch offices first. Afterwards, you and I should go to Albuquerque and pay Marie Lonewolf another visit. Maybe we can talk to

Adam and get some kind of response. With a little luck, we might be able to jog his memory and get a reaction."

"If the doctors allow it."

"It's worth a try, don't you think?" Ella asked.

He nodded. "I'll be ready to roll whenever you are."

Ella found Justine in the lab and, shortly thereafter, they left the station. As they headed down the highway she listened to her voice mail.

"What's going on?" Justine asked.

"Vandalism again. We'll get the details when we arrive."

Silence settled between them as Justine drove. Knowing her partner as well as she did, Ella could sense something was bothering her. "What's up, cuz?"

"Benny . . ."

"Mr. Romance! So what's been happening?"

"I like him, Ella—a lot. He came over to my house last night after that chapter house mess and cooked a late supper for me. He did all the work and wouldn't even let me lift a finger. The bad part was he can't cook. He burned everything and the smoke alarm went off from the trout he was cooking. We also had to clean up the stove when his 'special' sauce . . . shall we say, erupted? But he was trying so hard!"

"It sounds like a disaster," Ella said smiling, then, focusing back on business, opened her small notebook to check her notes.

"He makes me laugh, Ella, and that counts for a lot," Justine said, glancing over at her. "And dessert was fabulous. That man looks incredible without his shirt. And Ella, he doesn't wear underwear."

"Whoa! Too much information!" Ella said, looking up suddenly. "You realize that next time I look at him, that's what's going to pop into my head?"

Justine burst out laughing. "I was kidding! I just wanted to know if you were listening to me."

"I owe you one, partner. Remember that," Ella growled.

"But the dinner really was nice, Ella. The food was awful, but he's really sweet."

"And you're not, so like they say, there's balance in that," Ella answered with a chuckle.

Shiprock was a small town, so they arrived at the tribal offices less than five minutes later. As they walked into the front lobby, Alfred was there to meet them.

"It took you long enough to get here," he snapped.

"We came as soon as you called, and that was only about ten minutes ago, Councilman Begaye. Now what can we do for you?" Ella asked.

Billy came out of his office, halfway down the hall. "Finally! I left four messages for you. We're going to need more protection!"

"From what? Slow down and tell me what happened," Ella said, her voice cool and calm as she looked from one to the other.

"Come out back to the staff parking lot," Alfred said, motioning them to follow.

"Fill me in on the way," Ella said.

"No. I want you to see this yourself," Alfred answered flatly.

Once outside, Begaye led her down a row of parked vehicles, then stopped and gestured toward his luxury sedan. "Look."

Ella saw the car and had to suppress a smile. The sedan's driver's side window had been smashed, which was unfortunate, but the interior of the car had been crammed full of tumbleweeds—prickly weed. As she drew closer, Ella sneezed. She'd always been allergic to the danged things.

Almost on cue, Alfred and Billy began sneezing as well. Only Justine seemed to be immune. Grabbing a tissue from her pocket, Ella took a careful look around. No windows from the building faced this area, but there were security cameras in place. "I'm going to need the footage from those," she pointed up along the roof level.

"I've already had our future former security guard set aside this morning's footage for you," Alfred said. "Damned idiot never sees a thing. I want whoever did this prosecuted."

"I want them shot," Billy said, sneezing again.

Ella bit back a smile, then sneezed. "Justine, will you take a look inside the vehicle and see if anything else has been left there?" she asked, then sneezed again.

"My car's worse," Billy said, pointing across the lot. "They decided to save time by smashing the windshield instead."

Wanting to get it over with so she could get away from the weeds, Ella glanced at Justine. "Take the other car, partner. I'll search this one."

Ella put on a pair of latex gloves, hoping to minimize the scratches, then opened up the car door and began removing one tumbleweed at a time. The stalks were dry and brittle and the branches snapped as she made her way farther into the interior.

It took them less than three minutes to confirm that nothing except tumbleweeds had been left behind. But, by then, Ella's eyes were swollen and she couldn't stop sneezing. Ticked off, she glanced around. "Do I remember seeing a pharmacy around here?"

Alfred nodded and gestured across the street. "But I've got some over-the-counter stuff that works," he said, then sneezed. "Okay, it sorta works—that's if you can get away from these weeds."

"I'll take yours," she said, then walked back inside with Justine. They followed Begaye to his office, took the pills, then asked for directions to the security office where the surveillance footage was being prepared for them.

Justine was quiet as they walked down the hall. Ella

continued sneezing, and by the time they reached the security offices, she was in a foul mood.

The uniformed guard reminded her of Rudy Nez. Seeing his name tag through her tear-filled, swollen eyes and noting that his name was Darwin Nez, she had to ask. "Are you related to Rudy?"

He grinned. "Yeah, he's my cousin. I couldn't work at the casino because my religion prohibits gambling, but after I left the Air Force I needed a job—something I could do instead of construction work or sitting at a desk for eight hours. He told me about this job, and here I am."

It appeared that Darwin wasn't the only one who'd come out a winner from the deal. Rudy had a source placed in the same building as a tribal council member and most local government officials. Score one for Rudy.

Ella sat down to view the footage, and before long found what they were looking for. Unfortunately, it wasn't going to be enough. The two figures, the smaller of them possibly a woman, had deliberately kept their faces away from the camera and were wearing cowboy hats, pulled low over their eyes. She watched them bring a ladder close to the camera, then spray paint the lens. From that point on, they had nothing.

"How come you didn't notice this was going on?"

"When I come on duty, the first thing I do is conduct a foot patrol inside the building, checking all the doors and locks. They must have known that," he answered with a shrug. "When I got back to the monitors I saw something was wrong, but before I could go outside to check, Councilman Begaye called me to his office. He told me someone had vandalized his car and ordered me to get the surveillance video ready for you. He said I should leave everything out there exactly the way it was until you got here."

"There might be cameras outside the bank across the

street," Justine said. "If so, maybe we can get something from those."

"Good thinking, partner," Ella said. "But the bank doesn't have to cooperate with our investigation. We might need a warrant."

"Nah," Darwin answered. "My older brother works security there. He won't give you any problems. Just tell them I sent you."

Ella thanked Darwin. This was the way things often worked in this small community—everyone knew someone who knew someone else. "I'll go talk to him."

As they went back outside and crossed the street, Ella started to feel the effects of the allergy pills. New energy was pumping through her and she'd stopped sneezing. At least the pills weren't the kind that made a person sleepy. That, in her business, could mean a one-way ticket to an early grave.

"You're not exactly Rudy Nez's favorite person," Justine noted as they crossed the street. "You think Darwin will call his cousin? If he finds out we're not exactly best buds with Rudy, by the time we reach the bank things could become a lot more complicated."

"Walk faster."

When they arrived at the bank, Victor Nez came out to meet them. As was customary on the Rez, he didn't offer to shake hands.

"I heard you were on your way over. Come into my office, and I'll get the footage you need."

Ella and Justine followed him inside an office that was the size of a small closet—probably because it was also a storage area. There wasn't enough room for all them to stand side by side, so Justine stayed a step behind Ella as the video feed played.

"I don't have a plush office like my little brother does, but the equipment . . . ." Victor glanced back and gave them a happy smile. "I love all things electronic, and what I get to play with here is perfect."

Ella looked at the screen. The camera lens was directed in a way meant to keep any ATM customer in the center of the frame, but with no one standing there, she could see the parking lot across the street. Yet the angle was still wrong, so she couldn't get a fix on the area she wanted. "Do you have a second camera? I need to see more of the parking area's south side," she said, pointing to the screen.

"There's a second camera that monitors our employee parking lot, and it's aimed in that direction," Victor said. "Let me see what kind of clarity I can get for you."

They waited another few minutes for Victor to find what they needed. "This is the best you're going to get," he said, replaying the footage. "Remember that the camera is centered on our own lot, not the one across the street. The images will be small."

Ella studied the background, then moved closer to the screen. "There! Is it possible for you to enlarge and clear up that portion of the image?" she asked, pointing.

He gave her what could only be described as a completely contented smile. "You're about to see why I put up with an office the size of a bathroom." As he touched the screen with his index fingers and spread out his hands, the section she'd flagged became larger and clearer. "How's that? You can even read the plates on the pickup as it comes back into the street."

Ella glanced at the equipment with a touch of envy knowing that her department would never have state-of-the-art electronics like this. "I wish we could positively ID the two suspects inside, but at least we have a hit on the truck," she said, writing down the plate number.

Victor made a quick copy of the video segment, signed and dated the DVD, and promised to keep the original in the safe.

After thanking him, Ella called the information in as

they walked back to the tribal unit across the street. They were getting into the car when Ella got her response.

"You're not going to believe this, partner," Ella said as she fastened her seat belt. "We need to pay the Morgans a visit."

Justine gave her a surprised look. "*They* did this? Neither of them seemed the type."

"Those were Chester's plates, and the vehicle is registered to him and Trina. It's possible that one of their clan members works in the building and knows the guard or has been watching Begaye and Garnenez," Ella said. "The problem is that although we have enough to place them at the scene, we can't prove they committed the crime."

"So we'll push them—hard," Justine said.

"Even if they confess, we'd still be playing right into their hands," Ella said. "They want a martyr for their cause."

"We don't have a choice. You heard Begaye. He wants whoever did that to his car to pay," Justine said.

"And Garnenez wanted them shot," Ella said. "Looks to me like we're not going to make either of them happy."

They spent nearly twenty minutes in relative silence, but as they drew close to the Morgan home, Justine spoke. "What's eating you?"

"I think we're letting these vandalism incidents throw us off track. We need to stay focused on the money Adam was carrying. What was Adam doing with that cash, and how is that connected to the person or persons who paid to have him shot? I have a hard time thinking that the Morgans, or Emerson Lee, had anything to do with that. They don't have the money it takes to pay for a professional hit, nor do they have seventy-five grand lying around. But the Prickly Weed Project does have some major backers with that kind of money at their disposal. Someone in that league is bound to have equally powerful enemies, too."

"Taking things a step further, it's possible that one or more of the Prickly Weed backers will end up bankrupt if the project's shelved. If that's so, the person behind the hit may have decided to push things and ruin his enemy. He may have thought that getting rid of Adam would be enough to kill the deal. He was the tribe's contact with IFT. With him gone, Tribal Industries might have just called everything off rather than throw somebody new into a deal that was already on shaky ground," Justine said.

"What we need to do now is find out which of the Prickly Weed backers is on the edge financially, or has invested more than they should have. That means looking into the finances of the tribal president, of our attorney general Robert Buck, of Billy Garnenez, and Abigail Yellowhair, even Kevin," Ella said.

"There are also a host of other smaller business people who are associated with the Prickly Weed Project," Justine said.

"It's not going to be an easy job. There could also be a strong backlash, especially from Abigail, once we start poking around, but we have to do this." Ella picked up the phone, dialed Benny Pete, and filled him in. "Get Joe and Marianna's help on this. I want everything we can dig up on these people. And try to identify any enemies they've made along the way."

"How soon will you need this? To go past the surface, we're going to need time," Benny answered.

"Start on it right away and do your best. Also make sure to keep this as quiet as possible. I don't have any problems outing bad guys, but the department needs to avoid lawsuits."

"About Kevin, do you want us to dig into his background, too, or leave that part to you?"

"No. Dig away. Everyone gets the same treatment," she answered.

As she hung up, Justine glanced over at her. "Have you

seriously considered the possibility that Kevin might be involved?"

"My personal opinion is that he's not, but we'll scruti-
nize him as closely as the others. I'll be pushing him for more
answers about his enemies, too, but somehow, I doubt the
Aspass brothers are behind the shooting. Instinct tells me
this case isn't about revenge. It's about money and power,"
Ella said. "We need to start thinking outside the box. For
starters, I'm going to go with Blalock to pay Marie another
visit. My gut tells me that she knows more than she realizes."

"If I had a dime for every person who had held back information just because they didn't think it was important . . ."

"Yeah, exactly," Ella said; then, seeing the Morgans' home
come into view, she shifted the focus of her attention.

Less than ten minutes later, they were seated inside the
Morgans' small living room. Trina eyes were red and swollen,
her nose red, and she had a tissue box beside her. Ella might
have attributed it to crying if she hadn't seen Chester's equally
swollen nose and witnessed his sneezing. Both had scratches
on their wrists where the gloves hadn't protected them completely.

"There are allergy pills for that," Ella said, unexpectedly
feeling sorry for them.

"We took them. Nothing happened," Chester said. "Well,
no, Trina stopped sneezing. I haven't."

"You know why I'm here," Ella said.

Neither moved a muscle.

"The bank across the street also had a camera." As she
said it, Ella saw alarm flash across Trina's face, but Chester's
remained impassive. That told her that, despite everything,
Trina didn't want to be arrested.

"So what? We drive all around Shiprock," Chester said
with a smug smile.

"Try again," Ella said. "You were in the staff parking

area of the tribal branch offices and that's restricted to employees. Why were you there?"

"You're wasting your time—and ours. If you had something, we'd already be under arrest," Chester said.

"What if I tell you that the camera across the street recorded you breaking the windows and putting all those tumbleweeds in Garnenez's and Begaye's cars?" Ella said.

He shook his head. "It can't be all that clear-cut, or we would have been in handcuffs by now."

"You're playing a game you can't win. No amount of publicity is going to change the facts. That grazing permit—or lack of one—is going to be your downfall eventually," Ella said. "Have you heard anything more from the tribe about the compromise I suggested?"

"No, but Garnenez doesn't really plan to offer us a deal. One of our clan members overheard him talking to Frieda Beard last night. He told her that he would have promised us a brick hogan with marble steps just to get out of there in one piece. He wants the tribe to kick us off the land and take it all."

"Let me do some pushing of my own," Ella answered. "An agreement is still possible—I think."

Trina gave her a puzzled look. "Why would you do that for us—the people you came to arrest?"

"I work for the tribe, and that includes you two, and your father."

"If they agree to the compromise you suggested last night, there's no more cause for trouble. We'd take the deal," Trina said in a firm voice, then looked at her husband.

Chester shook his head. "You're both dreaming. They want the land, the house, everything. They won't settle. They don't even want to discuss it. Their minds are already made up."

"We'll see about that," Ella said.

TWENTY-ONE
------------ ✕ ✕ ✕ ------------

When they reached the house, Ella saw Rose entering through the back door, still wearing her gardening gloves. She'd probably been tending her new tumbleweeds, most already waist high. Even the sight made Ella's nose itch. At least the patch was on the opposite end of the house past the corrals.

While Justine fiddled with something at the vehicle's computer terminal, Ella went ahead. As she stepped through the front door the first thing she noticed was Dawn's absence. Whenever her kid was gone, even during school hours, the house seemed to hold its breath. Dawn gave it life with her constant activity and laughter.

Mack Kelewood had seen them arrive and gave her a nod from where he stood beside the curtain. Then Two, Rose's dog, came up, tail wagging, and Ella bent down to pet him. The dog was very protective of their household and had the uncanny ability to know friend from foe. Much to her mother's chagrin, the dog still refused to stay in the same room with Abigail Yellowhair. He'd growl softly, then leave and watch her from the closest doorway.

When Justine came in, a moment later, Two greeted her enthusiastically and Justine also bent down to pet him. "Do you mind if I go into the kitchen and raid your fridge? I'm starving. I only had a tortilla with some butter on it for breakfast, and half of it had to be tossed 'cause it had something gray and kinda furry growing on it."

Ella winced. "Gross, partner."

Justine shrugged. "It was either that, or three-day-old slippery leaf salad."

Rose poked her head out from the kitchen. "You get in here right now, child. I'll fix you something decent to eat."

Leaving them, Ella went into Dawn's bedroom, where Kevin was working with his daughter's laptop.

"What brings you here in the middle of the day?" he asked looking up.

"I need a favor," she said, and explained.

"This kind of thing usually works better in person, but I can make a few phone calls for you."

"Phone work's good, but make sure nothing you say gives away your location."

"I understand," he said. "So how's the case going? Have you found any connection between Adam and the casino? They're the ones with the bucks, Ella. The Prickly Weed Project could—someday—make serious money for us, but at the moment, it just sucks it in. Think of it as a financial black hole."

"Yet there's that seventy-five thousand in cash Adam was carrying," she said.

He took a deep breath and let it out slowly. "I've been giving that a lot of thought. Is it possible Adam was bringing that money back here to hire surveyors and support staff for IFT?"

"The deal wasn't cinched until *after* you guys got back— after the shooting, that is. Under those circumstances, to hand someone—anyone—seventy-five thousand in cash . . ."

"You're right. It doesn't make much sense. You don't pay contractors and white collar workers in cash—not in a deal this big," Kevin said. "When you hear about couriers who are carrying that much money, it's usually related to drugs, bribes, or money laundering."

"Drugs don't apply and there's no evidence to support money laundering. If there'd been any signs of that, we would have found out by now. Blalock and the FBI have been checking into it."

"You trust him?"

"Blalock?" she asked, surprised. "Yeah, with my life. He's a professional who likes to close his cases. Dwayne works long hours to make sure that happens."

"I'll talk to different people and see what I can get once I'm up and about. And speaking of that, I think you should consider allowing me to go home now that I can walk around a little better." He paused, then added in a growl, "I hate hiding out, Ella."

"You *cannot* leave. O'Riley's still out there. Since we haven't established who the primary target was, you'd be putting a bull's-eye on yourself and hoping for the best."

"I'd be careful."

"I thought you liked it here," she countered.

"I do, and that's the problem," Kevin said softly. "I'm getting used to being here and having my daughter around every day. That sense of family—it feels . . . really good."

"I hear you," Ella said softly, "but leaving now is a bad strategy. If I have to worry about Dawn going off and trying to find you, and you at a less secure or remote location, I'll be too distracted to give this case my undivided attention."

"All right," he answered after a momentary pause.

Ella stood. "I better get back to work."

"Before you go, there's something else we need to talk about. Dawn really wants to go to that private school in D.C., the one I mentioned, what, a lifetime ago? It's the same school some of the presidents' children have attended, Ella. We can't even begin to imagine the opportunities that would create for her. It's not just the education, but the people she'd meet. Those contacts could open doors and give her advantages neither one of us could ever provide."

"Don't try and pressure me. I haven't decided yet whether I'm taking that job in D.C. or not."

"Fair enough. But if you decide to take it, I'd like you to consider sharing the apartment the tribe leases for me there. I could move my office, and you could have your own room and Dawn hers. It's a large place."

Ella heard far more than his words. He'd spoken like a dad who wanted to play a bigger role in his daughter's life.

"Dawn's torn between us, Ella. She wants her father *and* her mother. If you allow it, we could become a bigger part of each other's lives—for her and for us."

"Dawn's fine. She doesn't lack a thing," Ella said.

"It's not about lack, it's about adding to what she already has."

"Nicely worded argument, Counselor," Ella replied, "but we've had this discussion before and . . ."

Before she could continue, Justine poked her head in the room. "Your mom wants to know if you would like a stuffed burrito. I said that you did, okay? So if you don't eat it, I will."

Laughing, Ella stood. "On that note, I better get going."

Ella and Justine were on their way back to the station fifteen minutes later when her phone rang. It was Blalock.

"Big Ed's about to call a meeting," he said. "I thought you'd want to know."

"I'm on my way in right now," she said.

As soon as she hung up, the phone rang again. Ella wasn't surprised when she heard Big Ed's voice on the other end.

Moments later, as she put the phone away, Ella updated Justine. "The chief wants answers, but I have none to give him."

"Maybe once we're all together, we'll come up with

something," Justine said, but her tone didn't reflect the confidence needed to make her words convincing.

By the time they met in the chief's office, Ella could feel the tension in the room. The chief wanted to hear that progress had been made, but none of them had anything solid to give him. All they could do was report what steps they'd already taken to move the investigation forward.

"My team's been doing background checks on everyone involved with the Prickly Weed Project. Specifically, we've been looking for anything that would link Adam, the money, and the shootings," Ella said, then nodded to Blalock.

"My people have been checking Lonewolf's contacts in D.C. We've searched for any signs of money laundering or drug trafficking activity that might explain the cash, but got nowhere," Blalock said. "Lonewolf's contacts are clean—or at least none have any charges or indictments against them right now. Of course with big business or big government, that's always subject to change."

"What about Tolino? Adam was working for him, at least recently and while in D.C. Maybe he talked Adam into carrying that board game, saying it was going to be a surprise for his daughter. It's possible Lonewolf had no idea what was inside that box," Big Ed suggested.

"If that had been Tolino's money he would have carried it himself," Blalock answered. "It's a lot of cash. Besides, the Bureau looked in on what Tolino does in D.C. and who his contacts are. He meets with lawmakers concerning legal issues that affect the tribe as a result of legislation and new government regulations. It's not the kind of thing that opens itself to bribes. He's an analyst who prepares reports and offers advice, none that have a direct tie to any particular business."

"And if he's been taking bribes, there's no trace of that money in any of his accounts, nor does his lifestyle reflect it," Marianna said.

"Could all this be totally random—like Adam getting

somebody else's cash by mistake, then having them come after him?" Joe said.

"Then why didn't they make a move to get it back?" Ella countered. "When Adam and Kevin went down, the shooters didn't advance to pick up the dropped briefcase. They concentrated on trying to pump more rounds into the victims."

"You drove them back, Ella. They knew their body armor would protect their torsos, but a head shot . . . ," Justine argued.

"I don't see it that way," Ella said, shaking her head. After a moment, she looked at Big Ed. "I know you're getting pressured to provide tribal leaders with answers we don't have yet, Chief, so you might remind them that Adam's the key. That's why we have to proceed very carefully. We don't want to risk doing anything that'll tarnish the reputation of a hero, particularly one believed to be dead and unable to defend himself."

"That's a good argument. No one wants to take on a legend—which is what Adam Lonewolf has become to The People," Big Ed said.

After the meeting closed, Ella met with Marianna in the hall. "Stay on Hattery, I want to know where he's at every minute. He's been getting his tips from someone on the inside. If you need backup, pull Joe in."

As soon as Marianna walked off, Blalock caught up to Ella. "You mentioned wanting to go to Kirtland Air Force Base, so I've arranged to get us a ride on a DOE utility aircraft that just dropped off some bureaucrats scheduled to inspect the new generating plant. That'll eliminate any possibility that we might be tailed and save us some time, too. Since everyone wants answers yesterday, the Bureau agreed to cover the expenses."

Less than an hour later, they were headed southeast on the twin-engine Department of Energy aircraft. It was just them and the pilot, who was up in the cabin, so they spoke freely.

"So what's your plan once we get there?" Blalock asked.

"I'm going to do my best to jog Marie's memory," Ella said. "I'll have to get her to relax first though, so I'm going to take it nice and easy."

"What if she doesn't know anything?"

"Then we're out of luck. But my gut tells me she knows more than she realizes."

"Adam may remember something by now, too, but from the updates I've been getting, we shouldn't count on him," Blalock said.

They landed in Albuquerque a half hour later. Thanks to Blalock, who'd contacted the base commander, a car was waiting.

"I'm here to drive you anywhere you need to go, on or off the base," the young airman said.

"Thanks. We'll start with the base hospital," Ella answered.

The old base facility, in existence since the early '40s, was less than ten minutes away. As they walked inside the military-gray-and-green structure, Ella noted the disinfectant smell, a blessing to the ill when used effectively, but unpleasant nevertheless.

Blalock asked to see to see Adam's physician, and several minutes later a young military doctor approached them.

"I'm Captain Marcus. I've been instructed to give you my full cooperation."

"Can we question Mr. Lonewolf directly?" Blalock asked, going right to the heart of the matter.

"You may have heard that the patient's regained consciousness, but the trauma damage was considerable and progress has been slow," Captain Marcus said. "Also be advised that only bits and pieces of his memory have returned. He recognizes his wife and parents, and that's about it."

The doctor led the way down a short hall, then, after two turns, pointed ahead. "Keep things calm and don't upset him. If he gets agitated, that'll be the end of the questions, clear?"

"Not a problem, Doc," Blalock said. "Will the family be here?"

"No, not until visiting hours. They've gone to their quarters for some rest."

They presented their IDs to the uniformed AP at the door—a woman in her twenties with a sidearm at her hip—and went inside. Adam was sitting up, resting his bandaged head on a stack of pillows. He looked terrible, and was staring blankly at a TV placed high on a shelf in the corner of the room, where a talk show was in progress.

As he noticed Ella and turned his eyes to look at her, there was no sign of recognition on his face, only vague curiosity.

"Adam, it's me, Ella Clah, the tribal police officer," she said softly.

"His memory of recent events has suffered the most," Captain Marcus explained. "But basic cognitive functions have begun to return. He's starting to remember the hospital staff—at least their faces. You might want to ask him a yes-or-no question. He can't speak, but he's learned to tap his finger once for yes, twice for no. If he doesn't know the answer, he taps three times."

Ella looked down at his right hand, resting on the top of the blanket. "Do you know who I am, Adam?"

He waited a moment, then tapped his index finger.

Ella breathed a sigh of relief. "Good. Adam, do you remember what happened to you, how you got shot?"

She waited, watching his hand, then shifted her gaze to his eyes. He seemed to be struggling—confused. He tapped twice—then three times. Adam groaned, then tapped three times again.

"It's okay," Ella said, not wanting to upset him. "Do you remember carrying your briefcase?"

His eyebrows furrowed as he thought about it.

As Ella watched him she didn't get the impression that he was eluding her question, but rather trying hard to remember. He tapped his finger once.

"Your wife bought it for you, didn't she?" Ella asked.

Adam tapped once, blinking his eyelids, like a nod.

"You were supposed to be protecting someone during the flight home. Do you remember who it was?"

He hesitated, then tapped twice.

"Think hard, Adam. Could it have been Kevin Tolino?"

He stared across the room, his eyes darting from place to place as he fought to remember. Then he tapped three times, his face contorted. A tear fell from his left eye, and he tried to wipe it away, but didn't have the strength to complete the gesture.

The doctor stepped forward. "Don't let it concern you, Adam," he assured. "It will take time for your memory to return."

"Just keep getting better," Ella said gently, reaching down and giving his hand a squeeze. "When you remember more, have someone call me," she added, and placed a card next to him on the bed stand.

Adam looked up at her, blinked his eyes, then tapped once with his fingertip before looking away toward the TV.

Once they'd left the room, the doctor stopped and looked at Blalock first, then Ella. "Memory's a tricky thing. It may all come back to him in an hour, or it may take years."

"Thanks, Doc. An update if he makes more progress would be appreciated," Blalock said, giving him his card.

The doctor placed it inside his coat pocket. Just then his pager went off. He looked down at the display. "I've got to go." Without further word, he hurried to the end of the hall, joining a nurse with a cart full of medical gear. They disappeared around the corner a second later.

As Ella and Blalock returned outside to the parking area, their driver held the car door open for them.

"We need to find Sergeant Lonewolf's wife, Marie, next," Ella said, climbing in.

"I have the address of their guest quarters. I was told you might want to go see the family as well," the airman said.

After a short drive down a busy avenue, they arrived at a generic, one-level home at the end of a street just beyond the northern perimeter of the base. The building, virtually identical to those around it, had a southwest-landscaped yard with native plants. The neighborhood looked quiet and well maintained.

Ella walked up to the porch with Blalock, and before she could knock, Marie Lonewolf opened the front door.

"I heard the car and saw you getting out. Is something wrong? Is Adam . . ." Her voice broke, and she stared at Ella, fear etched clearly on her face.

"He's still hanging in there," Ella said quickly. "We just came from visiting with him, and he was able to answer a few questions."

Marie breathed a sigh of relief, and dropped back against the door frame. "You nearly gave me a heart attack. Call next time and let me know you're coming."

Ella smiled. "Sorry about that," she said, following her inside.

Marie led them to the fabric couch in the living room. "My father-in-law and mother-in-law aren't here. They went for a long walk over to the Veteran's Memorial. You don't know how hard this has been on both of them. At their age . . ." She shook her head. "But you came to talk. What can I do for you?"

"We need some straight answers," Blalock said, with his usual bluntness.

Marie blinked, taken aback.

Ella fought the urge to give Blalock a swift kick in the shins. "He meant that we'd like you to fill in some gaps in the information we have, just some details we're missing. For example, what can you tell us about the time Adam spent in

D.C.?" Ella said, then smiled and continued in calm, conversational tone. "That's such a crazy place. Everyone's always in a hurry. There are so many interesting places to see, too. Have you been there?"

Marie smiled, sitting back again. "Adam gave me what he called 'the tour' right after he got that job, then again a month ago on our anniversary. Both times it was like visiting another planet. Everything there is so different. On the Rez you see people walking down the side of the road fifty miles from the nearest town. They don't pay any attention to the cars racing past because they're never in that much of a hurry. In the cities back east, the cars flash by and so do the people. They walk as if the ground beneath them is on fire."

"That's the way it was when I was there, too," Ella said. "I like the Rez a lot better." As she spoke, Ella realized how true that was. Yet there was no denying the many opportunities Virginia and the urban environment around the capital could offer Dawn. Quickly bringing her thoughts back to the business at hand, Ella continued. "Does your husband like traveling?"

"Yes, he loves seeing new places and dealing with anything that offers a challenge. That's why he accepted the job with the tribe. It gives him both."

"What does he like least about his new work?" Ella asked, taking advantage of the fact that Marie seemed more relaxed now.

"He hates being told how to do his job. He figures that if they hired him, they should also trust his skills."

Ella nodded thoughtfully, then, playing a hunch, added, "Does he ever talk about the people at IFT?"

"Some. I know there's one man my husband particularly dislikes. His name's Williams. My husband said that the man's lower than a rattlesnake, because the snake at least rattles before it strikes."

Ella laughed. "I've never met Williams. Have you?"

She nodded. "He was at a party my husband took me to last time I was in D.C. He only talked about himself—and money."

"When we spoke back in Shiprock, you mentioned that your husband thought he was going to lose his job. Do you think he was seriously worried about that?" Ella asked.

"I'm the worrier, not him. My husband's the kind who jumps in and, one way or another, settles the problem," Marie said with a sad smile. "I warned him before he took that job that Washington was full of crooks, but he said he could handle the pressure without selling out like so many over there end up doing."

"Those are pretty strong words," Blalock said, "particularly in a business where there are few—if any—moral absolutes."

"Money doesn't matter to my husband as much as doing something that makes a real difference. That's why he enlisted and why he took the job with the tribe after his discharge. He wants his life to count for something, and that's what drives him."

They continued to ask her questions, but after twenty minutes it was clear they were only going over old ground. Marie had told them all she knew.

They waited until Adam's parents came back from their walk, then Ella and Blalock spoke to them. They had no additional information to share, but wanted answers and demanded that she find whoever had shot their son.

"We *will* find the ones responsible," Ella assured them, unable to tell them about Carl Perry's fate. The plan to keep Carl Perry's connection to the shooting under wraps until they had O'Riley in custody was still in operation.

"What happened to my son—does it have anything to do with that Prickly Weed Project he was promoting?" Lila Lonewolf asked.

"Did he talk to you about that?" Blalock asked.

"No, but we've been hearing all about that from the ones back on the Rez," Lila said.

Ella's heart froze. "Have you been in contact with people back home?" she asked quickly.

"No," Melvin Lonewolf said firmly.

Lila Lonewolf stared at the floor.

Ella held her breath. "Ma'am?"

When she said nothing, Melvin looked at his wife curiously.

"We have to know, ma'am. This is extremely important. You might have inadvertently given your location away," Blalock said immediately.

"I only spoke to my brother," Lila whispered. "He's been so worried about my son."

"We need his name," Ella said.

"*Anádlohí*," she answered.

It meant "one who laughed." But he wouldn't be doing much of that after they spoke to him. "We'll need his Anglo name," Ella insisted.

"Fred Benn," she whispered.

"Did you warn him not to tell anyone where you are?" Ella asked quickly.

"Yes, and he swore he'd keep our secret. That Anglo TV reporter who's been talking to people on the Rez goes to visit him ever so often, so my brother's decided not to come here. He's afraid the reporter will find out."

Ella exhaled loudly. "You *cannot* have him come here—not under any circumstances. He might be followed, and that could place your son—and all of you—in danger."

After they left the house, Ella felt Blalock's anger as clearly as she did her own.

"You see this all the time with protected witnesses," Blalock grumbled as the airman drove them back to the restricted portion of the shared military and civilian airfield.

"They just can't resist the temptation to contact people back home."

Ella called the station and spoke to Big Ed, adding her suggestion. "I should have expected this, Chief, but I didn't see it coming."

"No one did," he said. "But on the Rez, family's everything, and having them contact one member back home . . . it *was* only one, right?"

"Yes, sir."

"Good. We'll contain the situation," Big Ed said.

"You might consider sending my brother to talk to Mr. Benn. Clifford wouldn't arouse any suspicion. Though I haven't confirmed it for him, I'm certain my brother already knows that Adam's alive."

"Do you want to ask him, or shall I?"

"I can take care of it, Chief," she answered.

Ella hung up, pressed the button for automatic dialing, and called her brother's home. Clifford, to this day, still refused to carry a cell phone. He had a million excuses, but the bottom line was he didn't want to be available constantly. She didn't blame him. There were times when she would have cheerfully chucked her cell phone out the nearest window.

It was on the flight back, about ninety minutes later, that Ella finally reached her brother. "I need a favor," she said, explaining. "The most important part is finding out if Fred's told anyone at all."

"I'll go, and I'll also make sure I'm not followed or seen," Clifford said.

"The presence of a *hataalii* at the house shouldn't be cause for alarm, but you'll need to make sure no one overhears your conversation with him."

"I'll take all the precautions necessary," he said, then after a brief pause, added, "Before I go, there's something you should know. Earlier today I heard that IFT's project director, a man named Williams, is flying into the Farmington airport tonight. Things have been really buzzing at the landowner's place ever since the news got out, too."

"How did they find out about this?" she asked.

"An article written by that Anglo reporter came out in the *Diné Times*."

After hanging up, Ella looked at Blalock and filled him in. "I need your help, Dwayne. I want you to use Bureau sources and get me all you can on Hattery. If he's got an Achilles' heel, I need to know."

"Done."

Ella stared out the small plane's window, her hand on the badger fetish. Every muscle in her body felt tense. She hated that airstrip at Shiprock, and would never forget how things had gone from normal to total chaos in a matter of seconds. Although it wasn't likely to ever happen again, she couldn't quite erase the memory or the fear that came with it.

Trying to push back her uncertainties, she thought of her daughter, of Rose and Herman, and even Kevin, all safe back home. Family. She couldn't really blame Lila Lonewolf wanting to reach out to blood at a time like this. Sometimes family was the only thing that kept you strong. Without them, there was no walking in beauty.

As Blalock spoke on his cell phone, Ella glanced at the badge on her belt and quietly replaced the standard-load magazine in her handgun with the armor piercing rounds.

TWENTY-TWO

———— **✕ ✕ ✕** ————

Ella wasn't at ease again until they landed at the Shiprock airstrip sometime later. Justine was there, waiting. While Blalock took off in his own set of wheels, Ella joined her partner.

"Everything's coming to a head here this evening," Justine said as Ella fastened her seat belt. "The Morgans know that IFT employees are coming to do some survey work and that Charles Williams, their project director, plans to take a closer look at the site. The Morgans have already posted clan members around the property, practically daring anyone to trespass. The survey crew and Williams have been advised to remain off the site, but Big Ed wants you to make sure Williams stays safe."

"How, exactly, are the Morgans planning to stop IFT's people?"

"I don't know. Williams isn't scheduled to be here for another hour, so I figured you'd want to go have a look for yourself," Justine said.

"Good idea. Let's go now."

"I brought a couple of Tasers, just in case," Justine said, gesturing to the back.

Thirty minutes later, when they reached the gravel road

leading onto the Morgans' land, Ella noticed at least a hundred sheep and goats foraging on the native grasses and shrubs. Closer to the house were several pickups with stock racks and a long trailer beside several large and small canvas tents. There must have been fifty people gathered around one open tent where food was being prepared on large, commercial-type grills. It was like a church picnic, if one could overlook the rifles and shotguns several of the Navajo men carried.

"Oh, crap," Ella muttered. "Half the clan is here. If those surveyors come down this road there's going to be one major confrontation."

Justine slowed as they passed the onlookers and continued directly to the Morgans' house. Before they'd even parked, Emerson Lee came out, followed by Chester Morgan. Both were holding rifles.

"Let's get this on video *and* audio," Ella said.

Justine placed a video camera on the dash, turning it on so it covered a large arc in front of the vehicle, then pulled out her audio recorder. "All set."

"Put down your weapons," Ella said, getting out of the car.

Emerson leaned the rifle against a post on the porch, and Chester did the same. "We're not at fault here. The one that's to blame is that snake, Billy Garnenez," Emerson said, purposely using his enemy's name. "He pretended he was going to work *with* us, but all he did was lie, hoping to keep us quiet for a while." He waved his hand toward the section of land closest to the house, which was now filled with livestock and his supporters. "But we aren't going to go down easy. My clan's here and the press is due shortly. We called them, too."

Even as Emerson spoke, Norm Hattery came out of the house, aiming what looked like a cell phone on steroids. A cameraman followed, filming with more conventional equipment bearing the logo of the Farmington television station.

"What are you doing here?" Ella asked Hattery. "When did you become so interested in tribal business?"

"Since I found out it's linked to a shooting incident that left one man dead, Officer Clah," Hattery replied.

"Have you been withholding evidence that suggests a connection between this and the shooting?" Ella countered.

"You're the one who's been withholding information from the public. We'll be presenting the details on the evening news. You might want to tune in and learn, Investigator Clah."

Ella turned back to Emerson, who'd now been joined by his daughter, Trina. "You were supposed to receive an offer from the tribal government, a compromise land deal," Ella said. "What happened?"

"When I asked Billy Garnenez, he said that the survey work IFT was doing was just groundwork for the inevitable," Emerson said, turning toward the camera. "He also told me to face facts—that, one way or another, the tribe was going to take back our family's land."

Ella was still trying to figure out how to respond when her cell phone vibrated. She ignored it, but then Justine's rang.

Her partner answered it, then came forward and handed the phone to Ella. "You need to hear this."

When Ella answered, she heard Kevin's voice on the other end. "It's a done deal," he said. "The Morgans will get a fair amount of land—and a fence—but only if they allow Williams to complete what he came to do, which includes surveying the land to be set aside for them. The paperwork's been signed and it's on the way over by tribal courier. All Trina Morgan has to do is countersign and date the agreement. I'm sending the key points to your cell as a series of text messages."

"Thanks," Ella said. "Your call came in at just the right time."

"I know," Kevin said.

"How?" Ella asked immediately.

"There's a Web feed on the computer," Kevin said. "You're coming through live on our daughter's laptop."

Ella looked at Hattery, and even though he hadn't heard the other end of the conversation, he smiled. "Yeah, I'm running a live feed to my station's Web page. You should stay tuned, too. I've got some news you're really going to want to see."

Ella gave him a look of complete disgust, then focused on Emerson and told him what she'd just learned, speaking loudly enough for everything to be heard clearly on the TV feed. "The tribe has offered you a good compromise. It's a win for everyone. The paperwork's on its way and ready for your signature."

"Is it the deal you'd suggested before?" Trina asked.

Ella showed her the highlights by retrieving the text messages in sequence. "You'll be able to see the complete document for yourself soon enough."

"If the document contains all this, we'll take it," Trina said.

When her husband looked at her and started to protest, Trina shook her head. "If we turn this into an outright war, we'll lose. The police will move in and the tribe will take everything. This way we get to keep what's most important to us—our home and enough land to meet our needs. We'll accept the compromise," she repeated, looking into the big camera.

"The Salt People Clan have won a victory for The People," Emerson said loudly, but after he spoke, his head sagged and his eyes grew moist. Being forced to accept a partial victory had killed something inside him.

Trina and Chester left to tell the rest of their supporters and the reporter followed. Emerson remained behind, staring at a distant mesa. Ella felt sorry for the old man, but at least this issue was settled and nobody had gone away empty-handed.

"Let's go," Ella said, turning to Justine. "Mr. Williams should be able to conduct his business without getting shot now. I'm still going to ask Big Ed to provide him with security, just to be on the safe side, but our work here is done."

"Where to next?" Justine asked, as they climbed back into the SUV.

"Back to the station. From the evidence we've gathered and what we've seen of Emerson and his supporters, I'm more convinced than ever that none of them were involved in the airport shooting. They would have gone for Garnenez and Begaye, not Adam, and they would have done it themselves. Hiring talent—particularly Anglo talent—would go against the grain for this group," Ella said. "What's worrying me now is Hattery's so-called news. When he mentioned it, Norm had this smug look on his face that practically begged for a knee to the groin. I'm absolutely certain he's found out something that's going to complicate our investigation."

On the drive back to Shiprock, Ella's cell phone vibrated. When she picked it up, she heard her brother's voice. "We have to meet. There's something you need to see. I'm close to the station right now. When will you be there?"

"In about ten minutes," Ella answered. "Is this connected to your meeting with Fred?"

"Yes."

"Has he told someone else about his sister's whereabouts?" Ella asked instantly.

"Not on purpose. I'll explain when I see you."

Ella closed up the phone and told her partner what Clifford had said. "Step on it, partner. This isn't good news."

Clifford entered Ella's office a short time later. Before she could say anything, he held a finger to his lips and placed a small listening device on the table.

Ella recognized it instantly and mouthed the word "Fred?"

Clifford nodded.

Justine put on a latex glove, picked up the device, then walked down the hall to the lab.

"Okay, brother, tell me how and where you found that."

Clifford took a seat. "I went to speak to the hero's uncle. All in all, it was an interesting visit."

Ella didn't interrupt the silence that followed, but her patience had been stretched to the limit already today and it took all her will power to keep quiet.

"The man had a prairie dog he'd befriended," Clifford began. "It was apparently born below the deck of his screened-in front porch, and though the mother and the rest of the litter moved on, the pup stayed around and has become a pet. It's even allowed inside the house."

"That's not good. They can carry things like rabies and plague," Ella said.

"I mentioned that, too, but he said that when the vet pays a visit to his neighbor's horses, he also comes by his home and makes sure everything's okay."

Ella said nothing, but the idea of turning a wild creature into a pet still bothered her.

"While he and I were talking, I asked him about his sister. He said that she'd called because she'd needed someone to talk to since her husband never has much to say. He assured me that neither of them mentioned where she was," Clifford said. "Relieved, I was getting ready to leave when I noticed the half-chewed, button-sized piece of metal on the floor. At first I didn't realize what it was, but when I got close, I knew. I have no idea where it had been placed originally, or if it's still working, but I knew you'd want to see it."

"My guess is that the prairie dog found it, chewed on it, then lost interest. Did you ask your host if he knew what it was?"

"Yes, but only *after* I took it to my truck," Clifford said. "He'd never seen it before, and told me that he had no idea where the prairie dog had found it. The only other guest he'd had in the last few weeks was the reporter."

Ella sat back in her chair, wondering if there was something her brother had missed or Fred had forgotten to mention. It was possible—maybe even likely—that Hattery's promised newsflash was connected to the device.

Justine came in a short time later. "The microphone is damaged beyond repair, but it's the type of device that can be purchased easily over the Internet. It transmits to a recorder placed in another location, up to a mile away under optimal conditions. Unfortunately, that doesn't narrow the field much. There's a lot of ground to cover."

"Tell Neskahi about this. He might be on duty elsewhere, but I want him to drop whatever it is and go see if he can turn up anything like footprints or vehicle tracks at Fred Benn's place."

"Once the listening device was damaged, Hattery probably picked up the equipment and moved on. You *are* thinking he was the one who planted the device, right?" Justine asked.

Ella nodded. "Have Joe try anyway."

Clifford stood. "If you don't need me anymore . . ."

"Have you been able to get any leads on the money the shooting victim was carrying?" Ella asked her brother.

"No. All I can tell you for sure is that the hero isn't a gambler. In fact, he won't even buy a state lottery ticket or a scratcher. I know he met the Anglo head of casino management once at a tribal function, but they didn't talk for very long, according to my source."

"Good to know, brother. Thanks."

"You want me to keep at it?"

"Yes. There are still too many unanswered questions about the hero."

After Clifford left, Ella leaned back in her chair. Maybe

it was time to look more closely at the time discrepancy surrounding the IFT deal. Garnenez had said one thing, Begaye another. The difference wasn't just a few hours either. It was at least a few days, and in that gap of time Adam and Kevin had both been gunned down.

"Quick, log on to the net," Justine said, hurrying into the office and over to Ella's desk. "The Farmington station's Web broadcast is running live again, and you're not going to like it."

As they watched, Ella saw Norm Hattery break his exclusive, stating that Adam had been carrying seventy-five thousand dollars in cash at the time of the attack, and that the money was now in the custody of the police. The bulletin finished, then repeated itself, going into a loop.

"Any idea how he found out?" Ella asked her partner.

"Someone in the know either screwed up or leaked it on purpose."

"So let's go down the list. We can rule out everyone in our team. Nothing to gain, everything to lose. Next comes the Lonewolf family. I doubt any of them knew about it, but even if they did, they wouldn't have publicly discredited Adam this way. Ford knew, but he wouldn't have told anyone. Clifford and Kevin also knew, but I trust both men. That leaves Kevin's boss, Robert Buck. He's more politician than lawyer, but I don't see what he might have to gain, at least in the short haul."

"Me neither," Justine said. "We've done background checks on all the players, and turned up nothing, so let's try a different approach. My sister Jayne's best friend, Dena Bileen, is Buck's office assistant. Let's see if we can get something from her via Jayne."

Ella tried to remember if she'd ever met Dena, but nothing came to her.

Seeing her partner trying to put a face to the name, Justine continued. "Dena's eminently forgettable. She's about as ordinary-looking as you can get, and has no charisma. But according to Jayne, she can type a gazillion words per minute and multitask like a mainframe computer. The perfect assistant—that's what Jayne says."

"Okay, see what you can do."

SATURDAY

The following afternoon Ella stopped just outside Big Ed's office, took a breath, then knocked on the semi-open door. She could hear him on the phone, and as Big Ed gestured for her to take a seat, her hope that he'd just wave her away vanished.

"We're doing our best to uncover the leak, and I assure you it didn't come from our department." Big Ed paused then added, "Yes, sir, I'll keep your office in the loop." After barely resisting the urge to slam the phone down, he walked to the door and shut it. "That was the tribal president, Shorty, and he's angry and embarrassed by the suggestion that our best-known Navajo warrior since the time of the Code Talkers has now been branded as a criminal. Do you have any idea how this got out?"

"Our best bet is Robert Buck, or someone connected to him, but we haven't been able to nail it down yet."

He rubbed a hand through his hair, then sat back. "Have you got anything new for me on the core investigation?"

She told him about the discrepancy in dates. "I'm hoping to make some sense out of that, but one of the problems on a case like this is that it doesn't travel in a straight line. We don't even know if the apparent contradiction is relevant."

After a knock sounded on Big Ed's door, he boomed out a "come in."

Justine entered, a big smile on her face. "We got a break. I know how Hattery learned about the seventy-five thou," she said. "Jayne told me that Norm's been dating Dena Bileen, Robert Buck's assistant. Dena was convinced that she and Norm had something special going on. He apparently promised he'd take her with him when he left the Rez."

"And she believed that slimy con artist?" Ella asked, shaking her head.

"The guy's smooth," Big Ed said with a scowl. "He plays everyone he meets, apparently."

"Dena's in a mess of trouble right now. As soon as Robert Buck heard about the leak, he took a closer look at his assistant, too. She's the only other person in his office who knew about the cash. Although it didn't take him long to find out that Dena was dating Hattery, he still can't prove she's the leak. Hattery protects his sources, too, so chances are Buck will never know for sure."

"Let's move on, then," Ella said. "I'm going to talk to Begaye and Garnenez once more," Ella said, standing.

"Keep me in the loop, Shorty. And good work, Officer Goodluck," Big Ed said, leaning back in his chair.

As Ella opened the door, she nearly collided with Benny, who was about to knock.

"Bad news boss, other boss," Benny announced, holding up a newspaper. "Adam Lonewolf's clan is up in arms. They called Jaime Beyale of the *Diné Times* to give their take on the cash inside the briefcase. Fred Benn—the uncle—has been quoted as saying this is our department's way of discrediting Adam and shifting the focus away from our own bungled investigation. Fred also suggested that the money belonged to Tolino and that it was a bribe he'd received from Grady, the Anglo casino boss. He claims that if Adam was carrying that money, it was undoubtedly on Kevin's orders."

Ella muttered a curse. When Kevin read that story . . . She hadn't even finished the thought when her cell phone vibrated. She didn't answer it.

Big Ed slammed his fist against the desk. "We're going

to experience the mother of all backlashes, folks. The public's going to buy into the uncle's story because they want to believe in Adam's innocence."

Benny Pete cleared his throat, and they all braced themselves, realizing that he had even more to say. "I've been studying Adam Lonewolf's notes in detail," he said. "Though he'd made every concession he was authorized to make, Adam was certain that IFT was going to turn down the tribe's final offer. The company wanted more money, but the tribe's budget was stretched to the limit and there were no more resources they could tap into to sweeten the deal."

"If that's true, then what made IFT change their minds? Adam was carrying the money *back* to the Rez, not delivering it to Williams or whomever," Justine asked.

"Good point, partner," Ella said. "Let's go talk to Begaye and Garnenez. Benny, I'd like you to check with Agent Blalock and see if anyone has come up with a lead on O'Riley." She glanced back at Big Ed. "Blalock's been directing a multi-agency task force and they've been checking out fast food outlets, gas stations, bus terminals, apartment landlords, and cheap motels. Even rest stops and parks. If O'Riley is in the area, he still has to eat and find a place to sleep."

Big Ed glanced at his three officers. "Keep me updated. And, Shorty, work fast," he said, reaching for his phone.

Benny returned to the lab as Ella walked with Justine down the hall. Before they reached the side door, her phone began to ring.

Ella sighed, expecting it to be Kevin, ready to sue Adam's in-laws. To her surprise, it was Sheriff Taylor, who'd often worked with her on cases that overlapped tribal and county jurisdiction. "Ella, I got a call from the chief of security at the tribal casino, Rudy Nez. He just reported a death at the Alan Grady residence just east of the Hogback—on county jurisdiction. There's a possibility this might be connected to the shootings you've been working on, so I'm extending you a courtesy. I'm en route now, about a half hour away. Can you meet me there?"

"I sure can. Is Grady the victim?" Ella pressed.

"Yes, according to Nez, who says Grady asked him to come over. Nez claims his boss was dead when he arrived at the residence. If you get there before our units, would you secure the scene and keep him out of the way? I've come across Nez before, and he's a pain in the butt."

"Roger that. I should make it in ten, maybe fifteen."

"Fine." Taylor ended the call.

Ella gave Justine the highlights as they left the building.

"I wonder if Nez had anything to do with this? Or maybe O'Riley decided to take out his boss—if Grady is behind all this," Justine said.

"Whatever the case, we need to get over there pronto. I'd like to question Nez before the sheriff and his team show up."

They arrived at the house just north of the river within twelve minutes. Grady lived in a large, modern home on land that had been part of an enormous apple orchard during Ella's childhood. Developers had changed the entire valley. The housing area was nice, and all the yards had manicured lawns, but they were built too close together for her tastes. As they pulled up, Ella saw Rudy in the front yard, waiting beside his mustard yellow pickup.

"Not surprised to see you here, Clah, though this is county jurisdiction, not tribal. Sheriff Taylor call you?"

"Something like that," Ella commented. "You've already been inside, right?" she added, stepping up the porch.

"Yeah, and you might want to take a look for yourself before the deputies arrive. Someone went to a lot of trouble to stage this," he said, waving toward the open door.

"How far in did you go?"

"No more than a few steps," Rudy said. "Didn't want to contaminate the scene. Once you get into the living room, look to your left. His office door's open."

Ella glanced inside, and at first, all she saw was an expensively furnished living room in some modern style requiring chrome and leather. Looking down at the carpet, she checked for trace evidence. Seeing nothing, she took two steps into the room and looked to the left as he'd suggested. Grady was slumped over his desk, a pool of blood around his head like an unholy halo. A revolver lay on the floor below his outstretched hand.

"It looks like he committed suicide, but that doesn't make any sense, considering his call to you," Ella said, stepping back out.

"Not at all," Rudy responded, adding a shrug.

"I'd like to take a closer look at all those papers scattered around the desk," Justine said, having come up alongside her.

"Not until Sheriff Taylor arrives," Ella said, stepping back outside and off the porch. "This is his turf."

Sheriff Taylor, the county sheriff and an old acquaintance of Ella's, arrived only a few minutes later. Hearing Rudy Nez's story, he glanced at Ella, who shook her head and shrugged.

"You're welcome to work the crime scene with us, Ella. You, too, Officer Goodluck," Taylor said as his own crime scene team arrived in their big van. "I've been following the case you've been working and also helping Blalock with the search for O'Riley. Is there any chance Grady was involved in the airport shootings?"

"I don't think so. Although I hadn't ruled the man out, I have stronger evidence against some of our other suspects."

"All right then, let's get started," he said.

Ella pulled on the first of two pairs of latex gloves—a practice most Navajo officers followed. Traditional Navajo beliefs held that touching anything that had come into contact with the dead was highly dangerous. The *chindi*, the evil side of a person that remained earthbound after death, would be nearby, waiting, and eager to create trouble for the living. While Ella struggled with the second pair, she listened to one of the deputies questioning Rudy.

"About fifteen minutes ago, Alan Grady asked me to come over to his house in Fruitland," Rudy explained. "He claimed that someone was watching his home and tailing him whenever he left. I told him to call the sheriff's department— that I worked for the casino—but he insisted. Since he signs my paycheck—at least up to last week—I gave in and drove over. It only took me ten minutes, but when I got here, the door was unlocked. Inside I found Grady, freshly dead. Gunshot wound to the head, it looks like.

"I came over as soon as I could," Rudy added, "but there was no one around. My first thought was that Investigator Clah or one of her team was watching the house, and that's who Alan had seen, but I looked around carefully as I drove up and all I saw was a male pheasant standing in the tall grass."

Ready now, Ella followed Taylor inside, and although most of the evidence pointed to suicide, experience had taught her that first impressions couldn't be trusted. She took in the room slowly, studying the scene from ceiling to floor as the photographer worked. Once he moved away, she drew closer to the papers scattered on the expensive Ganado-style Navajo rug. Most were articles on the shooting at the airstrip and Kevin's casino management investigation.

Ella looked up when one of the crime scene investigators shifted the body enough to lift a cell phone from Grady's pocket.

"What was the last number he dialed?" Ella asked her.

The tech, a small Hispanic woman, checked and read off the number. "It's the same number on his last three calls."

"That's my cell," Rudy said from the living room.

Ella nodded absently, and began looking around again, when Sheriff Taylor called her. "I think you'll want to see this." He stepped back, showing her what was inside the office closet.

The first thing that caught her eye was the .223 Arma-Lite assault rifle. The model AR-180B appeared identical to the ones used in the airport attack. There also was a box of ammunition, two twenty-round magazines, and a bullet-resistant vest.

Ella picked up the heavy vest, noting the impact marks and the ceramic plates inserted within. Hearing a light thud, she looked down and saw a smashed bullet on the floor. "I hit whoever was at the airstrip, but he didn't go down. . . ."

"We'll check that and any other rounds we find against those fired from your weapon," Taylor said. "Do you think Grady got spooked figuring you were getting too close, and decided to end it on his own terms?"

"Not unless he taped, then untaped both his wrists first," Justine answered from across the room. "In my opinion, the entire scene was staged."

Ella drew close and studied the victim's arms, noting the irritated skin and duct-tape glue that was still stuck to Grady's arm hair. "You're right. His hands were bound at some point."

Sheriff Taylor glanced at Ella and cocked his head toward the door. "What do you say we go talk to his neighbor?"

"Good idea. People who live this close probably know more about each other than anyone realizes," she said, walking out with him.

"I think having these four- and five-bedroom McMansions so close together gives the residents the illusion of protection," Taylor said. "But that's just this working man's opinion."

"A working man who wisely carries a gun. The *illusion* of protection doesn't carry much weight in our game," Ella said.

They knocked at the neighbor's door, and moments later were shown inside by a silver-haired Anglo woman wearing jeans and a red UNM Lobo sweatshirt. She led the way to a large leather couch and gestured for them to take a seat. "I'm glad you officers finally got here. I've been scared out of my mind since I heard those shots. In fact, I was getting ready to call 911 when that armed security man from the casino drove up in the yellow pickup. He showed me his ID and told me not to worry, that he'd take care of everything. But you county people took forever to get here."

"Tell us what happened," Taylor said.

"About an hour ago I heard what sounded like a back-fire from somewhere down the street, but when I looked outside there were no cars anywhere. Then I heard the second bang and realized gunshots were coming from inside one of the houses. That's when I got scared and called Alan, my closest neighbor. He didn't answer. I knew he was home because the tribe had put him on leave, so I went to check on him. There was the sound of a car in the alley, but then the security man from the casino drove up, so I never went to look to see who it was."

"You sure you heard *two* shots?"

"There were two identical loud sounds."

"One right after the other?" Ella asked.

"No. I heard one, then about three minutes later, the second."

Taylor took the rest of the information, then walked back with Ella to Grady's home. "The back door was un-locked, so we know how the killer made his escape. Looks to me we've got a clear case of murder on our hands."

"Let's take a closer look at the crime scene, and see what else we can uncover," Ella said.

TWENTY-THREE
— ✖ ✖ ✖ —

Sheriff Taylor was about her height, and Ella was able to match his strides. "Your medical investigator will have to send the body to OMI headquarters in Albuquerque, and getting answers will take time," Ella said. "Since the deceased was employed by the tribal casino and the tribe has an interest in this case, we could ask Dr. Roanhorse to take charge. Then everything would be done here and we'd have answers a lot quicker."

"That's fine with me. I'll call our deputy medical investigator and tell her not to respond."

"I'll call Dr. Roanhorse," Ella said.

After getting the Navajo Tribe's medical examiner on the second ring, Ella explained what she needed.

"I'll be there in twenty minutes," Carolyn answered.

"Good," Ella said. "The county's crime scene team is ready to wrap up."

"Thanks for calling me in on this, Ella. There hasn't been much to do lately, and I was getting restless. When I'm restless, I eat. I think I've put on ten pounds this past month," Carolyn said.

As far back as Ella had known her, Carolyn had been a large woman, and though keenly aware of all the dire warnings about obesity, she very simply enjoyed eating too much to curtail her appetite. The fact that she was a pariah on the Rez, where the dead and anything connected to them were assiduously avoided, undoubtedly was a big part of the problem.

Ella moved closer to one of the crime scene techs, who was speaking into a digital recorder, and listened. "No defensive wounds," the tech said. "Reddish brown liquid spreading outward from the wound."

Techs working a crime scene never listed anything as blood. Until it was tested, it remained a "liquid substance." Ella's attention was suddenly diverted when another tech reported a new discovery—a second bullet in the sofa cushion.

"Two rounds were fired from the gun found beneath the vic's hand," Taylor said, coming up to Ella. "And the serial numbers were filed down on the revolver, which means it was stolen. If the ME confirms this was murder, not suicide, we can get a forensics expert to try and restore those numbers."

"Maybe we'll find latent prints on the weapon, too," Ella said, though she knew it was a long shot that would require a great deal of luck. Unless the suspect had touched smooth metal, like the slide or barrel, handguns usually weren't very productive when it came to latents.

Minutes later, hearing a vehicle arrive, Ella glanced out the closest window and saw Carolyn pulling up in what the tribe's ME had dubbed the "body bus." The joke had been lost for most people on the Rez. Nobody liked talking about death.

As Ella watched her longtime friend get out of the van, it struck her how much Carolyn's split with her husband had aged her. Feeling guilty, Ella found herself wishing that she'd had more time to spend with her. Carolyn had even fewer close friends on the Rez than she did, but since they both had extremely demanding jobs, neither of them had much time to socialize.

"Hey," Ella said, going to greet her.

"Where's the body?" Carolyn asked, already focused on what lay ahead.

"Inside—still seated at a desk in the first room to the left. Indications are that the suicide was staged."

"I'll let you know," she replied.

Ella moved aside. Carolyn was in full ME mode. She could hear it in her friend's voice. Although police work required a strong stomach and steady nerves, Carolyn's work was on another level entirely. She'd often wondered how Carolyn stayed sane.

While Carolyn worked, Ella watched the techs finish searching the sofa where the second round had been found. "Will you be using a laser trajectory kit to track the position of the gunman?" Ella asked.

The young woman nodded. "It might also help us establish the sequence of events."

As she spoke to the tech, Ella had one eye on Carolyn. "I'm going to need to know as soon as possible if the slugs caught by the vest came from my service weapon. My partner will provide you with comparisons."

"Good. I'll let you know as soon as I have something," the woman said.

While Carolyn worked, Ella made herself useful by helping the county team continue to gather evidence. The back door knob was clean of prints, and was of a type that could easily be "bumped" open by any competent burglar. It was clear how the killer had gained entry. When she returned to the living room, she saw that Carolyn had already persuaded two sheriff's deputies to load the body into the van.

"It's sure easier to get help out here," Carolyn said as Ella came up.

"From what the crime scene unit has pieced together, it

appears that the victim was shot, then the shooter placed the gun in the vic's hand and fired off a second round. That way there'd be powder residue on the vic's hand," Ella said as she walked with Carolyn to the van.

"That'll leave clean patches on the victim's skin—places where the gunshot residue was blocked by the suspect's hand. I'll look for that. With that cheap old revolver, there should be plenty of residue. I'll let you know my findings as soon as possible," Carolyn answered.

"You and I . . . We always say we're going to get together, but our jobs keep getting in the way," Ella said.

"I know. That's why I decided to get a new best friend and roommate." Seeing Ella's surprised look, Carolyn laughed. "I've adopted a guinea pig. One of the nurses bought it for her daughter, but it created havoc with the kid's asthma. Anyway, GP and I are perfectly suited. He loves to eat, and will sit on the couch and watch TV with me at night. During the day when I'm gone he munches on alfalfa and takes his power naps." She paused. "I've decided that in my next life I'm coming back as a guinea pig."

"Just make sure to stay in *this* country. They're dinner in some others."

Carolyn laughed. "Call me later and I'll have some prelims for you."

As Carolyn drove off, Sheriff Taylor joined Ella. "We're dealing with murder, so I'm going to need whatever you have that pertains to the vic."

She nodded. "You'll have it as soon as I do. If I'm right, the primary suspect's on your turf. My hunch is that O'Riley's our man and that he planted the ArmaLite and the other items here to try and confuse the evidence," she said, giving him the pertinent details. "I think Grady's death was nothing more than another attempt to misdirect our investigation. Whoever's pulling O'Riley's strings wants me to believe that Grady was the other shooter at the airstrip."

"Send your ballistics data on the rounds from the airport shooting to our crime lab and we'll see if anything matches the .223 in the closet," Taylor asked.

"I'll have Justine get on that, but my guess is we'll get a hit. That's all part of the gunman's plan."

"What makes you so sure Grady wasn't involved in the shooting at the airstrip? The shooters wore masks, correct?"

"Yes, but Grady is too short, and besides, we've checked out Grady's alibi. The man was in his office at the critical time. Several people at his workplace confirm that he was there, though it was Sunday, and surveillance images for that time period verify it."

"He still might have hired O'Riley and Perry. And now that Perry's dead, maybe his partner decided to eliminate the only loose end that can point to him," Taylor suggested.

"It's possible, I suppose, but my gut tells me that the casino theory is taking us in the wrong direction," Ella said. "And with that, I'd better get going."

A short time later Ella and Justine were on their way back to the reservation. Justine seemed upset and Ella noticed it almost immediately.

"What's up? Did you have a disagreement with one of the locals on the scene?" Ella asked.

"No, it's not that. Abigail Yellowhair called. She wants to fund a public memorial service for Adam Lonewolf, and won't take no for an answer. She really leaned on me for a contribution, but I told her I wanted to spend my money helping the family once they returned from seclusion."

"Any idea why she's being so pushy about this all of a sudden?"

"No, not a clue," Justine said, "though she's paid a special interest in this from the beginning. Remember her showing up at the hospital, obviously going there directly from whatever business trip she'd just made? Her carry-on was still in the car."

"I remember her asking if Adam was still alive." Playing a hunch, Ella called Marianna Talk next. "Give me a twenty on Norm Hattery," she said, asking for a location.

"I've stayed with him for most of my shift. He met with Jaime Beyale for about fifteen minutes, then closed himself off in his motel room—alone. That's where he's been for the last few hours."

"Stay with him," Ella said, then after hanging up, glanced back at Justine. "I'd love to be able to assume that he's taking a nap, but that doesn't sound like a man trying to land a network news job."

"A couple of hours. . . ." Justine mulled it over. "If the motel has Internet service, my guess is that he's updating the station's Web news or blogging on his Web site. Probably both."

"Terrific," Ella snapped. "More trouble. I can feel it in my bones."

They arrived at the station ten minutes later, and Ella accompanied Justine to her office. The lab's computer was the fastest available. "I want to see everything Hattery's showing online: video, photos, blogs, whatever," Ella said.

"What are you hoping to find?" Justine asked, sitting at her computer.

"A reason for Abigail's interest in the Lonewolf family. She's never been a people person unless there was a power or profit issue involved."

A few minutes later, Justine logged on to Norm's Web site. They found nothing of particular importance there, nor at the Web site for the television station where Norm worked. Then they followed the link at the bottom to Norm's home page and found his blog.

"This is bad news," Justine said. "Hattery's checked out all the funeral homes in the area and knows no one has processed Adam's body for burial or cremation. Since the family's nowhere to be found, he's suggesting that there's more to Adam's alleged death than the department has said."

"Check out the quote marks around the word 'death,' not to mention his use of the word 'alleged,'" Ella added. "Now we know why Abigail was calling you. She's using that memorial service angle to try and figure out if Adam's still alive. You wouldn't pay to honor a dead guy you *knew* was alive."

"In that case, I blew it," Justine said. "But we've got a bigger problem. If the one who hired O'Riley and Perry gets wind of this, he's bound to start looking for Adam all over again—that is, if Adam was ever really the target."

"Blalock's going to need to alert the people at the base," Ella said, picking up her phone.

The agent answered on the first ring. "I've been keeping an eye on Hattery's blog, so I've handled that already," he said.

After she hung up, Ella continued staring at the phone, lost in thought. "Why is Abigail still so interested in Adam's real status?" she asked at last. "The Prickly Weed Project is back on track and her investments are looking up again. So what are we missing?"

"Maybe you're complicating the issue too much. Abigail likes knowing what's going on because it makes her feel more in control."

"I have a feeling there's more to it than that. The woman never does anything without a specific reason—and she's got a lot of money invested that could disappear if everything did go south." Ella stared at the wall, thoughts racing. "Let's go talk to Teeny. He has his ear to the ground and has access to all kinds of information."

They were inside Teeny's warehouse east of Shiprock twenty minutes later. Teeny had just handed Ella a plate of homemade fudge. "Eat. It's quick energy and you both look like you could use some of that."

Ella, who felt totally worn out, took a small bite then . . . heaven. "These are *wonderful*."

"It's my own recipe. I use fresh cream, cream cheese, and walnuts in addition to the usual ingredients. When I'm dragging but I need to keep going, it's the perfect cure."

Ella took a second one while Justine was still eating her first. It was too bad that Teeny didn't give out his recipes. She would have loved to have this one.

"Grab a bigger handful of those, and take them with you. You, too, Justine."

He didn't have to ask them twice. "Thanks," Ella replied. Justine, her mouth full, just nodded.

"Now tell me what I can do for you law ladies."

"Something weird's playing out with Abigail Yellowhair. Is there anything you can get me that might explain it?" Ella asked him.

He swiveled his chair around until he faced the computer screen, and began typing. "I drove past the turnoff to her new place yesterday on my way to Beclabito to meet a client. Did you know she's got two garden patches set aside for prickly weed? She told one of her neighbors that she's a consultant on the project."

"That I know. My mother's doing the same thing. She's got an entire field in back of the house where she's growing row upon row of that blasted weed."

Teeny focused on the screen, typed a few strokes, then glanced back at her. "I recently had reason to take a closer look at Abigail's finances. She'd been trying to convince a client of mine to invest in a wholesale jewelry operation of hers and he wanted to know the state of her finances."

"And?" Ella pressed.

"In spite of her big reputation, Abigail's barely solvent. Her previous business venture, the satellite phone deal that was supposedly going to make a fortune, sank without a trace after the tribe dropped out. Now she's got a quarter mil invested in the Prickly Weed project, basically the balance of her fluid assets. Since she sold her cabin in Colorado last week for about fifty percent of its appraised value—a huge loss on paper—my guess is that she's having severe cash flow problems."

"I knew that she'd sold the family home and moved into that smaller place, but I thought she was just trying to leave old memories behind," Justine said. "She's in a lot deeper than I realized."

Still checking his computer, Teeny glanced at Ella, and added, "The deal on her Colorado home closed last Saturday, the day before you got back from D.C."

Ella was still considering the possibilities when her cell phone rang. It was Sheriff Taylor.

"We've got a possible twenty on Shawn O'Riley," he said. "We've had an ATL on him ever since that incident outside Bloomfield and it looks like it finally paid off."

The successful "attempt to locate" was music to her ears. "Where's he at?" Ella asked.

"According to my deputy, who made the ID at a gas station, the suspect's traveling west out of Farmington on 64 in a dark brown pickup, old model, maybe 1990 Ford. He seems to be taking his time, staying well under the speed limit to avoid gathering any attention."

"Good. Have your officer stay on him, but give him plenty of room. We're on our way."

"Done. My officer's a detective in an unmarked vehicle. That should help."

Ella and Justine had reached the main highway and were racing east when Ella's cell phone rang again. It was Big Ed.

"Dispatch just got an anonymous call advising us that Shawn O'Riley's en route to a bar called C. O. Jones located outside of Kirtland," Big Ed clipped.

"Was the caller male or female?" Ella asked.

"Dispatch couldn't confirm either way. The call was grainy and the number was restricted. It's out of our jurisdiction, so Sheriff Taylor's been notified, but I want you and Justine there, just in case."

"Taylor's got a detective tailing O'Riley as we speak," Ella said. "My partner and I are already on our way."

Ella updated Justine as they raced down the highway.

"I've heard of that place, and it's not exactly a family establishment. They serve truck drivers and oil field workers, mostly," Justine said. "It's aptly named for the crowd it attracts."

"Is C. O. Jones someone I should know?" Ella asked.

"If you put it all together, it spells *cojones*, 'balls' in Spanish."

"This just keeps getting better and better," Ella muttered, calling Sheriff Taylor for an update.

"Your suspect just turned south off 64 onto the old highway leading into Kirtland. If he's headed for that C. O. Jones place, he'll have to turn north again in a few miles. There's some road work that'll slow him down, so his ETA at the tavern is ten minutes, give or take," he said.

"We can beat that time and get into position," she said.

"I'll be there ASAP, maybe twenty. I'm in an unmarked."

As they raced east down 64 along the northern perimeter of Waterflow, Ella felt her body tense. Slow, painstaking investigations intermingled with moments of sheer adrenaline made her job unique. What made her especially good at it was her ability to stay focused both during the slow times and when everything exploded into total chaos.

As they approached the establishment, represented by the image of a long-legged, winking cowboy, Ella quickly surveyed the parking lot, then contacted Sheriff Taylor and verified O'Riley's ETA.

"He's turned north and is coming up that street," Ella told Justine seconds later and pointed to a residential road that intersected Highway 64 at a stop sign just to the west.

"We only have a few minutes. Park around the back on the east side."

As they drove around the front of the building, which faced north, Ella recognized Begaye's late model luxury sedan parked near the entrance. What cinched the ID was the word Emerson Lee had scratched on the driver's side door. It had been painted over, but the rush job hadn't cured enough yet to completely conceal the damage.

"Could be a meeting—or a hit. Either Alfred is the next target or he's the one who's been pulling all the strings. How do you want to play this?" Justine asked, choosing a parking space that gave them a view of the entrance and Begaye's vehicle.

"Go in, locate Alfred, but don't make eye contact. If he sees you, ignore him and come back out. If he doesn't, stay on him. I'll watch for O'Riley. Backup's on the way, but be ready to use your weapon at any time. O'Riley likes to shoot people."

"Gotcha, boss." Justine stepped out of the vehicle, and, using the side door, went inside.

Ella climbed out next and looked around. Although there were more customers there than either of them had expected this time of day, the dinner crowd hadn't arrived yet.

Ella walked to a big Dodge pickup parked closer to the entrance and watched over the hood, across the lot toward the west. The sun was low in the sky now, but with her sunglasses on, it wasn't too bad. In another half hour, all she would have been able to see was a blurry silhouette backed by blazing heat.

A few minutes went by before Ella finally saw O'Riley's Ford pickup approach the stop sign. When the truck turned in her direction, she stepped back into the Dodge's shadow. Hopefully its owner wouldn't come out anytime soon and wonder what she was doing.

The pickup was slowing to make the turn when Alfred

came out of the bar, saw O'Riley's vehicle, and stopped on the sidewalk, apparently waiting. Justine stayed inside, pretending to be buying a newspaper from a vending machine but in position to watch through the glass panels of the foyer.

Ella, pistol in hand, made sure she was blocked by the rear roof pillars of the pickup's cab, then took a quick look to the west, wondering how close the deputy was following.

Instead of pulling into one of the parking slots, O'Riley wheeled his pickup sharply, facing east, then stopped behind Alfred's car, blocking it.

Leaving the truck running, O'Riley stepped out and came around to the front of his vehicle as Alfred walked over to him. O'Riley had his right hand inside his jacket, and from her angle, Ella could see the semi-auto jammed into his waistband. His shirt was also bulky underneath—he was wearing a vest.

"Where's the money?" O'Riley said, looking around slowly.

Ella froze, knowing any movement might reveal her presence.

"Here," Alfred brought an envelope out of his inside suit jacket pocket. "Take it and go. People know who I am."

"Hand it over and I'm out of here."

Alfred took two more steps forward, and handed O'Riley the envelope. Without checking, O'Riley shoved it into his own jacket pocket.

"You *sure* you weren't followed?" O'Riley asked.

"No way. I'm alone."

O'Riley looked to the west, then, as he turned to check the road east, a shiny black-and-white state police unit with a big gold badge on the door turned off the highway into the parking lot, heading right toward the empty slot next to Begaye's car.

O'Riley turned his back to the cop and drew his pistol.

TWENTY-FOUR

—————— ✖ ✖ ✖ ——————

"**Y**ou bastard," O'Riley yelled, shooting Alfred at point-blank range.

Too late to save Begaye, Ella fired two shots at O'Riley's head. He jerked once, then collapsed in a heap just as Justine rushed out the tavern's entrance in a crouch, pistol in hand.

The state patrolman whipped his unit around in a cloud of dust, then slid to a stop. As he dove out his door, using the cruiser as cover, Ella stepped into full view.

"Hold your fire!" she yelled, grabbing her badge off her belt and holding it high over her head. "We're tribal police officers!"

Seeing the big muzzle of the state patrolman's twelve-gauge shotgun over the hood of his vehicle, Ella placed her own weapon on the ground, then stood still, badge still up in the air.

Justine followed suit, laying down her weapon, then holding up her badge as she rose to a standing position.

"I'm Investigator Clah of the Navajo Tribal Police," Ella called out. "That's Officer Goodluck. Two suspects are down, and we need to get the EMTs here fast."

The black-and-gray uniformed state police officer came

out from behind his cruiser slowly, weapon waving back and forth between them. As he took a step forward, the deputy in the unmarked car pulled into the lot, emergency lights flashing.

A second unmarked cruiser, flashing light on the dashboard, wheeled into the lot, adding to the confusion. Sheriff Taylor, in his dark county uniform, stepped from that unit and identified himself. As the state patrolman lowered his weapon, Justine retrieved her weapon then ran over to Begaye, who was face down on the asphalt.

Taylor glanced at the gunshot victims, then strode over to meet Ella. "I saw the state police unit at the last minute, but there was no way to call him off in time."

Ella brought out her cell phone as she watched Justine, who was on her knees beside Begaye. After a long pause, Justine looked back at her and shook her head.

Ella put away the phone, retrieved her own weapon, then walked over to the state patrolman, a short, brown-eyed Hispanic who couldn't have been much over twenty-one. His hands were shaking and she couldn't blame him. Truth was, she wasn't far behind him on that score herself.

"You okay, Officer . . . Ramirez?" she asked, reading his name tag. A lot of officers shaved their heads close these days, but all it did for Ella was create the impression they were rookies. The style belonged to another generation, she decided, suddenly feeling old and tired.

"What did I step into here? I was just pulling in to take a code seven," he said, his hands tightly gripping the department-issue twelve-gauge pump.

"It's over now. Time to cool down," Ella said. She turned to check with her partner, who was examining O'Riley. From Justine's expression it was clear there was no need for a rescue unit.

"My crime scene team's en route," Taylor said, coming

over as his deputy stopped several tavern patrons who'd come out to gape. "I don't think we'll have any problems establishing what went down. It looks like a clean shoot," he added. "You need some time, Ella?"

She shook her head. "I'm better off busy, working the scene. Later, it'll hit me."

"Always does. Feel free to step away anytime. I'm sure the witnesses will confirm what happened. Lethal force was necessary here," he said.

Ella nodded, and, putting on her gloves, braced herself as she approached O'Riley's body. Though she thought she'd been prepared, seeing him up close was more than she could take. What was left of his face was an image that would haunt her nightmares for as long as she lived. She swallowed convulsively, pushing back the burning, acid taste that stung her throat.

"You sure you're okay?" Taylor asked quietly, coming up beside her.

Ella nodded, then shook her head and ran around the corner of the building to the garbage bins to throw up.

No one commented when she returned to the scene. Every experienced officer there had been through that before—whether at a TA, mobile home fire, or a shooting. Though she desperately wanted time alone, Ella knew her job was just beginning. The crime scene team was busy, and as Ella drew near, she saw the tech reach into O'Riley's pocket, pull out the envelope, and count the bills.

"How much?" Ella said, noting that her voice still wasn't back to normal.

"Two thousand dollars in hundreds, fifties, and twenties," she answered after a moment.

Ella nodded and stepped back, letting the techs complete their work. Begaye's body, a few feet away, was less messy, though he'd been shot at point-blank range in the heart.

Taylor came up and joined her. "You made the right decision taking the head shot. You'd already faced this guy before when he was wearing body armor."

Overhearing them, the tech by O'Riley's body confirmed it, opening O'Riley's shirt. "Looks like law-enforcement issue—still has a serial number on it. Probably stolen from some officer's vehicle," he said.

Leaving them to their work, Ella returned to the tribal unit and wrote the statement she knew Sheriff Taylor would be needing. Justine joined her about ten minutes later, sliding behind the wheel. "I'm guessing Begaye was paying O'Riley for the Grady hit, and when the state cop showed up, O'Riley thought he'd been ratted out. We already know O'Riley was involved in the airstrip shootings, so it all fits."

"No, not all. Grady was capped to throw us off, and it looks like Begaye set up that hit. But why shoot Adam when the IFT deal was still up in the air—something Begaye was pushing for? And what does this have to do with the briefcase of money Adam was carrying?" Ella asked. "We're still missing some key information."

"My people have things under control here," Taylor said as he approached. "I know you want to get rolling, so once you two write up your statements, you can leave. We know where to find you."

Ella had already finished the paperwork, so after Justine was done they got underway. "It's past office hours, but we need to get back to Shiprock and go through everything in Begaye's office," Ella said.

As Justine drove, Ella tried to concentrate on the case and block out the image of the man she'd just killed. "I've got a theory to run past you, partner," Ella said.

"Shoot . . . uh, sorry. Go ahead."

"I keep going back to the money Adam was carrying. Everything we know about him tells us that he's a straight arrow. So let's say he was given that money to deliver to IFT as a bribe. Maybe it was to the seal the deal with that Williams fellow he seemed to dislike. Then, somewhere along the way, Adam decided that he couldn't go through with it."

Justine nodded slowly. "Yeah. That theory fits in with what Adam told Marie about doing the right thing, and the possibility that he might lose his job. But that still doesn't answer the big question—*who* gave Adam the money?"

"Begaye? Or maybe it was Adam's closest tribal contact, Billy Garnenez. We've got too many bodies . . . not enough answers." Taking the job in D.C. working for John Blakely suddenly didn't seem like such a bad idea.

"Partner, are you *really* okay?" Justine asked gently.

"For now. I should be able to keep it together as long as I stay focused on the case. Later . . ."

"Yeah, I know," Justine murmured, looking down at the missing digit on her right hand. "There are some things that are impossible to forget. We just have to learn to deal with them."

"Yeah," Ella answered in a barely audible voice.

An hour later, they were sitting at the video monitors inside the tribal building's security office. They'd spoken to the security guard on the evening relief and obtained surveillance camera disks dating back a week prior to the Sunday shooting at the airstrip. Ella was hoping to find evidence of a meeting between Begaye and either of the shooters.

Ella watched the images from the lobby camera, which covered the front interior and the main hallway junction, while Justine, at a second monitor, went through parking lot surveillance. Although the going was slow and the work tedious, Ella couldn't face going home despite the late hour.

Taking a break she walked outside, leaving the security chief and Justine to continue. Ella stood a few feet from the side door and took a deep breath. Nightmarish images pushed from the edges of her mind, but with a burst of will, she forced them back. She had to close this case once and for all. She'd know no peace until she did. Afterwards, there'd be time to figure out what to do about her life. Working any-place far from the source of her nightmares was becoming more tempting with each passing hour.

Hearing footsteps behind her, Ella spun around in a crouch, and reached for her weapon.

"Easy, partner," Justine said quickly.

"Sorry," Ella muttered. "Still jumpy, I guess. Did you find something?"

Justine smiled. "Yeah, on the parking lot video. You're going to want to see this for yourself. It covers the last time Adam met with Begaye and Garnenez before returning to D.C., and matches the schedule Teeny unscrambled for us from Adam's BlackBerry."

Ella followed Justine back inside, then stood behind her, watching as the guard ran through the digitally recorded im-ages time-stamped the day prior to Adam's last trip to Wash-ington. As she watched, Adam Lonewolf arrived, crossed the parking lot carrying his briefcase, then went inside and out of view. The guard fast-forwarded five minutes, then Begaye ar-rived.

"Regular speed now," Justine said.

Begaye climbed out of his luxury sedan, reached for a large paper sack on the seat, then walked inside, carrying the bag by its two handles.

"Run Alfred crossing the lot again, but slow it down. And can you clear up the picture?" Ella asked.

"Some, but not much," he warned.

Ella wished the equipment here could have had half the capabilities of the one at the bank, but it wasn't to be. The guard worked with the screen until, at long last, the image cleared, and, when he paused the frame, Ella caught a glimpse of the box sticking out of the bag.

"M-O-N-O," Ella said. "Monopoly."

"And did you notice the shine—from the plastic wrap?

That's got to be the board game that had the money hidden inside it," Justine said. "We probably can't prove that, but it fits. Begaye passed the money to Adam, and now we know when that took place. Do you think Adam was unaware of what he was carrying?"

"And was he just volunteering to deliver a gift from Alfred to someone in D.C.? Then why bring it back? No, Adam knew," Ella said. "Later, he either decided to keep the money, or return it to Begaye and blow the whistle, knowing it would probably cost him his job. Considering what we know about Adam, the last option seems most likely."

As the digital images continued rolling, they saw Adam leave, again carrying his briefcase. Billy left a few minutes later, but all he was carrying was a small folder and a laptop under one arm. Begaye came out almost an hour afterwards, empty-handed except for a soft drink.

Ella asked the security guard to take a walk and give them some privacy for a while. Once he was out of earshot, she sat back, gathering her thoughts. "Okay, from what we've seen and the timing, we can assume that Adam was slated to deliver that game, and bribe, to someone at IFT. The way the money was packaged was brilliant, too. It made it through airport security—twice."

"But there's a flaw in our theory. The bribe was never made, yet the deal still went through. What happened?" Justine asked.

"Either the bribe wasn't needed, or someone else managed to come up with enough money to grease the right palms at IFT," Ella answered. "Remember the discrepancy about when the deal was sealed. That's the key. We now know that Adam was supposed to deliver the bribe, but he didn't. Whoever was supposed to be getting that money—most likely Williams—must have complained to Begaye or whoever else was working with the councilman. Then the second payoff attempt was made *after* the airport shooting. That one succeeded and that's when the deal went through. But there's still another player we haven't identified. The person who tipped us off today was hoping that things would end badly for O'Riley. He wanted to destroy any trail that might lead back to him. He also knew that even if Begaye wasn't hurt, he'd be implicated and out of the picture."

"That plan had a good chance of succeeding. O'Riley was a loose cannon. It certainly didn't take much to set him off."

"And whoever it was knew O'Riley well enough to figure that into the equation," Ella said. "But there's also a chance that O'Riley was sent there to kill Begaye, and the patrolman showing up only hastened the inevitable."

"That's possible, too."

The security guard returned and made them a copy of the DVD, identifying and signing it out to them to maintain the chain of evidence. Once it was in their possession they went out to the parking lot.

"What about Billy? He was also in the building at the same time that the game was given to Adam. Chances are he's our other player."

"I know how to find out for sure." Ella considered it for several moments. "We have reason to believe that the bribe *was* paid—in one form or another. That either required an electronic transfer through a financial institution, which would leave a trail, or a quick trip to D.C., which can also be traced. Go to Blalock's office. We'll need his clout now."

About an hour later, Ella sat across from Blalock's desk. Justine was pacing.

"Sit down, Justine," Blalock growled, looking up from his computer terminal. "You're driving me crazy."

Justine sighed, then did as he asked.

"No money was transferred from either Begaye's or Garnenez's accounts," Blalock said. "Neither of them has that kind of money anyway, not unless they happened to have seventy-five K stashed in their mattresses. My guess is that someone else rounded up that cash, then hurried to D.C. to hand over the replacement bribe right around the time Adam got back. But who on the Rez would have that much cash lying around?"

"We don't know that the second amount totaled seventy-five thousand. It might have been a lot less, with a promise of more to come," Ella said.

"But Dwayne still has a point," Justine said. "Who around here has that kind of cash?"

Silence stretched out until Ella finally spoke. "Abigail Yellowhair's home sale—actually for her cabin—closed the day before we came back from D.C.," Ella said, remembering what Teeny had told her. "She must have received a fat check."

"I've got some travel records here. Both Alfred Begaye and Abigail Yellowhair flew to D.C. and back around the time you did," Blalock said. "Begaye left two days before your return, and came back the same day you did, Sunday, only later. Abigail flew there on Saturday, the day before your return, and came back on Monday morning."

"Yeah. Her luggage was still in her car when she dropped by the hospital to check on Adam's condition, remember? I'm going to need a warrant to go through Abigail's financial records," Ella said.

"Let me go to my grandfather on this. I think he'll move quickly for us," Justine said.

"Go. I'll stay with Blalock," Ella replied.

"Let's say that we're right and Abigail's behind the bribe. Why would she risk *everything* for something like this?" Blalock said, thinking out loud.

"Abigail likes power, and that comes with money. Her funds have been really depleted by her recent business failures, so this might have been a desperate attempt to gain some lost ground. She's already sold her high-end home and moved into a modest three bedroom, and now her cabin is gone—at a loss, according to my source. With her last remaining bundle sunk into the Prickly Weed Project, she couldn't afford another financial hit."

"What about Begaye?" Blalock asked. "What's his role in all this?"

"The Prickly Weed Project was his brainchild and, politically, he couldn't afford to lose, so when their lobbyist failed to deliver the bribe, Adam became a problem for both him and Abigail," Ella said, then after a pause, continued. "Although Begaye handled the payment to Perry and O'Riley, getting rid of Lonewolf and misdirecting the investigation by killing Kevin, too—that part of it has Abigail's handwriting all over it. The woman knows how to plan an operation."

"Begaye was used. Is that what you're saying?" Blalock asked.

She nodded. "When Adam refused to deliver the bribe, Abigail realized that the project would probably be dropped, but Begaye was desperate, too. He had his credibility—the heart of his political career—riding on it. That gave Abigail the edge she needed to manipulate him and take control of the situation."

"And existing issues, like the fight over the land, the casino lawsuit, and so on, would serve to lead us away from the real motive for the hit?" Blalock asked.

"Exactly. Having Kevin killed in addition to Adam also held an extra bonus for her—payback. Remember I put her adopted daughter, Barbara, in prison. She wanted to take something from me, but failing that, leaving *my* daughter without her father was a good second."

"What about the hit on Grady? Another misdirection?"

"You got it. Abigail had Grady killed and had one of the weapons used in the airport attack planted in his closet along with the vest to seal the frame against him. I believe Grady got caught up in something that had very little to do with him or his problems with Kevin and the tribe. This case was all about Abigail's quest for power—and her vendetta against me," Ella said. "It was personal."

SUNDAY

After a wake-up call to Big Ed, who'd returned to the station despite the fact it was nearly 2:00 A.M., they had the warrants needed to legally verify the state of Abigail's finances.

Back in the chief's office, bleary-eyed and coffee-stoked, the group of four discussed the revelations of the past several hours. Blalock was the first to point out that their case still had flaws. "We can't arrest Mrs. Yellowhair, or even take her to court with what we have right now. She'd walk," he said.

"It's hard to nail mud to the wall," Ella muttered, taking another sip of cold coffee.

As silence fell over the gathering once again, Ella realized they were out of energy and options. "We have one shot. It's a crazy idea, but I think it'll work," she said, filling them in.

Once she finished speaking, Ella glanced around the room. No one even looked up, and the silence was deafening. "You guys still awake, right?"

Blalock sat back in his chair rubbing his chin. "Hell, it might just work, and at the moment it's all we've got. I say we go for it."

Big Ed nodded slowly, then stifled a yawn. "Okay, Shorty. I'll back you up if things go south."

"We'll need someone who can pass as Adam," Ella said. "Any suggestions?"

Justine sat up straight in her chair. "How about Benny?

They're about the same size and weight. Same Army buzz haircut, too. If we obscure his face with some bandages, he'll pass."

"You're right," Ella said after a beat. "The key will be getting Marie Lonewolf to cooperate."

"Once she hears the whole story I think she'll be willing to help us out," Justine said. "Marie wants all this to be over with, I'm sure."

"Now we need a reason to bring Charles Williams in. I don't care if it's speeding, or for spitting on the sidewalk," Ella said.

"Leave that to me," Blalock said. "I can be downright creative when the situation calls for it, and if there's any way to put some additional pressure on him, I will."

"You're good to go then, Shorty. Keep me updated," Big Ed said.

TWENTY-FIVE

✖ ✖ ✖

Just before eight in the morning and already exhausted, Ella picked up the phone. The thought of making any kind of deal with Norm Hattery went against the grain, but he was the only logical choice. Once he leaked the story she was about to give him, it would hit the Internet, the press, and the media all about the same time. She pulled out his business card and called his cell number.

Hattery picked up on the first ring. "Investigator Clah, you're the last person I expected to hear from so early this morning. You must want something from me and are finally ready to trade."

His reporter's instincts were right on target. She hoped that hers, as a police officer, would turn out to be as good. "I'm calling to offer you the story of a lifetime, but I'm going to need something from you in exchange," she said, then explained. As she spoke, she could hear him typing.

"I'm putting this up on my blog right now under breaking news. Then I'll call Jaime Beyale and tell her I got it from one of my most reliable sources. Your name will never come up," he said. "Basically, my story will reveal that war hero Adam Lonewolf is still alive, out of danger, and on his way back to the station to help identify his attackers. I've also said that he's bringing evidence that'll break the case wide open and implicate an important and respected member of the tribe."

"Perfect."

"You see? I told you we'd both benefit from some cooperation. This way, justice is served and we both come out ahead."

Ella tried to ignore the bad taste the creep left in her mouth. "In a few hours, we'll announce a mid-morning press conference here at the station."

Ella called Teeny next, and after a quick update, added, "I need you to prepare an audio that will use Begaye's and Abigail's voices." She continued, describing the contents of the conversation she had in mind.

"That's all, huh?" Teeny asked, chuckling after she finished. "And let me guess. You want it yesterday."

"Even with your toys, is it possible, or do I need a new plan?"

"I can get voice samples from Justine—she tapes all her interviews, like you should, by the way. In addition to the right toys, I also have access to a professional impressionist who does voice-over gigs on movies that have to be cleaned up for network TV. That means I can do this with my eyes—ears—closed. But you're going to owe me big time."

"Deal." Ella hung up, wishing she didn't know that Teeny had probably faked other conversations in the past. Still, if there ever was a good time for deception, it was now. She'd heard from Blalock a while ago, and he had good news about Charles Williams, but they'd still need a little more to nail the key player still in the picture—Abigail Yellowhair. She was slippery, and they needed to come from all directions or the woman might just get away.

Justine walked in a half hour later, and her expression

was grim. "I have some bad news—in more ways than one. We may be close to losing Adam. He's gone into surgery again. He's bleeding inside the brain and it doesn't look good, but he's got the best doctors in the state working on him, so there's still hope. Marie was already en route here, so she's decided to stick to the plan. There's nothing she can do at the hospital, and, according to her, this is the best way to honor her husband, no matter how it turns out."

Ella sighed. Just when they were getting close. "I agree. In the meantime, let's do what we can to nail these lowlifes. Keep working on the details with Benny."

"I'm on that," Justine replied.

"Good. Once everything else is set, we'll go pay Abigail a visit," she said just as her phone rang.

Ella looked at the caller ID. It was from the hospital at Kirtland AFB—Captain Marcus. Ella thought of Adam, and his family, then brought the phone to her ear.

"With Blalock's big score this morning, we've got enough to arrest Abigail right now. But I'd sure like to nail her for every crime she's committed. What if she doesn't take the bait?" Justine asked, as they got into the tribal cruiser. It was nearly noon, and the operation was underway.

"A lot has changed in the past few hours, and we'll have to make the most of what we have. Ever play poker? Think of this as the hand of a lifetime," Ella said. Over the years, Abigail had been a formidable opponent, but her time had run out. At long last, Abigail was going down.

As they traveled along the road, Ella studied the sunlit mesas, nature's apartment complex, housing thousands of other heartbeats. Among the millions of hiding places, large and small, were those of coyotes and rabbits, burrowing owls and bats, hidden deep inside rock crevices and caves, waiting for the right time to come out and hunt.

Ella thought of the rhythm and cadence of the desert—life and death, heat and cold, night and day, even the cycles of drought and monsoons that linked all of life, human and animal, together. Here on the Rez, Navajo ways taught that everyone and everything was connected. Those beliefs, as old as the tribe itself, renewed the courage of the *Diné* daily, even in the toughest of times. Today a measure of balance would be achieved, though harmony often came with tragedy in its wake.

Years back, eager for adventure and the opportunity to explore a world she'd barely known, she'd left the Rez to join the FBI. Now, with every breath she took, she could feel her ties to this land, bordered by the sacred mountains.

More than ever, she wanted her daughter to grow up appreciating who and what she was. On the outside, prejudice still existed, and she didn't want her daughter to hear others devalue what it meant to be a Navajo before she could fully understand the treasure it was.

Though Kevin's argument for sending their daughter to school in D.C. had many valid points, it was one based on an Anglo's definition of success. Ella suddenly realized that she knew what her answer to the job offer would be.

"Thinking this might be a good time to take that job offer in D.C.?" Justine asked.

"I suppose," Ella said. "But neither one of us should get sidetracked now. Concentrate on Abigail and the plan. Our only chance to put her away for good depends on what happens in the next hour."

They arrived at Abigail's home a short time later. The curtains were open and they could see someone inside, moving about. Before they'd even parked, Abigail came to the front porch and waved them in, cell phone still at her ear.

As Ella approached, Abigail smiled and placed her phone on a side table. "The news is all over the Four Corners. Adam

Lonewolf is alive and starting to recover—though you knew about that all along, no doubt. I understand he's going to be present at a press conference within the hour. If what I've heard is all true, you should be able to close your case before too much longer. Hopefully, Lonewolf will be able to fill in the missing questions you and the department have been asking yourselves since the shootings."

"Which brings me to the reason I'm here. I suggest you come down to the station of your own volition. It'll look better that way," Ella said.

"You're not serious. You think Adam plans to implicate me?" She laughed. "For what crime? You and I have a long history, Ella, but I think you can definitely file this under 'wishful thinking.'"

"I'm not here to arrest you, Abigail. I have no idea what Adam's going to say. My visit is simply a courtesy to my mother's friend, and someone whose work has had a great impact on the tribe. I figured you would like to be present in case your name comes up. You had ties to Councilman Alfred Begaye, and as you undoubtedly already know, he was murdered yesterday afternoon."

"I knew Begaye, but our only connection was that we both invested in the Prickly Weed Project. All your suspects are dying off, dear, but if you're looking to me to fill the holes in your investigation, you're grasping at straws. I know nothing that can help you."

"If you're so sure of yourself, why don't you follow us to the station?" Ella countered smoothly.

"Of course. This is something I wouldn't miss."

Abigail was true to her word, though Ella kept her sedan in sight the entire trip, just in case she decided to make a run for it. The drive took less than fifteen minutes, and when they arrived at the station, the press and media were already crowding the front and side door. Among them were a hundred or more onlookers, some waving small flags, and most carrying digital cameras and cell phones, waiting to capture the historic moment when Adam arrived.

Ella and Justine walked over to join Abigail as she got out of her car.

"Making people believe that Adam had died probably saved further attempts on his life," Abigail said softly, waving at someone in the crowd. "And, with him coming back today . . . well, The People *do* need their heroes."

Ella realized that Abigail had known all along that Adam hadn't died in Shiprock, merely been relocated somewhere she couldn't penetrate. It shouldn't have surprised her. Informants were everywhere. For a price, one could buy almost anything these days. The question now was, what else did Abigail know?

Seeing the look Justine gave her, Ella shook her head. She didn't want to give Abigail any more information. She had enough already.

Ella stood beside Abigail as Marie Lonewolf pushed the wheelchair containing the expertly bandaged Benny Pete into the crowded station lobby. Cameras went wild and there were so many lights and flashes that Ella found it difficult to see.

Standing beside the undercover officer, who was slumped down, his head resting on his shoulders, Marie held up her hand. The gathering went dead quiet within seconds. Tears filled her eyes—it wasn't an act—and for a while she couldn't speak. Everyone remained silent, respecting her situation, but cameras continued to flash.

Finally Marie found her voice. "My husband was brutally attacked, and for his protection he was moved to a hospital in Albuquerque. We all went into hiding, unable to tell anyone—even our closest friends and relatives. For that, and for the lies that had to be told, we apologize and ask for your understanding. But now we know the truth behind what happened to him and Mr. Tolino, and those responsible will soon face arrest—and justice."

More camera flashes went off, and cell phones were aimed, recording every second in photos and video. Ella's gaze drifted to Abigail, who was trying not to look too interested, but it was clear she was hanging on every word. Then Ella noticed Abigail glance to the left, where Martin Tallman, the attorney, was standing. He nodded slightly, and Abigail switched her gaze back to Marie. Abigail had probably been on the phone with him this morning. The Yellowhairs had a sixth sense for danger, and always lawyered up when trouble loomed on the horizon.

Marie continued, shifting her attention back and forth between the media cameras. "I'm speaking on behalf of my husband. Afterwards, I'll try to answer some of your questions."

Marie gave them a brief rundown of what had happened, then according to Ella's plan, added, "Adam couldn't remember anything connected to the shooting for days. Then his memory began to return just as the doctors said it would. But there were still a lot of gaps in what he recalled. That's why he didn't think he'd be much help to the police. All he could do was tap his finger—once for yes, two for no."

"What changed?" one of the Anglo reporters called out.

"Yesterday, I began sorting through some old mail I picked up on a secret trip back home. That's when I found a small package Adam had mailed to himself—a memory card full of audio recordings." She held up the small memory chip so everyone could see and photograph it. "Once I realized what it was, I called the police immediately," she said, then taking a breath, continued. "Although we were asked by the authorities to keep this private for now, we've decided against that. Too many questions have been raised about my husband's loyalties, so we wanted to set the record straight once and for all. Someone betrayed my family and the tribe in the process. I want that person unmasked now in front of everyone."

Marie stuck the memory card into a small handheld player, then turned up the volume.

First they heard the voice of Councilman Begaye explaining that the bribe money hadn't been delivered. That was followed by Abigail Yellowhair, demanding to know what had happened to the money, and saying that, one way or another, she'd make sure that her investment in IFT paid off. The recording was slightly muffled to make appear as if it had been made by a handheld device hidden, maybe, inside a pocket.

As the recording continued, those familiar with Abigail's voice turned toward her. By the time the brief conversation ended, everyone's attention was focused in her direction.

Tallman came over. "Tell everyone the truth," he advised, placing a hand on Abigail's shoulder.

"That's a fake. I never had that conversation," Abigail said confidently, directly into the cameras. "This is a scam played out by police officers who don't have a clue about what's really going on."

Ella watched her play it cool—all self-righteous indignation without any trace of hesitation. Unfortunately for Abigail, her voice matched the one they'd just heard on the audio recording. Even her lawyer had seemed surprised at first, though he'd quickly recovered.

Benny raised his arm, very slowly at first, struggling. He managed to get it up nearly to his eye level, then held out his hand. He wiggled his finger twice. Marie started crying, and Blalock, who'd come up beside her, put his arm around her shoulders with surprising tenderness. Sheriff Taylor was there as well, his eyes on Ella, in on the plan and waiting for the reaction.

Chaos erupted as reporters yelled yes or no questions, each louder than the last.

Abigail took a step forward and pointed her finger at Benny, pure hatred on her face. "You're a fake and a liar. The real Adam Lonewolf died this morning during surgery!"

"How did you know, Mrs. Yellowhair?" Ella spoke, realizing she had to use the evidence they already had on hand. "Another spy you've paid off? I'm taking you into custody right now. Even if you somehow manage to avoid a life sentence for the murder of a tribal hero, we already have enough to send you to jail for a long, long time. Somebody in your little conspiracy decided to cut a deal this morning."

Ella motioned toward the booking area, where Justine was standing. Next to her was IFT employee Charles Williams, the county's district attorney, and another man in an expensive suit that screamed lawyer. Williams didn't look happy at all. Justine was in a good mood, however, and smiled as she removed a set of handcuffs from Williams' wrists.

Abigail managed a laugh, though her bluster was rapidly fading. "Lying to save his own skin, no doubt. You'll never make any of those accusations stick," she said. "You have no idea who you're dealing with, Clah. I've lost my husband and two daughters trying to better myself *and* the tribe. I've given everything I had, even my fortune, for others. You've given up, what, a few weekends on the job when you couldn't go for a hike with your little girl? Prepare for the biggest fight of your life. I'm not rotting away in some jail cell."

Ella grabbed Abigail's wrists and slapped on the handcuffs tightly. "That's a sad excuse for all the harm you've caused to innocent people. She's all yours, Agent Blalock. Her interstate crimes place her under federal jurisdiction."

Anger flashed in Abigail's eyes. "You and I aren't through,

Ella Clah. I have a *long* memory. Tallman, get me in front of a judge. I want to be home before dark."

Blalock stepped forward, then turned Abigail over to Sheriff Taylor and Sergeant Neskahi. The officers motioned her toward the entrance, currently blocked by photographers with flashing cameras. Abigail stopped and turned around one last time. "Don't think you've won," she said, glaring at Ella. "The tribal chairman won't want this cloud hanging over him. You'll need more information than you've got, and I'm your only hope of getting that."

As Abigail was taken away, Ella knew she was right. Somewhere down the pike, Abigail would be back—with a vengeance.

"Looks like you've made yourself another enemy. She'll be gunning for you the second she gets a chance," Blalock said.

"She'll have to take a number," Ella said. "By the way, Dwayne, getting Williams to spill his guts was a real gift, and at just the right time. How did you get him to fold like that?"

"Once I showed him the cash withdrawals from Yellowhair's accounts, copies of her flight itinerary, and told him we had surveillance of his last meeting with the woman, he crumbled like fresh cornbread. With aggravated assault and a murder now connected to his actions, he faces conspiracy charges and serious jail time. We could also nail him for accepting kickbacks, soliciting and accepting bribes, and a host of other civil violations—not to mention informing the IRS about illegal income he had no way of declaring. So I got him, his lawyer, and the DA on the phone together and suggested a deal. I said he could turn back the clock by returning the money and cooperating with us in nailing Mrs. Yellowhair. He accepted the offer before I'd even finished talking."

"Nice. We don't really have surveillance video of that meeting, do we?"

"No, but from the way he cringed and came forth with

the details of his meetings and conversations with Mrs. Yellowhair, I figure it must be on somebody's video somewhere," Blalock said, chuckling.

Big Ed came up and shook FB-Eyes' hand before turning to her. "Good work, Shorty."

"You've got the hard part, Chief," she said gesturing to the crowd of reporters on a feeding frenzy, including Norm Hattery, who was at the front of the pack. "When Adam Lonewolf died this morning in surgery, our plan was suddenly turned upside down. You're going to face some tough questions from the Traditionalists for the way we used his death to catch his killers. The tribe has lost a real hero—twice."

"I can take the heat. My heart goes out to the victim's loved ones. His wife showed a lot of courage this morning, going through the act like she did. I respect her for that. Marie Lonewolf needs a reminder of our gratitude—and an escort back to her family."

"I'll take care of that, Chief," Ella said. "It'll be my honor."

Three days passed. Ella was helping Kevin gather his things while Dawn, upset that her father was leaving, had barely said a word to either of them.

"I'll always find time to come and see you," Kevin told Dawn, who was standing in the doorway to her room as if to block the way. "There's no need for you to be upset."

"It's just not fair! You two like each other. I know you do," Dawn said.

"Yes, we do," Ella admitted, "but a man and a woman need more than friendship to make things work."

"No, they don't. *Shimasáni* says that only the Anglo world believes in romantic love and that's why they're always getting divorced."

Kevin laughed and looked at Ella. "She's got a point."

Ella scowled at Kevin, then glanced at Dawn. "Your father and I need a chance to talk. Isn't it time to groom Wind?" Ella said, referring to Dawn's beloved pony.

Suddenly Dawn's expression brightened and there was a hopeful gleam in her eye. "Wait—are you saying that you two need time alone? No problem. I'm outta here."

Ella sighed as her daughter hurried off. "I should have phrased that differently. You need to quit giving her false hope, Kevin."

Kevin stopped packing and, for a moment, met Ella's gaze. "Think about it, Ella. She's right, you know. The things that used to separate us . . . they aren't there so much anymore."

Ella remembered the days when Kevin's career ambitions had been the focal point of his life. Even Dawn had come in second. "You still spend a lot of time in Washington. Not that I blame you. Working in and around the nation's capital must bring an incredible level of excitement and satisfaction. The position I was offered over there is pretty much a dream job—"

"So you *are* going," he said, interrupting her. "That's going to be great for your career. I think you'll find that life in D.C. is addictive in its own way. *I'm* sure going to miss it— and the chance to be around Dawn a lot more."

She'd been folding one of his shirts, but suddenly stopped and looked up. "Wait. What?"

"I'm not going back. Remember me telling you about those vibes I'd been getting from my bosses? Well, it turns out that with all the irons in the fire, the tribal council has decided we need to cut the budget and reduce expenses. We've had some major capital outlays recently with the casino, the generating station, and that new uranium extraction operation. At least that's the tribe's position. Personally I think it's because of pressure from Councilman Natani, who resents the bad name I've given the casino."

He gave her a wry smile. "I can't win for losing, huh? We're switching long-distance job locations, and now Dawn will have to fly home to see *me*."

"No, that won't be a problem. I'm not going to D.C. either. What I was about to say was that something that seems too good to be true—generally is. My *career* might be better off elsewhere, but I've realized more than ever that my *future* is here, with my family and The People. I'm keeping my job with the tribe. For once we've both come out ahead—you for doing your job so well, and me, well, for wanting to do the job here instead of back east."

He smiled slowly. "Finally. We'll both be in the same place at the same time—here on the Rez."

"Yes!" They both heard Dawn's excited whisper from just outside the door.

Ella went to the doorway and saw her daughter standing out in the hall.

"I'm going to brush Wind right now," Dawn said, backing up a few steps. "I can hear him calling me," she added, then took off running.

Kevin met Ella at the doorway, suitcase in one hand, cane in the other, supporting his bad leg. "Don't worry. I'll explain things to her later."

"What, exactly, will you explain?" Ella asked.

"That although you can—and should—take a shot at your dream, life always has the final say."

Ella walked him outside to his car, where Mona Todea, his assistant, waited behind the wheel.

Turning to face Ella one last time, Kevin brushed her face with the palm of his hand. "And you know what? When it comes to us, life hasn't had the last word."

Ella was watching Kevin's car go down the driveway when Rose came out to join her. As they stood side by side, Ford's old pickup came over the hill, approaching from the east. Both vehicles stopped, and Ella saw Ford climb out of his car, then walk around to the passenger's side to talk to Kevin.

The men were there for a few minutes. Then Ford got back into his truck and headed up the dirt road leading to the house.

"Was the preacher supposed to visit *this* afternoon?" Rose asked.

Ella nodded. "He wanted to go horseback riding with my daughter after she got home from school."

"I didn't know he could ride," Rose answered.

"Neither did I," Ella said.

"There's still an awful lot you don't about him," Rose said softly. "But here's something you can count on. Neither of those two men are prepared to share you. You'll have to choose, daughter."

"I know, Mom, I know. Just be ready for the possibility that it may end up being none of the above. But let's not talk about that today. How about some of your herbal tea?" Ella placed her arm around her mother's waist, and together they walked back inside.

Turn the page for a sneak peek at
Aimée and David Thurlo's new novel

Black Thunder

Available Fall 2011

ONE

——— ✖ ✖ ✖ ———

Tribal Police Investigator Ella Clah stood next to her department's cruiser, a dusty, white SUV that had more miles on it than a Two Grey Hills sheepdog. As she stood beneath the shade of the Quick Mart station's island, watching the dollar amount shoot past fifty as the pump fed regular into the tank, her second cousin and partner, Justine Goodluck, was busy cleaning the windshield.

"It's been so quiet lately," Justine said. "I hate slow days. I'd rather be up to my ears in an investigation than catching up with paperwork. It's nine in the morning and it already feels like we've been on duty all day."

"I hear you," Ella answered. "At least we're not behind a desk."

Justine stopped working on the windshield and looked directly at Ella. Although among Traditionalists that would have been considered extremely rude, tribal cops had learned to walk the line between the old and the new, adapting to a reservation in transition.

"What's eating you, partner?" Justine asked. Seeing Ella shrug, Justine added, "Don't try to tell me it's nothing. We've known each other too long."

There were many advantages to working with a close partner but the ability to second-guess each other was often a two-edged sword. With some partnerships, familiarity bred contempt, as the old saying warned. Yet Justine and she had found a middle ground. Though they weren't what Ella's daughter would have termed BFFs, they'd become attuned to each other in a way that gave them a distinct advantage out in the field.

Ella was still thinking of how to answer that when a call came over their radio. "S.I. Unit One, see the clerk at the First United Bank on Highway 64, east of the bridge. He reports a man posing as Chester Kelewood is trying to cash a two-hundred-dollar check. The clerk will try to stall the subject until you arrive."

Ella hung the gas nozzle back onto the pump and reached inside the open window to pick up the mike. "Unit One responding," Ella said as Justine paid the bill.

"We're less than a mile from there," Justine said, slipping behind the wheel. "How do you want to handle this?"

Ella began accessing information on the MDT, Mobile Dispatch Terminal. As her partner eased out into downtown Shiprock traffic, she answered, "Chester Kelewood has been on our missing persons list since last June second, and in these situations the bank always flags their accounts. Let's go in silent and try to get next to this scam artist before he catches on."

A few minutes later, Justine dropped Ella off near the bank's front door, then headed for the closest parking slot. As Ella approached the entrance, an anxious-looking man stepped outside—not Kelewood, judging from the image she'd just viewed on the terminal. She hesitated, wondering if this was the suspect or just another patron.

His gaze shifted to the badge clipped to her belt and a second later, he spun around and bolted down the sidewalk.

"That's him!" a man in the foyer yelled.

Ella raced after the man, who darted around the corner of the building.

Although he'd only had a slight lead, the man moved like the wind, fear of arrest undoubtedly motivating him. He reached the back corner of the bank, then disappeared down the alley to his left.

Just as Ella appeared in the alley, he reached a six-foot cinder-block wall. Seeing her closing in, he scrambled clumsily over the top.

Ella followed, jumping up, then over. This was a lot easier than the ten-foot barrier at the county police academy's obstacle course. Dropping to her knees to absorb the shock of landing, she searched the perimeter and quickly spotted the suspect. The Navajo man was hightailing it down a dirt road.

She hit Justine's speed-dial number on her cell phone, slowing just enough to make the call. "Justine, I'm in pursuit. Drive down the ditch road and try to cut him off. He's heading north through the brush."

"Roger that," Justine replied, then hung up.

Ella continued pursuit into the *bosque*, the wooded area that lined the riverbanks. She knew she couldn't match his sprint speed in a 440 or less, but she was sure she could wear him down cross-country, providing she could keep him within sight or track him. Even as she processed this thought, the man raced fifty yards down the road, then cut right and disappeared into a clump of twelve-foot-high willows, red and gray-green from their early summer growth.

Less than ten seconds behind, she ducked in after him. Ella could hear his labored breathing and the thump of his boots on the sand as he ran parallel to the San Juan River, here only about a hundred yards wide. Although there were steep bluffs on the opposite shore, on this side there were many possible exits back along the north bank. She'd have to be careful he didn't slip back into town. Hopefully, Justine would see him if he crossed the ditch road.

The path the suspect had chosen kept him close to the river. The chase required constant swerving and twisting to avoid getting whipped by the long willow branches or tripping on a tuft of salt grass. Ella found herself constantly ducking and throwing up her right or left arm to avoid being, literally, bush whacked.

She'd already eased into her long-distance running rhythm: two strides, inhale, two strides, exhale. She knew from her regular conditioning runs that she'd be able to keep up this pace for miles. Even with the heavy ballistic vest she always wore under her shirt, she'd catch up sooner or later. Unfortunately, the moment he realized that, he might turn on her, so she'd have to be ready.

Still on his tail, she remained alert, forcing herself to keep her breathing smooth and regular. Even if she hadn't been able to hear him crashing through the brush like an enraged bull, his tracks were easy to follow. Soon she noticed that he was angling steadily toward the river. The bluffs a quarter mile farther down were lower and receded from the banks, leaving easier access to the shore and possible escape. Maybe he'd decided to swim for it next—though it was probably more of a deep wade or wallow unless he dropped into a pool or undercut in the bank.

Suddenly Ella stopped hearing his footsteps. She slowed to a brisk walk and listened carefully. Almost instinctively, she reached up to touch the turquoise badger fetish hanging from a leather strap around her neck.

Her brother, Clifford, a medicine man, or *hataalii* as they were known to the *Diné*, the Navajo People, had given her the Zuni-made fetish years ago as a gift. Since that time, she'd noticed that the small carving invariably became hot whenever danger was near. Right now it felt uncomfortably warm. Though she'd never been able to explain it, she suspected that the heat it emitted might have something to do with her own rising body temperature in times of crisis. Either way, she'd learned to trust the warning.

Ella stopped and slowly turned around in a circle, detecting the acrid scent of sweat—not her own. Before she could pinpoint it more accurately, a man burst out from behind a salt cedar, yelling as he swung a big chunk of driftwood like a baseball bat.

Ella ducked and the wood whooshed over her head, missing her skull by inches. Before he could take another swing, Ella drew her weapon and aimed it at her assailant.

"Drop the stick, buddy, now!" she ordered.

The man dropped the branch, but dove to his right, rolling into some tall grass. Then, leaping back to his feet, he sprinted away.

"Crap!" Ella holstered her gun and took off after him again. No way this jackrabbit was going to get away from her.

Running out of steam, the panting suspect tried to leap a fallen cottonwood branch, but caught his toe, or misjudged the jump. He fell to the sand, face-first.

Ella caught up to him a second later, but he swung around, still on his knees, and dove for her feet. He grabbed her boot and twisted her leg, trying to knock her down. Ella broke free and recaptured her balance just as the guy leaped up and lunged.

Ella kicked him in the chest with her heavy boot.

The impact stopped him in his tracks, and he gasped. He was wobbling back and forth, but somehow he stayed on his feet. He took a step back, then held up his fists, waving them back and forth like a fighter working out in a gym as he took a bob-and-weave defense.

Ella kept her fighting stance. "Stop. I'm a cop. Don't fight me. You'll go down."

"You wish," the Navajo man yelled, his face beet red from exertion.

"Have it your way," Ella said, and reached for the canister of Mace on her duty belt. She had it halfway up before his fists suddenly opened up. Showing his palms and outspread fingers, he took a step back.

"No, stop! I'm allergic to that stuff. Really. I give up."

Ella immediately spun him around and cuffed him. "If you run for it again, I'll Taser your ass."

Taking him by the arm, she informed him of his rights as she guided him east toward the dirt road that paralleled the *bosque* along the irrigation ditch. As he stumbled along she asked him for his name, but all she got was a request for an attorney.

By the time they reached the road a patrol cruiser was waiting, having come from the north. Justine was inching up from the south in her unit, less than fifty yards away. Ella looked at the uniformed officer climbing out of the cruiser. She recognized Mark Lujan, a young cop with about four years on the tribal force. "Thanks, Lujan, but I've got him now. My partner and I will take him in," she said, seeing Justine climbing out of the SUV.

"Let the officer take him, boss," Justine said, leaning her head out of the SUV. "We've got another call."

"What's happening, partner?" Ella asked, climbing into the vehicle.

Justine turned the SUV around, then spoke as they drove toward the highway. "A Navajo crew was replacing fence posts on the Navajo Nation side of the border, just the other side of Hogback, when they found a body."

"On tribal land—they're sure of that?" Ella reached for a tissue from the glove box, then wiped away the perspiration from her brow with one hand and redirected the air-conditioning vent toward her face and neck.

"Yeah, from what I was told. They called 911 and dispatch called us immediately."

There was no direct route to the site. When they passed

through the wide, river-cut gap in the Hogback, the long, steep-sided outcrop towering above the desert for miles, Justine had to continue east off the Rez. Their intended route required them to circle back to the northwest along the old highway, which came much closer to the spinelike ridge.

There was a dirt track that ran along the north-south fence line through an old field and former marsh, and the ride was extra rough. Trees and brush dotted the area, thickly in some places, and it took a while to spot the tribal truck, which was in a low spot. The tailgate of the oversized pickup was down and the bed filled with coils of wire and fence posts.

"Where's the crew?" Ella asked, looking around.

"Way over there," Justine said, gesturing with her chin, Navajo-style, toward a shady spot beneath an old cottonwood at least a hundred feet northwest of the pickup.

Ella wasn't surprised. As a detective on the Navajo Rez, she usually didn't have to worry that a murder scene would be contaminated by the Navajo public. Whether they were Traditionalists, New Traditionalists, or Modernists, fear of the *chindi* was a fact of life here.

The *chindi*, the evil in a man, was said to remain earthbound waiting for a chance to create problems for the living. Contact with the dead, or their possessions, was a sure way to summon it to you, so avoidance was the usual strategy.

The foreman, a short, muscular Navajo in jeans and a pale blue tribal-issue shirt, came to meet them as they parked and stepped out of the SUV. His yellow straw cowboy hat was stained with dust and sweat. It was getting hot already here in northwest New Mexico. "We called you as soon as we realized what we were digging up. You can see what's left of a human hand down there. It's over by that spot where we were taking out some fill dirt."

"Thanks. We'll handle it from here," Ella said.

Justine joined Ella and they approached the location

he'd pointed out. A shovel had been left beside the area where sand had been scooped out, probably to fill around a newly planted fence post about ten feet away. The original ground had been eroded by heavy rain and the old post still lay nearby, the wood badly rotted away.

Ella and Justine moved carefully, stepping only in the fresh shoe and boot prints left by the work crew and making sure no other potential evidence was disturbed.

"Our crime scene team is on the way," Justine said, looking down at the dark, leathery-looking, dried out remnants of what was clearly a human's right hand. "Benny's driving the van. Ralph Tache wants in on this, too. He said he can't dig—doctor's orders—but he can collect evidence and document the scene."

"I don't know about that," Ella said, giving Justine a look of concern. "I'm not sure Ralph's ready. This could be labor intensive, and we'll have to do it all by hand. We can't bring in a backhoe, and all that bending over . . ."

"Ralph's had a lot to deal with after all those surgeries. That pipe bomb incident at the college did more than just put him in the hospital. But he's spent months in rehab, and needs to get back to work, Ella. His doctor's given permission for him to resume field duty, and the chief agreed. Let him have this assignment. He's not cut out for a desk job, and we need our best personnel on this."

Ella nodded. Although Ralph had already made it clear he wasn't ready to take up his bomb squad work again, he wanted to get out of the station and take part in field work.

"After all those months of recovery and therapy, I thought for a while he'd just take an early retirement and go on to consulting work," Ella said. "He was a veteran cop when I joined the department."

"I think police work's in his blood, Ella, and he needs to reconnect." Justine glanced down at the missing joint on her index finger, recalling the brutality of her kidnappers years ago. "We all pay a price for what we do, but police work's a calling. That's why we're drawn to it so much."

Ella said nothing. Justine was a devout Christian and her religious beliefs shaped her views. Yet no matter how Justine defined it, she lived and breathed the job, too. It was that dedication to the tribe and the department that made all of them overlook the downside—like the crappy pay and long hours.

"I'll start with photos," Justine said. "I want shots of the tire tracks on the dirt trail leading in. I saw two distinct, fresh sets as we were coming in, and there's only one tribal vehicle here."

"Good eye. I'll get statements from the crew," Ella said.

As she walked over to the men clustered in the shade of the cottonwood, Ella understood the wariness in their eyes. She spoke to the foreman first and he pointed out the two men who'd found the body. One of them, a stocky Navajo in his early twenties wearing a turquoise and black Shiprock High School Chieftains T-shirt and worn jeans, stood fingering the leather pouch at his waist.

Recognizing the medicine bag for what it was, an essential personal item for Traditionalists, Ella decided to speak to him first.

She introduced herself without using names. Traditionalists believed that a name had power. To use it needlessly deprived its owner of a personal asset that was his or hers to use in times of trouble. Asking to see his driver's license, she took the necessary information off that.

"I got too close to that body," he said, explaining that he was the first to uncover the still-attached hand, and that the shovel left at the location was his. "I'm going to have a Sing done. Your brother's the *hataalii* who lives on the other side of Shiprock, off the Gallup highway, isn't he?"

"Yes, he is," Ella answered, not surprised he'd made the connection. Despite the vastness of the Navajo Nation, theirs was a small community, and she'd been part of the tribal police department in this area for nearly fifteen years.

"I came ready for work, but this . . ." He shook his head, then kicked at a clump of dry grass with the toe of his worn lace-up work boot.

"Why did you happen to dig at that particular spot?" Ella said.

"I needed fill dirt so I picked a spot where there wasn't much brush. It was pretty loose and easy to scoop out, so I dug deeper. Then the shovel snagged on something that looked like a leather glove." He swallowed hard. "I reached down to pull it out when I saw that it was a hand—still attached to an arm. I backed off, fast." He avoided eye contact with Ella out of respect for Navajo ways. "Do you think the whole body is down there?" he asked in a strangled voice.

"We'll know in a bit."

"Do we have to stay around while you . . . dig it up?"

"Not for that long. I'll need to take statements from everyone and make sure I know where to find each of you in case we need to talk again. Once that's done, you'll all be free to leave."

"Good. I don't want to stick around."

Ella couldn't help but notice that the entire crew seemed anxious to leave, even those who appeared to be Modernists—their curiosity, their more relaxed expressions, and the absence of medicine pouches at their belt or in hand easily identified the Modernists.

Going about her business, she spoke to the other men, but nothing new came to light. Nobody seemed to know anything about the extra set of vehicle tracks. The foreman also made it clear that he didn't think any other tribal employees had visited the site before them. Their job here today had been part of regular maintenance and scheduled months ago.

Shortly after the crew left, her team arrived. Ella watched

Ralph Tache climb out of the van. Though he still moved slowly despite having lost at least thirty pounds in the last year, determination was etched in his deep-set eyes.

She knew that look. The need to restore order so all could walk in beauty was more than just a concept. It was the way of life on the *Diné Bikéyah*, Navajo country.

The crime scene team quickly cordoned off the area, using the boundary fence as the eastern perimeter. They each had specialized jobs, but no one would touch the ground around the hand until every square inch had been photographed from all possible angles.

While Ralph helped Justine take photos, Sergeant Joe Neskahi brought out two shovels and stood them against the van for future use.

Soon afterwards, Benny Pete and Joe surveyed the ground outside the yellow tape looking for tracks, trash, or anything out of the ordinary. If the scene needed to be expanded, they would be the first to make that determination.

Joe was a longtime member of the team, but Benny, their newest member, had fit in almost instantly. He'd come to them as a temporary transfer, then had opted to remain with their team. They'd all welcomed him after seeing his skills, particularly when it came to spotting even minute details.

"What's the M.E.'s ETA?" Ella called out to Justine.

"Ten minutes," Justine called back, not looking up from her work.

Looking over at Ralph, Ella saw him taking a photo of something off in the direction of the highway. "What'd you see, Ralph?" she asked, walking over.

He shrugged. "Someone was over there, standing by a white sedan, watching us through binoculars. I saw his reflection off the glass and it caught my eye. It was probably just a curious motorist, but you know what they say in Crime Scene 101."

"Yeah, sometimes perps hang around to watch the police work the scene—might even volunteer to help," Ella said.

"I'll also be taking shots of every car that stops to check us out. You never know," he said.

"Sure would be nice to get lucky," Ella said, "investigation-wise," she added quickly, seeing Ralph's eyebrows rise.

Hearing someone clear their throat directly behind her, Ella spun around. "You don't make a lot of noise when you walk, do you?" she said, glaring at Benny.

"Sorry about that, boss," he said. "We looked around for footprints connected to that extra set of tire tracks, but there isn't anything fresh. The driver must not have exited the vehicle. We did find something interesting—another set of fresh prints that clearly belong to a child. They're along the fence line and elsewhere, but not close enough to the tire impressions for the child to have been the driver or a passenger."

"So the only adult prints belong to the work crew?"

"That's right," Benny said.

"The next thing we'll need to do is check on kids who live in this area. Anything else?" Ella asked him.

"So far we've found the usual windblown debris of candy and food wrappers, paper cups, and the kind of stuff we'd normally find alongside the highway. But something struck me as particularly odd."

"What is it?" she pressed.

"I'd rather show you," he said.

"Lead the way." This was going to be one of those cases where nothing fit the norm. She could feel it in her gut.